Forlorn Hope

Book 3 of the Branwell Chronicles

Judith Hale Everett

Evershire Publishing

Published by Evershire Publishing, Springville, Utah
ISBN 978-1-7360675-6-7
Library of Congress Control Number: 2022904140

To Amy
who knows a thing or two about challenges

To my readers:
Make sure to read the Author's Note in the back for historical
information on concepts and events described in the story.

Books in the *Branwell Chronicles* series:

A Near Run Thing
Two in the Bush
Romance of the Ruin
Forlorn Hope
A Knowing One
Piqued and Repiqued

To get *A Near Run Thing* for free and to find out more about the series, go to judithhaleeverett.com or scan the QR code below:

Forlorn Hope

Prologue

IT WAS PLAINLY his sister's fault that Geoffrey had forgot his boots in the woods, since it was she who had dared him to wade across the stream and onto the haunted Chandry estate. He had not even hesitated to remove his boots and take the dare, for if he had, Clara would have thought him a coward. But he was not a coward, as he had showed her well enough, tossing his boots and socks onto the bank and splashing through the stream to stride manfully into Sir Anthony Chandry's wood. Clara had waited, white-faced and wide-eyed, as Geoffrey had stood in the shadow of the hulking trees, his shoulders thrown back and his head held high to disguise the frantic beating of his heart.

Unfortunately, after barely a minute a loud crack had sounded, followed by a sudden rush of movement in the brush behind him, and all Geoffrey's bravado had fled. Clara had instantly hared off home, and Geoffrey was not far behind her, leaping the stream in two bounds and forgetting his boots and socks on the bank in a headlong flight to the safety of Gracely Hall. Geoffrey entered the house through the tall French doors that opened onto the sitting room, and discovered that Clara, hen-witted as she was, had blurted out the whole story to their mother, who sat livid with outrage on the sofa.

"Geoffrey!" Mrs. Mantell cried, turning flashing blue eyes upon him. "How dare you step foot in that horrid, nasty place! Never mind these ridiculous rumors of hauntings—depend upon it, that disagreeable Sir Anthony has spread them on purpose to affront the decency of his neighbors! He is an odious, vile man, who doesn't scruple to have dealings with every sort of low, vulgar person, and you're never to associate with him, no, nor cross the boundary of the estate again! I shall never forgive your grandfather for having done nothing about this deplorable situation, before leaving your father to inherit, for all he does is wink at it! It is not to be borne! Good heaven, where are your boots?"

His father had just then entered the room, drawn by his lady's shrill expostulation, and Geoffrey, shamefaced, was obliged to confess before the Colonel that he had left his boots at the stream out of fright. Mrs. Mantell's irritation was unpleasant enough, but his father's disgusted mutterings, followed inevitably by his brother Francis' mockery, set the seal upon Geoffrey's mortification.

It was with a view to proving himself that Geoffrey set out for the stream the following day. At the bank, he took up his boots, slinging them by the laces over his shoulder, but rather than obey his mother's injunction to return instantly home, Geoffrey hopped across the stream and into the Chandry wood, intent upon tramping right up to Chandry Manor and touching the haunted house itself.

A hundred yards or so into the wood, the sound of unearthly

singing stopped him still. The hairs raised on the back of his neck as he scanned the near vicinity, clutching his forward boot tightly and making a plan to flee at first sight of any ghostly figure. None appeared, but the song floated enticingly to him, from somewhere off to his left. It occurred to him that to confront the phantom singer would be even more brave than to touch a moldy tower wall, and he followed the sound deeper into the wood.

The song seemed to be emanating from the other side of a mass of brush and trees that formed a sort of hedge and, when he put an eye to a gap in the foliage, he discovered that it hid a small clearing, the drooping tree branches forming a low roof and bushes grown up around as walls. It also hid, to Geoffrey's not inconsiderable disappointment, no ghastly spirit but merely a girl, thin and pale, with large mournful eyes and lank blond hair tied back inexpertly behind her ears with a ribbon, and who sang the haunting melody to herself as she puttered about.

His first inclination was to slink back the way he had come, grateful that Francis would never know of his stupidity, but then the girl shifted, revealing an intricately detailed faerie village in the shrubbery, created with twigs and leaves and twine and clay. Fascinated, Geoffrey crouched down and watched her work for several minutes, amazed at her cleverness, but all at once his muscles seized with cramp and he lost balance. His body pitched forward, crunching against the hedge, and he uttered a surprised cry as the branches scratched his face and tore at his coat. With a thrash, he scrambled up and peered back into the clearing, but the girl had gone.

Curious, he made his way around the bower until he found a large gap through which he could enter the clearing. He sidled in and stopped, falling to his hands and knees to see into each cunningly wrought little house in the girl's make-believe village. They were each unique, some suspended in the brambles and others reposing on the mossy ground, some with slate-like roofs and others with thatch. The girl had used twine to hold small, straight twigs together in a frame, then clay to bind bark and leaves for floors and walls, and straw or shale for the roofs. They were sparsely furnished as yet, with a few tiny beds and tables and chairs made of the same materials.

But the most astonishing part of the village was its inhabitants. They were tiny people made of twigs and acorns, with grass and leaf clothing, and hats of seed pods. They posed as if at daily tasks amid their dwellings, one bending over a child in bed, another stirring a pot on the hearth. A tiny man sat atop a cart harnessed to a miniature horse, while another mended a one-inch high stone wall surrounding a mossy field wherein tiny sheep made of catkins grazed.

Geoffrey had never seen anything so wonderful in all his life, and beyond his shock and amazement that it existed at all was his disbelief that it could do so here, on the forbidding Chandry estate. If he had not seen the girl with his own eyes, he would have imagined the village to be the work of fae creatures. But seen her he had, and he determined that she must be the rumored daughter of Sir Anthony Chandry, whom none of his fellows had ever seen in the flesh, but whom, contrary to popular opinion, was not kept locked up in a cell in the garret.

Determined to be part of this magical world, Geoffrey set to work on an addition to the village that, he hoped, would recommend him to the girl, and induce her to accept him. It took him some time, with the aid of his penknife and the ball of twine the girl had left behind, but at last he was finished and placed his offering so as to be seen, before retiring from the clearing to go home to dinner.

He returned the next day, and the next, but it was yet another day before the girl came back to the bower, silent and cautious as a deer. She froze when she saw the clumsy twig horse placed beside one of her empty huts, and she stared at it for many moments before bending cautiously to pick it up and take in all its details with her large eyes. Smiling, she replaced the horse and scanned the surrounding bushes as if for another sign of the trespasser, but Geoffrey, suddenly shy, pulled his head back from his peep-hole, holding his breath as her glance swept past.

When he dared to peek again, the girl was crafting a miniature figure with long hair and a leaf dress to ride on the horse. Just as she had finished, a distant gong sounded, and she put down her handiwork with a regretful sigh before making her way out of the clearing and toward Chandry Manor.

Geoffrey wanted no more encouragement. He slipped silently into the clearing and gathered twigs and clay to create a tiny boy with bark trousers. He set the boy next to the little girl on horseback and gazed thoughtfully at them, then wove a little basket and put it in the boy's arms. Slipping back through the bushes, he ran to the stream bank and searched until he found a lovely white pebble shot through with milky swirls, and took it back to the clearing. He placed it in the basket, considering a moment more, then scratched a message in the dirt by the feet of the boy—"Friends?"

The next day, when he made his way to the hedge-wall and peeked in, the girl was there, busy about the houses. He saw that his boy was still in his place, the basket in his hands, but the strange girl held the white stone, rubbing it between a thumb and forefinger.

Deciding the time was right, he lightly rustled the bushes, inquiring, "May I come in?"

The girl whirled to face the sound of his voice with both her hands up in a warding gesture and her eyes wide with uncertainty.

He said quickly, "I mean no harm. I only want to play."

She slowly lowered her hands, her large, gray eyes searching the hedge. "Who are you?" she asked, in a gentle voice hardly above a whisper.

He advanced slowly through the opening and sat down cross-legged just inside. "I'm Geoffrey Mantell. Our property is next yours. That way," he said, pointing back toward the stream.

She smiled faintly, swallowing. "I am Emily Chandry."

Geoffrey thought she looked as fragile as one of Clara's porcelain dolls. Cautiously, he pointed to the pebble she still worried in her hand. "Do you like it? I found it in the stream."

She nodded, coloring faintly. "It's lovely." She placed it back into the little basket as he inched forward.

"Your village is so clever. I wanted to try something like it," he said, gesturing to his horse and boy.

Dropping her eyes, she murmured, "Your horse is wonderful."

"Not as wonderful as yours," he said, eying his lopsided animal a little dubiously.

"No, no! It's grand!" she said, reaching out to touch it. Still averting her eyes, she murmured, "I should like some help in the village."

Geoffrey grinned, releasing a contented sigh. "I'd be glad to help!"

She looked up, her smile brightening, and her shyness seemed then to be dispelled.

Once he had gained her trust, Geoffrey scarcely saw the timid, frightened Emily again. She accepted him whole-heartedly, and depended on him to both create new additions and watch over the village with her. Her vibrant imagination was a never ending source of amazement to him, as was her tender heart. Whenever he was low, she helped him to recover his spirits, singing in her faerie voice or inventing silly stories with the village people. And if ever Francis or his father had belittled him, she listened patiently to his rantings, soothing his frustration by saying gently, "Please, Geoffrey, you mustn't mind it so. They do not mean it—or if they do now, someday they will not."

As everyone knew Sir Anthony to be an odious miser who entertained all sorts of low persons at the Manor, with no apparent regard for his daughter's delicacy or safety, it was astonishing that Emily should possess so forgiving a nature. One need only look at her old, worn gowns and her unkempt hair to know that her father took little thought for her comfort, and Geoffrey often wondered that such a creative, friendly spirit could reside in so forlorn a figure.

He came to consider her his best friend, and the most interesting person of his acquaintance; however, he dared not reveal his friendship with her. His family, he knew, held the Chandrys as cheap as dirt, and his mother would forbid him from seeing Emily again should she discover where he went nearly every day. Francis would think him touched in the upper works for spending his time with a girl, and even Clara would likely tease him endlessly for playing with dolls.

And if Geoffrey considered speaking of Emily to his friends, he never did so again after one day in town when two of his fellows began talking of the Waif of Chandry Manor.

"I've heard its moaning myself, late at night," said Shelby Frean, the Squire's son, relishing the rapt attention of the other boys.

"Well, I've seen it!" put in Billy Thornton, puffing out his chest. "Pale and skinny thing with huge eyes like a frog's."

Shelby waved him away. "No, that's just the daughter."

"Sir Anthony don't have a daughter, clodpole!"

"Of course he does," said Shelby in an authoritative tone. "She's the reason Lady Chandry's dead, and that's why the old gadger keeps her locked up, because he can't stand the sight of her, you gudgeon!"

"Well, if she's locked up, then why'd I see her with my own eyes, eh, cawker?"

"Because she's made a pact with the Devil, and can move through walls, but only when the moon is at the full, you—"

But the others never heard what name Shelby had concocted for Billy for, in a trice, Geoffrey was on him, pummeling him with his fists and shouting, "Take it back, you snake!" The other boys were no more surprised than Shelby, who only had sense enough to curl up and yell, "Gerroff!" while the others stared slack-jawed. Were it not for Colonel Mantell's groom, who came striding across the street at that moment to grab up Geoffrey by his coat collar, there may have been very little of the Squire's son left unbruised by the encounter.

Unceremoniously dumped into the chaise next to his rigidly disapproving mother and morbidly delighted sister, and forced to endure Clara's sniggering all the way home, Geoffrey thought to beat a hasty retreat to his room upon reaching the Hall.

But in this he was forestalled by his mother, who halted him with the words: "No, no, Geoffrey! You shall not get off that easy. Your father will wish to see you, instantly! What can have possessed you to behave in such an oafish way? I declare, I was stared out of all countenance! All the village high street gaping at us, no doubt wondering what back slum you were brought up in! Oh, I shall never live it down!"

The boy had no choice but to go directly to his father's domain, a study on the first floor whose walls were adorned with various hunting trophies and a life-sized painting of a more youthful Colonel

Mantell in full military regalia, medals glittering upon his manly chest. A single bookshelf was full of manuals on hunting, boxing, riding, and all other forms of outdoor sport, and a fine oak case held an assortment of guns, some antique, others glaringly new.

Geoffrey stood in embarrassed silence, eyes flicking about this shrine to masculinity, until Colonel Mantell raised his eyes from the letter in his hand only long enough to ascertain the identity of his guest. Lowering them again, he said, "Well?"

The boy cleared his throat. "I was in a fight today, sir."

The Colonel immediately put down his letter, an eyebrow raised at his son. "A fight you say? What sort of fight?"

Geoffrey swallowed and looked at the floor. "An affair of honor, sir. With Shelby Frean."

"The Squire's son?" His father stared at him for several interminable seconds, then suddenly threw back his handsome head and laughed out loud. "I knew you had it in you, boy!" he crowed, wagging a finger in his son's direction as he stood and strode around the desk to stand in front of the utterly surprised boy. "Who was in the right, son?"

Geoffrey gulped. "I believe I was, sir. He—Shelby—said something—I mean, insulted a lady, sir."

The Colonel's eyebrows shot up and he whistled low. "Ah, that's the landscape is it? I should think at ten years of age you're a little young to notice the females."

His son flushed scarlet. "She's not a female! I mean—we're just friends, sir!"

The Colonel chuckled knowingly. "Well, well, my boy, and who is this lady?"

Geoffrey glared at his toes. "Emily Chandry, sir," he mumbled.

"What was that? Speak up, boy!"

He threw back his shoulders and looked defiantly into his father's eyes. "Emily Chandry, sir!"

A slightly pained look crossed his father's features but was quickly replaced by an indulgent smile. "No matter, son, it's a good start! She's not quite a lady, but it's the thought that counts!" He took his son's hand and pumped it in both of his, then ruffled the boy's hair and, with a final chuckle, went back to his letter. Thus dismissed, Geoffrey fled to the refuge of his room to contemplate the perversity of parental priorities.

Subjected thereafter to many grins and knowing looks, and the occasional clap on the shoulder in passing, Geoffrey tried in vain to reconcile his father's spirited support of his exploit with the conviction in his heart that his defense of Emily had been honorable. But rather than satisfying his desire for his father's approval, the Colonel's baffling manner served only to reduce the nobility of the deed to mere posturing, thus tarnishing any satisfaction he could have gained from it, and rendering the thought of repeating the action untenable.

His friends, too, seemed unable to comprehend his actions, and save for Lawrence Simpford, who was too easy-going to think very long on any subject, they regarded him with misgiving for weeks to come. This resolved him never to speak of his friendship with Emily to anyone; however, he would not give up his time with her in the faerie clearing. It was the one place he could be entirely free of the baffling complexities of life, and Emily—though unacceptable to others—was his dearest friend.

It was not to last, however. At the end of the summer, Geoffrey was summoned to his father's study, and he obeyed with some trepidation. Colonel Mantell glanced up from the newspaper he was reading, adjuring Geoffrey to sit down, then shuffled the pages a bit and muttered over their contents before at last folding the paper and gazing thoughtfully at his son.

"Well, my boy, you're nearly eleven."

"Yes, sir."

"Your mother and I are agreed that it is high time we sent you off to school."

Geoffrey gasped. "But Mother said I am to have a tutor, sir!"

His father harrumphed in disgust. "Tutors are for weaklings, and I'll not have a weakling for a son! You're no more sickly than Francis was, whatever your mother wishes to believe, and Miss Gillies, though a fine governess, cannot teach you forever. Besides, the gamekeeper has seen you trespassing on Sir Anthony's land, and though I couldn't give that for the old curmudgeon, I won't stand your mother having the vapors over the business."

Geoffrey went pale, horrified that he and Emily had been found out, but his father merely pushed himself to his feet and began pacing behind his desk. "This nonsense has driven home to me that you must get away. You showed spirit when you flattened young Frean last May, but with your mother's continued interference, I've no doubt you'll become a milksop by and by. School has done well by Francis, and it will do well by you."

Though relieved that his father knew nothing of Emily and the village, Geoffrey had no wish to leave them, and strove to convince his father of the desirability of engaging a tutor and allowing him to stay at home.

But Colonel Mantell turned a severe eye upon him. "That is precisely the kind of claptrap I mean to cure you of, son, and no nincompoop tutor will do it for me. We must cut the apron strings, and the sooner the better. You will go to school, and learn what it means to be a man!"

Geoffrey, surrounded by the fruits of what it meant to be a man, and facing his principal example of what manhood had to offer, believed he could do very well without it, but there really was nothing he could do. Within two weeks, he had been fitted out with new clothes and books, and prepared as much as was possible by Miss Gillies for what challenges awaited him. He deeply regretted being made to leave Emily without warning or explanation, but he was utterly forbidden to wander in the woods, and being unwilling to divulge his secret, had no way to deliver a message.

On the fateful morning, the Colonel bid him goodbye with a buffet on the shoulder, while his mother adjured him not to act in any way unbefitting his station, and with a mournful wave to Clara and Miss Gillies, he mounted into the chaise and set off toward Shrewsbury School in Shropshire.

Chapter 1

Ten years later

THE PROPRIETOR OF the Blue Pig Inn in Southam, Warwickshire, stepping outside the stuffy confines of the taproom for a breath of air, congratulated himself on the taproom being full, and the best four rooms besides—a circumstance which was rare enough in that village, though it was on the post road. Smiling into the dimming light, he perceived a post chaise and four rumbling down Oxford Street and considered whether he ought to wave it onward, for there wasn't but the two pokey rooms under the eaves, which wouldn't do for the occupant of a coach with four horses. Expanding his chest with importance, the proprietor ambled the remaining ten steps to the road, only to scuttle backward as the coach swept past, not slowing at all.

The innkeeper's chagrin at having lost the opportunity of puffing off his own prosperity was unobserved by the single occupant of the coach. Lieutenant Geoffrey Mantell, having been three years abroad in the army, was lost in amazement at how little Southam had changed while at the same time seeming quite foreign to him. The arid climate of central Spain, with its adobe and stone cities only recently burned and pillaged, and its countryside bearing the fresh scars of battle after battle, was entirely dissimilar to this peaceful and untroubled town surrounded by verdant farmland.

Eying the spire of St. James's church, he endeavored to recall the twists and turns of the footpath behind to the Holy Well without much success. He had passed so little time in Southam since he had been sent to school, his mother's aversion to their neighbor, Sir Anthony Chandry, driving her to insist upon her family's traveling during the bulk of the school vacations. By the time Geoffrey had gone up to Oxford, this habit had been ingrained, and he had found it natural—and much more enjoyable—to take up the offers of his friends to visit their country homes rather than return to Gracely Hall during term breaks.

A slight easing of the coach to the east as they reached the Coventry road pulled his thoughts from what he could not recall, and he bent forward to catch a glimpse of the Horse and Jockey on the far side of the street. His last drink before leaving Warwickshire for the Peninsula had been at the Horse and Jockey, and Lawrence Simpford had offered odds to Shelby Frean that Ensign Mantell would fell Old Boney himself and return to all them sorry fellows a hero.

Sitting back against the squabs, Geoffrey smiled ruefully. Lawrie had lost that bet, for the lieutenant had been stationed in Spain at the moment of the Emperor's abdication in Paris, and had had nothing to do with his exile to the Isle of Elba. Indeed, other than staying the course, Geoffrey felt he had done nothing in the Peninsula that could reasonably be construed as heroic. He had attained the rank of lieutenant, which he supposed was good for something, but with feats of true heroism abounding all around him in the fight against the French, he could not in good conscience claim such an appellation as hero.

As the coach rumbled through the cobbled high street, past the Squire's residence, and out into the open country once more, the Lieutenant reflected that, after all, he was much the same Geoffrey Mantell who had taken up a pair of colors three years ago, if a bit less hasty and far more cheerful. War was not a thing to make a man careless of life, and Geoffrey's gratitude to be alive had cultivated in him a pleasant, easy temperament that he hoped would serve him well during his furlough at home.

Some miles out of Southam, the neat walls of orderly farms gave way on one side to an extensive thicket of bramble and hedge, and Geoffrey spied the lodge gates of Chandry Manor amidst the overgrowth. Eying the dark, rutted lane that wound away into the gloom with distaste, he wished for the hundredth time that Sir Anthony would be sensible of his duty—if not for himself, at least for his little Emily. Geoffrey's memory of her was vague indeed, for he had not been allowed to step one foot on Sir Anthony's land again after that summer with her, much less been given the opportunity to revisit the faerie clearing, and he had not met with her anywhere else.

Though time and occupation had eventually dulled his yearning for the clearing, he had always regretted having left Emily alone. But as he had entered his awkward teens, it had seemed unreasonable for him to think of renewing the friendship, partly from respect to his mother's wishes and partly from the conviction that Emily was not the sort of acquaintance one could easily explain to one's associates. Now, with the crumbling walls of Sir Anthony's property passing by, he wondered what had become of her.

The chaise turned in at the lodge gates of Gracely Hall and tooled up the drive, slowing on the sweep, and as Geoffrey gazed up at the gray stone walls of the mansion he reflected how often he had felt akin to Wordsworth's vagrant, as "homeless near a thousand homes I stood, and near a thousand tables pined and wanted food." The youthful infatuation that had brought his parents together had long ago given way to antipathy, and the growing coldness between themselves had bled into their interactions with their children. The three young Mantells had grown up more or less friendly to one another, but their dispositions were too disparate to allow of forming a strong bond. Francis, the eldest by several years, took too well after his father, and Clara, though closer in age and in sentiment to Geoffrey, had shown over the years an alarming similarity to her mother. Geoffrey did not expect that he should ever be close to either.

As he descended from the coach, a footman came forward to retrieve the baggage strapped on behind the coach, and the butler stood ready at the door to welcome him.

"Grimsley! How good to see you," said Geoffrey. "And how does Mrs. Grimsley?"

"Very well, Master Geoffrey, I thank you," returned the butler, bowing slightly. "May I say it is good to have you home again, sir."

He allowed the butler to take his traveling coat and cane, consigning his hat and gloves to a second footman, and after a cursory glance around the hall, which had not changed a whit, he trod up the steps directly to his old room. He was somewhat astonished to discover that it had been furbished up in the latest mode, with new Sheraton furnishings and a fine blue paper on the walls. At first inclined to be moved by the circumstance, he was persuaded upon reflection that it had been done not, as one might expect, in honor of his coming, but simply for his mother's consequence—for how often had the room been wanted as a guest chamber during his absence?

Changing from his traveling clothes and running a comb through his rumpled blond locks, he cast a longing glance at the bed, feeling tired to the bones, but went dutifully in search of his family. They were to be found in the drawing room, his mother sitting with her embroidery frame before her, and his father leaning against the mantelpiece, contemplating the fire.

The Colonel stepped firmly forward, shaking his son's hand and saying, "So you're back. Well, well." He followed this effusion with desultory inquiries on his journey and the state of the roads before turning him over to Mrs. Mantell, who gave him her hand and allowed him to kiss her cheek before remarking that she could not comprehend how he could have been so dilatory in his travel.

Geoffrey sustained this moving welcome with fortitude, having expected nothing more. "Forgive me, Mother, but I was obliged to spend some days in London with Commander Sir Edwyn Stanhope, for it was on his ship I found passage home, as I wrote to you from Plymouth."

"You stayed with Sir Edwyn Stanhope?" repeated his mother, looking up. "Lord Chesterfield's cousin? You did not mention it, for I should have remembered such a detail. Of course, that was quite proper to pay your respects. You stayed, I suppose, with Lord Chesterfield, for Sir Edwyn has not a house in town, I think."

"Certainly, Mother. Lord Chesterfield most kindly invited me, though he has recently lost his lady, for I am a great favorite with little George, as you must know."

"Dear George! So tragic to have lost his mother so young. Perhaps we may pay him a visit when we are in town next spring."

"He should be delighted, I have no doubt." Clasping his hands behind his back, Geoffrey cast a look around the room, with its gilded portraits of the stern Mantells of the past, and inquired, "Where are my brother and sister? Or are they not come to meet me?"

"Clara has been these four days at a house party at Black Oaks," replied his mother. "We did not think it quite right to bring her away early, for the Drayfords are such excellent people. You do not yet know Miss Drayford! A delightful girl—twenty thousand pounds and the granddaughter of an Earl! You may meet her when you go to fetch Clara Friday next, for I do not like to send a servant for her."

Nodding acknowledgment to this hint, Geoffrey said, "As you wish, Mother. And Francis? I had a notion he had come down from London, for I did not meet him there."

"Francis will be along," said the Colonel with a wave of his hand. "He had some excellent sport this morning, hunting with Wraglain's pack. He has bought a capital hunter—one which I should not disdain to own—and is trying him out, but the whole business has put him behind. No matter."

Geoffrey could do no other than agree, and he took his seat beside his mother on the sofa. "How does Clara, Mother, now that she is come home from that Bath seminary?"

"She will do very well, I am persuaded, and will not shame us on her come-out this season. Her drawing has come a long way since last you saw her, and her performance on the harp is exquisite. Her Italian is not quite what one could wish; however, her French is as lovely as ever, thanks to our incomparable Miss Gillies, so we need not repine."

"Is Miss Gillies in the neighborhood?" asked Geoffrey. "I believe you wrote me that you had found her another position nearby."

Mrs. Mantell sniffed disdainfully. "I had, however it went off. Mrs. Carruthers had promised absolutely to take her, but then the niece of her cousin—an encroaching woman, to be sure—applied and took the position right from under my nose. But Mrs. Carruthers has her reward, for if her eldest son does not get into a scrape with that sly little piece, I am much mistaken."

A huff from the Colonel drew Geoffrey's eyes thither, and the appreciative curve to his mouth gave Geoffrey to understand that his father rather approved of the sly little piece.

Thinking it wise to put the subject behind them, he said, "And what of Francis? Does he still contemplate a stay at Weymouth next month?"

"Weymouth?" exclaimed his father. "What's to do at Weymouth at this season?"

"His friend Mr. Brandley invited him, Robert, do not you remember?" said Mrs. Mantell, continuing her embroidery with brows imperiously raised. "There is to be quite a select party of young people gathered—a most advantageous situation, to be sure."

The Colonel grumbled, "Advantageous, my eye. A pack of whey-faced females ready to pounce on my son and heir, no doubt!"

"Miss Brandley is far from whey-faced, Robert," replied Mrs. Mantell in arctic tones. "She is quite a lovely creature, and is her uncle's favorite niece besides."

"Uncle? Oh, Lord Pattinson! He is pretty warm, and if he leaves it all to her—I suppose it wouldn't be such a bad match. What does her father give her?"

"Five thousand or more, depend upon it."

"Very well, very well."

After this, the conversation languished, and Geoffrey excused himself to return to his room to rest until dinner. But he lay atop the coverlet for some time, considering that home was not, under the surface, much more gentle or human than the battlefields of the Peninsula. Indeed, the only material change at Gracely Hall had been to increase the distance between himself and his parents and siblings, and he conjectured that the time was not far distant that he should feel completely shut out from their affections. If coming home was to become akin to entering a stranger's house, perhaps it would be better that he make a change in his estate, and seek to establish a home of his own.

Giving up sleep, he got up and dressed for dinner, coming out into the hall just as his brother rounded the corner at the top of the staircase.

"Francis!" he called, quickening his step to shake hands.

Francis Mantell grinned, striding toward his brother with a hand extended. "Geoff! Sorry I wasn't on hand to welcome you back to the ancestral home! Capital sport with Wraglain, you know. Simply couldn't get away until we saw the thing through."

"Certainly, brother. No harm done," was the easy reply, born of long experience.

At that moment, a winsome little maid came down the hall, and Geoffrey could not mistake the coquettish glance she cast at Francis.

"I see you're up to all your old tricks," he said.

Francis laughed, swiping a hand through his rakish brown locks as he turned to watch her down the hall. "She's willing enough, to be sure, but I wouldn't dare! Not in this house. One whiff of scandal and Mother'd give little Janet the sack, and then what would I do? At least Jane leads me a dance, and I've a need for diversion just now, I tell you. Father's been after me to manage the estate—says Brompton ain't what he used to be and needs watching. You'd not believe the number of ledgers I'm made to pore over! It's enough to give one the mopes."

"This won't be the first time I'm glad to be second-born," said Geoffrey. "I'll take the army over ledgers anytime."

Francis stopped him with a hand on his arm, gazing at him with uncharacteristic gravity. "I'm an ass to have made you say it, Geoff. It must have been hell for you these three years."

Though surprised, Geoffrey was not unmoved by his brother's apparent sincerity. "It was the best schooling a man could have had."

"Better you than I, Geoff." Francis's lips twisted in self-derision. "I'd not have stood the nonsense, and where would the Mantell name be, I ask you? In the mud somewhere about Ciudad Rodrigo, I expect. But come into my room and we'll catch up while I dress."

He began talking of Charles Wraglain and his hounds, but Geoffrey made a mental note not to underestimate his brother. Perhaps something could change at Gracely Hall after all.

They met the Colonel and Mrs. Mantell in the drawing room and were immediately called down to dinner, which was laid out on the long table in the formal dining hall, as it had been before Geoffrey's joining the army. It suited his mother's consequence to put on such a parade, and if the dishes were not always warm when they came to table, he had learned long ago not to mention it.

As Grimsley presented the dishes in the old-fashioned style, Colonel Mantell questioned Francis regarding his luck with the hounds, and Geoffrey was glad to sit quietly as his brother reiterated his exploits. This subject spanned all the first course, but with the second, Mrs. Mantell turned to Geoffrey. "Now that you are home, Geoffrey, you must think of settling down."

"Time enough for that, Anamaria," said the Colonel. "Let him enjoy the Peace for a time! Now is the best time to be in the army— all the glory and none of the danger. Nothing to do but reviews and drills, balls and parties." He raised an eyebrow at his son. "Plenty of beautiful women in Spain, eh?"

Geoffrey politely concurred, but his mother said petulantly, "It is very well to talk of it, Robert, but you would sing a different tune if next he came home with some French dairymaid on his arm!"

The Colonel barked a laugh. "Depend upon it, my dear, the day Geoffrey shows any such spirit, I'll be liable to crow. However, you need not be anxious that either of our sons would so far forget himself as to marry such a girl."

Francis raised his glass in approbation.

"And I suppose you have no objection to their littering the countryside with their by-blows, rather than settling down and producing legitimate heirs?" cried Mrs. Mantell, angrily waving away a dish of stewed cherries which Grimsley was offering to her.

"Spare my blushes, Mother," said Francis, his sangfroid a trifle strained. "You are well aware that I have yet to produce even one by-blow."

Pointedly ignoring him, she said, "Geoffrey will do better to put his energies into securing a good match while he still can."

"Now what are you on about?" grumbled the Colonel. "It is not as if he is doddering into his grave, my dear."

"You mistake me, Robert," said his wife, glaring at him from down the length of the table. "He may yet be in his salad days, but that will change if Bonaparte should escape his exile. By the grace of God Geoffrey has survived this war without disfiguring injury, but were there to be another battle, he may not be so lucky, and then what eligible female would have him?"

Geoffrey felt his jaw tighten and reached for the burnt cream pudding, heaping a healthy portion onto his plate, as the Colonel embarked on a pithy defense of military life, which went on until Mrs. Mantell rose with a huff to take herself to the drawing room. The Colonel, calling to Grimsley to bring the good port from the cellar, sat staring gloomily at the table top for some time, while his sons avoided each other's eyes.

At last, when the port had been brought and poured and Grimsley had retired, the Colonel raised his glass and said, "To untrammeled bachelorhood! May you enjoy it while you can."

"Hear, hear!" replied Francis, downing his wine in one gulp, while Geoffrey merely smiled wanly and thought fondly of a little cottage far from Gracely, where one might enjoy a peaceful evening with one's loving wife.

Chapter 2

DETERMINED TO CARRY her point, Mrs. Mantell swept next day into the drawing room, where Geoffrey and Francis sat reading the paper, and stated that they would attend her on her morning visits. Francis, instantly rising, checked his watch and announced that he was to meet with Brompton in ten minutes, and so, regretfully, could not attend her. Geoffrey, however, acquiesced, and as he held the carriage door open for her, he considered that both Francis and the Colonel would think him as milky as ever could they read his mind at that moment.

Though his parents' marriage was a disaster, he had known enough of other marriages to be reasonably certain that if one chose a female whom one cared deeply for—and who reciprocated these feelings—one could rub along quite nicely for the remainder of one's life. As satisfaction in family life had eluded Geoffrey at Gracely, he rather thought he should like to discover if such a thing were possible elsewhere.

Their first visit that morning was to Mrs. and Miss Thornton—the latter of whom Geoffrey had remembered as a teasing little girl with brown curls and an irritating pout. Miss Arabella Thornton had since learned to turn her pout to her best advantage, with lips that had become full and ripe and cherry-red, and which, when paired with her melting blue eyes, were a combination sure to make men's brains stutter to a stop. Geoffrey was not immune to these charms and, after recovering his senses, immensely enjoyed the half-hour, during which Arabella listened to Geoffrey's stories of the Peninsula with her blue eyes wide, and her pretty mouth forming a delicious O, and her lace scarcely hiding the palpitations of her generous bosom.

Their next visit was to the rail thin Mrs. Seely and her conversely sized—but, his mother had informed him, impeccably pedigreed—niece, who seemed intent upon consuming refreshment enough for herself and five aunts. Geoffrey, though at first quite shocked at her immoderate behavior, thought after a while that perhaps he might comprehend her feelings; he fancied that Miss Seely was merely compensating for her anxiety at being on display. This made conversation somewhat unwieldy, however, and he was not reluctant to depart when his mother rose to take their leave.

After these meetings, Geoffrey was released from his mother's service with an hour or two to spare before dinner, and he seized the opportunity to stretch his legs, striking out across the lawn and through the summer garden. Entering into the quiet and peace of the wood, he breathed in the sweet, warm scent of summer grasses and the cool, earthy scent of the trees. His feet carried him down a familiar path through the trees, over hillocks, and to the stream, and without a thought, he forded the water in one long leap, continuing on into the trees on the other side.

Before he could think where he was, he had arrived at a hedge that he knew at once; here was the bower where, years before, he had discovered his neighbor, Emily Chandry. He gazed at it for some moments, amazed that he could still recall the place after so long a time, and curious to see the rest. Making his way around the shrubbery, he found the entrance and came into the clearing.

The place had changed scarcely at all. There was the faerie village he and Emily had built together, expanding it almost across one side of the clearing. Little creatures reposed everywhere between the houses and shops and tiny bushes and trees, and as he gazed about, memories flooded back. The dragon he had made to roast the knight that Emily had said was so full of himself that he ought to be eaten. The faerie queen who sat on a throne and wisely ruled all her people. And the little horse and girl and boy that had begun his friendship with Emily.

Geoffrey turned himself about, gazing at all of it with a drawn out sigh of wonder. Emily must have continued to come here over the years, keeping everything in order as if she had expected that he would return. He experienced a pinch of guilt at that—he had hardly thought of this place, after the first few years. Indeed, his childhood had been over before he had had much time to be a child.

But now that he had returned, he perfectly recollected the joy of that summer and the pleasure of this secret world where he could be whatever he wished to be. And Emily had been the perfect companion, a friend to fill the lack of familial affection. The village itself had been the vehicle for his now innate optimism to blossom and grow, for it was in the building and playing that he and Emily had found the endurance and the humor to deal with every situation.

As he looked all around, his gaze fell on a broken lock box that he had saved from the woodpile to put their oddments and treasures in.

Enthralled, he knelt down, his hat and gloves forgotten beside him as he opened the box and peered inside. They were all here—the motley assortment of rocks, sticks, and other long-forgotten treasures, each one evoking a memory and a smile. The minutes passed as he reverently fingered the objects one at a time, occasionally exclaiming over one thing or another.

Suddenly a soft sound behind him brought him out of his reverie. Turning, he found a slight young woman in an ill-fitting walking dress standing at the opening to the clearing, a round bonnet framing a heart-shaped face with luminous gray eyes—eyes that he wondered he could ever have forgotten—that were fixed in shock on his countenance.

"Emily?" he inquired, not daring to move, for she looked poised to flee. "Miss Chandry—it's Geoffrey—Lieutenant Mantell."

The gray eyes blinked at him, and the rigid body relaxed a trifle. "Then it is you."

"Yes," he confirmed, rising slowly to his feet. He felt as though he towered over her, for though she was of average height, she was thin and delicate. He dared not approach her.

"It is good to see you," he said.

Her pale lips formed a smile, and her eyes took in more of his face before she answered. "You are so changed, and yet you are not. I thought it was you from the way you handled our treasures, but I could not believe it."

"After such an age, you might justly have thought me dead," he said.

She dropped her eyes, the smile disappearing from her face. "I did hear that you had gone to the Peninsula, and I feared that very thing."

He had forgot even her tender heart. "You are good to care for a prodigal friend."

There was a long pause before she looked up at him. "And I rejoice in his safe return."

He felt another pang of guilt. "I did not wish to stay away."

Emily held his gaze, searching his eyes intently, then sighed and nodded. Her resignation cut him to the heart, but what else could he say to her that would not sound like a flimsy excuse?

Bending over the box, he pulled out a rough-hewn whistle. "This quite took me back to that summer. Do you remember? I made you this whistle so you could frighten away your father's friends should they distress you, but the whistle frightened you almost more than his friends."

"It was so shrill. The sound chilled my blood at first." She raised her eyes again with a little laugh. "But you may recall that I learned to use it."

"That you did, to the detriment of my ears!" Pleased at the smile returned to her lips, faint though it was, Geoffrey dropped the whistle back into the box and took out a forked stick. "Do you remember what this was?"

"A two-headed snake that attacked our village," she said without hesitation.

He nodded. "But the faerie queen mesmerized it, and it became—"

"Her pet," they both finished together.

He gazed at her, the memories that had flooded his mind striving to reconcile with the young woman before him, who was so familiar, and yet a stranger. He replaced the stick and sifted through the box, searching. "Where has the moon stone gone?"

There was a pause, then she said, "It is here."

He turned, and saw that she had pulled a chain out from beneath her fichu, suspended from which was the milky white stone he had offered in his little woven basket. "Friends," he murmured.

The word seemed uncertain somehow, as it lingered in the air between them, and he felt shame that it had been so long neglected.

"It is a pretty stone," he offered, "eminently suited to a necklace."

"Yes," she answered, replacing the chain under her fichu. "But that is not why I wear it. You were my only friend, you see."

He could have wished she would not speak so bluntly, but it was nothing but the truth. Even had her father allowed her free inter-course with the other children in the neighborhood, there was hardly a soul who would not have looked askance at her, with her ghostly looks and skittish manner.

He stepped forward, taking her hand. "Oh, Emily, forgive me for leaving you. You cannot conceive of how heartily I wish it had not been so, and I beg you to believe I did not do it by choice."

Her fingers trembled slightly in his clasp. "I do now, though at first I did feel betrayed. It was terribly lonely after you went away. But I became reconciled, and had only to come here when-ever I wanted to remember you, my friend."

"It hasn't changed a whit," he said, in a heartening tone. "You've taken such care of it."

She smiled, reclaiming her hand and bending to sit down before the village. "One could not always say so, for you were not the only one to go away."

"You got away from your father? A lucky thing!" Geoffrey sat beside her. "Where did you go?"

"Mrs. Marsden, our housekeeper, managed to convince my father that it would be better for business were he not to have a young girl about the house. He sent me to a seminary in Warwick, where I boarded for three years."

"I am excessively glad of it. Any reprieve would be a good one, in your case."

She huffed. "What sort of reprieve is the backboard, and endless practice of etiquette? Yet those were peaceful years. And I learned much that has enabled me to endure what I must."

Geoffrey was quiet for some moments. "Has your father not changed, then, even a little?"

"I do not think it is in my father's nature to change," she said, picking up a villager and looking at it. "But it is not so bad as it was used to be. I am a grown woman now, and have a better understanding. I have learned the right way to deal with my father's associates, and though many of them are vulgar and coarse, they no longer frighten me."

A far off bell sounded and she closed her eyes against the sound, her shoulders tightening. "I must go."

He helped her to her feet but retained her hand in his grasp. "You do not convince me that all is well."

"You are too kind, but do not worry yourself over me," she said, returning the pressure of his hand. "It is well enough."

"I am on furlough another two months—perhaps we may meet again."

She smiled, but he thought her look belied a lack of faith in him, and before he could say more, she darted past him and was gone.

Their meeting weighed upon him for the remainder of the day. His conversation over dinner suffered from frequent abstraction as he relived in his mind the delights of their childhood friendship, and he was near silent while he sat at port with his father and brother, guessing at the sober realities of her life, now and in the intervening years. Even as he played billiards with Francis, he could not keep from considering how wrong it was that such a gentle and timid creature should be born into such infelicitous circumstances.

"What, has my mother got her way?" cried Francis, when Geoffrey's absence of mind had led him to another losing hazard. "Tell me you aren't mooning after the Thornton chit."

Blinking himself from his thoughts, Geoffrey swiftly put Francis's mind at ease on that head.

"A good thing," said Francis, "for I'd have thrown you over sooner than have her for a sister-in-law. Looks aplenty but dead boring!"

"What do you know of it?"

Francis leaned on his stick with a satirical look. "How do you think I've been spending my time the past three years? While you've been making yourself heroic on the Peninsula, I've been made to dance attendance on my mother and sister at any number of balls and routs and fetes and dinner parties—it is enough to run one mad. Somehow I must make it plain to our dear mama that she may leave off trying to make me respectable, for I've not the least turn for it."

"So I am your scapegoat?" asked Geoffrey, smiling.

"Oh, yes! I rely upon you to keep her entirely engrossed until I may once again escape to Leicestershire or London or wherever I may find to disappear for several more months."

"What of Weymouth?"

"Heaven preserve me from Weymouth and Miss Brandley!" Francis cried, lining up his next shot. "I'd sooner go to Hell than to Weymouth in that train! But no tattling to Mother, I beg! Let her trust till the bitter end that I've no other view in mind, while I toddle off to Bookerton's hunting box."

They played their turns, and Geoffrey asked, "Is there truly no lady that tempts you to marry, Francis?"

"None. They are either too plain to interest me, or too birdwitted to hold my interest. And those with money are all the worse, for their other attractions suffocate in their own consequence. You can have no idea of how Miss Simpford's bloom faded, like a lost sunset, upon her inheriting her aunt's property."

"Miss Simpford?" inquired the lieutenant. "But she is married these two years at least, or am I mistaken?"

Francis laughed. "Indeed, she is Mrs. Crawford now, but not before our dear mother forced me to wait upon her fifty times, as if the repeated exposure would deaden me to her lack of charms. Unfortunately for mother's feelings, I was not so impressionable."

"Nor, it seems, was Mrs. Crawford," observed Geoffrey blandly, leaning on his stick. "I suppose you'll end in marrying the upstairs maid."

"Father was right that I'll take good care not to be driven to that, if I am driven to marriage at all. I'm content to enjoy the fair bits who wish to dally, and leave the odium of respectable marriage to your lot."

"If you are content with my son succeeding to your honors, I suppose I cannot argue," answered Geoffrey, to which his brother laughed heartily, and they finished their game.

Far from being daunted by Francis's claims, Geoffrey happily obeyed his mother whenever she called upon him to accompany her on visits, and thus came in the way of several eligible young ladies in the neighborhood. Miss Thornton was, perhaps, his favorite, for her cherry lips and the mischievous dimple in her cheek were delectable to behold while she talked. But on the third visit in twice as many days, he began to see that Francis had not been trying to impose upon him, as he had at first conjectured.

Miss Thornton, turning on the sofa beside him to grant him a perfect view of her pretty face, said, "Do tell me again about the Peninsula, Lieutenant! I long to know how society is there, and if any of the rumors are true, that the Empress Marie Louise wears the most ravishing gowns!"

"Well, Miss Thornton, I cannot tell you of the Empress, for she was in Paris, or hiding in Blois, while I was fighting in Spain. They are not so close together as they might appear on the globes. Perhaps you had better tell me what you have heard of her, for it is certainly more than I have seen of her."

She tittered. "Oh, sir, I know perfectly how far it is from Paris to Madrid. But you would not have me believe that all the camps did not daily receive reports of what was going on in Paris! Why, I have heard that all the newspapers in Europe carried descriptions of the Empress's gowns, so how could you be ignorant of it?"

Geoffrey blinked at her. "Well, Miss Thornton, there were more pressing matters to attend to than the fashions of Bonaparte's wife. The reports we received were of quite a different nature than what you imagine."

"But did you not read the newspapers?" she pouted prettily. "What, pray, can have kept you from that? You have said yourself you were in those horrid camp for weeks on end, and yet you could not find time to relieve the boredom by looking at the newspaper?"

Scratching his side whiskers, Geoffrey replied that she must pardon him, for though he had often read the newspapers in the camp, it had not occurred to him to look at the fashion columns, for which he assured her he was now very sorry.

"I could tell you of the Spanish fashions, however," he offered. "For I was often in company with Spanish ladies, and I believe, though I am no judge, that their dress was quite lovely."

Miss Thornton shrugged at this, saying that Spanish fashions were nothing to French ones, but allowed him to describe what he could in the time left to them.

Chapter 3

THIS INTERVIEW LEFT Geoffrey less than satisfied, and he reflected on it that afternoon as he wandered again in the wood. It was unsurprising that Miss Thornton was unable to comprehend the complexities of military life; even men of information were often sadly lacking in that area. However, Geoffrey still was disappointed. Miss Thornton had shown an interest in his stories as long as they were full of adventure and heroism, but she seemed indifferent to his more prosaic contributions to the war effort. As these made up the majority of his three years' service, it was disheartening to think they could be so easily cast aside.

His steps naturally led toward the faerie clearing, but before he had reached it he was brought out of his reverie by the vaguely familiar sound of singing near at hand. He turned to see Miss Chandry round a corner on the path.

She hesitated, then came forward. "Forgive me, I fancied I was alone."

"I had forgotten that you sing," he said with a smile, bowing. "But how delightful to meet you here, of all places, Miss Chandry!"

"Indeed, I did not think to meet with you again." She colored, looking down. "Though this is the country, and we are old friends, you must own there is some impropriety in my meeting with a gentleman, alone."

He blinked, having never considered the matter, for she was nothing to him but a childhood friend. Nevertheless, he could not but recognize there was much truth in what she said.

"I wonder if I could persuade you to walk with me a while, Miss Chandry," said Geoffrey, gesturing to the path ahead. "If we are in motion, there is no impropriety."

Her warm look and acquiescence was his reward, and he offered his arm. "Do others walk here?"

"No, not often. At least on our property. In a moment we will cross over onto your property, and then we will have less privacy. It is still one of my favorite ways to wander," she explained, ducking under a tree branch. "There is nothing so peaceful as the wood after an unpleasant scene—" Her voice became suspended, though her footsteps continued on their unhurried way.

"Forgive me, Miss Chandry, if I am impertinent," he said quietly, "but are you often obliged to seek solace from home?"

She was some time in answering. "You must not imagine that my life is unbearable, or even that my father is—is—" She paused, as if considering her words. "He is disagreeable, but not violent. He simply does not understand people—at least, he does not understand me." She walked on in silence before adding, "It must be a very hard thing to have so odd a child."

Geoffrey's brow creased as he recalled with a pang that he had spent the majority of his youth allowing himself to believe her odd. And yet she had once been his dear friend, and now was as enjoyable a companion as any of the young ladies whom he had recently entertained.

His attempts to formulate a suitable reply were in vain; however, she asked him suddenly if he would mind very much telling her about Spain. Glad to turn both their thoughts away from her depressing situation, he readily obliged her, giving her a word picture of the varied landscape of the Peninsula, with its deserts and mountains and orange groves and brightly costumed people. He dwelt on the beauties and curiosities he had seen during his sojourn in Spain, thinking this would be more to her taste, as it had been to the other young ladies of his acquaintance.

"It must have been horrible to see such things destroyed, as no doubt they were, during the battles," was her response.

He glanced at her, startled at this unexpected comprehension of the matter. "Yes, there was much waste and wanton violence, looting and—other terrible acts. But there was also much heroism and kindness and sacrifice. That kind of beauty never can be destroyed."

She looked up and said, "It is a mercy, I believe. Where there is pain and terror, there is also some sort of blessing to soften the hurt."

He stopped to regard her, persuaded that not one young lady in a thousand would think of such an answer. It spoke to that part of his soul that had formed a bond with the peoples on the Peninsula, and that strove to make sense of their suffering.

"I should not wonder that you would see things so, Miss Chandry," he said at last. "You ever had a tender heart—though I never could comprehend it. You have experienced more discouragement than most people."

"I am not so elastic as you may think," she said, with a slight, rueful smile. "I have shaken my fist at Heaven in my time, but I know it avails me nothing. I must bear my troubles as best I can, for who knows but what I will be made stronger from it all."

"I have no doubt of it," he said, patting her hand where it rested on his arm.

They talked on as they wandered, of his time in the army and of her favorite haunts in the wood, until Geoffrey, remarking the extension of the shadows under the trees, checked his pocket watch. Exclaiming at the time, he looked around, getting his bearings.

"We ought to be getting home. May I escort you?"

"No, I thank you," said Emily, and at his further insistence added, "My father does not like to see strangers on his property."

Geoffrey was obliged to give it up. "Do you know your way from here? I believe we are on my father's land."

"Yes, I know the way well," she said, smiling and extending her hand to him. "Thank you."

He took her hand, thinking how restful a female she was, and impulsively kissed her fingers. "It was lovely, meeting you today. I hope to have the felicity of doing so again, someday soon."

She ducked her head to hide a blush and a widening smile, but returned the pressure of his fingers before turning away and disappearing into the trees.

As he had promised, Geoffrey went to retrieve his sister from Black Oaks, an elegant Georgian mansion on a prosperous-looking estate in Northamptonshire. Lady Drayford had condescended to have a nuncheon prepared for him, which was excellent—most especially his view of the fair Miss Angeline Drayford, whose beguiling dimples continually invited him to admire her. He was able to indulge her amply in this, as her ladyship sent the three young people out on a tour of the grounds, and Clara laughingly declared that she had rather walk with the gardener than remain as a third to so cozy a couple as Miss Drayford and Geoffrey were.

Geoffrey passed an enjoyable evening, which was marred only by the discovery by Lady Drayford that he was not Clara's eldest brother, causing that matron's pleasant smile to dim somewhat, but not enough to affect her young companions. Indeed, the following morning, she made a show to coax her young guests to remain another day, but Clara, though she "so dearly loved her dear, sweet Angeline, and should wish to stay for a hundred million more days with her," was packed and ready to depart directly after breakfast.

As the carriage swept away from the mansion, Geoffrey observed how his little sister had grown into a woman over the past three years. She was just turned eighteen, and was bidding fair to be a great beauty, like her mother, with glorious golden ringlets and deep, blue eyes, and he wondered if she would prove to have her mother's ambition as well.

"Did you enjoy your stay, Clara?"

"Oh! Prodigiously, Geoff, thank you," she said with a gaping yawn. "Only the men left yesterday, and Angeline is a dead bore, forever prosing on about gowns and balls and offers—she will be having her first season this winter as well, and we shall be great friends in Town."

Geoffrey gazed at her, bemused. "Do not you like gowns and balls and—and wish for offers?"

"Certainly, but I do not wish to be forever talking about them. There are so many more interesting things to be doing, especially when the gentlemen are about, however secretive one must be."

He raised an eyebrow. "Secretive about the gentlemen—or with them?"

She laughed, a musical tinkle made—he assumed—disastrously alluring by the impish twinkle in her eyes. "With them, but it is not what you suppose. How fast you must think me! I ought to be scandalized and fall into a swoon of maiden mortification. But I never swoon, and neither am I often scandalized."

She worked the gloves off her fingers and laid them in her lap, then pulled the pin from her hat and removed it, breathing a sigh of contentment. "Journeys of forty miles ought never to be attempted whilst wearing headgear, do not you agree?"

Geoffrey's forehead creased in his effort to get his sister's measure. She had written to him many times while he was on the Peninsula, but this strange mixture of worldly wisdom and disregard for decorum had not come through the letters. She seemed a most unconventional female, and he could not quite make her out.

Seeing his confusion, she laughed again. "You do not agree! You must pardon me. But do not fear, dear brother. I shall obediently don my hat and gloves before we stop to change horses, and no one shall be the wiser. I never disappoint my family, nor do I needlessly mortify my companions."

He smiled at this, saying, "You relieve my mind, though not entirely; dare I ask what interesting things you like to do, with or without the men?"

"To be sure! Without the men, I do what every other gently-bred female is wont to do: practice my instrument, sketch, embroider, and a thousand other dull things." She flashed him another of her impish looks, but this time it measured him, just as he had been measuring her. "With men, I like to bring them round my little finger and flirt and drive them mad. They can be so easily led, you know, though you will likely disagree with me. I imagine you are one of the less biddable sort, like Francis, who merely flirts back."

"I cannot tell," he said, chuckling at this very odd picture of himself.

"It does not signify," she said good-naturedly. "But you may see why I must go about these things in secret, for young ladies whose mothers go to great lengths to secure the society of several eligible gentlemen for a house party are not, in general, amused when another young lady sweeps in and singlehandedly captivates them all."

Geoffrey gazed at her in astonishment and she waved her hand, as if brushing away something inconsequential. "But now you know all there is to know about me, dear brother, and I know hardly anything of you. How do you go on here, without your regiment about you?"

He told her, and they talked of all that had happened since their last correspondence, while Geoffrey reconciled himself to having a hardened flirt for a sister. It was all of a piece, he reasoned, for Francis was cut from the same cloth, and he would count himself amazed if his mother and his father had not been entirely the same in their youth.

They arrived at Gracely Hall to the warmest of receptions: the Colonel was gone to dine with an old crony, Francis had sent his apologies as he had elected to dine with Charles Wraglain, and Mrs. Mantell greeted them with the information that they had obliged her to set dinner back an hour and would not they make haste, or all the evening would be ruined.

Clara, exchanging a look with Geoffrey, kissed her mother's cheek and said, "Hello, Mother. Yes, I am very well, and Geoffrey too. Our drive was splendid, with only the slightest difficulty in Weedoft, where they gave us the veriest slug of a wheeler, and thus we are late."

Mrs. Mantell sniffed and said, "You left Miss Drayford well, I hope."

"Oh, blooming; however, I imagine you had better let Geoffrey tell you how charmingly she looked." And with a saucy look at her brother, she withdrew to dress for dinner.

Geoffrey was able, through some adroit handling, to extricate himself from any firm commitment as to Miss Drayford's charms— for he had not mistaken the very civil dismissal in Lady Drayford's manner, and would not for the world lead his mother to believe he had any hope there. Then he went away to his rooms, inventing in his mind some horrid revenge upon his sister which would at once mortify and chasten her, while somehow keeping her regard. Upon reaching the drawing room a mere twenty minutes later, however, his vengeful thoughts gave way to complete amazement in finding Clara, in full dinner dress, already ensconced in a chair by the fire, virtuously conversing in low tones with her mother. This absolute departure from his mother's habit of taking an hour to dress for dinner led him to consider again that Clara was an extraordinary female.

This conviction was borne out on the following day when she appeared in the drawing room, dressed in something like a riding habit without the full skirts, and asked him to take her shooting.

He stared at her over his newspaper. "Do you mean with the dogs?"

"Oh, no! Only with a pistol or two. You need not shoot if you do not wish it. I merely must practice, but I cannot convince Morley that I know what I am about."

Geoffrey, in absolute agreement with the gamekeeper, asked her if she had been in the habit of shooting before.

She rolled her eyes, with that same impish look. "Good heaven, Geoffrey. You could not believe I would be so hen-witted as to go shooting willy-nilly."

"Then with whom can you have gone out?"

"Lawrence Simpford has been so obliging as to take me out once or twice, but I fear he has not the patience to continually tutor me. But you have always been my teacher in things such as this. I must take advantage of you while I can."

This was said with such sweet cajolery that Geoffrey groaned, laying aside his newspaper. "Heaven defend those poor sots in London, who know not what calamity awaits them!"

Geoffrey unearthed his pistol case and met Clara, who was holding a small bag under her arm as she drew on a pair of worn leather gloves. He did not ask after the bag but led her out the side door and across the lawns to the wood. It was not a long walk to an open area where Francis and Geoffrey had often practiced shooting, and Clara seemed familiar with the path. When the trees opened up before them, Geoffrey glanced about to ensure the marks were set firmly on their poles, and turned to see Clara removing a wooden case from her bag. To his utter amazement, she withdrew a handsome pistol from the case and set about loading it.

"Where had you that pistol?" inquired Geoffrey.

"From London," she said blithely.

"But you have not been to London."

"No, Francis purchased it for me." She looked at him askance, her eyes dancing. "To put it truthfully, I cozened and cajoled, wheedled and teased him until he purchased it for me and taught me to use it."

Geoffrey stared at her. "I distinctly recall your saying Simpford taught you—Francis never had the patience to teach you to shoot."

She laughed. "Only to hold the pistol, and to load it. He informed me in no uncertain terms that I should have to find others to teach me to shoot."

"Thus poor Lawrie. Was he very shocked?"

"My friends are never shocked, Geoff. I take great care that they are not."

Geoffrey shook his head, again pitying the poor gentlemen whose misfortune it would be to meet with Clara during her London season, and readied his pistol. "Is this another occupation that you must hide from the eyes of others?"

She made a sound of disgust. "It is, for I have discovered that females generally are expected to go into the vapors over guns, which I cannot comprehend at all, for what could one be afraid of? Unless the person handling the gun is an absolute ninnyhammer, and has no notion how to go on—but one simply does not trust such a one with a firearm."

Geoffrey found that he agreed with this great good sense, and asked Clara if her aspirations extended to the hunt.

"Oh, no, for where is the adventure in that? Hunting is entirely predictable, and a dead bore. Why one would wish to stumble about the countryside in all weathers simply to shoot at anything that moves, is beyond my comprehension. No, I had rather face a worthier foe, such as a highwayman or a cutthroat, or some other sort of villain, if only to see his face when I coolly pull out my pistol and point it at his heart." The faraway look in her eyes gave way to a smirk and she said, "And if I must wrap a man around my little finger to learn how to do it, all the better."

"I suppose it is my duty to teach you then, and save one or two of my fellowmen the ignominy of being made a fool of," said Geoffrey wryly.

Clara agreed archly with him, and they began the lesson. She had a good eye and a natural talent, and as she did not start or jerk away at the explosion, she bade fair to become a very tolerable shot.

After much of the morning had been whiled away in this manner, Clara suddenly let her gun arm fall and tilted her head, saying, "What do you think that can be, Geoff?"

He listened and heard ethereal singing. Turning quickly, he saw a slight figure with pale features half hidden in the trees. "Miss Chandry!" he exclaimed, then putting down his pistol, he made his way toward the figure, calling to her so that she would not run away.

Clara ran to catch him up. "Miss Chandry?" she hissed. "And what do you know about her, Geoffrey, pray? Mother expressly forbade intercourse between our two families, ages ago!"

"We met as children, Clara," Geoffrey said impatiently. "Besides, that is all past."

"But Mother and Father hate the Chandrys—Is this a romance, Geoff? Like Romeo and Juliet?"

"Their quarrel is with Sir Anthony, Clara, not with his daughter. She is our neighbor, and we will be civil."

"But you must be on such terms with her to merit a meeting—"

"She is an old friend, Clara, nothing more. She walks often in the wood, and I have met her once or twice."

By this time, they had come close enough to Emily to require an end to their whispered conversation, and Geoffrey greeted her. She stood uncertainly, looking at Clara with both interest and trepidation.

"This is my sister," supplied Geoffrey. "Miss Chandry, this is Miss Clara Mantell. She is eager to meet you."

Eying Emily with fascination, Clara shook hands, saying brightly, "It is strange, is it not, that we have never before met, Miss Chandry? Fancy being neighbors a whole lifetime, and not knowing one another."

"Yes, well, I am not much in society," said Emily, looking down and smoothing her dingy dress.

A silence ensued, and Geoffrey cut into it by saying, "You are on another of your walks, I see. It is fortunate that you came this way, so that we could meet you."

"I heard the shots," said Emily, with a conscious smile. "I was a little curious to see who it was. I have often seen your brothers and father here shooting, Miss Mantell, but I own I was surprised to see a female with a gun."

"I am a little unconventional, I am told," said Clara glibly. "But so you seem also to be. Are not you afraid of gunshots?"

Emily smiled. "I do not like loud noises in general; however, I have often wished to learn to handle a gun."

Clara eyed her with something like respect, and then the impish smile came over her lips. "Geoffrey would be pleased to teach you, I am certain."

Chapter 4

EMILY STARED AT Clara, her cheeks reddening. "I do not wish to disturb you. I will be on my way. I am delighted to have met you, Miss Mantell."

"No, no!" cried Clara, taking her arm and leading her back toward the shooting range. "Geoffrey has been teaching me, and is ready for a new pupil, I am certain. Are not you, Geoffrey?"

He was indeed willing—surprised as he was that Emily should desire to learn such a shocking sport—and gave her to understand as much. "We are already prepared with ball and pistols, Miss Chandry. Now would be an excellent time to teach you."

Emily only said, "You are too kind, and I am much obliged for your offer; however, it is my furthest wish to put you to so much trouble."

But Clara led her to the tables where the pistols lay. "You must use my pistol, Miss Chandry, for it is made for a lady, and is excellently balanced for a small hand."

Emily relented, taking the pistol and hefting it, and listening as Clara pointed out the various parts and mechanisms to her. "However, Geoffrey must teach you to shoot, for I am a mere beginner, besides being a woman," Clara said, lowering her lashes demurely and backing away.

Geoffrey, inwardly groaning at Clara's misapplied maneuvering, nevertheless stepped forward and assisted Miss Chandry to properly hold the pistol, to cock it, and to aim. She was fairly tense as he adjusted her arms, but he assumed she merely was as embarrassed as he to be in so intimate a posture with one whom she had always considered an old friend.

"Now steady yourself and prepare for the explosion and, when you are ready, you may pull the trigger," he said, his hand at her back for support.

She took a breath, closing her eyes, and squeezed the trigger. The pistol fired, and Geoffrey, anxiously watching her face, saw that he need not have feared; she smiled as she opened her eyes.

"How exhilarating!" she cried, heaving a happy sigh.

"You must continue!" said Clara, encouraging to the utmost. "Here, Geoff, I'll show Miss Chandry how to load it, then you may support her again as she shoots."

By the time they had repeated the exercise four or five times, all Miss Chandry's anxiety seemed to have gone, and she was laughing and looking with equal enjoyment on both her companions. But a distant gong sounded and she put the gun down directly, turning to Clara.

"I must go. Thank you, Miss Mantell, for the loan of your pistol," she said, putting out her hand for Clara to shake. "I shall never forget your kindness."

Turning to Geoffrey, she thanked him too, though with only a curtsy. Then she went back the way she had come, and Clara and Geoffrey watched her out of sight.

"Well," said Clara, when she had gone. "That is something I thought never to do."

"Meet our neighbor? I suppose it was unlikely, as things stood."

"Certainly, but it is too bad there is no romance between you. Goodness, Geoff! She did not even look coyly as you practically hugged her!" She sighed her disappointment.

Geoffrey merely shook his head.

"She seems genteel enough," Clara went on, "though her gown was the shabbiest thing I've ever seen. I suppose, however, that Sir Anthony's parsimony is to blame for it."

Geoffrey agreed to it, and they gathered their things. As they walked back to Gracely Hall, Geoffrey wondered idly if he might prevail upon Miss Chandry to take another lesson, while Clara lost interest in their neighbor altogether and talked of how to better her aim with the pistol.

With Clara's return, Mrs. Mantell could no longer require Geoffrey to accompany her on visits, but her intervention was unnecessary; he was not disinclined to be civil and accepted every invitation from their neighbors. Thus, the succeeding days found him at an al fresco picnic given by Mrs. Seely, walking the winding path to the Holy Well with a lively group gathered by Mrs. Thornton, and playing Speculation at the Simpford's. There were many pleasant young ladies at these outings, and pretty ones too, though none could rival Miss Thornton for pure beauty.

However, he could not hide his disappointment at their understanding. If one proved herself able to converse on a subject outside fashion or London seasons, she seemed uninterested in the realities he had experienced in the army. When he talked of his encampments on the Peninsula, she said it sounded romantic, and when he spoke of the challenges still obtaining in France, she squealed and tittered about the balls in Paris. With no desire to relate every dreary occurrence in Spain, and a deep-seated optimism for the future, Geoffrey nevertheless found it wearing to participate in conversation after conversation in which his experience was treated lightly, as if the war was simply a succession of playground battles over and done, and not soon enough forgot.

A sennight of these entertainments saw Geoffrey drawn away again to the clearing, where he sought both solitude and rest, but his entrance into the little bower surprised Emily at work amongst the villagers.

"Lieutenant Mantell!" she said, startled but not unwelcoming. "I wondered if you had forgot this place, you have been gone from the wood so long."

He removed his hat, turning it in his hands. "Forgive me, I have been otherwise engaged. My mother feels it is high time I was married, and has thrown herself into introducing me to all the eligible young ladies in the neighborhood."

"I see," she said, turning back to the villager she had been repairing.

He settled himself against a tree trunk and sighed. "I do not mind it so much, for I should like to have a wife, and they are very amiable girls; however, after some of these entertainments, I feel world-weary—as if I were a hundred years old."

She did not answer immediately, but when she did, she kept her back to him, continuing her work. "I imagine that one who has seen as much as you have could not help but feel weary."

"Yes," he said, gazing into the middle distance. "It is hard to come away from turmoil and violence and danger to be civil and proper and quiet. I ought to be relieved, and I am—so relieved that I often do not believe it is over. The memories of battle and privation are always underneath my thoughts, and will not be suppressed forever. I need to see them, to feel them, and sometimes even to speak them, in order that I may know they are past and done. But they seem to have no place in civil conversation."

Her hands stilled as she bowed over her work, and silence settled over them for several moments. Then she turned to look at him.

"You may speak them to me," she said, "if you wish."

He settled his abstracted gaze on her, seeing the tender concern in her large gray eyes. "You are always so good, Miss Chandry, but I do not wish to burden you so. You have already enough to bear."

She shrugged. "A shared burden may strengthen both parties."

"I could have guessed you would answer me so," he said, smiling and looking away again. "But you are right. There was a soldier on the battlefield after Toulouse, who had lost a leg and an eye in the fighting. I had sustained only superficial wounds, but was weak from the loss of blood. He reached and grasped my hand as we lay awaiting rescue. I never felt so strong."

His gaze shifted again to her. "You said once before that there are mercies in every horror. You were right."

"That is why I cannot view any one of my difficulties as so very bad," she said. "There is always something good, however small, or however late, that comes of it. And there is always someone whose difficulties eclipse mine."

Then she coaxed him to tell her more of the experiences that haunted him, and he felt lighter and more free with every disclosure.

But at last, the gong sounded and he was forced to acknowledge that she must go.

"And here we have been, ensconced alone again," he said lightly, helping her to stand. "But I trust you will not mind it, for we are such old friends that I do not think of the conventions when we are together."

Her gaze faltered, and she removed her hands from his grasp. "Of course not. Here in the faerie clearing I feel in a different world, and almost feel a different person. Though perhaps we ought, in future, to take care, for there is no saying what others, who do not know the peculiarities of our situation, may think."

"I do not see that as very likely, for who comes to this part of the wood but ourselves?" he said blithely, settling his hat on his head and allowing her to proceed him from the clearing.

They parted, and Geoffrey made his way back to the Hall, refreshed and ready to accompany his mother and sister to a card party that evening. There he conversed easily with the young ladies, finding their naivete about the war only a trifle bothersome after the tonic of his dialog with Emily in the wood. He could even appreciate Miss Thornton's flirtatious sallies, believing that as long as he had a friend to whom he could occasionally unburden himself, a pretty wife would be quite a satisfying companion.

A few more days of Southam society, therefore, took him again to the clearing, but it was empty this time. Upon close inspection, however, he instantly saw signs that Emily had recently been busy there—and intriguing signs they were. Removing his gloves, he crouched down to inspect a new little building that bore a small wooden plaque with the inscription, "Post Office." Inside, there was tucked a note.

> *Let it hereby be known that this Post Office shall be for*
> *sundry correspondence, including that which will be for*
> *the information of all the inhabitants of this village, to*
> *make them aware of the movements and intents of those*
> *concerned in their welfare, and to publish such tidings as*
> *will enlighten and amuse them.*

Grinning, Geoffrey refolded the note and tucked it into his pocket. Emily had ever been the clever one. Her anxiety over their accidental meetings in the wood being detected and construed as improper he considered unfounded, but he found her solution impressive. The post office was a most suitable means of communication between them, being indirect correspondence that could not be looked on askance. Indeed, it was child's play—but most useful, for it would both answer his need to share his memories with someone, and further their friendship, whether or not they met again.

Pulling out his pocketbook, he scratched a note to leave in the post office.

> *To whom it may concern: One who is concerned in the*
> *welfare of this village wishes to declare his approbation*
> *for this edifice and its purpose, and promises to both*
> *contribute to its usefulness and partake of its offerings.*

Though Geoffrey's leave was half over, Mrs. Mantell was by no means discouraged in her quest to find a suitable match for her military son. His imminent return to his regiment was of little consequence; even should the war resume, he could easily take a bride with him to the Continent. Paris had been little ravaged by the war, and a young military bride could enjoy herself reasonably while her husband went about his duties. And if he was injured in a battle, well, he had already got a wife, who could do no other than remain at his side, whether she thought him hideous or no. But if he were wise enough to make his choice from among the eligibles his thoughtful mother had thrown in his way, money would no longer be an issue, and his wife might manage to convince him to sell out before any calamity had befallen him.

Thus, Geoffrey's insistence upon walking out in the wood became a distress to her, for though she saw nothing in it at first, the buoyancy of his spirits upon his return seemed inconsistent with one who had merely communed with nature. When she could not find out that any high-born heiresses were apt to appear with regularity in the wood, she began to have dark suspicions of his activities therein, and at last she stooped to the expedient of sending Morley to spy on him. Her worst fears were justified by his report that the lieutenant had gone to meet with a shabbily dressed young woman whom he believed to be Sir Anthony's daughter.

This was enough to strike horror in Mrs. Mantell's maternal breast, for Sir Anthony, having denied all claims to delicacy and breeding by keeping low and vulgar company and treating his neighbors with disrespect, could never produce offspring of any worth whatsoever. This girl of Sir Anthony's was undoubtedly a designing hussy, intent upon trapping Geoffrey in some way. That the game keeper never again saw the young woman was immaterial to Mrs. Mantell, for he had said that the lieutenant returned always to the same spot—and Mrs. Mantell had long ago lost all illusions when it came to the voracity of the male appetite. He would not return if it was not to meet the girl, and Mrs. Mantell could see all her carefully laid plans crumbling into dust.

Geoffrey was quite unaware of the vexation he had caused, for his mother was ever temperamental, and he detected no alteration in her manner toward him from one day to the next. He therefore continued to visit the clearing whenever society had proved too much for his patience, and to write out his memories as stories for the villagers. This habit so relieved him of care that it further fortified his bond with the clearing, and though he had determined at first to go only occasionally, he was drawn thither almost daily.

There were other inducements for him to visit the faerie village, for his memory-stories were joined by others—detailing the adventures of a young inmate of an ogre's castle—and he came to comprehend more fully what was Emily's situation. The ogre, of course, was Sir Anthony, and there were goblins and hags and giants who figured as his odious guests, and whose execrable manners toward the young inmate confirmed many of his suspicions regarding the challenges of Emily's youth. There were some faithful retainers in the castle who did what they could for the safety and well-being of the child, but one by one they were let go, and the child was forced more and more often to fend for itself. As time wore on, it was made to become a servant, because the ogre could not be bothered to care for the child or the house, but the child had become wise beyond its years and learned magic charms to make the work light and to make itself invisible to the ogre's horrid guests.

These stories soon expanded to include others of the villagers and their kingdom, and Lieutenant Mantell joined whole-heartedly in the game. It was a secret life that he relished, and strove, though insensibly, to keep it from the knowledge of others. How could he explain himself to any of the young ladies who tittered and dimpled and gazed up at him, or his friends who laughed and quizzed him about sport, believing him to be a man of sense and rationality? No one need ever know of the faerie clearing and his pursuits there, he reasoned within himself, for it was merely a game to help him transition from war to peace, and would, by and by, cease to be necessary to him.

But as the game went on, his enjoyment of it grew, and his curiosity to see what might be found in the post office continued to draw him there. Once there was a small piece of rose quartz, with a note proclaiming the joy of the faerie queen that her heart stone had been reclaimed. This occasioned his creation of a pedestal upon which to place the heart stone, which was accepted by the queen with a posy of tiny flowers, gathered from the edges of the clearing and placed at the foot of the pedestal.

In his turn, he left a little booklet with a story of the wreck of a faerie ship on the great river which flowed nearby, complete with what he deemed to be cunning illustrations. A eulogy on the perished seamen appeared in answer, pronouncing them to have been pirates in disguise, and the survivors to have fought them bravely before abandoning them to the sinking ship. So Geoffrey added, one by one, a small regiment of faerie soldiers, with a captain to lead them, sword held high. This, however, had apparently distressed the villagers, who submitted to the post office an inquiry regarding the regiment's intent. A soothing letter of introduction from the newly styled Duke of Wellington followed, which served so well to ease the worries of the villagers that they hosted a Grand Fete, complete with flower crowns for the soldiers and a banner declaring "*Pax Aeternus.*"

All this—which Geoffrey insisted to himself was a delightful game and nothing more—produced in him such a flow of spirits that his family could not but remark it, and his mother was vexed enough by this time that she shared her maternal frustrations with her husband.

Colonel Mantell merely scoffed, saying, "If you'd give him his head as you should have done long ago with Francis, he'd come about. It's my belief you've driven him to it, Anamaria."

"How can you say so, when all I've ever done is to put some eligible girls in his way?" she demanded. "And very eligible girls, I must say—not a one with less than five thousand pounds, and all of them very pretty."

"Humph! That Leamington chit looks like a horse," replied the Colonel, picking up a newspaper.

"That is neither here nor there," sniffed Mrs. Mantell. "What I wish to know is what you intend to do about Geoffrey."

"What about Geoffrey?"

"His horrid habit of haring off into the wood after some hussy!" cried Mrs. Mantell.

Colonel Mantell straightened his paper with a snap. "Nothing, my dear."

"Nothing? Nothing? Have you no pride? Have you no consideration for your name, or for your son's prospects? How can you tell me you intend to do nothing?" she fairly shrieked.

"I wish you will stop behaving like a fishwife, Anamaria," said the Colonel, glancing down the advertisements in the newspaper. "What Geoffrey is doing has no bearing on my name or my pride."

"It will soon enough, when Sir Anthony is on our doorstep claiming his daughter has got with child by our son!"

He cast her a deprecating look. "Your imagination is by far too active, my dear. Geoffrey will take good care that does not happen."

Mrs. Mantell stared at him. "Then what do you think he is doing?"

"He is doing what every other young man of his age does with too much time on his hands and a marriage-mad mother breathing down his neck. There are methods of prevention he is no doubt aware of. Leave him be, for heaven's sake, Anamaria! He must report to his regiment in two weeks, and then there will be an end to it."

She whirled and stomped away, feeling him to be far too sanguine on the matter for her comfort. Having one son follow in his father's footsteps had been bad enough, but to have two was insupportable. And Geoffrey had promised so well—but she would not dwell on what was past. She had long ago developed a resolve only to look to the future, for the past held only mistakes that made one despondent and prone to the discomfort of self-examination.

Chapter 5

GEOFFREY WAS NOT insensible that his family took an interest in his proceedings. Francis had more than once twitted him on what he supposed were amorous rendezvous in the wood, and made it plain that he approved. This Geoffrey determined to let pass, for he fancied that Francis could not truly believe him capable of something so improper.

But he was shocked and dismayed one afternoon when Clara, clipping roses while he held her basket, said, "I know what you have been doing in the wood, Geoffrey. I confess, I had not thought you the sort of man to engage in such activities."

He gazed sharply at her, his brows lowered. "I imagine you have been listening to Francis, and wonder at your having paid any heed to him."

"I never heed Francis. He is a rake and a libertine, and his light-skirts seem incapable of enlightenment."

"Clara!" cried Geoffrey, shocked. "You are not so indelicate as to address his—his companions on this matter!"

She shrugged, reaching into a bush with her shears. "One does what one can, but in the end, it is out of one's hands. However, I flatter myself that you, my dear Geoffrey, are still within my reach, and so I shall endeavor to reclaim you."

"Your solicitude is moving," said Geoffrey, irritated. "But what my movements can have to do with Francis's proclivities, you must explain, for even had you the effrontery to follow me into the wood, you cannot know the whole."

"It was not necessary that I follow you, Geoffrey," she said, casting him a deprecatory look. "I have an excellent memory, and perfectly recall making the acquaintance of a certain young lady, whom you owned to meeting in the wood, over a fortnight ago. When your predilection for wandering in the wood became impossible to ignore, I determined to see if I could discover the cause—and I did. Mother would be most shocked."

Geoffrey's jaw worked. "Because I am not so detestable as Francis?"

"No one is so detestable as Francis—excepting our father, of course." She tilted her head to look up at him. "I fully comprehend your keeping it a secret from Mother and Father and Francis, for they have very little imagination. I, however, have a prodigious imagination, and am horribly wounded at your selfishness in keeping your creation from me."

His outraged response died on his lips. "My creation?"

"That miniature village is astonishingly clever, Geoff. Just how you managed to build it eludes me—those clumsy fingers of yours. As a boy, perhaps, you were more deft with your hands, but now—" She huffed at the thought, eying his large, gloved hands where they held the basket. "I imagine the chief of the buildings were done that long ago summer, wherein you also wandered much in the wood—you see, I do have an excellent memory—and you have merely been furbishing them up since your return."

Taken completely aback, Geoffrey stammered that it was the case, and asked her pardon for believing her to have had a very different idea.

Clara laughed. "Oh, you must not beg my pardon, for I did have a very different idea. Indeed, I was certain you had a lover, and wondered if it might not be Miss Chandry, for which I would have taken you to task, Geoffrey, for though she is Sir Anthony's daughter, she is not vulgar in the least, and it would be shocking for you to take advantage of a gently-bred young lady in that way. But as not even Francis would dare to do such a thing, I assumed it was some willing village maid, for Francis and Father were full of knowing looks and manly chuckles whenever you were gone out, which could mean only one thing. You have risen a rung or two in their estimation, and only think what should happen if they were to discover the real cause of your clandestine outings—"

He exclaimed, but she put up a hand, stopping him. "Do not fear my apprising them of the true nature of things, Geoff. Though I am disappointed at being excluded from your confidence, I cannot but put it down to our not knowing one another well—your having been on the Peninsula and I having been at school these three years—and I should never be so mean as to expose you to Father and Francis for that."

"Thank you," he managed.

Clara placed a few more blooms in the basket and turned back toward the house. "I shall prove my good faith with a promise not to go to the clearing without your express invitation, and I will not mention the matter again. Having thus satisfied you as to my trustworthiness, dear brother, I hope to be better used in future."

This was said with an impish sideways look, but she did not wait for an answer, merely walking on into the house, and Geoffrey remained silent, uncertain whether to be grateful for her secrecy, or angry that all of them had so easily believed him to be lacking in virtue. His instinct was instantly to undeceive his father and brother, but when given the opportunity, he discovered he was reticent to do so. He was uncertain as to how to explain matters without bringing Emily's name into it, for though Clara was content to believe he had all along been going to the clearing alone, Geoffrey knew that Francis and the Colonel would never credit it—indeed, they should think him a madman to be playing at dolls.

Perhaps it was for the best that they remain deceived. As long as the Colonel believed Geoffrey to be engaged with an unknown village girl in a harmless flirtation—Geoffrey did not allow himself to consider exactly what the Colonel would think harmless—the remainder of his stay would be pleasant. And when he left to rejoin his regiment, his supposed activities would become a mere memory, with no stain attached—inasmuch as his "lover" remained incognito.

His next visit to the clearing found Emily there, singing quietly as she tidied up the debris left by a small summer storm of the previous night. Made conscious by his family's misconceptions, he paused at the entrance.

"Good morning, Miss Chandry."

She turned quickly, but her wariness dissipated upon perceiving him. "Lieutenant Mantell. It is lovely to see you, but you are a day early for the festival."

At his questioning look, she gestured to the post office. "There is a notice of the Midsummer's Eve festival to be held tomorrow, but it could easily be changed to today."

"Is it Midsummer's Eve?" he asked, confused.

"Not precisely," she said, returning to her work. "It was last month, however we missed the day. Therefore, the villagers voted that the festival shall be held late, and in your honor."

"The honor is mine." He smiled at this simple solicitude, which he had come almost to expect in her. "Tell the queen the celebration need not be moved. I shall return on the morrow," he said with a bow.

She glanced quickly up at him, as if to say something, but merely nodded and turned back to her work with a small sigh.

Geoffrey considered her, sensible that she was not comfortable being alone with him, but conscious of the droop to her shoulders and the resignation in her sigh. Perhaps she regretted that he should be gone so soon. There could be no harm in their taking one half hour together, here in the magical clearing, where convention held no sway.

Removing his hat and gloves, he stepped into the clearing and knelt by her side. "We must make haste if we are to be ready for so august an occasion."

She stilled for a moment, but then her bearing softened and she smiled, and he suddenly felt as if the sun had come into the clearing.

"Very well, Lieutenant," she said. "Many hands do make light work."

"Even such clumsy ones as mine?" he asked with a wry grin.

She answered only with a smirk, setting back to work with vigor. They worked busily together, and after almost an hour—and thanks in large part to Emily's small and nimble fingers, which undid any damage Geoffrey's ineptitude caused—the decoration was completed.

They sat back, admiring their work, and Emily clapped her hands, turning to him with a laugh and delight shining in her large gray eyes. He had never seen her look so well, and he thought that she should be made to laugh and smile more often.

Emily's eyes searched his for a moment, then she stood and dusted off her shabby gown. "I must be going. My father will wish his dinner soon, and we have lately lost our cook."

Geoffrey jumped up beside her, handing her gloves to her. "You will be looking for a new cook, then?"

"Oh, no. My father feels that I have little enough to do, and so he may as well save the money," she said, studiously adjusting the buttons at her wrists.

He regarded her averted face with chagrin. "It is infamous of him to do so." She did not respond and he asked quietly, "Do you mind it very much?"

Her eyes flew to his, and he suspected that she did mind, but she said, "Not very much. It is good to be useful, and to have employment when the days are so long."

He watched her final preparations with vexation, the story of the inmate of the ogre's castle flitting through his brain. As she extended her hand to take her leave, he took it and pressed it. "Sir Anthony does not deserve so good a daughter as you."

Her color heightened as she withdrew her hand and quitted the clearing, and he watched her out of sight through the wood before making his way back to the Hall. He was mildly comforted by the thought that at least she had the Midsummer's Eve celebration to look forward to.

This celebration passed differently than he had anticipated: Emily was not there. She had set out a small feast of cold meat and fruit, tartlets and a tiny pudding, the procurement of which, her note said, was thanks to her recent assignment as cook, and so he must not repine at her elevation to the post. He ate it for her sake, wishing that she were there to talk to him, but recognizing that it would have been no less than what his misguided relations expected if he had made an assignation with her.

His modest repast finished, he lay back on the ground and gazed up at the bright blue sky that peeked through the trees above the bower, and considered what awaited him in his future. The war had ended, but it had ended many times before, and things were so unsettled on the Continent that there was no telling whether another war would not break out. He had hoped to find a lady to follow the drum with him, but if he was truthful, none of the young ladies he had become acquainted with over the last two months had convinced him she was the one. Perhaps he wanted more time, or perhaps he might find the perfect young lady in Plymouth, where his regiment was stationed, at one of the many assemblies and parties to which he, as an officer, would no doubt be invited.

His thoughts were interrupted by a light step nearby, and he turned to see Emily come into the clearing. He moved to stand up, but she knelt beside him, begging him not to trouble himself, for she would stay only a moment.

"I was not going to come," she said in her gentle way, "however, I found that I could not stay away. This may be my only opportunity to bid you farewell."

"I am glad you have come, Miss Chandry, for I would deeply regret not taking proper leave of you."

She averted her eyes. "I wish to thank you, Lieutenant. You have been such a friend to me, indulging my childish flights and oddities. You have brought me so much joy—you shall never know how much."

Reaching quickly, she plucked the faerie queen's heart stone from its pedestal and put it into his hand. "Take this, please, for me. To remember me by."

"Certainly. I shall have it set in a pin," he said, closing his hand over the stone.

She looked at him then, and her large eyes held such a contrariety of emotions—sorrow, gratitude, hope, and resignation—that he was moved to say, "You are not an oddity, Miss Chandry, nor do I consider what we have done here childish in the least. You have given me back my childhood that was lost all those years ago, and helped me to make sense of my present situation! You have a magic about you that defies disappointment and pain, and fills everyone around you with wonder. I would not have you altered for the world."

She smiled a little at that. "You and our faerie villagers, I suppose, for my father merely wonders what can be wrong with me."

He shook his head. "Sir Anthony cannot know what a treasure he has in you, Miss Chandry. I pray someday he will."

Coloring faintly, she thanked him in a muffled tone, and he took her hand and kissed it, pressing it for good measure. "I wish you happiness, Miss Chandry. I wish for you to prevail over the ogre, and to find your prince, and to escape into the bright horizon to be happy forever."

She blinked quickly at him, and her throat worked as she swallowed. Her gaze searching his face, she said, in a suffocated tone, "Thank you, sir. May you find happiness as well."

Then, her eyes shining with tears, she bid him goodbye and fled the clearing.

❧

His final evening at Gracely Hall, Geoffrey's mother remarked at dinner that she would say her goodbyes tonight, as she could not be expected to rise as early as he would be leaving. After her retirement from the dining room, his father produced a very old bottle of port that he had desired Grimsley to bring up from the cellar, to celebrate his son.

Pouring out generous libations for the three of them, Colonel Mantell congratulated Geoffrey on weathering the visit so well.

"For I'll not scruple to say your mother can be downright bull-headed sometimes. What fustian to be throwing at your head every eligible young lady in the neighborhood, when she knows full well you intend to return to France. Nonsense to get leg-shackled just so you can leave your lady behind, for only a cod's head will drag his wife all over the Continent keeping the peace. All a soldier needs is a female squawking over billeting arrangements or servants or food. Best stay single and carefree yet a while."

Francis sipped his port. "I wonder if she ever guessed how futile her arrangements have been all along."

"Oh, she did guess!" said the Colonel, laughing heartily. "You've the true Mantell mettle, Geoffrey, to disregard her machinations so completely."

Geoffrey glanced warily from one to the other. "If any of the ladies had taken my fancy, I should have thanked my Mother, but such was not the case."

"I'd say not," said Francis, rolling his eyes. "What hen-witted crea-tures females are, forever believing men to be pining for marriage!"

"It's the doom of every gentleman, my boys, but it need not be entered into too soon," opined the Colonel. "Better to enjoy your salad days without the baggage."

Francis toasted untrammeled bachelordom, and Geoffrey mechanically raised his glass, wishing his early departure next morning was an acceptable excuse for retiring betimes. His father, sensing his reticence, scowled at him.

"Don't tell me you've fallen for the chit, Geoffrey."

Geoffrey's gaze snapped to his father. "What chit, Father?"

"You know very well what chit, son, and I say it won't do, so don't even think it. She's all very well for a flirtation, but more would disgrace the Mantell name."

As Geoffrey stared in horror at his father, Francis came to his side, slapping his back. "Come, Father, you know he'd never consider such a thing. Not with that drab little piece."

Pushing Francis away, Geoffrey said tautly, "What drab little piece?"

"The Chandry girl, Geoff!"

"She's Sir Anthony's child, Geoffrey," put in the Colonel, pouring another glass of port. "The man's a commoner, no matter his title, and though she's been dashed convenient for you, put upon as you've been by your mother's matchmaking, I'll not countenance more than that."

"I do not have the pleasure of understanding you, Father," Geoffrey ground out, his fists clenched tightly. "Miss Chandry is the daughter of a baronet, and is a gently-bred young lady. In what way does her upbringing open her to insults of this kind?"

"Come now, Geoff," interpolated Francis. "No insults intended. If you don't want your lady fair's name dragged in the mud, we'll not say a word about it."

"She is not my lady fair!" cried Geoffrey, shooting to his feet. "What can you have been thinking? That I have been dallying with our neighbor's daughter? Playing fast and loose with a virtuous young lady?"

The Colonel narrowed his eyes but said, "If you've no more interest in her than a neighbor, then why the devil have you sneaked off into the wood after her every day? Come now, Geoffrey, you can't bamboozle us into believing you've chivalrous intentions."

"I've not!" Geoffrey thundered, then caught himself with an oath. Gritting his teeth, he said, "Miss Chandry is my friend, and is the gentlest, sweetest creature imaginable. She has been a companion and a kindly listener, but that is where it ends. What you suggest is so wrong, so evil in connection with her, that I can scarcely keep from striking you down as we speak!"

Colonel Mantell stood slowly, leaning both hands on the table before him. "If Miss Chandry, as you call her, is such a lady, why has she met with you, unchaperoned and unprotected, in a lonely spot out of the public eye?"

"Doing it too brown, Geoff," drawled Francis, taking a sip of his port.

"Who told you we have met?" demanded Geoffrey.

"Morley saw you, more than once."

Geoffrey silently cursed all interfering game keepers and coarse-minded fathers and brothers in the world. Taking a shuddering breath, he said distinctly, "My relationship with Miss Chandry is that of brother and sister, for we were friends as children, so there was no impropriety. Her meeting with me those few times was accidental, and her being unaccompanied is no worse than any other young lady who walks about alone in the country; indeed, Sir Anthony does not keep a maid or other servant to act as her chaperon. The clearing where we met was our old play place, and nothing happened, I swear it! Miss Chandry is always and forevermore a lady, and I respectfully request that you will take back your vile insinuations, sir!"

The Colonel's brows lowered at his son. "All this over a rag-tag female with no prospects and no charms to recommend her. I tell you I was amazed at your choice of entertainment, but I overlooked it for your sake. But now you'll have me believe that nothing happened? I'll tell you what it is! It's a hum to soothe your namby-pamby conscience, and I've nothing to take back, for I'm devilish certain I've hit upon the truth, and you're not man enough to own it!"

Geoffrey brought his glass down onto the table with a crash and quit the room, flinging the door shut behind him, but not before Francis's words floated out to him.

"'Methinks the lady doth protest too much.'"

The Colonel's shout of laughter was loud enough to penetrate the closed door, and it followed Geoffrey up to his rooms, and kept him tossing and turning far into night.

Chapter 6

GEOFFREY WISHED HEARTILY when he woke the following morning that his father and his brother would not bother to see him off, for he was not of a mind to treat either of them with respect. His chagrin on finding Francis in the breakfast parlor, therefore, was great, and was scarcely disguised by his cold greeting.

Francis, gorgeous to behold in a dressing gown of blue embroidered silk, watched him over the rim of his coffee cup, waiting as he filled his plate with ham and eggs and a buttered bun before saying, "I was a coward to take Father's side last night, Geoff. I beg your pardon."

Pausing only momentarily, Geoffrey remained silent as he turned to place his plate carefully on the table and pour himself a dish of tea.

"You may see why Father never pushed me into the army," remarked Francis, still gazing at Geoffrey, who studiously stirred sugar into his tea.

"You are not only a coward, but a blackguard as well," said Geoffrey, placing the spoon carefully next to the cup.

Francis huffed, a tiny smile curving his lips. "I am. But you need not regard it. Only know, Geoff, that I'll do what I may to turn Father's attention away from Miss Chandry, so that no rumors get about to soil her reputation."

Geoffrey's brow creased as he fought to reconcile this repentant man with the careless brother of last night. He cut fiercely into his ham, saying, "I only hope you may meet with success." He ate in silence for some time, then said firmly, "I did not lay with her, Francis. She is no trollop."

"I did not think you had." Francis traced the edge of his cup with a finger. "You are a better man than I, Geoff. I have always known it."

Geoffrey finished his breakfast in a subdued mood, then stood, taking up his hat and gloves which rested on the table's edge. "Do you go to Weymouth?"

Francis huffed a weak laugh. "Yes, by way of Leicestershire. I go tomorrow."

"Happy hunting," said Geoffrey, with a half smile. A heavy silence ensued and he looked out the window and sighed. "I must go if I am to meet my regiment at Plymouth tomorrow."

Francis stood, extending his hand. "Goodbye, Geoff."

"Goodbye, Francis." Geoffrey shook hands with him, smiling with some real warmth, and left the breakfast parlor.

Clara came running down the stairs to see him off, and Geoffrey's mood was so improved that he could even forgive her thinking ill of Miss Chandry, and gave her a parting embrace. She followed him onto the porch steps and stood waving as his carriage rumbled down the drive, and he shook his head, wondering at the strangeness of his relationships with the inhabitants of Gracely Hall.

❦

Though Francis's promise did much to quell some parts of his anger, Geoffrey's spirits remained unquiet, for he knew now, more than ever, that he would never call Gracely home. How could he, if he was required to defend himself against the base assumptions of his relations, and to deflect their effects from innocent others? That his father could wink at his son debasing himself was disgusting to him, and he wondered that he was of the same stock. His mother was not much better—she looked no further than fortune and birth in a prospective wife for her sons. It was unsurprising that Francis and Clara had turned out as they had.

But what of himself? He had dismissed Emily's concerns at meeting clandestinely in the wood as baseless, with the outcome that she now stood on the brink of ruin if Francis was unsuccessful in curbing his father's ribald tongue. Geoffrey thought himself a gentleman, and yet had compromised an innocent girl's reputation through mere carelessness. By the looks of things, he was no better than his siblings. It was lowering and humbling to contemplate, and he prayed that Francis would come through, and not forget his promise.

He arrived at Plymouth, where his duties as lieutenant served well to redirect his thoughts, and for some weeks, he was kept busy enough to have very little time for quiet reflection. Social engagements claimed him as well, as the officers were eagerly sought as guests at dinner parties, assemblies, and routs, as well as card parties. But he could not enjoy these as he had done in Warwickshire, for whenever he became annoyed at the young ladies' naivete, there was no Miss Chandry to ease the perturbation of his spirits, and he lost his taste for female company. There was time and to spare to find a wife, he reasoned, and threw himself into hunting and sports.

Thus the autumn passed, and his brother officers began to talk of going home for the winter, while Geoffrey considered a sojourn in London for Clara's season. But then his regiment received notice of Bonaparte's escape from Elba, and of their assignment to intercept the French army in Belgium. The renewal of war—which brought the very real possibility that he may never return from the Continent—was daunting, but his honor and restless spirits were eager for action, and he took leave of England in March of 1815 without much regret.

As Bonaparte's army marched toward Belgium, and Wellington's troops readied themselves outside of Brussels, Geoffrey wondered if he ought to write to Emily, if only to say goodbye. He would write to Clara and his mother as well, of course, but Emily was foremost in his thoughts, and he was uncertain as to why.

It was not until he lay bruised and bleeding on the battlefield at Waterloo, after the endless attacks of the French had felled thousands upon thousands of his brethren, and the certainty of death had hovered over him even as Blucher's army arrived to ensure the final defeat of Napoleon, that Geoffrey began to understand. In the minutes that seemed like eternities as he awaited his fate, he thought only fleetingly of Clara and Francis, for his mind revolved upon one face: it was not Miss Thornton with her cherry mouth, or Miss Drayton with her beguiling dimples—but Miss Emily Chandry, her luminous eyes filled with unfailing sympathy and tender care.

In the haze of pain and exhaustion, the wish uppermost in his thoughts was that Emily could be transported to his side, to hear of his exertions, his triumphs and his mistakes, to tell him that she had prayed for him and hoped for his return, and to make him see the good that would come of all this horror. For he was certain there would be good, if he could live to see it, for Emily had said so, and he believed her with all his heart.

He did live to see it. He saw the people of Brussels band together to care for the wounded and to bury the dead. He saw the joy of the people of Belgium as the Allied army marched through the countryside toward France, cheering and crying and waving banners to proclaim the end to Bonaparte's rule. He watched the result of the signing of the Treaty of Paris, where the weary Continent could at last hope for prolonged peace.

Through it all, though months elapsed and his injuries healed and his duties resumed, he thought of Emily—how she would wish him to carry on, and to see the beauty in ashes, and eventually, to return to her. This became his intention, for he recognized now that he loved her. Those weeks that he had sought to recommend himself to various damsels, that he had searched for a wife, he had been searching in the wrong places—his best hope for happiness, his perfect companion had been all the while next door, in the faerie clearing.

He had been a clodpole not to see it before. He had grown into love with her so gradually and quietly over the weeks of his leave that he had not recognized it as love, and perhaps never would have, had his father not made such vile insinuations against her. It was the Colonel's vitriol that had shattered all Geoffrey's pretense at caring for anyone but Emily, and since that day he had not been able to think of another female.

His bravery at Waterloo—coupled with his survival—earned him an advancement to the rank of Captain and a commission to remain as part of the Army of Occupation, whose duty it was to keep the peace until the new French government was established, and to see that reparations were made. This commission he greeted with mixed emotions. It was an honor, and ensured his continued employment, for the war had cost Britain a great deal, and many soldiers were to be turned off. But it would mean he must put off a reunion with Miss Chandry, for leave was difficult to obtain at that moment. He could, however, declare his feelings and be assured of their return, even if they could not be together until the end of the Occupation. So he accepted the commission and wrote to Sir Anthony to request his permission to address his daughter.

In the months that he waited for a reply, Geoffrey received many letters from Clara, and even some from Mrs. Mantell. His mother wrote to inform him of a seizure his father had sustained, and which had rendered him weak and unable to speak above a whisper—a circumstance which prevented the Colonel from expressing his congratulations on Geoffrey's rank advancement with his own pen. This news caused Geoffrey some concern, but he doubted not that his father, with characteristic mulishness, would not succumb to a weakness of this kind.

Clara wrote to tell him of the beaux she had collected during her London season, of house parties and balls, and of her improvement with her pistol. But Geoffrey waited for Sir Anthony's reply in vain. Two months lengthened into three, and three into four, during which he reasoned that either the letter had gone astray in the post, or that Sir Anthony had burnt it rather than lose his unpaid servant.

He sent another letter, with the same result. Clara wrote to apprise him of the several marriages of the young ladies he had known while last in Warwickshire, rallying him that their numbers would steadily dwindle if he did not soon return home. Mrs. Mantell wrote to inquire as to the eligible young ladies she knew to be in Paris with their military fathers, and to beg him to send her the latest fashion magazines. Nothing came from Sir Anthony.

Geoffrey, in a final effort to communicate his feelings to Miss

Chandry, sent an undirected letter under cover to Clara, begging his sister to deposit it in the post office of the clearing, and requesting that she not tease him as to the recipient's identity. When nothing came of this, he could only assume that Sir Anthony's disdain for his neighbors had decided him against any sort of alliance with them, and that Geoffrey would be obliged to wait until he could speak with Emily herself before making his intentions known.

Soon after arriving at this conviction, Geoffrey received a note from his mother with the intelligence that the Colonel's condition—contrary to his belief—had lingered for over a year until it had worsened suddenly, culminating in his death and leaving Francis as head of the family. She requested that he do his duty to his family and return home, as Bonaparte was certain to be better guarded on St. Helena and so ensure the continuance of the peace. Geoffrey, a little stunned, immediately resolved to make arrangements to comply with her request, but an unexpected order from the War Office to end the Occupation made this unnecessary. He took his opportunity and applied for half pay, sailing from Bordeaux in October of 1817, and after delivering his report in London, he arrived at Southam in the golden days of November.

As the chaise rumbled past Chandry Manor, Geoffrey wondered what sort of reception he should receive there, if he were to go tomorrow. He had often considered what he must do to win Sir Anthony's approbation once he had returned home, but had not yet hit upon an answer. He was undecided as to whether a siege or a direct attack would bring about the desired outcome, but was determined that his first action must be to make contact with Emily.

He ruminated over this as the coach swept up the drive and stopped before Gracely Hall. Grimsley met him as before and, having divested him of his traveling cloak in the hall, informed the captain that Mrs. and Miss Mantell awaited him in the small saloon.

"And where is my brother?" Geoffrey asked, handing the butler his hat and cane.

"To my knowledge, sir, he is closeted with Mr. Brompton in the library. They have much to discuss regarding the tenants on the long acre, I believe. He will no doubt meet you for dinner."

He thanked Grimsley and ascended the staircase to make his way to his rooms near the back of the house, changing out of his travel-worn garments and allowing his batman to bring his unruly locks back into a semblance of order before presenting himself to his mother and Clara in the small saloon. If he had cherished any uncertainty of his reception there, it was unfounded, for scarcely had he opened the door than Clara jumped up and threw herself into his arms, her dove-gray bombazine dress whispering around them both.

"Geoffrey! You are come at last! I declare, if you had been one more minute, I should have died of boredom! I was just telling Mother that the only explanation for your tardiness was that you had forgotten us entirely and made up your mind to live in London."

"Nonsense," said Mrs. Mantell, receiving her son's kiss. "Depend upon it, he was delayed by that odious Lord Bathurst at the War Office."

"Nothing of the sort, Mother!" said Geoffrey. "I dealt merely with an undersecretary, who took my report and sped me on my way. Only, young George, Lord Chesterfield could not let me go."

Mrs. Mantell's disapprobation melted away. "He is lonely, no doubt. No child should lose both his parents so young. And within two years of each other! How is the dear boy?"

"Extremely well, considering he cozened my solicitude into taking him to all sorts of places his parents would never allow him to go. I declare, if his guardians ever got wind that I had taken him to the Peerless Pool, they may bar me from the house."

"Surely you apprised Sir Edwyn of your outings!" cried his mother.

Geoffrey laughed. "Sir Edwyn is excessively careful of his lordship, but he need not be always in residence, for George has a steward and a bailiff and a butler—who is as fierce as any mastiff, I tell you— and a housekeeper and a nurse—who both coddle him as much as his mother—beside a tutor and a man who I suppose is something of a valet-in-training. Not to mention any number of disinterested hangers-on such as myself, who undertake to entertain him in his lonely hours."

His mother only pursed her lips and took up her embroidery, while Clara laughed, taking his arm and pulling him down beside her on the chaise longue. "I am persuaded you take great care of little Lord Chesterfield, so we will tease you no longer. How was your journey?"

In detail sufficient for his sister, he described his passage across the Channel and overland to London, not neglecting several colorful persons he had met with along the way, until the door opened and Francis entered the room in dinner dress.

Geoffrey stood to greet him, holding out his hand. "Out of purgatory at last, eh, Francis? How is old Brompton?"

"I thought he'd never stop prosing on! I must pension him off before he's gone queer in his attic," said Francis, shaking his hand. "You look terrible, Geoff! If I'm out of purgatory, you're straight out of the jaws of Hell! How's it feel to be on English soil again?"

"I've not the courage to treat it as more than temporary. If Boney slips his guard again, they'll be calling me up as quick as you can stare. But I must have some sort of living, else I'll be living entirely out of your very respectable pocket."

Francis gave him a horrified look. "Heaven forfend I become respectable, just through inheriting an estate! No, once I've got a new land agent, and as soon as the rents are flowing in, I shall become an absentee, and fly away to London."

"To game away all your father's money, I expect," said his mother tartly, "and leave nothing for your poor sister and mother to live upon."

Francis poured himself a brandy. "Never, Mother. I cannot touch your jointure, and Clara's dowry is safe from me as well. My esteemed grandparents made sure to tie your funds up so neatly as to make it impossible for me even to get a finger on it. Do not you remember the terms of the settlement?" He tossed down the brandy. "The lawyer laid it out in great detail at Father's death. I could not forget it if I cared to."

Mrs. Mantell sniffed and changed her embroidery thread. "I very much hope you will not, Francis, for you have never been used to think on anyone but yourself. Clara and I depend upon you now."

Francis turned so that his annoyance was visible only to Geoffrey, but as Grimsley came at that moment to announce dinner, the subject was mercifully dropped.

"And what do you think I have been doing while you were away, Geoff?" inquired Clara as she served herself from the pork medallions in wine sauce.

"I know very well, my dear, for your letters were most informative. Tell me, has Mr. Frant recovered from his disappointment?"

She laughed. "There was nothing in that. It was calf love, and he should have fallen out of it within a week if I had continued to encourage him."

"Ah. And what of Mr. Spelling? You cannot tell me a man of eight and twenty could feel only calf love."

"He! If he could feel love at all, it would be no better," cried Clara with a roll of her eyes. "His entire object was to secure my fortune, I am persuaded—and a biddable young wife."

"Then you have saved him from a bitter disappointment. Not that he would have been choused out of your fortune," he clarified, directing a sardonic look at Francis.

Clara tugged on his sleeve to return his attention to herself. "But you have said nothing of my head!"

Geoff glanced at his sister's head. "You have not lost it, I perceive."

"Do not be vexatious! Is it not the most ravishing style?" She turned so that he had a better view of a twist of short ringlets high on the back of her head, and tight curls pressed closely to each side of her forehead. "I had it cut by a Frenchman who was used to attend the Princess Charlotte! Sarah has kept it up since then, for I begged her to watch his every movement, and she has done quite well, for only a lady's maid."

"It is charming, Miss Mantell," said the captain, with formal civility. "I can see now why you have captured so many hearts, obliging you to leave them pining in your wake."

She flashed him a roguish look and turned her attention to the asparagus being offered by Grimsley.

After the ladies had withdrawn, Francis tossed off his port, heaving a great sigh and pouring another. Geoffrey eyed him warily.

"Only six months as master and you're already chafing?" he asked.

Francis flicked a glance at him. "I've had good cause to stay as far away from Gracely as possible, for you see she cannot leave well enough alone. I cannot conceive of how my father stood it, and for so many years."

"It seems a small enough price to pay for such a fine inheritance."

"Jealous, Geoff?" He huffed, eying his brother. "No, I daresay you are not in the least. But you were never wont to run in Father's traces."

Geoffrey watched Francis toss back the wine and reach again for the decanter. "Perhaps you ought to weigh the disadvantages of appearing in my mother's drawing room drunk as a wheelbarrow before you refill your glass, Francis."

"Ah, but I won't be appearing there, Geoff. I've been wise enough to teach the ladies not to expect it, and so it is seen as a great conde-scension when I do. No, tonight I shall retire to my room, where I may depend upon finding little Janet lingering in the alcove by the door."

Geoff averted his eyes with a tired smile. "The willing maid? Or is this a new one?"

"The very same," said his brother, rising and loosening his necktie. "I have taught her well—showing females their proper place seems to be one of my talents."

And with a smug grin, he quitted the room, leaving Geoffrey to contemplate the tragedy of a life without true love.

Chapter 7

THE FOLLOWING DAY, Geoffrey slipped out the side door of the Hall and made his way through the fading garden and into the wood, treading the path that had become so beloved over two very distant summers. As he neared the hedge-wall surrounding the faerie clearing, his heart began to pound. Emily may be within, as she often had been when he had come before. What would he say to her? How would she look at him?

Overcome with eagerness to be with her again, Geoffrey quickened his steps and entered the clearing. It was deserted, and looked to have been so for some time. Leaves and debris from several seasons had accumulated on the ground, nearly burying the little village, and hiding all its inhabitants from view. The post office had been uncovered recently, but it was in a sorry state, and with a sudden foreboding, he bent to look inside, pulling out his letter to Miss Chandry.

He gazed at it, slightly moist and yellowed in his hand, with a small dusting of grime. It had not been read. Miss Chandry had not been to the clearing in quite a long period, perhaps even since he had left before Belgium. What had happened to make her neglect her lifelong pursuit—her one resort of peace and happiness? Had Sir Anthony sent her away again?

Unable to answer these questions, he left the clearing and went home to consider his next step—he must confront Sir Anthony. It was almost as daunting a prospect as battle, but for this he at least could plan, which he did for two days in between waiting on his mother and sister on visits and at entertainments when Francis could not be prevailed upon to do so.

"I wash my hands of him, Geoffrey," declared Mrs. Mantell in the carriage one day, on their way to visit Mrs. Frean, whose niece had inherited ten thousand pounds and was in the care of her aunt for the winter. "If he does not wish to look about himself for a suitable wife, then there is little one may do for him otherwise. I need not repine! No, I have my jointure, and Clara is certain to make a good match, for she, at least, knows her duty to her family. You may think her no better than a flirt, Geoffrey, by your looks, but you will see! She will take her pick of the rich men in her way in good time, and will be well settled, you may depend upon it." She sighed and looked with injured dignity out the window of the chaise as it bumped along the lane. "And then I may retire in peace to Fern Lodge, and watch from afar as Gracely goes to the devil at your brother's hands."

Geoffrey wisely refrained from comment on such tirades, common as they were. His mother, he believed, felt threatened by the alteration in her position, and with her querulous temper and nice notions of filial duty, time only would convince her that the world was not about to collapse about her ears. The unsettled state of her mind was enough cause for Geoffrey to maintain silence on the matter of his intentions toward Miss Chandry. Even if Emily accepted him, his mother would be horrified by the connection. All that was known of Emily Chandry was that she was the daughter of the most greedy and disgraceful man in the neighborhood, who was hated by everyone, and there was no cause to believe his daughter was any better. It would take a deal of work to convince his mother and sister, not to mention their neighbors, that Miss Chandry was nothing like her father, and therefore a fit and proper wife for Captain Mantell of Gracely Hall. But first he must convince Sir Anthony.

Thus, it was not until the third day of his return that Geoffrey resolved to make the dreaded visit to Chandry Manor, whether his mother approved it or no. He found his parent in the saloon, replacing the flowers beneath the black-draped portrait of his father when he had been made Colonel.

"You take such care of his memory, Mother," said Geoffrey, watching as she painstakingly arranged the flowers in the vase. "One can hardly credit that he has been gone these six months."

"No, but so he has, and six months more before I may put off mourning," observed his mother. "The flowers do not do well in this room—I believe it to be the lack of proper light just here. When the six months are out, I shall remove the vase to another spot." She glanced over the room. "Over there, on that table by the window. The clock may go here then."

Blinking at this display of tender emotion toward her dead spouse—though it was no more than what he could have expected—Geoffrey asked, "Have you any errands in the town? I am going to visit Sir Anthony and am at your service."

"Sir Anthony?" Mrs. Mantell flicked him a disapproving glance. "You've no need to call on Sir Anthony, for he has never shown the least civility to us. Indeed, why should you wish to, when there are any number of amiable persons in the neighborhood who would welcome a visit?"

Geoffrey straightened his cravat with what he hoped was a nonchalant air. "He is our nearest neighbor, and I do not wish to be remiss."

"I suppose you will next be wishing to visit old Mr. Crane at the Blue Pig Inn, or that horrid harpy Miss Spiddle," sniffed his mother, "as you are being so punctilious."

"Perhaps I may," he replied, with a forced smile.

Mrs. Mantell gave the arrangement of flowers a last inspection before casting a look of resignation over her shoulder and saying, "What you choose to do is none of my concern, but if you go as far as the town, I wish you will go a bit farther and take a basket to poor Mr. Noyce."

"Mother, Mr. Noyce is nothing like poor."

She shrugged, not looking at him. "He is lonely and crippled, which merits more of our charity than that odious, vulgar Sir Anthony. Besides, Wesley Abbey is just the other side of Southam, and you did put yourself at my service."

"Very well, Mother, but I cannot imagine Mr. Noyce has the least need of a basket."

"Nonsense, Geoffrey. Of course he has not. It is merely a kind gesture, which he understands well enough. I have been meaning to send Hatten with it, but he seems always to be needed in the stables. Francis has brought down ever so many of his horses from London. I cannot imagine what he wants with them all."

"Better stable them here than in town," offered Geoffrey. "Far more economical."

"Oh, certainly," agreed his mother with a wave of her hand, "though I am much mistaken if your brother has given the matter any consideration at all. It is merely for his own convenience, I am persuaded—Francis never has a thought but for himself."

Murmuring sympathetically, Geoffrey escaped to the kitchen to retrieve Mr. Noyce's basket and to give orders for his horse to be brought round. He paused to inspect his appearance in the mirror in the hall, assuring himself that his new brown coat and snowy white cravat—with the heart stone pin set in its folds—were in spotless order, and his golden hair impeccably combed. He checked and double checked his teeth, smiled three or four times to ensure his look was natural, then put on his black gloves and hat and strolled out the front door to where his horse had been led by the groom.

"Thank you, Hatten!" He grasped the pommel and hove himself into the saddle. "Tell me, is the stable very full of Mr. Mantell's cattle?"

The groom handed up the basket. "No more than before, sir, what with the Colonel's hunters, and that fine pair o' grays he had for his curricle. And the bays for the phaeton."

"Yes, I remember. Whatever became of them?"

"The Colonel give orders they be sold off when he were dead, God rest him."

Geoffrey nodded. "I thought as much. You're a good man, Hatten."

With a gratified smile, the groom touched his cap, and the captain set his horse at a walk down the drive, the basket balanced on the pommel. With such a burden, it seemed he must delay his visit to Sir Anthony just a little while longer, a necessity which did something to steady his nerves. He turned onto the lane, breathing deeply of the bracing autumn air, hoping it would clear his head. As he passed the Chandry estate, he considered that he never had spoken to Sir Anthony in his life, and he felt almost as intimidated at the prospect as he had watching the advance of the French at the battle of Badajoz. But that had been his first battle, and he had been filled with fervor and excitement—emotions which he had quickly learned served no real purpose in war.

But just as battle had been necessary to bring peace, so too was a confrontation with Sir Anthony requisite to bring about what Geoffrey flattered himself would be Emily's lasting happiness, and he thought he could face any unpleasantness for her welfare. If he could only be certain of her feelings for him, he could be more sanguine, but though he felt assured of her sincere attachment, he could not trust that it extended to love. Because he had not thought of her as more than a sister during his last visit, he had never considered the depth of her affections until long afterward, when his memory was capable of deception. He could not depend upon Emily's accepting his addresses until he had talked with her again.

As he could not canter with the basket on his pommel, the ride to Wesley Abbey occupied the better part of a half hour, and Geoffrey's mind was so engaged with his proposed visit to Sir Anthony that he scarcely noted the time passing. Before he knew where he was, the walls of the Noyce estate rose up alongside him, and he could see the spires of the Abbey beyond the trees.

Mr. William Noyce was the last of a long line of landowners, descended—if the tales were to be believed—from the Normans, his family having received a gift of land from King Henry I. His property was extensive, his patronage much courted, and his political influence powerful. But even these testaments to his prosperity could not protect Mr. Noyce from the epithet "poor," for he had been a cripple from birth. A deformity of the spinal column caused spasms and stiffness in his legs, necessitating his use of crutches to walk. This misfortune had not dimmed Mr. Noyce's popularity, however, for his sunny disposition and ready humor had endeared him to old and young alike in the neighborhood, and he had enjoyed the kindness and generosity of every female whose path he had crossed since coming into the world some fifty years previous.

Geoffrey had hardly passed through the lodge gates when he was met by no other than the owner himself, cantering down the lane in very good style on a handsome black gelding. If the gentleman was somewhat ungainly on his own two legs, he was magnificent with four others beneath him. No other rider could outshine Mr. Noyce in the field, and none could compare with his seat on a high-bred hunter.

Mr. Noyce, on perceiving his visitor, pulled up his mount and turned his tawny-eyed gaze speculatively upon him. "If I'm not mistaken, you're a Mantell. Can't recall which one exactly, but I'll wager you're the one who's been on the Continent time out of mind," he said.

Geoffrey sidled his mount forward to shake hands with his would-be host. "Yes. Captain Geoffrey Mantell at your service, sir. I was used to climb your wall and walk along it, to the chagrin of my parents."

Mr. Noyce laughed heartily. "And to my great delight! The rare trimmings your mother was used to give me, when I'd not lift a finger to discourage you—for I'll have you know, young man, that is what I maintained that crumbling old wall for!"

"For me to walk along, or for the trimmings?"

"Both," replied Mr. Noyce with a broad wink. "Now, to what do I owe the honor of your visit, Captain?"

Geoffrey somewhat shame-facedly proffered the basket. "From my mother, perhaps in apology for all those trimmings."

Mr. Noyce gazed at the basket, and for a brief moment Geoffrey fancied the light had gone out of his eyes. But when they raised again to the captain's, they twinkled merrily. "I'm a great favorite with the ladies, you see. None can resist my charm." He took the basket, pulling back the cloth to reveal the contents. "Ah! My favorites. However do they know? Blackberry preserves and fresh scones. Potted meat—pheasant by the looks of it—and a pineapple! My! Even my own succession houses have not produced a specimen as lovely as this."

"I'd hazard a pony you want none of it, sir," said the captain with a wry grin.

Mr. Noyce waved the supposition away. "I never turn away excellent charity, young man. It would be ill-mannered. Besides, one must never contradict a lady, nor give offense where kindness was meant." He pulled the cloth back over the basket, settling it on the pommel of his saddle. His face going grave, he inquired, "How does your mother? It's been five, six months since she was made a widow?"

"Six, sir," Geoffrey said, his mother's words still fresh in his mind. "She's bearing up remarkably well, I thank you."

Mr. Noyce humphed his approval of this, his gaze dwelling on the captain's face, though unseeing. Then his usual joviality returned and he said, "You ought to be rewarded for your efforts, Captain. Come up to the house and take some refreshment with me. I've an excellent burgundy just waiting for a solemn occasion such as this."

The captain was sorely tempted to put his original errand off one more day, or even one more hour, for his anxiety regarding Miss Chandry's feelings came back upon him in a rush, and he did not know if he could go through with it. But he had faced down many an attack of nerves as a soldier, and with a smile and heartfelt expressions of regret, Geoffrey declined the invitation, determined to do now or die. Mr. Noyce, ever gracious, took this refusal in good part, turning his mount and walking him back up the drive to the house to dispose of Mrs. Mantell's basket.

Chapter 8

BURDENED NO LONGER by the basket, Geoffrey set his horse cantering up the road, hopeful that the exertion would bleed away some of his jitters. A mile short of Gracely, he turned onto the overgrown lane of Chandry Manor, slowing to a walk so as to avoid breaking his horse's legs in one of the many potholes. Soon a deteriorating manor house came into view, surrounded by unkempt lawns and riotous gardens which rather sadly complemented its shabby exterior. If the manor had changed at all, it was for the worse. Geoffrey's anxiety heightened, but he remained resolute.

No groom came out to meet him as he dismounted, but he was aware of Sir Anthony's impecunious habits and assumed that there was no groom employed on the estate. Tying his horse to a crooked tree beside the drive, he mounted the steps to the unswept porch and pulled the bell, but when no answering peal was heard from inside, he pounded firmly on the door. After what seemed an age, a decrepit old butler opened the door and stared mutely at him through cloudy eyes.

"Good afternoon," said Geoffrey. No visible response was evident. "Captain Geoffrey Mantell. From Gracely Hall?" He cleared his throat. "I have recently returned from the war and have come to call on my old neighbors." Still no reply. He raised his voice. "Is Sir Anthony in?"

The old man turned suddenly about and shuffled off into the gloomy hall. After a moment's hesitation, the captain followed him, only just thinking to shut the door. He was led to a shabby saloon with more cobwebs than drapery shrouding the grimy windows. Threadbare sofas and dusty end tables crowded in the center of the room, watched over by soot-blackened paintings of indistinguishable former occupants of the manor.

The butler shuffled out again, never uttering a word, and leaving his guest to decide whether or not to be seated. As he gazed about the room, Geoffrey admitted a little surprise at just how badly the house was kept, until he recalled that Emily was, no doubt, made to do it herself, thanks to Sir Anthony's parsimony. The housekeeper, he remembered from Emily's ogre story, had left them, and long ago, by the looks of things. He could easily imagine that Emily would have a great challenge in maintaining such a barrack of a house, and he resolved that if she would have him, her situation must change as soon as may be.

The door was flung open and a lean scarecrow of a man stalked in. He surveyed the captain from under bushy gray eyebrows, his eyes narrowed and piercing. "So you're young Mantell, are you? Back from the war, and I imagine you think you're better than all the rest of us now, eh?"

Geoffrey blinked at this attack, but maintained his calm. "I do not profess to such feelings, Sir Anthony, but I am only just returned from the Continent, and am reacquainting myself with English notions of civility. I trust you are well?"

The old man grunted. "Much you care. What do you want?"

Seeing that Sir Anthony favored the direct attack, the captain plunged ahead. "I have come to pay my respects to you and your daughter. Is Miss Chandry at home that I may visit with her?"

The bushy eyebrows arched, but Sir Anthony said nothing.

"I have something particular I wish to say to her, sir," the captain plunged on.

The old man crossed his arms and pushed out his thin chest. "I can't say if Emily is at home or not, because I don't know, nor do I care! She's been married these two years and don't bother to come visit—not that I want her to! Ungrateful wench, always was."

Sir Anthony may as well have planted Geoffrey a facer. This news so mentally prostrated him that he hardly knew how he remained upright in the minutes that followed. While the old man ranted on about his ungenerous offspring, the captain tried to regulate his breathing and stop the spinning of his mind. Emily—married! How could this have happened, and he not be told? Surely there was some mistake, or Sir Anthony was toying with him.

"Forgive me, sir," he finally managed to articulate, during a brief pause in the old man's mutterings, "but I do not believe I understand you. Your daughter no longer lives with you? She has married?"

The thin lips grimaced. "Got knocked on the head over there, eh?" He raised his voice and spoke slowly and distinctly. "Emily run off with Theobald Crowther nearly two years ago and ain't been back since." He nodded his gray head for emphasis. "And I say good riddance to 'em both!"

The captain's heart seemed to want to pound right out of his chest. Without regard for his host's wishes, he groped for a chair and sat, staring unseeing at the dusty floor at his feet. Emily—lost to him! It was all he seemed able to think.

Sir Anthony's eyes narrowed further and he stooped to look into the young man's face. "If you're going to go off in a fit or an apoplexy or anything like it, you'd better be off home, as I don't have the where-withal, or interest for that matter, to drag your carcass out of my house once you're dead. My constitution ain't strong, and I'll not sacrifice what health I've got to some idiot soldier." He strode to the door and held it open.

Geoffrey looked up at him, staring a few seconds more until he realized that he had been given his notice. In a daze, he stood, placed his hat on his head, touched the brim to his host, and quitted the room, making his way blindly to the door, and letting himself out of the house.

How he mounted his horse or set it walking, he hardly knew. When the horse dutifully stopped in front of the Hall, the captain looked about himself, coming back to the present as if out of a stupor.

Hatten ran up and took the horse's bridle. "All right, sir?" he asked, as Geoffrey mechanically dismounted and stumbled a bit on the drive.

Geoffrey blinked and shook his head. "I don't know, Hatten. Had a bit of a shock," he murmured, and declining assistance, made his way slowly into the house.

Clara was crossing the foyer, a bunch of flowers in her arms, bright against her gray mourning dress. "Hallo, Geoff! I declare, this house was never so cheerful when Father was alive!" But her saucy smile vanished when she saw the pallor of his face. "Good heaven, what is the matter?"

He set down his hat and gloves. "Why did no one tell me Miss Chandry was married?"

"Miss Chandry?" Clara was clearly taken aback. "Sir Anthony's daughter? Why, how were we to know you would care to be told? You were only barely acquainted—and you were in Belgium!"

The desolation on his face somehow stimulated her memory, and she dropped the flowers onto the floor as her hands flew to her mouth. "Oh, Geoff! She was your lover!" Her eyes flew wide, and she put her hands out to him, crying, "Oh, no, I beg your pardon—I did not mean—Oh, Geoff! How could I imagine—Geoff, do you love her?"

"Yes." He passed a hand over his eyes. "I know it seems ridiculous. By all appearances there was no reason for anyone to believe I could feel so." He forced a wan smile. "We were childhood friends, and when I came back before Waterloo, I fell in love with her before I knew what was happening—indeed, I didn't understand it fully until I was gone again to Belgium."

"A secret romance," breathed Clara, her hands pressing to her heart. "I suspected something of the sort, when you sent me that mysterious letter, but because she was married, I own I thought it was someone else."

"She had long been married by that time," said Geoffrey, more to himself than to Clara. "It has been more than two years, and I sent you that letter only in June. And Sir Anthony never answered because there was no point."

"Oh dear!" said Clara, pressing her hands to her mouth. "When you introduced Miss Chandry to me, I did not believe you could be in love with her!"

"It seems she also did not believe it." He closed his eyes. "I was her only friend. I suppose I presumed too much upon that counting for something."

He stooped and began mechanically to gather up the flowers Clara had dropped, feeling acutely his impudence at having believed all this time that she was his for the taking, merely because he had been her friend for a few short months.

Clara touched his arm. "Geoff, I'm so sorry. I am such a worthless creature, with so little real feeling—I cannot pretend to understand your situation—but I am most heartily sorry. I truly did not imagine she was so important to you."

"It's alright."

Placing the flowers back into his sister's arms, Geoffrey turned and made his way out the side door and over the lawn to the wood. He walked in a haze of misery through the trees, across the stream, and into the Chandry wood. He reached the clearing, which still looked quite as despondent as he felt, and slumping to the ground, he dropped his head into his hands and mourned that he had been so stupid. If only he had understood his heart while he had been at home, if only he had acted more quickly, as soon as he had known, to tell her he loved her, if only this Theobald Crowther had not appeared and taken her away. But it had all happened, and Geoffrey was too late.

He turned his head, blinking at the ruined village. It was a sorry sight, and looked like nothing so much as a child's discarded playthings, and he was a fool to have cared so much for it. What a waste, and what a shame for a fully-grown man to make so much of a pile of twigs and bark and clay! With a sudden rush of anger, he kicked at one of the sagging buildings, crushing it with a blow. He smashed another with his fist, and another, kicking and crushing them as he sought to obliterate the associated memories in his mind. He scooped up the villagers and their tiny animals, throwing them into the hedge, and would have destroyed the entire village but that his fury-dimmed eyes fell on the tiny horse and boy and girl that had begun his friendship with Emily.

He stilled, then took the little girl in his trembling hands and, sitting back on his heels in the moist undergrowth, he gazed at her bedraggled form. With shaking fingers, he tried to mend her, pulling the dry little wisps of grass that were her hair back into place and daubing mud to keep it there. His efforts, as had always been the case, were not half so nimble as Emily's, but he did what he could, then started on the horse, and then the boy. When he had done, he set them all carefully in their places and heaved a ragged sigh.

Standing slowly, he gazed about the clearing and felt suddenly how desolate it was without her. The irony of it was that she had felt this way after he had left, those many years ago when they were children. But it was only what he deserved. On this conviction, he found that he could bear to stay no longer, and he left the clearing.

Re-entering the Hall, Geoffrey ascended to his room and shed his coat, dropping onto a chair and fingering the heart stone pin in his cravat as he gazed out the window. Nothing had prepared him for this turn of events. When he had gone away three years earlier to the Continent, Miss Chandry had been unattached, and though he had told her he wished for her to find her prince, he had assumed she was destined not to do so. How could she, situated as she was—a servant in her own home, and excluded from society? He could have had no cause to believe she would be married within a year, before even he had known his own heart.

Who was this Crowther? It would be no cause for amazement had Emily met him after Geoffrey had gone away. Indeed, she may have met Crowther before Geoffrey's visit, and simply never mentioned the circumstance. She had said Geoffrey had been her only childhood friend, which did not preclude her having found another friend while he had been away at school, or in the army. Perhaps she had entered into marriage gladly, with every hope of happiness. Sir Anthony had said she had run away, after all.

As he ruminated over possibilities, he recognized that she could easily have met a gentleman while at the seminary in Warwick, but had been too young at the time for it to come to anything. Perhaps Crowther had fallen violently in love with her—which would be no surprise, so gentle and lovely as she was—and had bided his time until she was of age, and had come to claim her then.

But this notion could not comfort him. She had given no sign that she had been admired in Warwick, and had spoken of her time at school as merely not disagreeable, which did not suggest that she could have done anything so exciting as having met a man she would someday run away with. And she had not spoken of any other friend during all their time together. He believed it was impossible, therefore, that she had met anyone before his going to Belgium.

Which made his blindness that summer all the more tragic, for he, and he alone, was to blame for her running off with a man who could be no more than a chance acquaintance, for all he knew. Her circumstances were such that any man who promised to ameliorate them, and who was the least kinder than Sir Anthony, might easily have persuaded her to throw in her lot with his. She had no other prospects—Geoffrey certainly had never given her to hope that he thought more of her than a sister. Indeed, he shuddered to recollect some of his words to her, spoken in kindness, but so easily construed as dismissive.

No, he had never given her any reason to imagine that he could love her, and he could only despise himself for presuming that she should wait on his convenience forever, simply because she had so patiently endured all her life. Now he must accept that Emily was the property of Theobald Crowther, until the death of either, and Geoffrey must forget his love for her.

He tried not to think of how long the man's life could be, but was singularly unsuccessful, and when his thoughts turned to the many ways that life could be shortened, he was forced to get up and close the heart stone pin in his jewel case, ringing the bell for his batman to come distract his mind by helping him to dress for dinner.

Chapter 9

THE ARRAY OF dishes at family dinner served as an excellent foil upon which he could focus, so that he was able to appear tolerably composed. He need not even prevaricate, for his years in an army camp, often on the move, had significantly reduced his expectations at mealtimes, but his mother's cook had done much to restore his fascination with food, and tonight he dwelt verbally on the excellence of each dish with a vigor that caused his mother to raise an eyebrow.

"My dear Geoffrey, if I was in any way unaware of the talents of my cook, I should take these encomiums to my heart with gladness," she said blandly. "But as I am under no misapprehensions in this matter, I will desire that you forgo such effusions until I am no longer within hearing."

This effectively dampened Geoffrey's feigned enthusiasm, and Clara being similarly subdued, the conversation over the remaining courses consisted of trifling gossip from the village, or a bit of news from the Outer World brought by letter. This information was in no way interesting enough to engage the captain's mind, and his concerns regarding Emily's present circumstances again overtook his thoughts.

At last, unable to remain quiet, he inquired, "Tell me, Mother, is anything generally known of Sir Anthony's new son-in-law?"

His mother stared at him, her fork partway to her mouth. "Why should you care to know that, pray?"

Clara's gaze flicked between her mother and Geoffrey as he said, "Sir Anthony mentioned that Miss Chandry was married, and I was simply curious as to how it had come to pass. Miss Chandry did not seem to be the marrying sort."

Mrs. Mantell placed her fork carefully on her plate, directing an icy glare at him. "Certainly not. That she caught a man's fancy at all was a wonder! I declare, I was all agog to meet the man who would have her to wife! However, there was no party or gathering of any kind, in keeping with Sir Anthony's distaste for parting with his money, so we never were introduced to him, thank heaven. I do not even recollect the man's name."

"Crowther," supplied Geoffrey.

Toying with her food, Clara interjected, "I saw him in company with Sir Anthony in the village on one or two occasions, and other than thinking him far too old, and rather a vulgar person, did not think much of him."

Captain Mantell glanced sharply at his sister. "How old is he?"

"Perhaps as much as fifty."

Mrs. Mantell tutted. "I own I was surprised that any young lady could agree to marry a man so many years her senior, but it certainly was not the first time it has been done. But she is—what she is, and if there was any money in the business, then there is no mystery to it at all!"

Controlling himself with an effort, Geoffrey allowed this disgusting insinuation to pass and pressed on. "What, pray, gave you reason to think him vulgar, Clara?"

"It wasn't his dress, for that was respectable enough, I assure you," Clara said, adding with scarcely veiled revulsion, "but his features were soft, like porridge, with piggy little eyes and an enlarged nose that was perpetually red, as if—well, I am sure you take my meaning," she finished primly.

Geoffrey paused, assimilating this picture, which was nothing like what he had imagined for Emily. "One hopes there was strong love in the case. When was she married?"

"We did not hear of it until weeks afterward, I declare, for Sir Anthony—in true Chandry style—did not trouble to do the thing properly," answered his mother. "A notice in the bottom corner of the society page in the Gazette was what alerted us at last. It was the most irregular circumstance. If one had not seen this Crowther about town with Sir Anthony, one should have supposed it to be a run away match. But they were married in London, I expect."

It was not generally known, then, that Emily had eloped, which Geoffrey was glad of, for Emily's sake. But he did not at all like the sound of Crowther, and he knew he could not rest, or put his feelings for her to rest, until he knew just how the marriage had come about.

Francis having gone to dine with a friend, Geoffrey was left alone when his mother and sister retired to the drawing room, and he was able to give his full concentration to the matter. Crowther did not sound as though he was a lovelorn suitor; rather, he sounded to be one of Sir Anthony's associates, as Emily had called them. What, then, could have possessed her to consent to marry him? And why had they eloped?

The only answer was that Sir Anthony was a bully, besides being a miser, and his poor daughter had all her life been the worse off for his selfishness. Crowther must have taken a liking to her, and she had been persuaded that marriage to him would be better than lifelong servitude to her father. The elopement was also easily explained. Sir Anthony would never have consented to lose his cook and house-keeper. She had run off to London, and had been married by special license, so that her father could have nothing to say to it.

What Geoffrey could not know, without further inquiry, was what about Crowther had made her trust him. His looks, by the sound of it, were enough to give any gently-bred maiden pause, but this could merely have been a misfortune, hiding a kind and friendly soul. However, Geoffrey found it difficult to reconcile this picture with that of Sir Anthony's usual guests, who were shifty and vulgar and generally disreputable. It bothered him, for he wished to believe Emily was happier now, but he could not, given the evidence.

He adjourned at last to the drawing room, but the quiet pursuits of the evening only exacerbated his feelings, and even after he had taken himself off to bed, his mind could not let the subject rest. No matter how often he told himself there was nothing to be done, his thoughts churned around and around, and he knew that he must somehow discover all the details of the marriage arrangement, to find if there was any glimmer of happiness available to Emily, or he would run mad.

At breakfast the next morning, Geoffrey announced "I intend to call on the Simpfords this morning. Would either of you care to join me?"

His mother looked pained. "Diedre Simpford is the most odiously boring gossip, Geoffrey. Though Lawrence is your friend, it amazes me that there are no other families to interest you."

"The Thorntons, for example," offered Clara, who had regained her spirits. "Arabella will be home for Christmas, I am certain, and you will want to have ingratiated yourself to her family by then, Geoffrey."

Geoffrey deigned not to answer this and politely addressed his mother. "When there is something to interest me at any other house in the district, you may rest assured that I will present myself instantly. But today, I wish to visit the Simpfords, and if you do not like to go, perhaps Clara will bear me company."

Clara smilingly agreed, for though Mrs. Simpford was rather long-winded, her excessively malleable son was down from London, and Clara would not lightly pass up an excuse to flirt with him.

The two set out in the Colonel's old curricle, the captain graciously allowing Clara the handling of the ribbons, and apart from nearly clipping a fencepost, which she declared had been set too near the road anyhow, she earned his unqualified approval on her skill upon her driving them safely to Gosley House, the seat of Mr. Simpford and his mother.

After sending in his card, the captain and Miss Mantell were ushered into a sunny sitting room, where the lady of the house and her handsome offspring were receiving visitors. Mr. Simpford greeted his friends and proceeded to recount old times, a conversation that boded ill for Geoffrey's purpose. But after very few minutes, Clara drew Mr. Simpford's attention to herself, suggesting they take a walk into the conservatory, where he promised her the sight of some exceedingly rare blooms. Geoffrey was a trifle relieved at this fortuitous happening, and lost no time in embarking upon the subject he had come to pursue.

"So much has changed since I went away to war, Mrs. Simpford. I find there are new neighbors moved in and old neighbors moved out. You may imagine my surprise to find that Sir Anthony's daughter had married."

Mrs. Simpford nodded her plump head. "Oh, my, yes, Captain. I had no inkling that would ever happen! That poor, drab little thing, so quiet and never saying a word. She hardly ventured out of her house except upon errands for that bully of a father of hers. Pardon my saying so, Captain, but you know as well as I do that Sir Anthony has always ruled the roost in that house, and likes to throw his weight around! And poor Mrs. Crowther—Miss Chandry then—forced to keep house for him with only the paltry sum he gave her. Why, I remember one time in winter I met her in the town and though I greeted her very kindly, she started as if I had roared at her like a lion. Poor mouse, she was coming to buy necessities, which she could have sent a servant to do, if Sir Anthony would spare a few shillings to hire one, and I told her, 'It's too chilly to be out and about without a shawl, my dear,' and she answered that she had no shawl because the moths had gotten to the one of her mother's that she was wont to wear, and—though she didn't say it in as many words—Sir Anthony forbade her to spend money on a new."

The lady paused for a breath and Geoffrey dove in, trying to steer the conversation back. "Perhaps it was in hopes of a better situation that she married Mr. Crowther?"

"I wouldn't doubt it, though she chose poorly in my opinion. None of us had a chance to properly meet Mr. Crowther, because Sir Anthony is too clutch-fisted to host an engagement party, or a neighborly dinner, or even a cozy gathering for cards! But I met him in the village a time or two, and though he had manners enough, they were not what I would call well-bred, to be sure. And old enough to be her father! If it had been a love match, I could have believed it better, but that was not the case here, I tell you. From what I observed, he was in his cups far more often than is seemly, especially for a gentleman considering marriage, and in the middle of the day more than not. Poor Mrs. Crowther cannot have known this, or if she did, perhaps she was too desperate to care!"

Again she paused for a breath, and Geoffrey snatched his chance. "I cannot help but wonder how the marriage came about. Have you any idea how Miss Chandry met with Mr. Crowther? For I had no knowledge of him before coming home."

She leaned forward, her voice lowered, "She met him in London." At Geoffrey's look of astonishment, she continued. "Yes, in London. There was some important matter that needed attending to, and Sir Anthony was taken suddenly ill—I had it from the apothecary's apprentice. Took to his bed, as he's wont to do occasionally, on account of his dyspepsia, but was so set on this matter being settled that he went anyhow and took his poor daughter along to be his nurse. And all the way to London, too, though she don't travel well, poor thing, and Mr. Crane at the Blue Pig said Sir Anthony engaged four horses to the post chaise, so you know it must have been prodigiously important. Not two weeks after they returned, Mr. Crowther appeared, and the next thing we knew, Miss Chandry was gone and married to him!"

"Perhaps Mr. Crowther has a fortune that tempted her to accept his suit?"

"Not that I could discover. Crowther'd not the airs of a rich man. London was the only residence he mentioned, and that is where they were married. Private ceremony, there in the church. And Sir Anthony is as clutch-fisted as ever, so it seems there was no generous settlement for him. No, it's my belief that Miss Chandry took Mr. Crowther's fancy, and Sir Anthony would as soon save money on housekeeping altogether, because now she's gone, it's only he and that old butler Marsden with one foot in the grave, and Mrs. Clark coming in twice a week to do for them, with nothing put aside for the care of the estate that I can tell."

She rattled on for some time, but there did not seem to be much more to the story, and when she again paused for breath, Geoffrey indicated his desire also to view the rare blooms in the conservatory. She graciously consented to his finding his way there, and he took his leave. His true purpose in going, now that he had what information he could get, was to rescue Mr. Simpford from Clara's clutches, and when he found them in a far corner of the garden room, Clara gazing up at Mr. Simpford with roguish blue eyes, he congratulated himself on his perspicacity.

"I expected a rise in temperature in this room, but was not prepared for quite this much," he said dryly.

Mr. Simpford jumped away from Clara, who rolled her eyes in Geoffrey's direction. "Mr. Simpford and I were merely deep in conversation, Geoff."

"It must have been an excessively interesting topic, to be sure. Shooting, perhaps?"

Mr. Simpford laughed nervously. "You've not seen her skill since coming home, Geoff! You'd be astonished at her improvement."

"I can see it with my own eyes, Lawrie," said Geoffrey, taking his sister's hand and placing it firmly under his arm. "We must be going. We hunt on Friday?"

"And you'll come to dinner, Mr. Simpford?" added Clara with a coy smile.

Mr. Simpford confirmed both these appointments, and Geoffrey and his sister went out to the curricle, Clara handsomely relinquishing the ribbons to him for the ride home. She tried a time or two to prise what he had learned from Mrs. Simpford, but he did not engage to satisfy her curiosity, much as she had been helpful to him, for what he had learned engendered feelings which were better kept to himself.

Clara, sitting back in her corner of the curricle, sighed gustily, animadverting on the cruelty of brothers who not only had led far more exciting lives but who nursed broken hearts and would not allow their sisters to pour in the balm of sisterly consolation. Geoffrey did not respond to this more than to look askance at her, and she pursed up her lips, flouncing out of the curricle as soon as it had come to a stop in front of the Hall.

Knowing her annoyance did not run deep, Geoffrey let her go and made his way to the library, where he poured himself a brandy and settled heavily into a chair by the fire, to ease his heartache as he contemplated the flames crackling in the hearth.

Not only was Crowther a drunkard and a crony of Sir Anthony's, it seemed he had also orchestrated the marriage, which suggested an ulterior motive. Geoffrey did not like the idea of Emily being used to further someone else's ends, however it had improved her situation. He had hoped she had at least found happiness in her marriage, but he could not imagine that the happiness of a wife of convenience would be of paramount importance to a man who would stoop to transacting business with Sir Anthony. She must certainly have been desperate. Geoffrey closed his eyes against the vision of a vulgar-speaking man in fine clothes, with a drunkard's nose and piggy eyes, taking Emily's hand in the church. It was enough to turn his stomach, and he set his glass on a side table, breathing deeply through his nose.

It appeared that knowing more regarding Emily's marriage had done nothing toward encouraging him to let her memory go; rather, it had deepened his worry over her. She deserved to be happy, but he could not imagine that she would be cherished or even considered as she ought in such a marriage, and it tortured him to think of it.

But she had made her choice, and he had only himself to blame. What was done was done, and he must find a means of putting his feelings for her behind him, for they had no place now. His only course was to look to his own future—one without Emily.

No matter how often he repeated this refrain to himself, aloud or in his mind, however, his stubborn thoughts continued to wander back to the faerie clearing, and Emily seated at his side, her fair hair coming loose from her bonnet and her luminous gray eyes fixed on his face as she listened and comforted and sympathized. At last he stood and strode to the sideboard, carrying the brandy bottle back with him to his chair, so that he could sit comfortably by his fireside and drink himself into oblivion.

Chapter 10

DURING THE FOLLOWING sennight, he was singularly unsuccessful in his resolve to forget Emily, though his mother resumed her previous habit of requiring his company on her visits. The various young ladies who had remained unmarried during his years in France were again paraded before his view, but none could captivate him in his fresh grief. He was all that was civil and kind but no more, and Mrs. Mantell, sensing his reluctance, increased her demands to include his attendance in her drawing room when she received callers, but though he was all obedience, she could not rejoice in her success.

On the seventh day, he came dutifully into the drawing room to find only his friend Mr. Simpford chatting agreeably to Mrs. Mantell, and his relief was so patent that Mr. Simpford, after suitably greeting his friend, said with a mischievous twinkle in his eye, "Poor Geoff! You must be bored to tears with no young ladies to entertain you!

Come, Mrs. Baldwin has two lovely nieces staying with her, and with ten thousand apiece!"

"I had not heard Mrs. Baldwin was entertaining her nieces," said Mrs. Mantell with a sniff. "Ten thousand—well, Geoffrey, if you should like to go with Mr. Simpford, I would not object. We have no expectation of callers at present, and Mrs. Baldwin is a very good sort of woman, and I daresay would not entertain her nieces if they were not a very good sort of girls. Their birth is not what I would have wished, precisely, but it would do very well, I fancy."

After taking their leave of her, the two young men were out onto the drive before Geoffrey took Mr. Simpford's arm and said, "You are the best of good boys, Lawrie! I shall never forget that you perjured your soul for me!"

"Who said I perjured my soul?" said Mr. Simpford, with a look of angelic innocence.

"Lawrie! Never say these young ladies are real?"

Placing his hat jauntily on his head, Mr. Simpford said blithely, "Oh, they are real, my dear Geoffrey, and they are visiting their aunt; however, we shall not meet them today, for I never said we would, and besides, we are going to the Horse and Jockey."

Geoffrey slapped his friend on the back and happily accompanied him to the stables, where they both were mounted and rode away from everything that was civil and proper and worth several thousand pounds a year. The scheme worked charmingly to relieve Geoffrey's anxiety for that day; however, he knew he could not always run away from his duty. He must forget Emily, and to do so, he must find a wife, preferably from among the young ladies nearby—for if he thought to go to London, where society was infinitely more broad, he invariably began to think of Emily, wondering where she lived, and that would never do.

The Christmas party held at Gracely Hall was always a splendid affair, but Mrs. Mantell, with two unwed sons and an eligible daughter just out of mourning, had outdone herself this year. The house was packed with guests for two full weeks, and if there was not a ball every night, there were always enough couples to get up a dance when the young people had had their fill of cards and round games. Mrs. Mantell, still in half mourning, was a willing martyr to her own cause, and plied her fingers at the keys of the pianoforte for as many hours as her sons required to partner every young lady in the room twice, for she knew from experience that dancing was only a step from falling in love.

Francis, though flirting shamelessly with every young lady in the house—save his sister—knew his company enough not to go beyond the line of what was pleasing, and more than one matronly bosom swelled with the notion of her daughter's being the lady who tamed the rich Mr. Mantell at last. A rake, it seemed, would always be intriguing to a certain sort, especially once he had inherited a very fine fortune.

Geoffrey, being a mere captain and second son, drew less interest; indeed, the air of grim determination with which he had prepared for the party was carried with him into the company, daunting to all but the most assured of young ladies. However, the whispers that he must suffer from post-war melancholy—which often afflicted soldiers just returned home—increased his fascination, and many a lady, young or old, approached him with no other aim than to assure him of his worth and their general approbation. In the company of so many amiable and solicitous persons, his natural good humor soon began to reassert itself, and he was able, in large part, to make himself agreeable.

It was uphill work, nonetheless. A pair of gray eyes turned to him in just such a way made him forget what he was saying as his mind turned to the many times Emily had looked at him so. A walk in the wood near the fording of the stream between Chandry Manor and Gracely Hall had the power to silence him for many minutes. And a casual reference to the glorious battle of Waterloo and its aftermath had the effect of chasing him from the company altogether.

Each morning, as he sat at his dressing table, he was obliged to give himself a stern lecture on the vital importance of sticking to one's resolve, while his batman eyed him askance. Chalmers, who had been assigned to Captain Mantell at his latest advancement, was not unobservant, and thought he knew in which quarter the wind lay. The confined spaces in which he and his master had been billeted in France during the Occupation had made an education in the captain's private affairs inevitable, but the occasional heartrendings after too much blue ruin or the mutterings during sweat-inducing nightmares had enlightened him tenfold. Events in the first weeks of their residence at Gracely had not, therefore, passed unnoticed, and he had watched his master's moods with tender vigilance.

Thus, handing Captain Mantell a fresh neckcloth on the fifth morning of the house party, Chalmers observed, "It ain't always to a man's taste to be forever obliged to do the civil. It's a clear day. P'rhaps a jaunt into town for a quiet game of cards at the Horse and Jockey. I imagine it will set you up nicely."

The captain, intent on pushing through another day, was at first inclined to reject this advice out of hand, and said as much—though kindly—to Chalmers. But after breakfast, during which a scheme had been got up by four or five of the younger set to sneak onto Chandry Manor and try if they could not spy the White Lady, who was said to walk the grounds at all hours, he had a change of mind. Mrs. Mantell scotched the ill-judged scheme instantly upon Geoffrey making it known to her, and as she set about placating the disappointed youths by organizing a game of lottery tickets, he slipped out to the stables.

The day was gloriously clear, with a pale sun shining over the fields of winter wheat and turnips and cabbage. Geoffrey rode at a walk, gazing ahead at the spire of St. James's church and thinking of walks to the Holy Well, tea with the vicar, his prosy sermons—anything but of Emily. He was very nearly successful, but as he came into town and saw a simple woolen shawl hanging in a shop window, his mind at once reverted to Mrs. Simpford's story of Emily without one in chilly weather. He was contemplating the wisdom of purchasing the shawl to send to Mrs. Crowther when a cheery voice hailed him. He turned to see Miss Thornton with her head out of a carriage window, her blue eyes bright and her golden ringlets bouncing from beneath a very fetching bonnet.

"Captain!" she cried again, as he walked his horse to greet her. "It is an age since last we saw you, I declare, and here we are just getting back from a visit to my aunt in York. What a lucky circumstance! "

Peering past her in the coach, he saw her brother William, who nodded curtly.

"How can you be such a stick, Billy?" she said, that pretty pout on her lips. "The captain has been our neighbor time out of mind, and still you cannot be more than civil to him?"

Geoffrey laughed. "I fear it is because I have been your neighbor time out of mind that he does so, Miss Thornton. There is too much history between us to make Billy easy in my company."

"Pooh! What can have happened to warrant such reserve? Even had you been sworn enemies, are we not all grown up? It is absurd.

Mr. Simpford has every bit as much history as you do, Billy, and yet he shows no such formality."

Mr. Thornton, increasingly annoyed at this speech, leaned across her to shake hands with Geoffrey. "Do not regard her, Geoff. She's no notion what it means to be grown up, having not yet experienced it. How do you do?"

"I am very well. And you?" returned Geoffrey with smiling civility.

"I shall be better once our interminable journey is at last done and I can be free of this ridiculous child's chatter."

Miss Thornton glared at him, her blue eyes flashing. Turning to Geoffrey with a very different look, she said, "You see what I have been made to endure, Captain. But it could not be helped. Aunt Albinia was most insistent that we come to her before Christmas. She is a sad invalid, and is quite alone three parts of the year. It was the least we could do to keep her company and raise her spirits. Is that not so, Billy?"

"Forgive me if I cannot agree with you that a journey of four days either way was worth a three-weeks' stay in a drafty castle with a harpy of a woman whose only recommendation is an unsettled fortune of fifty thousand pounds."

"Billy!" cried his sister, her cheeks coloring hotly. "Aunt Albinia is not a harpy! We were treated with the utmost civility—when her gout did not give her pain. You are too unfeeling not to make allowances. And if you disliked staying in that drafty old castle, then you ought to consider how she must bear it year in and year out!"

"I could consider it better would she use some small part of her considerable means to improve the place," he muttered.

Miss Thornton huffed, turning back to Geoffrey. "My brother will give you a wrong idea of us. Truly, I look forward very much to our visits to my aunt. The castle is drafty, but it is not so bad in the summer, and the moors are so wild and exciting! And Aunt Albinia is generosity itself, despite her ill crochets. I love her dearly." She turned back to her brother. "And not on the hope of her fifty thousand pounds!"

Geoffrey was impressed, for Miss Thornton had been far less thoughtful when last he had met her. The blue eyes that now gazed into his were eager still, but not, he was persuaded, for mere flirtation.

"You need not fear me, Miss Thornton," he said, bowing slightly and smiling back at her. "I should never think ill of you. And I know your brother well enough to believe it is exhaustion talking and not his heart."

"You are too kind, Captain," she said, her answering smile giving him a warm glow. "But you were ever so. I do hope we may further our acquaintance, now you are back."

"It is my greatest wish, Miss Thornton," he said, and it was not very far from the truth.

Her dimpled blush moved him to kiss her fingers in parting—despite her brother's disapproving look—and he watched the carriage out of sight as it rumbled southward on the Coventry road. He had not thought of Miss Thornton since his return from Belgium, her absence having excluded her from his mother's schemes, and he was obliged to own she looked well. Very well, in fact, and he fancied that she had indeed grown up over the past three years. Her self-possession did not diminish her beauty—if anything it increased it—and as he considered the short meeting, he flattered himself that she did not seem indifferent to him, though he was a mere captain and second son.

He turned his mount and walked it toward the Horse and Jockey, his thoughts more agreeably engaged than they had been in some weeks. He had despaired these many days of ever mastering his hopeless love for Emily and moving on. Perhaps here was a lady who could do the thing.

When the turn of the year saw the last of the house guests, Mrs. Mantell was not dissatisfied with the result, for Geoffrey had lost his manner of gritted teeth midway through the party, and had become almost lively again. She began to consider which of her fair guests had caught his fancy, and how soon she could expect a declaration, but no one lady came to the fore. When it came to her attention that Geoffrey had taken to riding over to Thornton Park, she was surprised, for he and William Thornton had never been close, and Arabella Thornton had not been of the party at the Hall. But it soon became apparent that Geoffrey was favorably inclined toward Miss Thornton, which was annoying, for he had come to it without his mother's assistance.

However, she could not admit to more than trifling disappointment. If he had formed a tendre for Miss Thornton, however it was done, Mrs. Mantell's work was done. His future seemed tolerably assured, for Miss Thornton apparently returned his regard—and she had six thousand pounds, and very likely more, if the rumors of the rich and childless Yorkshire aunt were true. Mrs. Mantell began to think on how an acquaintance with the aunt could be contrived, and if the aunt survived past the marriage, how to encourage Geoffrey to cultivate it.

Francis had his own opinions regarding his brother's sudden interest in Miss Thornton.

"I never imagined you'd be such a cawker, Geoff. If you don't take care, you'll be leg-shackled within the month, and for what, I ask you?"

Geoffrey shook his head. "Have no fear for me, Francis, for that's not far from my intention."

"You cannot hope to make me believe you have fallen for all that mummery!" cried Francis. "Not you!"

Shrugging, Geoffrey said, "Have it as you will, Francis, but with or without the mummery, I am persuaded I could not do better than Miss Thornton."

Francis made a sound of derision in his throat and marched to the brandy decanter, pouring himself a finger and downing it in one gulp. "If your intention is to please my mother, Geoff, I beg you to reconsider. The sacrifice is not worth her pleasure—she never stops! Now it will be marriage to some rich lady, and tomorrow it will be attaining the rank of Colonel! Better to keep her expectations low, I tell you. Eventually, she'll come to a right way of thinking and leave off."

"But I wish to have a wife," said the captain reasonably. "And I do intend someday to become a Colonel, so what's to lose?"

Francis stared at him, then barked a laugh. "I ought to have known it. You were ever incomprehensible. You will pardon my saying, that whatever your views on marital felicity, I find your present capitulation disappointing."

It was, perhaps, natural that Geoffrey should resent somewhat his brother's prejudicial views, but Clara evinced her support of his endeavors by declaring that she hoped he would scandalize the neighborhood by dancing three times with Miss Thornton at Lady Geffington's ball.

"And if Arabella happens not to be there," said Clara, as she seated herself at the harp, "I shall undertake to swear to your having spent the whole of the evening propping the wall and gazing with undisguised boredom on the entire company, no matter how many lovely girls you choose to dance with."

Geoffrey, meanwhile, wanted no encouragement to further his acquaintance with Miss Thornton. He was a frequent guest in her mother's sitting room, and on fine days, he could be seen riding in the fields with Miss Thornton and a groom. Once, when the weather was particularly warm and dry, they went as far as St. James' church, where they tied their horses and took the footpath to the Holy Well.

The way meandered along the river Stowe, under the bare branches of overhanging willow and birch trees, and through pastures and fields. They came to the well, which had been surrounded by a picket fence to keep cows out, and Geoffrey opened the gate, allowing Miss Thornton to precede him through. The well, its three masks spewing the clear water into a trough, was full, the spring having never failed, presumably, since the day St. Fremund struck the ground with his sword and washed his decapitated head in the resultant gush of water.

Miss Thornton sat on a wooden bench near the wall at the back of the well, observing, "That legend is so horrid. It all but ruins the beauty of this place. But it was likely begun by an odious boy, for they always wish us to believe that history was filled with blood and swords."

"Unfortunately, Miss Thornton," said Geoffrey, sitting beside her as the groom took up a position on the far side of the well, "history is filled with blood and swords, however we wish it were otherwise."

She gave him a sidelong look. "Yes, I suppose you are right, and it is merely my wish that such things would be done away. If only men such as Bonaparte would be satisfied with ruling their own kingdom, and not thirst after everyone else's."

"That would be preferable, certainly," answered Geoffrey, "and would save us all much trouble. But that is why I love the legend of this well, for St. Fremund's sword created the well, which has stood for centuries after, and his blood helped to feed the fields we now see. It is an example of how blood and swords may be turned to account."

"I suppose so. However, I am persuaded it would be better not to have swords at all."

Geoffrey let this go, apprehending that, in her innocence, she could not understand that such a thing would never come to pass, and so it was ineffectual even to wish it. "The healing properties of the well must have merit in this discussion, I think," he said, rising and removing his glove to dip himself a drink of water in his cupped hand. "If my eyes deceive me, they will no longer."

Miss Thornton gazed at him from beneath her lashes. "And do you fancy your eyes deceive you, Captain?"

"If they do, I will not repine," he answered, and offered his cupped hand to her.

She smiled and stood to receive some water from his hand, and then, noting the sun had gone behind a cloud, shivered and suggested they return to the church. Geoffrey instantly complied, leading her out of the gate and down the path.

Geoffrey could not be entirely satisfied with their interview, for he was a soldier, and any young lady aspiring to be the wife of a soldier must accept that war was inevitable. Indeed, she must support the fact of his being called up to fight at any moment, and in any place. War was hell, and Geoffrey could not wish for it, but it was his duty, and his vocation, to fight against whatever force threatened the peace of England or her allies. It was a fine balance, and he was obliged by this to wonder how Miss Thornton would take to it.

Chapter 11

IN THE FIRST week of February, Clara sought out Geoffrey in the stables, whither he had gone to sort out his feelings for Miss Thornton in the soothing presence of mute animals.

"I have just heard the most interesting news, Geoff." Her eyes flicked to the groom in the next stall and she lowered her voice. "The Crowthers have come to stay at Chandry Manor."

Geoffrey straightened. "Both—Mr. and Mrs. Crowther?"

"Apparently. I would not care that that vulgar man is back in the neighborhood, but he has brought along his poor wife—" She leaned nearer to whisper, "You must admit it to be an interesting turn of events, Geoff."

"Not in the least," said Geoffrey, stoically returning to the task of grooming his horse. "It is a sad thing when a man cannot bring his wife back to her childhood home without being looked at askance."

She tossed her head. "Well, if you will not say it, I will! I think it an excellent opportunity for you, if you will take it."

His shoulders stiffened and he paused his work. "I see no opportunity in this, Clara, other than to make the acquaintance of a man I am most curious to know."

Clara pursed her lips, making a frustrated noise in her throat. "If you will be obtuse, then I wash my hands of you!"

She flounced out of the stables, leaving Geoffrey to the companionship of the interested groom and his own thoughts. These last were far from complacent, for the shock of hearing that Emily was within a mile of him had been overwhelmed by the insinuation Clara had made—an insinuation which he was horrified had been whispered in his own mind. Had he not escaped the taint of the Mantell blood after all?

He moved as if in a dream, mechanically grooming his horse and breathing in and out as he swung from yearning to see her instantly to planning to flee the county for his own good. A thousand questions filled his mind, and he could not answer a one of them. Could he trust himself in Emily's presence? What of Miss Thornton? What if Crowther proved to be as odious as he was thought to be? How could he not see Emily?

The rhythmic brushing of his horse's coat at last brought some semblance of calm to his brain, and Geoffrey began to order his thoughts. Emily was Mrs. Crowther now, and he could not change that. Moreover, he could not hope to avoid her for the rest of his life. If she heard that he was in the neighborhood and did not visit her, she would be injured, and he could not bear to cause her pain. She deserved his support now more than ever. His best course was to put love of her behind him, by coming as a friend to meet her husband and to wish her well. His mother certainly would not do it, and Francis had gone to London. It was up to him to be civil to Sir Anthony's daughter and son-in-law.

Two days elapsed, however, before Geoffrey was master enough of himself to implement this plan. He set out for Chandry Manor on a bright winter day, with a chilly breeze undercutting the vague warmth of the sun, and it was all he could do not to take it as foreboding. He was admitted by Marsden, the ancient butler, who once again left him in the cheerless saloon to await the master. This time, Geoffrey wandered about the room, preparing himself to appear nothing more than a neighbor on a visit during the bleak winter months. His eyes took in the derelict state of the room—cobwebs clinging to an empty corner vase, an unswept grate, patched and faded curtains—and he steeled himself not to hate the man who had brought Emily back to this horrid place.

After several minutes, the door opened and a thickset man with lank brown hair and small, deep-set eyes entered the room. Geoffrey instantly connected him with the vision of Mr. Crowther that Clara's description had given—his nose was rather fleshy, with red veins lacing the surface, and his eyes gave him a piggy look. But this man was no thoughtless ruffian, of that Geoffrey became convinced as his host gazed at him in an expectant manner, his lips fixed in a rather oily grin and his hands worrying together.

"Captain Mantell. Welcome, welcome!" he said, his arms going wide for a moment, then returning to their fidgeting. "You'll have the goodness to excuse Sir Anthony. He is indisposed, and it is left to me to introduce myself. I am Theobald Crowther, Sir Anthony's son-in-law."

The captain said, "How do you do," then stood fingering the hat in his hands. "Pardon me, I did not know Sir Anthony was unwell. I will return another time."

"No, no! Sit down, sit down. No need to toddle off," said Crowther, trundling a bit closer. "He's well enough—only not home to visitors. Mrs. Crowther is attending to him—an old complaint, soon mended. You know his way, no doubt. It needn't keep us from getting acquainted! I've a mind to know my father-in-law's neighbors, for if I'm to have this place when he goes, I may as well get accustomed to it."

Geoffrey raised an eyebrow at this, deciding that "vulgar" was not an unfit descriptor for him. He sat on the sofa, while Crowther took a wing chair opposite, never taking his eyes off his visitor.

"I only just became aware of your marriage to Miss Chandry," began the captain. "Pardon me, I should say Mrs. Crowther. How does she?"

"It's kind of you to ask. Her health don't permit of much travel, for it knocks her up terribly, but only for a day or two. She insisted on coming, though, for Sir Anthony's sick as a horse, and she's mighty loyal to him, despite what happened." He cocked his head, as if to ascertain how much Geoffrey knew of the circumstances of his marriage. "Your estate marches with Sir Anthony's, does not it? You know her well, I suppose, being near neighbors."

Geoffrey hedged around this by saying, "Mrs. Crowther was near my sister in age. Perhaps you will tell her Miss Mantell is well?"

"Yes, yes, I'll tell her," he said, his oily smile returning. "The missus is well enough, just her nervous condition—she never takes well to the road, nor to any new place. Better to keep her safe at home, I say, but she would come. A good daughter, to be sure."

"Undoubtedly. I remember she was quite a fragile young woman, but I have not seen her for many years. It is good of you to take such care of her. I hope she does not find it a hardship to care for her father."

"None at all," said Crowther, smiling widely to show crooked teeth. "Em's the most obliging creature in the world—does her duty and more and don't complain a bit. Makes me proud."

Geoffrey returned the smile, though it cost him some pain. "I have always thought much of Miss Chan—Mrs. Crowther. I must congratulate you on a union which brings you so much satisfaction. Do you mean to stay long in the neighborhood, then, Mr. Crowther?"

"As long as we can be of use to Sir Anthony," he said, his small eyes intent on Captain Mantell's face. "Oughtn't to take much longer, but we'll see it through."

"I hope that Sir Anthony is soon on the mend."

"Oh, he will be, to be sure. Trust Em's nursing to that."

The captain nodded, becoming unnerved by the man's interested gaze. It was as if he wished to peer into the depths of his soul, but Geoffrey could not conjecture why. He shuddered involuntarily, prompting his host to apologize for the lack of a fire.

"My father-in-law has strange notions of economy, as you may well guess. I'd have ordered a fire if this were my own house, but I've no wish to overstep myself."

Geoffrey nodded his understanding, resolving to end the visit as soon as possible.

"Your father died recently, I believe," said Crowther in a matter-of-fact tone. "God rest him. Leave you the whole of the estate, did he?"

Geoffrey's brows raised again. "You mistake me for my elder brother, Francis. He inherited the bulk of the estate, whereas I have been left only an independence."

The small eyes did not even flicker. "Fine thing for him, to be sure. I'm the first one to congratulate a good man who's got a good inheritance. However, I can't say but I should try to make good by my second son, if I had an estate—this one, for example—and two sons, so as neither had cause to take a pet. There's nothing more shameful than bad blood between brothers."

"One hears of the tragic effects; however, I have no personal experience with such things, myself. Francis and I have ever been on amiable terms."

Crowther nodded sagely. "None could think ill of you, Captain. An upright gentleman such as yourself—and no doubt your brother is just such a one—wouldn't hold a grudge against your own relations, no matter the provocation. I expect you're naught but an honorable man."

The conversation had become excessively uncomfortable to Geoffrey, and he resolved upon instantly taking his leave, when the door to the saloon slammed open, and Sir Anthony staggered over the threshold, wearing a tattered dressing gown, and so haggard-looking and emaciated that the captain scarcely recognized him.

"The devil—Crowther—" Sir Anthony gasped, reaching a claw-like hand toward his son-in-law, who had leapt up with the captain at his entrance.

A servant whom Geoffrey did not recognize careered into the room. "He got hisself up, sir—" he cried, but the guest's presence in the room silenced him instantly.

Sir Anthony swayed alarmingly, and Crowther moved to catch him, but the old man stumbled to the side, waving his arms wildly at his son-in-law and the servant. "Don't touch me—" Then he crumpled into the captain's arms.

The shock of having Sir Anthony fall senseless was enough to confound Geoffrey, but the proceeding events compounded his distress. Crowther aided Geoffrey in lifting his burden onto the sofa, whereupon the unconscious man was violently sick, inducing his companions to consider the wisdom of removing him to his bedchamber and consigning him to the care of Snipson, the servant.

"But Mrs. Crowther was attending him," said Geoffrey in confusion. "Where is she?"

An answer was made unnecessary by that lady's precipitate entrance into the room.

"Crowther—my father is gone again—do you know where—" she cried, then stopped still as a stone as her frantically searching eyes found Geoffrey.

The world spun and Geoffrey's heart constricted as he drank in Mrs. Crowther's presence: her silver-blond hair, now worn under a neat white cap; her glorious gray eyes, wide with astonishment; her trim figure, enrobed in a clean and stylish morning gown. Her features, so dear to him, were burned into his memory anew as he returned her shocked gaze without thought for his companions.

His abstraction was broken when Crowther stood and went to his wife, taking her hand.

"Sir Anthony got away from Snipson, my dear, and came to us. Got out of his head again, and took a dislike to Snipson."

She jerked out of her trance, gazing somewhat blearily at Crowther. "I only went to make a tisane—the one he was used to ask for."

Crowther patted her hand and led her to a chair. "Yes, yes, my dear. No harm done. He will take a pet, and it's no fault of yours. He's been unwell, but Captain Mantell—say how do you do to the captain, my dear! For he came to pay his compliments to you—I say he has been excessively obliging and offered to help me to get Sir Anthony up to his rooms, however now you're here to entertain our guest, Snipson and I will manage it."

He signaled to the servant to take Sir Anthony's legs, and grasping the unconscious man under his arms, carried him from the room. Geoffrey turned to Emily, rapidly gathering his wits and intent upon being civil and friendly, but her look of near despair almost undid him.

"Mrs. Crowther, pray be easy," he said, moving to sit by her. "You have had a shock, I know. Your father will be better presently."

She kept her gaze on her hands, which were clenched tightly together in her lap. "I have never seen him so ill, Captain. I fear he will never recover."

"Do you wish me to go for the doctor?" inquired Geoffrey. "I will go instantly."

She looked at him then for a long moment, then away again. "Yes. Please go for the doctor, sir. He would not have one before this, but I own it would give me great comfort to have him seen."

"I am at your service, ma'am," said Geoffrey, rising and bowing.

He had got to the door when she spoke again. "Captain—it was good of you to come."

"I could not stay away," he said, with perfect truth. Then he added, with less truth, "I wished to congratulate you on your marriage. I did not know of it until recently."

She shook her head, looking down again. "No, I cannot imagine it would have reached your ears in France."

"Mrs. Crowther," he said impulsively, starting forward, "are you happy with him? Does he treat you with—with kindness?"

She huffed a tiny laugh, looking up again with a faintly bleak gaze. "He is not unkind. As you see, he pays me more attention than my father ever did. I have pin money and a maid and a housekeeper, just as he promised. No, he is not unkind. I have nothing to complain of, and much to be grateful for."

Her uncomplaining disposition he had heard praised by Mr. Crowther, and he did not like to hear from her own lips that she was merely well enough. Crowther was not unkind—tepid praise indeed. But before he could press her further, or discover more of her situation, Mr. Crowther entered the room again, dusting his hands together.

"He's all settled, my dear. Stirred at the end and told us to go to the devil, but seems to be resting now."

Mrs. Crowther stood a little jerkily. "Captain Mantell has very obligingly offered to go for the doctor. It would make me easier to have the doctor."

"Certainly, my dear, certainly. Captain Mantell is all kindness. The best of neighbors, to be sure. You look worn to a frazzle, my dear. Go on to your room and lie down. Allow me to see you out, sir, while Mrs. Crowther rests herself."

Geoffrey bowed again to Mrs. Crowther, then allowed himself to be led out of the library and into the hall. Mr. Crowther was all solicitude and apology for what his guest had been so unfortunate as to witness, and took him to the door with many expressions of regret and assurances of his intent to provide Sir Anthony with the best care available.

"It's a recurring condition, sadly," said he, urging the captain out onto the steps. "I've never seen it firsthand like this, but have heard of it through Emily. She knows just what to do about it. If you'll only summon the doctor, we'd be so obliged, and you'll hear soon enough he's back in the stirrups."

Then the door was shut, and Geoffrey untied his horse and mounted, shaking his head to clear it so that he might arrive at the doctor's door in one piece. Never had he imagined that he could feel concern on Sir Anthony's behalf, but he knew that it was more than

⤳ 133

half out of anxiety for Mrs. Crowther. Her situation was distressing to him. Her father was terribly ill, and she was almost overcome with the worry, which her husband, with all his professions of concern, did little to alleviate. Crowther was not odious, precisely, but he was not what she deserved, and it pained him to think of her united to the man for all her life, when she could have been—here he forced himself to focus on the road ahead, lest he give way to despair.

He fetched the doctor and rode behind his gig to Sir Anthony's lodge gates, then turned his horse firmly toward home, where he stayed, pacing and fidgeting for three days, until his mother civilly requested that he go elsewhere until he could sit still for two minutes together.

"Is not Miss Thornton at home? Surely she will cure you of this monstrous indisposition!" she tersely suggested.

Geoffrey merely bowed and left the room to don his greatcoat and walk out the French windows and toward the wood. He had not thought of Miss Thornton in days, and it would do him no good to think of her now. Mrs. Crowther's face, her voice, her distress all crowded in his mind, and he was helpless to assist her. Crowther stood in the position of helpmeet to her, and yet Geoffrey did not doubt he was sadly lacking. There must be something Geoffrey, as her true friend, could do.

His steps led him to the faerie clearing, which looked even more forlorn than it had upon his return from France two months ago. He stood in the center, gazing about at the pathetic mess, knowing that it would pain Mrs. Crowther to see it so, should she come. The likelihood that she would come, especially should Sir Anthony die, was very great, for this was where she had always come to be comforted in her dismal life.

He removed his gloves and began to tidy the village, as well to ease her burden as his. Some of the tiny buildings he had crushed in his first grief, some leaned haphazardly, and the post office looked as though an animal had tried to burrow under it. The villagers had hardly fared better; several hung in the hedge where he had thrown them, others lay scattered about like skittles forgotten after a game. He did what he could for them, righting walls and straightening roofs, and propping the tiny people and animals in their proper places, but many structures were beyond repair.

"You need your mistress's nimble fingers, I'm afraid," he said aloud to the villagers, and somehow it relieved him to speak to them once more. He had not done so since before he left for Belgium, and the instant rapport he felt here soothed his ruffled spirits. The conviction followed that Mrs. Crowther would be soothed here as well, even as she worked to repair the damage that nearly three years' neglect had done, and he sighed. Emily had once said that the faerie clearing was its own world, and held the outside world at bay. Here he could be of use to his old friend, and he had not once thought of Crowther or his own forbidden sentiments.

Chapter 12

IT WAS NOT to be supposed that the serenity of the clearing would follow Geoffrey back to reality. Once in his home, he was accosted by his mother on one hand, insisting that he not neglect Miss Thornton, and on the other hand by the news that had come through the mysterious channels of the servants that Sir Anthony had been stricken down at last and was at death's door. His pacing and grim reflections resumed, until Clara cornered him in the library and all but dragged him out to shoot with her in the wood.

As they readied their pistols, she said casually, "I really am quite heartbroken that you will not repose trust in me, Geoff."

"What can you mean?" he muttered.

"I know that something momentous happened during your visit to Chandry Manor, dearest, for you've been moping for three days without telling a soul what you saw, and I'll no longer stand for it."

"Pardon me, Clara," said Geoffrey, his brows contracting, "but it is none of your business what happened there."

She rolled her eyes. "It is not as if it is secret! The whole town knows of it, for they saw you ride up like a madman to Mr. Sloan's house and follow his gig out of town. Then the apothecary has been mixing up powders and what-not and sending them daily to Chandry Manor, while no one within stirs. Surely you can tell me how it is there?"

"Clara," he said sternly, "this is not a romantic novel. It is a matter of great moment, and involves someone who is very dear to me."

She gave him a measuring look. "Mrs. Crowther. I thought as much. I thought you could not feel half so much anxiety over Sir Anthony." She loaded her pistol and continued, "Does his illness truly worry her so terribly? I should think that she, of all people, would be glad to see him go."

Putting down his gun, Geoffrey looked hard at her. "How can you say such things, Clara? Have you no proper feeling? Sir Anthony was a poor father, to be sure, but she has no other relation."

"I had not thought of that." She shrugged. "I did not mind so very much when Father died."

Geoffrey gazed at her, his consternation gradually dying away in the consciousness of his own guilt. "No, nor did I. Though I was far away when it happened, and so was spared the full face of it. We are all of us—you, Francis, Mother, and I—cold in our affections, I suppose. But Mrs. Crowther is a very different sort of person."

"Then I begin to comprehend your loving her as you do," she said, taking careful aim with the pistol. "It is double the blow I thought it was to you." She shot, and nicked the edge of the mark. "But Mrs. Crowther is not lost to you."

"I am not in a mood to listen to your nonsense, Clara—"

She cast him a deprecating look. "You have been on the Continent for a hundred years, Geoff. You must know by now that married women are not untouchable."

"Clara, if you were a man, I should call you out for such a remark," said Geoffrey, lowering his pistol and turning to gaze grimly at her. "How dare you suggest such a thing? Mrs. Crowther is not some flighty matron who has discarded her virtue as soon as she took her vows. I could never offer her such an affront."

"I see. And I honor you, really I do." She set down her pistol. "But I cannot help but wish you would reconsider, for I like you, Geoffrey, and I do not wish to see you kill yourself with pining, or worse, run mad."

He went with her to replace the marks on their poles, and as they returned to where their pistols lay, he said quietly, "It is not as though I do not try to move on, Clara. I simply do not know the way to go about it. Whenever I think I have done the job, I am confounded somehow, and I find that I am just as much in love with her as ever."

"But a declaration would wound her?"

"Terribly. How can you even doubt it?"

"And yet you cannot find the strength to hide your feelings." She loaded her pistol, shaking her head. "Honorable persons are inexplicable to me." She took careful aim and let off the shot, piercing the mark near the center. She turned back to Geoffrey. "If you care for Mrs. Crowther as you say you do, you cannot go on being confounded."

"I do not intend to, Clara, but I have already told you I cannot help it!"

She pointed a finger at him. "You cannot help it because you are thinking only of yourself, Geoff. Forgive my plain speaking, but if you search your feelings, you will find it to be true. Your chief concern has been your own disappointment, with scarcely a thought for how your actions will affect her, and if you continue in this way, it is she who will suffer most."

He blinked at her, stunned.

Clara continued. "You must resolve that she will never know you love her."

"After what I have just told you, you do not imagine I would be so crude as to tell her," he said, frowning.

"No, I do not," said Clara matter-of-factly, as she went about reloading her pistol again. "But I do imagine you to be fully capable of showing her if you do not take care. I have a wonderful imagination, Geoff, and I imagine you will go on visiting her and fetching the doctor for her and glaring at the mention of her husband until you make quite a fool of yourself, and all at her expense."

"Never," Geoffrey said emphatically. "I merely wish to see her happy."

Clara gazed dryly at him. "If you do, then you will see that your inability to stifle your feelings will do her as much injury as a declaration would. You must think of her, Geoff. As long as she has reason merely to think of you as her very dear friend, she may find contentment in her chosen lot. You must never do anything to destroy that contentment, Geoff. Make that your purpose, and you will find your strength, I am persuaded."

Geoffrey stared at her, his brow furrowed. He had not thought that his disappointment could cause Emily pain. He could not be certain that she had cherished more than friendly feelings for him, in the years before Belgium, but if she had, she had gone into her marriage believing them to be unrequited, and his revealing a partiality to her now would be tantamount to inviting an *affaire*. Her feelings would revolt, she would be mortified and wounded, and if the neighborhood were ever to hear of it—as they most assuredly would—she would be even more outcast than she was previous to her marriage. And he would be the cause—if he had not injured her by his rejection two years and a half ago, he would injure her by such a betrayal now.

"Indeed, as matters stand, Geoff," said Clara, more gently, laying a hand on his arm, "she is at worst disappointed, but she is not heartbroken."

"Nor shall she be," he said, loading a ball into his pistol. "You are right, Clara. I have been a selfish, weak excuse for a man. I am more like Francis than ever I thought." He aimed and shot through the heart of the mark.

"Do not refine too much upon it," said Clara, satisfied with his change of attitude. "We all have our shortcomings."

"I had rather mine was to fall in love and marry and settle down happily," said Geoff, beginning to clean his pistol.

Clara followed his example. "Even you could not wish so dull an existence as that, Geoff. Think of the heartburnings and rages lost. You must have something interesting to tell your posterity."

"If I ever have one."

"That is right! Angst and alt and tortured love!" She laughed, but then took his hand in a comforting clasp, looking at him with warm regard. "It will all work out in the end, you will see."

On the seventh day following Sir Anthony's sudden collapse, Geoffrey resolved again to call at Chandry Manor to assure himself of Emily's well-being and to offer what support he could.

"Then I'll go with you, Geoff," declared Clara. "If you will be a hero, then I may do my poor part and lend my support for the visit."

They took the Colonel's curricle, and Clara's eyes went wide at the sight of Marsden, who opened the door. Without pausing even to gaze blearily up at them, he shuffled off toward the saloon, and Clara leaned toward Geoffrey to whisper that she now believed entirely in the veracity of novels. Geoffrey, ignoring this, led Clara into the room and seated her in a comfortable chair, but he had scarcely seated himself, when the door opened again and Mrs. Crowther entered the room.

The effect was not so electrifying as it had been a week previous, for which Geoffrey's iron self-control was responsible. She wore a light calico morning dress with a high collar and long sleeves, and had a rough woolen shawl draped over her shoulders. Her eyes were even larger than he remembered—at least it seemed so, as they stood out in her drawn face. She also seemed more in command of herself as she walked toward them with a brave smile.

"Captain and Miss Mantell, how good of you to visit."

She sat opposite Clara, her thin hands clasped in her lap. "I fear I have no refreshment to offer you. My father—"

"Do not tease yourself, Mrs. Crowther," said Geoffrey quickly. "We did not come for refreshment, but to see how you get on. Is your father very ill?"

"You are too good! I am well enough, but my father, I'm afraid, is not—" She averted her eyes. "It is worse than ever before. He was always able to recover quickly, but nothing we have tried seems to relieve him."

"Does the doctor believe he will recover?" asked Geoffrey.

"He cannot say. Mr. Crowther has gone to fetch him now, though he does not trust he can do more than he has already done. Snipson, our man, has posted down to London after some powders Crowther has used with success himself. His is only a mild stomach complaint, however, and I cannot imagine—"

She suddenly choked on a sob and put a hand to her mouth, turning away from them to hide her distress. Clara, to Geoffrey's astonishment, went instantly to her, sitting beside her on the sofa and clasping one of her hands.

"You are overwrought, poor thing," she said, patting her hand soothingly. "How horrid, to be constantly on watch, without your servant to spell you, and likely the only female in this ramshackle house. No wonder you are worn to the bone!"

Emily gripped her hand in return. "I am excessively tired. My father is fretful and demanding, even in his lucid moments, and I can hardly keep my temper with him."

"You must not blame yourself," said Geoffrey gently, offering his handkerchief to her. "As you say, you are very tired, and have borne more than the best of daughters should be made to bear."

"Thank you. You are so kind," said Mrs. Crowther, drying her eyes. Then she stood. "I must go to my father. He is agitated if I am too long absent from his side. Thank you Captain Mantell, Miss Mantell, for your visit. It has cheered me."

She saw them to the door, and as soon as they were in the curricle and down the drive, Clara said, "You did well, Geoffrey. I was forced to leap into the breach and comfort her myself, however, or you would have had her in your arms in a trice. Perhaps you ought not to visit again, at least for some time."

Geoffrey was obliged to acknowledge this wisdom, and contented himself with sending some fruit from the Mantell succession houses to Chandry Manor, while visiting instead the faerie clearing. In the conviction that Emily would not leave her house until the crisis had passed—whether it was in death or recovery—Geoffrey allowed his feet to carry him thither most mornings, where he puttered at the old faerie village, mending the people and animals and houses as best his soldier's hands and penknife could do, so that when she did come, she would find comfort there.

It was on the morning of the tenth day that he came upon her sitting quietly in front of the faerie post office. On his approach she stood, dabbing at her eyes and welcoming him with a wan and watery smile.

"Captain Mantell. I had hoped you might come. I see you have taken your turn in keeping up the village. Thank you."

He swallowed down the lump that had leapt to his throat at sight of her distress and forced a smile of his own. "It was nothing. I simply could not stand to see it neglected." She looked away and he asked, "How does your father?"

She looked down at her hands, which were clasped before her. "He is dead."

"Oh, my dear Mrs. Crowther," he said, instantly betraying more feeling than he had hoped. "It is over, then, and you have done your duty to the last."

Her large eyes raised to his, and their pained expression nearly undid him. His hands went out to her of their own accord, and she came to him, but put out her hands to clasp his before he could do anything so improper as to embrace her.

"The funeral will be at St. James's church, on Wednesday," she said in a thickened voice. "As females do not attend, I cannot be there, and I do not know who can wish to go, other than Mr. Crowther and perhaps Mr. Noyce. He was always kind to father and me."

"I will go, if you wish it," said Geoffrey.

She smiled sadly up at him. "You were always kind, too, Captain."

As she pulled away, Geoffrey curled his fingers into his palms, to keep the feel of her hands in his. "Do you return to London after the funeral?"

She sighed, looking down again. "No. Crowther intends to remain here for the present, to settle the estate as is proper. I will do what I can to make the Manor more comfortable. I do not believe our house-keeper will come down from London." She looked up at him, a wry smile twisting on her lips. "My situation has reverted upon my coming back, it seems."

"Were you happy before—in London?"

"It is not quite to my liking, but I have learned not to be nice in my notions. I am very often alone, but for my maid, but it suits me quite well. Mr. Crowther is a restless sort of man, and I do not mind that he is away on business more often than not."

"You do not love him," Geoffrey said without thinking.

Emily's brow creased. "No. I did not marry him for love."

"May I ask—why did you marry him?"

"Because he offered, and I had no better." She crouched down to better arrange a group of villagers. "I met Crowther in London, and when he followed us into the country, he claimed to have taken a liking to me. I did not believe it then, nor do I now, though he professes such solicitude. But he promised to take better care of me than my father, and offered even to put it into writing. There was not likely to be a better way to escape my father, so I accepted him." She stood, shaking out her skirts. "He has kept his promises. He treats me much as he would a younger sister, which is far, far better than did my father. I cannot complain. It is well enough."

Geoffrey yearned to tell her that well enough was not accept-able, that she deserved her cup to be filled and overflowing with contentment and joy, and never even to think of enough. Her whole life had been enough, of patience, of fear, of loneliness, of slights, of unkindness, of drudgery. He had had enough of knowing that those who controlled her happiness would never see her as enough. He could never tell her enough of what he felt for her—but Clara had been right, and he would not destroy what little peace Emily had found by revealing to her what improper feelings he cherished for her.

Controlling himself, he said simply, "I am so glad. I have been worried for my old friend."

The gray eyes met his, and the resignation they bore nearly broke his heart. But there was no despair, no desolate longing, and this fact fortified him to take his leave of her with friendly assurances that he would attend Sir Anthony's obsequies, and no more.

As he walked away toward Gracely Hall, he thought how poorly he had hidden his feelings, and how unbearable it would be to see her thus frequently. For now that her father had died, the Crowthers would undoubtedly settle there permanently, and the encroaching Mr. Crowther would worm his way into neighborhood society, on the strength of Emily's acquaintance with Mr. Noyce and the Mantells, and then Geoffrey would see her, would see Mrs. Crowther, on the arm of her husband, painfully often.

Geoffrey knew then there was only one thing to be done; he must go away. He must walk away from the woman he loved, to save her from a broken heart and himself from never ending purgatory. He must let her live, and try to live himself, by putting enough distance between them to foster forgetfulness and encourage healing. He must resign himself that she would be well enough, and he must let her be so without possibility of upset.

Chapter 13

MRS. CROWTHER'S CONJECTURE regarding the attendance at her father's funeral proved correct: in addition to Mr. Crowther and Captain Mantell, only Mr. Noyce and Squire Frean were in attendance, and the squire, intent on discovering the political bent of his new neighbor, cornered Crowther after the service, and monopolized him for nearly a half hour.

Mr. Noyce made his way out of the church at Geoffrey's side, the captain slowing his pace to allow for his neighbor's more awkward gait.

"You're good to come, Mantell," said Mr. Noyce, when they had gained the open air. "I'd not believed your family to be on good terms with Sir Anthony."

"We were not, but Mrs. Crowther and I were childhood friends," answered the captain. "I thought it the least I could do, as she could not attend."

Mr. Noyce glanced sharply at him. "A lonely child, little Emily. I remember. More than once I came upon her in the village, and if I frightened her less than most men, I have my crippled legs to thank for it. We had something in common, she and I, you see. Both of us oddities."

"If the two of you represent the general run of oddities, sir," said Geoffrey, less quizzing than truthful, "I should call it an honor to be of your number."

Mr. Noyce chuckled and went on. "From what I've seen of Crowther, he seems a friendly enough sort of man. Puts one in mind of a pig, however."

"I believe Mrs. Crowther is content with her lot," was all the captain thought wise to say.

"Mmm," said Mr. Noyce, eying him askance.

The captain read perception in that gaze and looked off across the fields.

Mr. Noyce shrugged. "Barring anything extraordinary with the will, it seems apparent that Mrs. Crowther will inherit. Which means Mr. Crowther is now the owner of a very decent piece of property, for all the work it must needs have done. He will likely settle here."

Geoffrey could not resist a grimace. "I wish him joy of it, though I'll not be here to witness the business. I have resolved to remove to London for the season."

"Ah," said his companion. "Escort your mother and sister, eh? Very proper."

"No, my mother does not fancy Town this year, though she is only in half-mourning, and insists that there is no respectable female among her acquaintance who would take my sister for the season. I do not contradict her, for I have come to comprehend that Clara is a handful. But I suppose London may offer too much gaiety for a new widow."

"Hmm. A new come out for her, I believe," Mr. Noyce murmured, then was silent for some time. "Did not your father have a house in Town?"

"He always hired a house when he and my mother went to Town, for he never quite took to London."

"Perhaps you will press your brother to make the purchase, and so save you the expense of lodgings. Your mother will not always be in mourning, after all, and she and your sister cannot stay in gentlemen's lodgings when they go to Town in future."

"I doubt Francis could be prevailed on to purchase a house in London, for he seems to prefer an independent lifestyle there. However, it is nothing to me, for I have a good friend who is generally willing to put me up. George Stanhope, Lord Chesterfield."

"Young Lord Chesterfield, eh? No wonder you fancy Town! There's no such fine friends to keep a young man entertained in the country, I'll give you that. While there's plenty to distract a young man in London, eh?" He grinned, but his eyes were still keen, searching Geoffrey's.

"Yes, sir!" replied the captain, smiling back. "I wonder that you do not go to Town, and work your charm on all the females there. You could get you a wife! Or is fear of that what keeps you immured in the country?"

Mr. Noyce chuckled. "There is no deceiving you, I see. No, my charms would do me no good in London, my boy, for not just any wife will do for me. You may understand me, I fancy." And wishing Geoffrey a prosperous journey, he walked stiffly to his horse, was helped to mount, and rode away.

Geoffrey walked slowly to where his horse awaited him, but was halted by the sound of his name called from across the street. Looking up, he saw Miss Thornton crossing toward him with her maid.

"Captain Mantell! Oh, I've caught you at last." Her blue eyes shone and her cherry lips turned up in a smile. "It has been weeks since last we met, I declare! What has happened to you? Did you attend that odious man's funeral? It is good of you, though I suppose you only did so because he was your neighbor."

"Yes, but I am also acquainted with his daughter, Mrs. Crowther, who asked me specially to attend."

She became doubly interested. "Mrs. Crowther? The one who married that horrid man? I have never seen him—Oh! That must be he, speaking to the Squire. Is he as odious as he looks? He must be, to have married Sir Anthony's daughter."

Her beauty seemed to diminish as she spoke, and her words grated on Geoffrey's ears.

"Mrs. Crowther is nothing like her father, and is a very dear friend," he said succinctly.

The blue eyes flew to his. "Oh, pardon me, Captain. I would never think ill of a friend of yours. I am sorry for her, to be sure."

He thanked her, but though she would have kept him talking longer, he said he must go and mounted his horse. He did not look back as he set his mount at a trot up the road, for he was not certain he wished ever to see Miss Thornton's face again. He had thought her so pretty, once, but her beauty must have palled on him, for now she seemed almost ordinary. It was a pity, for he had once believed her to be the one who could make him forget Emily. He could only be grateful he had been undeceived before he had committed himself to a life with her, however, for it had likely saved him from the very mistake his parents had so foolishly made.

Within the week, Geoffrey was once more the guest of young Lord Chesterfield, who was at present endangering the pristine cleanliness of his nankeens and frilled shirt by hunting in the shrubbery of his magnificent gardens for a cricket ball. The captain, awaiting the retrieval of the ball, gazed off into the distance, his thoughts far from cricket, far from London even, in a decrepit manor, with a lonely young woman whom he must forget.

"Captain!" cried the young earl, his head swallowed up by the shrubbery. "I can't see it!"

The captain laughed, stepping forward and pointing. "It went in just there, to your right. Fish around with your right hand and you're bound to find it."

As his lordship flailed in the shrubbery, the captain tried again not to think of Mrs. Crowther, and was assisted in his effort by the sudden and distinct impression that eyes were upon him. Looking round, he perceived a pretty young woman gazing abstractedly out the window of a house opposite the gardens, her eyes fixed not on him, precisely, but beyond him. He regarded her with interest, imagining he knew just how she felt—settled physically while mentally miles off—and he wondered if what stole away her thoughts was as compelling as that which stole away his own.

He watched her for several moments, considering this possible similarity, until abruptly, the young lady's eyes snapped into focus. She looked wide-eyed at him, her hand flying up as if in apology for her staring, and Geoffrey, seized by an impulse engendered by fellow-feeling, tipped his hat in greeting. But the poor girl blushed furiously, disappearing from view an instant later, and the captain berated himself for a scapegrace. No well-bred gentleman would so force his acquaintance on an unknown young lady.

Abashed at his part in her mortification, Geoffrey watched for her return to the window, determined to indicate his contrition in some way, and to show her she had nothing to fear, but George called out again, demanding his assistance to find the ball, and with a regretful sigh, the captain strode out of view of the opposite house, removing his hat and diving into the shrubbery.

When the ball had been located they resumed their game, but cricket had lost its enjoyment for both of them, and after only a few pitches, the captain suggested to his flagging companion that they take a drive in Hyde Park, to see what high steppers were to be found there. This scheme was instantly approved, for George Stanhope, Lord Chesterfield, was horse mad—though only twelve years of age—and looked forward to his friend's visits chiefly because Captain Mantell was a right one, and thought nothing of gadding about the principal raceways and horse dealers with a youth at his heels.

Their turn in Hyde Park unfortunately yielded a longing in the young earl's breast for a showy chestnut touted to him by one Lord D'arcy as a prime goer, but Geoffrey, taking his role as de facto mentor more seriously than it appeared, only laughed at him and told him to wait a few years more until he could tell a breakdown from a prime beast before he spent all his allowance on cattle. George then demanded to be told what was wrong with the horse, and the captain—much to Lord D'arcy's discomfiture—obliged him, dwelling for some fifteen minutes on the chestnut's deficiencies. At the close of this instructive space, the earl had gained some useful information and lost his fancy for the animal, and perhaps feeling the effect of his mental exertions, declared himself famished. Geoffrey gladly took his young friend home, where dinner was awaiting their return.

After their repast, his lordship was taken away by his tutor, and Geoffrey was at liberty to retire to the library for a sip of brandy and a bit of repose. But as ever, when not fully engaged elsewhere, his mind wandered back to Warwickshire, and to Mrs. Crowther, and it was some time before he had recollected himself and jumped up to pluck a book from the shelf. He reflected that he must do more to restrain his thoughts from forever straying to Mrs. Crowther, which he knew very well was both fruitless and contrary to his purpose in Town, for he had come to get her and all associated with her out of his mind, and to look to his own future. It occurred to him then that keeping to the company of a small boy would do little toward his goals, and that he must be more active in placing himself in situations which were more conducive to falling in love.

Fortunately, the Season was beginning, and as he had advertised his presence in London to his various relations, he was assured of invitations to every sort of social event he could wish. He attended a card party that night, where he tried very hard to flirt with the young lady with whom he was paired at whist. This proved alternately diverting and exhausting, for the lady became so distracted by her coquetry that she quite forgot the game, and Geoffrey was obliged to recall her attention repeatedly to prevent her losing every trick.

To recover from these exertions, he played cards at his club until the early hours of the morning, then got up betimes to exercise Lord Chesterfield's horses with him in Hyde Park. That afternoon, he met Charles Wraglain at Limmer's, and engaged in a Council of War over which young ladies the captain was allowed to flirt with, and which were off-limits.

Another party rounded off the evening, at which Geoffrey girded up his loins and spoke with not one, but three eligible young ladies.

He possessed considerable charm, which he had had occasion to exercise while on the Continent, and found that with practice, it flowed quite effortlessly. The young ladies, moreover, were refreshingly well-educated, and could speak with eloquence on a variety of topics unknown to his female acquaintance in Warwickshire. One, unhappily, had gray eyes, and he found it rather disconcerting to be called to order for gazing rapturously into them, when he had in actuality been lost in memories of quite another lady's eyes.

By the next day, Geoffrey longed for a more solitary activity. Taking advantage of his host's generosity, he availed himself of the Stanhope box at the Covent Garden Theater, arriving fashionably late and taking his seat midway through the first act. The play was perhaps too well fitted to his situation, for it was a tragedy of no mean order, whose characters were made to bemoan the perversity of Hymen, the god of marriage, and Cupid, the god of love. He felt great sympathy with the characters until the falling of the curtain and the hiss of gas lights brought the theater alive for the interval, and he felt suddenly exposed in his weakness. In this dangerously maudlin mood, he was relieved when the curtains behind him parted, and Mr. Wraglain entered, followed closely by Mr. Simpford.

"Lawrie! I'd no notion you were in town!"

"Devil a bit, Geoff!" cried the newcomer, clasping hands with him. "You couldn't think me so poor-spirited as to lurk about in Warwickshire while you and Charles rake about town."

"I tell you, neither of you has anything to fear from me," insisted Geoffrey, grinning. "A captain on half pay is no match for the eldest son of a baron, nor the owner of a very pretty estate."

They both disclaimed this, stating his conquest of Miss Thornton as evidence of their danger, and the urgent beckonings of a matron in puce satin in the box opposite, accompanied by the blushes of a pair of very pretty girls who sat with her, only escalated their jocular debate. Geoffrey, determined to conquer his recent weakness, stated his intention of accompanying his friends to the matron's box and introducing himself to her companions, which earned him a severe reproach from Mr. Simpford and a declaration by Mr. Wraglain that he should plant him a facer if he tried. While Mr. Simpford made his escape, Mr. Wraglain detained Geoffrey with some unscientific jabs, and had just determined on a desperate scheme to keep him there, when a commotion in a box across the theater caught the captain's attention.

He scarcely noticed Mr. Wraglain's exit as he pulled out his quizzing glass to inspect the familiar face of a young lady whom a pair of what looked to be niffy-naffy fellows were putting to the blush with their overloud protestations. The young lady was the very one whom he had surprised at her thoughts in the window overlooking Chesterfield House Gardens, and as he watched with rising indignation, her two companions so far forgot themselves as to announce to the theater at large that she was minx—at which point her horrified gaze found his.

Instantly, he dropped his quizzing glass, sitting back in his chair and turning his eyes to the stage as if in anticipation of the second act. To have been caught once again behaving so ungentlemanly discomposed him exceedingly, and he wished even more for the opportunity to redeem himself. He could not hope to win the affections of a lady— any lady—if he appeared to have no self command, and he had twice now given this particular young lady every reason to believe him a coxcomb. Glancing quickly back at her, he saw that she was sitting very subdued in her box, with what seemed to be her mother hanging solicitously about her, and he was even more repentant.

Sighing, the captain could not but feel the irony of his situation, having just endured the rallying of his friends over his charm with the ladies, while placing one young lady—with whom he had fancied a bond of unrequited hopes, no less—in the intolerable position of having made herself ridiculous to a stranger. As the lights dimmed for the second act, Geoffrey dared another peek at the young woman's box, but her eyes were fixed on the parting curtain, and though he sensed her eyes upon him at various times through the performance, he could not bring himself to look at her again.

Over the following days, his gaze was often drawn to the young lady's window, whenever he strolled about Chesterfield House Gardens, or walked along Curzon Street in his way. He wondered if his actions had materially affected her composure, or if she had instantly dismissed him—both times—as nobody of consequence. But he had been mistaken before for Lord Chesterfield by those who were not familiar with the earl and his family, so he was more inclined to believe that she had done the same, and was suffering agonies of mortification for having exposed herself to so important a member of the *ton*.

He would have given much for an opportunity to undeceive her, but he knew not who she was, nor how to find it out, for she was not at any of the *ton* parties he attended. This was not surprising, for the Season was in full swing, and even he had been obliged to decline several invitations which overlapped those he had already engaged to accept. He could only hope that at some point soon they should both be at the same party, and he could make things right with her.

When he was brought to realize how constantly this nameless young woman was in his thoughts, he was not chagrined, as may be supposed—for he knew in general that it would be improper for him to entertain such an interest in a female to whom he was unknown. However, his was not a general circumstance, and he rather congratulated himself on his success in replacing other, more dangerous thoughts of another female. So he encouraged his mind to dwell on the stranger, and to wonder at his first impression that she also suffered under a disappointment, and to consider whether this hypothetical bond could be sufficient to overcome their separate losses and to ignite in either of them a lasting passion.

Chapter 14

ONE MORNING, SOME four or five days following his evening at the theater, Captain Mantell took his breakfast in the back parlor, glancing over the post as he sipped his coffee. Two invitations and a bootmaker's bill were set aside, for here was a letter addressed to him in Clara's neat hand, and after the exertion of putting Gracely and its environs forcibly from his mind for several days, he rather wished for tidings from home.

The letter ran thus:

> *My dear Geoffrey,*
>
> *No doubt you are too wasted with dissipation to give a thought to your poor sister, who must be resigned to her fate, and leads an uncomplaining and unvarying existence in the wilds of Warwickshire. Do not tell me, I beg, of all your parties and balls and entertainments, and of all the interesting people with whom you are undoubtedly*

thrown together, for I shall jump in the river if you do. Why my mother must adhere so strictly to the constraints of tradition just because my father is dead is a circumstance quite beyond my understanding, for while he lived, she lived only for society, and could not abide the country during the dead of winter. But it is not my place to wonder, nor to question the actions of my honored parent. Only assure me, my dearest brother, that there are no dashingly eligible young men on the town, and I shall be content.

One may wonder what I could find to entertain myself in this wilderness, with half the families in the neighborhood gone up to Town, and all of the amiable young men. You may tell Mr. Simpford from me that he is the greatest traitor imaginable to have followed you, and if he believes himself secure of my esteem after such a trick, he is much mistaken. But I am a young lady of great resource, and my nature is not one to lay down and die simply because I am forsaken by all I hold dear—excepting Mother, of course. None of this can come as a surprise to you, but the following may.

I have struck up a friendship with Mrs. Crowther. She called upon me one day after you had gone away and though she was exceedingly shy, we had a fine visit, eating plenty of cake and fruit to make up for the lack of conversation. I returned her visit in form, for though I am in general not given to charity, I am never rude. It occurred to me to try if I may discover more about her, including how she does not run mad in that house, a question which arose readily in my mind as I awaited her there in the most delightful saloon, whose furnishings and hangings are older than that butler, Methuselah or what's his name. She has done much to tidy it up, but there does not seem to have been any money spent on the endeavor. When she came in, I could not help but ask if she had plans to renovate Chandry Manor, and mentioned most helpfully that my mother could furnish her with the address of an excellent decorator, but this suggestion fell upon unfruit-ful ground. She said that Mr. Crowther has no plans to renovate at present, though they intend to reside there some time. It is a pity, but I suppose that Mr. Crowther, having been an old business associate of his poor father-in-law, is much like him, except that he is not dead.

This visit proved most interesting, for Mrs. Crowther was on pins and needles for the entirety, and I was on pins and needles to discover the cause. Was she in expectation of a terrible event? Did she suspect me of ill intent, or was it that some fearful incident had recently occurred in the house? Was that horrid manservant, who continually creeps in and out, spying on her? And consequently, was every word which passed her lips, though small in number, great with hidden meaning? I tell you, it was all I could do to end the visit within the allotted time, and carry myself out to the chaise with any semblance of decorum. There is a mystery in that house that wants solving, and if I, who have nothing else whatsoever to do, cannot untangle it, then I am not worth mentioning.

A full week passed before she called again, and this time, I was ready to burst with curiosity. I inquired very slyly about her life in London and if she missed it (no), and after blathering a bit about how much one loves Town and would die to be there, if only one's mother could accompany one, I asked how she liked to be at home (a rather mournful "it is quite changed"). Then, my piece d'resistance: I expressed a wish to be of service to her, to which she smiled rather forlornly and said that I have already been of great service in making myself her friend. What could I say to that, dear brother, but that I also took great delight in the acquaintance?

And it was not much of an untruth, for I am terribly curious about Emily Crowther—I know I need not enumerate to you, of all people, her charms, but I suspect she has much more substance than meets the eye. I know enough of her father to believe she has had much to bear, and have seen enough of her husband to imagine her burdens are not significantly lessened in that relationship. He is an odd man, and I wish I knew what he is about. His oiliness on our first meeting was excessively irritating, but I have met him only once since, as I came into his house to return Emily's second visit, and then he merely smiled like the lion at the Exchange and bowed me into the saloon.

Do not get on your high ropes and remonstrate with me for insensibility, for I will not listen. I have so little to distract me from the littleness of my life and the restraints of country society, that you cannot be so cruel as to deny me this one extravagance. Besides, you cannot deny that Crowther is very strange, and if his obsequious manner does not hide a dastardly soul, I shall be excessively disappointed.

Here, the letter seemed to have ended, but after a long dash, was begun again in a more agitated hand:

Good heaven, Geoff, you will never guess what has happened! After two or three more visits to Emily, I had come to believe my imaginings had got the better of me, and was ready to wash my hands of the whole affair, when I came into Chandry Manor and as I was being ushered into the saloon as usual, I heard raised voices in the adjoining room—I think the library—and though I am not by principle an eavesdropper, I could not but hear Crowther telling Emily that she was not worth marrying, and that he regretted his association with her father. You must believe that I was powerless to keep from hearing, for I was positively rooted to the spot, and old Methuselah merely tottered off to wherever he goes, so what could I do else but stay where I was put? Crowther carried on for some time, to the effect that if Emily did not know the whereabouts of some documents which were worth a great deal of money, he had wasted his time and thrown himself away in marrying her.

You may imagine my horror at hearing such things, but you will only be half right, for what should happen next but that the library door should be flung open, and Crowther himself came out, and Geoff, I have never before seen him so—a puffing, snorting bull with murder in its eyes! Before I could move or collect my wits to think of anything to say, the whole of his demeanor underwent a change so material as to give me quite a turn. One moment he was the murderous bull, the next a smiling lion, who took my hand and bowed over it—he smelled so strongly of spirits, I nearly swooned—and begged my pardon for having exposed me to a great deal of nonsense, for he was under tremendous pressure to sort out Sir Anthony's affairs, which had been left in such disastrous order that anyone might be driven distracted by it.

Well, I am grateful that I need not have replied to this, for Emily followed him directly and, taking me by the arm, pulled me into the saloon and shut the door. I tell you, I was terribly tempted to be impertinent and to pry into her affairs, but she saved me the trouble, and rather than engage in our regular, civil interaction, she took me away to the far corner and poured the whole of the matter into my ears. Never did I think my sustained efforts at neighborliness would be so rewarded! But I have been excessively generous and obliging, and so perhaps I deserve it. And the cream of it, brother, is that in telling you all I am merely doing my duty, for you will see that I have been implored to relay the information to you, as it is hoped that you might be of use. If not, I shall not be the only one to be disappointed.

It seems that Sir Anthony was incredibly rich, for all he pretended not to be, and owned quite a few properties in addition to Chandry Manor. These Emily had only a vague knowledge of, for she had been almost as deceived as we all were as to Sir Anthony's fortune. Then she met Crowther, who had convinced Sir A to make certain investments, which would tie up his capital for some few years but would (Crowther averred) yield great sums afterward. Then Crowther wished to marry her, and though they both knew Sir A would never allow it, Emily was so intent upon escaping the Manor that she consented, and can you believe it, Geoff—you must not be a prude and be shocked, or I will never speak to you again—they eloped! It is the most romantic thing. She thought it had all been a scheme for Crowther to secure Sir A's fortune to himself, for she knew she was to inherit, but it made no odds to her, for she could see no other way to freedom.

(You will and you must applaud my self-control at this point, Geoff, for it was on the tip of my tongue to reveal to her how horribly she was mistaken on that point. But I heroically did not utter a word, for I am determined to practice what I preached to you, and let her have her untarnished memories without the heartbreak of knowing just how close she had been to great happiness. May I say, dearest Geoffrey, that you really were a fool not to notice you loved her? But I digress.)

When Sir A died and the estate was settled, it was discovered that Chandry Manor is heavily mortgaged, and the rest of the estate worth far less than Crowther can account for. He is now convinced that Sir A took the money from the mortgages and invested it somehow, privately and without the knowledge of the solicitor, in an attempt to hide it from his son-in-law, as revenge upon he who cheated him so soundly. Crowther has been searching the Manor for proof of his supposition, but cannot find it anywhere, and is requiring Emily to assist him.

At the end of this recital, remembering her husband as the furious bull, I of course asked Emily if she was in any danger and she assured me she is not. She tells me that Crowther has often shouted at her, but he is not in the habit of offering violence to anyone, and has never raised a finger to her. He cares a great deal about money, merely, and has suffered a great disappointment. She said he would be chastened by the fact that I overheard him, and will be more circumspect in future, as he desires that Emily retain my acquaintance.

She was quite right. Crowther came in soon after this, and do you know what he said? He was excessively contrite, to me and to Emily, saying he was a scoundrel to have ripped up at her like that, and begging us both to forgive him. It was quite a performance—I do not think I shall ever dare to take him at his word again. But then he did an astonishing thing, and asked if I should very much mind informing you of his dilemma and asking for your assistance in discovering how Sir A had invested his money, for he was very tied up with the estate at the moment, and—he was very nearly in tears at this point, I tell you—if he could not get some money, he could never refurbish Chandry Manor for his dearest Em.

I of course engaged you to do all in your power— which I promised is considerable—to right this terrible wrong, and to sweep all Sir A's deceit before you. There, I have made you a knight errant, so you need not shrink to serve your married lady, for it will be with a pure and chivalric love that even you may honor.

Never fear, dear Geoffrey, that through this development my acquaintance with Emily will suffer, for I do not mean to abandon her at this most interesting time. Wild horses could not drag me away from this adventure, even if they were to take me to London! I will remain faithfully at her side until the last breath is wrung from my dying body—but that is the wrong symbolism, for I have quite given up the notion of gruesome secrets in Chandry Manor. Comfort yourself that we merely are looking for old, musty documents in this gloomy, neglected house, and do not imagine that Crowther is anything but a thwarted, oily businessman who is likely being dunned for his debts and feeling the pinch. We will find his nasty documents, and he will be happy, and Emily will be at peace once more, depend upon it.

In the meanwhile, Geoffrey, you are set the task of discovering what you may about the investments Sir A kept from the solicitor's knowledge. Is such a thing possible? I do not know what you can do, but I have promised Mr. Crowther and Emily that you will do it, and so you must. Sir A's solicitor is Mr. Windle, Jr., at Windle, Windle, and Findlay, in the City. Enclosed you will find a letter of introduction from Crowther for you.

It is a blessing, I must say, that you may serve Emily in this way, for there is very little likelihood that she will misconstrue it as love.

Yours ever, Clara

Chapter 15

IT WAS NOT to be supposed that Geoffrey should be much pleased with his sister after having read this letter, and his first impulse was to write instantly to her, as Clara had guessed, to chide her for treating Mrs. Crowther's trust so lightly. But a period of reflection recalled to his mind that Clara, much like Emily, had more substance to her than met the eye, and very likely would be made to feel as she ought through her proposed project.

Clara was also very correct in assuming his willingness to accede to Crowther's request, for he would do anything to ensure Emily's safety. He paced the room for a half hour, ranting to himself on the injustice of fate in awarding such a prize as Emily to a man who only valued her material worth and scrupled not to tell her so. Emily had insisted that she was not afraid of him, but even if he did not physically harm her, his words were violent enough, and Geoffrey was sickened by the pain and indignity to which she had been exposed by her desperate marriage.

Thus, the matter of Sir Anthony's property had not insignificantly piqued his interest. That Sir Anthony was capable of such a trick as this did not astonish him in the least—tales of his exploits had run rampant during his lifetime, and probably still did. But the mode of his revenge was exceedingly unique, and Geoffrey, now without a doubt as to Crowther's motive for marrying Emily, owned to a curiosity to see whether it could answer after all.

After having dispatched his now cold breakfast, therefore, he set off from Chesterfield House, hailing a hackney and giving the driver an address in the City. This was the office of his own family's solicitor, whose information enabled him to locate the firm of Windle, Windle, and Findlay, and gain an audience with Mr. Windle, Jr., in his small office at the back of the house. Their interview was short and to the point. Mr. Windle was not shocked to discover that his client may have invested monies without his knowledge—it had happened before, and was not difficult to do, nor was it illegal.

"Sir Anthony was a businessman, and did not feel it expedient to include me in every transaction," he explained primly.

"However, his daughter and her husband—his heirs—have the right to know the full extent of her father's property. I feel certain you will be able to put me on the track of someone who might be helpful in uncovering these private transactions," replied Geoffrey.

Mr. Windle seemed reticent to admit any knowledge of such information until the captain mentioned that he meant to retain the services of an investigator from Bow Street, at which point the solicitor, with a very sour look, said that he did happen to recall the names of some of Sir Anthony's former business associates, which he would be happy to divulge, provided no Runners invaded the firm. Drawing out a sheet of paper, he scribbled two names on it, with their directions, and slid it across the desk toward his guest. Geoffrey thanked him and took his leave, assuring Mr. Windle that he would discourage his Runner from paying any calls to the firm during the course of his investigation.

Another interview, this time at number 4, Bow Street produced the desired result: Mr. Adkins, a small, wiry man with bright eyes, was introduced as a most competent detective, and received from Geoffrey Mr. Windle's list—along with a guinea for his fee—agreeing to report to Chesterfield House with his earliest intelligence. There did not seem to be much more Geoffrey could do on Mrs. Crowther's behalf, though he wandered about Covent Garden for some time racking his brains for any further ideas, so he left the matter in more capable hands and repaired to his club for his dinner.

This little interlude had effectively halted his progress in forgetting Mrs. Crowther, and it was with some anxiety that he recognized he would not be able again for some time to put her from his mind, for he was in the midst of a commission for her husband, and must apprise him of circumstances as they arose. But as Clara had suggested, his honor could not be offended by these dealings, for though he pursued them for Mrs. Crowther's sake, they were at her husband's express request, and no taint of scandal could attach to them. Sir Anthony had made all the scandal, and Geoffrey was merely tasked with discovering the extent of it.

As he had done all he could for the present, however, he threw himself back into his activities in society, renewing his efforts to find some eligible girl with whom he could spend his life, if not fall in love. The Crowthers' investigation added an urgency to this enterprise, for he hoped to at least balance the resultant increase in his thoughts of Emily's welfare with an escalation in pleasant distractions. As his disposition was amiable and he enjoyed society in general, he found it only mildly difficult to succeed.

After several days, these efforts in society had begun to cast a haze over his thoughts of Emily at last, and though he was made to own his notions were still fairly nice regarding females to whom he was attracted—he preferred pale features to dark, gentle voices to bright, etc.—it was his hope that soon he would find one lady who excited his interest for longer than a day or two.

His attention was diverted from this purpose one day when Mr. Adkins' card was brought to him in the library at Chesterfield House. The Runner was shown in, and was brief and to the point. He reported that he had discovered the existence of a handful of investments, including three properties, all of them very large, but that at least one of them had since been sold off.

"I may, if your honor wishes, look into the disposition of the other investments," said Mr. Adkins. "But it'd take a bit of time, as they're spread over three counties, and the records ain't kept in London."

"I'd be most obliged if you did, Adkins," said Captain Mantell, handing over a few guineas to pay the Runner's expenses. "If you'll just keep me apprised of your progress."

"Certainly, sir," said the Runner, touching his hat and bowing himself out of the room.

In mid-March Geoffrey attended a soiree at the home of Lady Gidgeborough, an insufferably proud woman who was on intimate terms with Mrs. Mantell, and who had taken up her friend's cause in getting her second son suitably married. She had promised no fewer than three heiresses in attendance tonight, but as Geoffrey fancied he was acquainted with two of them, he cherished few expectations. He nevertheless dressed with his usual care, and after promising young George a ride in Hyde Park in the morning, set off to Gidge-borough House.

Arriving with military punctuality, Geoffrey found himself to be one of the earliest guests, a circumstance which recommended him to the Countess. She found him a delightful companion in Miss Marshall, a lively damsel of about one and twenty with whom Geoffrey was, in fact, previously acquainted. This put him more at ease and, perceiving that her eyes were often turned toward the door, Geoffrey conjectured that she awaited a gentleman, and teased her to divulge his name.

"It is nothing of the sort, Captain," protested Miss Marshall. "I look for one of my dear friends, whom I have not seen since Christmas. I am a trifle anxious for her, this being her first Season, for though she is of an age with myself, she has the strongest aversion to society, and had positively to be constrained to come to Town this year."

"Poor girl," said the captain, envisioning a girl much like Emily. "Is she so very shy?"

Miss Marshall giggled. "Not precisely, sir. When in company with friends, she can be the most diverting creature—one never knows what she will say! But it can be quite shocking, too, if one does not know her well."

"I see," he said, the picture of Emily wavering. "I am well warned."

"Oh dear! Now I have given you a wrong notion," cried Miss Marshall with laughing chagrin. "I beg you, sir, do not believe Iris—Miss Slougham, that is—is in any way improper, or indelicate. She simply cannot help it—she says whatever she thinks, and as she does not think as most people are wont, this is often very odd. It is the greatest affliction to her, I assure you."

Geoffrey chuckled. "I fancy I understand you. She sounds a most refreshing young lady, and I am impatient to meet her."

"Oh, but she does not speak so to men," said Miss Marshall. "Indeed, Miss Slougham cannot converse with men at all. It is quite impossible for her to do. You may stare, but it is true. That is the greatest cause for her putting off her Season, you see. She feels it a great waste of effort and expense to put her on the town, only for her to stand in rigid silence whenever in company of eligible young men." She shook her head. "But I am persuaded there must be a cure for her, and I mean to exert all my energies to see if it can be found."

Geoffrey, who had been quite amazed at this disclosure, blinked at her and expressed his hope that she would be successful in her venture. They were joined then by the daughter of their hostess, the handsome and distant Lady Athena—with whom Geoffrey was also acquainted, and to whose lofty elegance he knew very few could aspire, least of all he. She brought with her the dark-whiskered Major Lord Prewhurst, whom Captain Mantell had known on the Peninsula. The two military men briefly caught each other up on their movements since Spain, but the captain was quick to comprehend that the major's attention was chiefly at Lady Athena's disposal, and soon found his to be unnecessary to either.

Amused that a mere baron imagined himself in any way equal to the untouchable Lady Athena, Geoffrey turned to exchange a knowing look with Miss Marshall, but found she had left his side. Looking about, he saw that she had gone hastily to greet a thin, pretty girl with red-blonde hair and a vague air who had just been towed into the room by an equally vague-looking man and a harassed-looking woman—presumably her parents.

Intensely curious to see if Miss Marshall had exaggerated the case, Geoffrey watched Miss Slougham keenly. She did not appear, from a distance, to be so very different from Emily after all—less gentle and anxious, and more flighty perhaps. When Miss Marshall moved to guide her toward the group, she blanched and demurred, looking as though she sought for any excuse rather than to confront himself and Major Prewhurst face to face—a reaction, he thought, much in keeping with Emily's inclination. Miss Marshall was successful at last in bringing Miss Slougham within speaking distance of the group, but her silence was indeed rigid, and her eyes never raised from a rather intense contemplation of the captain's knees. Geoffrey's ready compassion was stirred, and he did his utmost to put her at ease, wondering if this was the way to heal his heart—to find a lady in similar circumstances to Emily, whom he could help to overcome her fears and find shelter in his protection.

But his sentiments found little favor with this notion, for the more he attempted to draw Miss Slougham out, the less did he feel attracted to her. He was easily able to comprehend the cause: he had not fallen in love with Emily out of pity. He had loved her fanciful imagination from the beginning, he believed, and then had grown to value the strength and beauty of her character as it had been slowly revealed to him. She was a woman in a thousand, and every other young lady would find it difficult not to be eclipsed by her.

This intense comparison with Emily had pierced the haze with which he had succeeded during the last weeks in surrounding her, and Geoffrey became lost in his thoughts. He was soon in danger of entirely nullifying the work of a fortnight, but was abruptly snatched from this eventuality by a request from Major Prewhurst that he corroborate something. He had not heard what had been said, and begged pardon, asking the major to repeat himself.

"Lady Athena believes all billeting arrangements to be horrid on campaigns, and will not believe that a lady could be comfortable following the drum—you must back me up, Captain, or all military men will evermore be thought savages, and then what is to become of us?"

"He can say nothing that will change my mind, Major," said Lady Athena, with an arch of her elegant black brows. "I have heard enough from my cousin about the dismal conditions prevailing during the War, and stand by my assertion that any woman of even mild sensibility should be shocked and horrified to even consider such accommodation."

Prodded by the major, Geoffrey said, "You are right in thinking, Lady Athena, that the conditions during a campaign are more harsh and uncertain than those during the peace, and I'd far liefer offer a lady accommodation on board a frigate at any time, for they are always very comfortable."

Major Prewhurst abused him for a fribble and a dandy, and Geoffrey explained, "The distinction must be made between a single officer's accommodation and that of a married officer, for the best places are always reserved for the wives and families who accompany their husbands and fathers. Very often accommodation can be found in a city or a town that is quite as clean and comfortable as any house in England, providing one does not expect much finery or elegance."

Lady Athena deigned to accept this possibility, and the major, believing he had won the point, waxed on in masterly style over the benefits of marriage to a military man, and Geoffrey, withdrawing once more from the conversation, was moved to feel gratitude to the major for having saved him from a most perilous foray into his memories. Further consideration of the matter was suspended, however, when Miss Marshall, who had gone to greet another friend, rejoined the group to introduce this young lady to their midst.

Geoffrey recognized her with a start. It was the young lady from the window and the theater, and she must instantly have recognized him as well, for the color rushed into her cheeks. Then she paled alarmingly, as if she were on the brink of a swoon, and he was glad that Miss Marshall's introduction was brief—"Miss Lenora Breckinridge, may I introduce Captain Mantell, who is at present residing with Lord Chesterfield?"—for he was able to take her hand in a firm clasp and prevent her sinking onto the floor.

"I believe we are neighbors," he said, as if nothing were amiss, and she acknowledged him gratefully, though by her looks she was deeply mortified. He felt responsible, more than ever, for her discomfort—for it was he who had behaved so ungentlemanly in their two previous encounters and brought such embarrassment upon her now—and he sought in his mind for the means to put her at ease.

By the time the others had lost interest in the mini-drama and engaged in a discussion of the merits of Kean over Kemble in their respective play houses, Miss Breckinridge had sufficiently composed herself, and he bent his head toward her to remark in a quietly conversational tone, "I fear you have been laboring under a misapprehension, and if I am right, I must admit it to have been a very understandable one, for who expects an earl to be twelve years old?"

This produced the desired effect, for she laughed and said, "You are too kind, sir, though I had not determined upon you being Lord Chesterfield, precisely."

He was curious as to what, then, had caused her so much mortification, and when her answer confirmed his conjectures on the matter to be true, he lost no time in exonerating her and taking all blame to himself. She responded just as he had hoped, allowing him to explain—with plenty of self-deprecating humor—the ins and outs of his relationship with Lord Chesterfield, until she had recovered herself enough to be led back into the general conversation of the group.

Miss Breckinridge was a pretty, well-behaved young lady, with dark hair and eyes, so it was without concern for his heart that Geoffrey acknowledged his interest in her and a wish to become better acquainted. As she spoke of her hopes for the season, he thought that he had been right in fancying that she had a secret—perhaps not a disappointment as he had first conjectured, but a hope that may be as distant as his could be.

By the end of the evening, he was certain that this was so, for while Miss Breckinridge did not say as much, she was possessed of a sort of anxious energy that was all pointed at something—or someone—that may or may not return her interest. He considered that she seemed to be at the precise point he had been three years ago—in Belgium, when he had determined to declare himself to Emily—and he wished for her sake that she would not meet with his fate. As he bid her farewell at the close of the party, he resolved that no one of his acquaintance should do so, if he could prevent it.

Chapter 16

THE FOLLOWING MORNING, Geoffrey received a letter from Mr. Adkins, informing him of his movements.

Dear Sir,

It seems that Sir Anthony Chandry was very busy latterly, for the first two of the properties it pleased you that I should investigate seem to have changed hands within the last two years. I have enclosed a listing. From anything I can discover, there was little profit to the business, so he must've been under the hatches, to go to all the trouble of selling them within so short a period of buying them. I'll go on to look at the other investments, though I've a notion it'll be the same as with these, but I'd liefer do the job proper and leave nothing to guess.

J. Adkins

Digesting this missive, Geoffrey was inclined to agree with the

Runner's estimation of the business, for Chandry Manor had been mortgaged, a usual step taken when one was in financial straits. Crowther, however, held Sir Anthony to have been a shrewd businessman, and was convinced that, contrary to the looks of things, he had secreted his money away from his son-in-law for revenge. His outburst on the uselessness of his marriage showed all too clearly his priorities, and Geoffrey feared what he would do should his expectations be vain. He considered the prudence of writing to Mrs. Crowther to warn her of what lay on the horizon, for though she had insisted that her husband never had laid a finger on her, he would rather she be prepared for the worst. But he quickly determined this would be foolish, for Mr. Crowther would no doubt discover the letter and take exception to Geoffrey's corresponding with his wife; therefore, he wrote to Mr. Crowther merely to inform him that the investigation was ongoing, and to ensure his further intelligence as it was received.

Cursing his helplessness to truly ameliorate Emily's circumstances, he changed his dress and walked out to call upon Miss Breckinridge. She, he was certain, stood in need of assistance, and if he could not lend his aid to the one he loved, then he would do what he could for those within his reach. She was at home, and Geoffrey found her every bit as conversable as the day before, and even more lively. Without the onerous presence of Lady Athena and Major Prewhurst to stare down their noses at her, it seemed she was free of consternation, and he began to trust that she would, in time, take him completely into her confidence.

Accordingly, Geoffrey's acquaintance with Miss Breckinridge prospered in a way that might have surprised some, had they not been aware of the rumor that the young lady had thirty thousand pounds, and were convinced that the captain must have had the earliest intelligence of it, so quickly had he made himself her friend. His chances with the heiress were sometimes spoken of favorably, and sometimes reduced to evens in the clubs, for she had at least two other persistent suitors who were neither of them second sons, and both had the added advantage of a title.

That these persons were fair and far off Geoffrey himself could have assured them, for though Lady Gidgeborough had given him a hint of Miss Breckinridge's expectations, he was no nearer after two weeks of their acquaintance to a proposal of matrimony than he had been at the outset. He enjoyed Miss Breckinridge's company more than that of any of the girls newly out on the town, and even more than those seasoned young ladies closer to his age, but very few would ever believe that his chief motive in singling her out was to discover what romantic hope she cherished in her maidenly bosom and how, unlike himself, he might ensure her achievement of it.

Geoffrey had the free but grudging use of Lord Chesterfield's phaeton, for George could not find it in himself to forgive his military friend for being strong enough to hold the two spirited chestnuts used to pull it.

"If you were a better whip, I could stomach it, but really, how's a man to abide such a cow-handed driver as you taking out such fine cattle?" cried his lordship, when apprised of the captain's plans to drive out with Miss Breckinridge.

"Well, George," said the captain, in full sympathy with his lordship, "only a gentleman could abide such a thing, as a favor to a friend. And perhaps you shall have the satisfaction of seeing my skill improve by your generosity."

Dubiously agreeing to this, George had allowed the loan—which he had never intended to deny—and Geoffrey soon found himself driving through Hyde Park, not quite at the fashionable hour, with Miss Breckinridge at his side.

"I prefer this hour to that of the promenade, Captain," she remarked. "To be forever in the public eye is quite exhausting, do not you think?"

"Undoubtedly, ma'am. In my experience, the scrutiny of the *ton* is quite as distressing as that of the defeated Enemy."

"Such a comparison is quite apt, though I am persuaded I cannot understand the half of what you mean. You were in the Army of Occupation, were not you?"

He acknowledged this. "It was, for the most part, a good experience, with many grateful feelings on both sides. But once, a farmer attempted to burn us alive in his barn, where we were quartered, and at another time, a lady endeavored to have myself and a fellow soldier executed for licentious behavior in which neither of us had participated. But we were exonerated in the end, and could not blame her for defending, though misguidedly, what she believed to be her country's rights."

This gave Miss Breckinridge to reflect upon the strange ways in which a person could feel justified in doing wrong, which Geoffrey felt to enlarge upon so ridiculously that the mood was considerably lightened.

A pause brought Miss Breckinridge to comment, "So you are relatively new to London, then, sir? I believe you were in the Peninsula before you were in France."

"Yes, I fought three years in Spain and Portugal before Bonaparte abdicated and was exiled to Elba. But it has been my custom to take London in my way home on leave, though I generally do not stay long."

"But now you have leisure to stay?"

He smiled ruefully, saying, "Yes, and must look about me for a wife."

"And it is a very good thing to do, sir, at your age. You must be five and twenty at least! If you do not take care, you will become a rake and a profligate, for that is what I have been taught is the fate of every man who eschews the married state in favor of his own freedom."

He agreed laughingly, observing to himself that she had taken no hint in his comment. Though he readily deprecated his being a second son and a mere captain, he nevertheless knew his charm to be not ineffectual among the ladies; thus he believed more than ever that she had another gentleman in her eye, and was intent upon discovering who he may be—for if her hopes were likely to be dashed, he wished to do all in his power to prevent it.

In an attempt to introduce the point with her, he continued, "If I am not mistaken, marriage is deemed most appropriate for young ladies as well, Miss Breckinridge."

"Certainly, Captain," she said, apparently unconcerned. "It is the aim of almost every young lady who comes to London."

"But not for you?"

She looked quickly at him. "I will marry, someday, to be sure. One must be patient, however, for only time may reveal the best choice."

He waited for her to elucidate, but she was silent, and he set his team at a brisker pace. "Time can be a friend, indeed, Miss Breckin-ridge; however, allow me to warn you that it may also be a foe. Pray do not trust only to time to show you happiness."

She nodded, seeming thoughtful, and he left it at that, trusting that time would be his friend in this case, and show him as a friend to her in his patience.

As thanks to young Lord Chesterfield for his generosity with his phaeton and pair, Geoffrey took him off to Newmarket, and on his return, he was to discover that time had been his friend. Walking with Miss Breckinridge in the Green Park two days after his return, she suddenly inquired if he had heard of the Englehearts of Helden Hall.

Instantly intrigued, he said that he had heard something of them, and she added, "They have a most thrilling history—full of betrayal and tragedy. I shall tell you the story, for I have no little interest in the Englehearts, and desire your advice."

"Certainly," he returned, gratified. "Anything in my power."

What followed, however, was unlike anything he had prepared for, and he was utterly taken aback. Her story had much the sound of a high romance, and the essence of it was that the Engleheart estate had been laid waste by the previous lord, who had died, and the heir had not as yet shown himself, leaving the estate to languish without his oversight.

"And what I wish to know, sir," she said at last, "is what can be done about it?"

Nonplussed, he walked on for some way, trying to comprehend her. Could it be that all this time he had imagined her to be pining for some beau, she had been pining for a ruined manor? She spoke with such emotion regarding the tragedy of the wasted estate, but with almost a detached curiosity about the man. If he had not a younger sister who had read Mrs. Radcliffe, he would never have believed it to be true, but he had seen firsthand the power of Gothic novels to work upon the minds of young ladies, and Miss Breckinridge seemed to have succumbed to their lure.

But whatever her fascination with this estate, or even if she had designs on the man, it could not warrant her involvement, and he told her so. They debated the point for some time, he becoming all the more confused as to her motives, for she was very spirited on the point of intervention being necessary, even confessing to having put her inquiry to no fewer than two other gentlemen. But he could not tell if it was for the sake of the property, or of honor in general, or of the man.

At last she said, "I cannot but feel compassion for the heir, sir. He may be secretly yearning for someone, anyone, to reach out the hand of friendship, to lend a listening ear, to give wise counsel, and to judge impartially."

Struck by the candor of this remark, he glanced at her askance. Perhaps she was in love with Lord Helden—or at the least, in love with the notion of being Lady Helden—but had lost herself in the notion of altruism. This realization did not injure her in his eyes, for it was one thing to aspire to the hand of a wealthy and settled lord, but another entirely to desire the welfare of a poor one. She was an heiress, he knew—and of no small fortune, if the rumors were true—and he thought it commendable that she wished to use her means to right the wrongs and ameliorate the situation of a man she had never even met.

Satisfied, he drew her hand within his arm and said, "Any man would be lucky to have such a friend as you, Miss Breckinridge."

"Do you think so?" she said hopefully.

"I do. And I think that it would be a shame to leave poor Lord Helden without one."

"Then you will help me?"

He smiled down at her, thinking that Lord Helden, wherever he may be, would be a gudgeon not to respond to such sincerity. "I will try," he said, and engaged to discover whether this Lord Helden had applied for his place in Parliament, that she could know if he meant to undertake his responsibilities, and perhaps get a name to identify him. He left her with a caveat that he could make no guarantees, as others had already tried and failed, and implored her to await his information.

This he hoped she would do, for though he did not doubt her earnest interest, he did doubt that she had considered the matter with any rationality. The story of the fortunes of the Englehearts, though romantic, did not bode well for the happiness of any respectable young lady who chose to insert herself into it. After he left her, his conscience strove with him to return to her instantly and withdraw his offer of assistance, for her dream, just as his had proved with Emily, was most probably a forlorn hope.

But as he settled himself in the library at Chesterfield House, a finger or two of brandy enabled him to recall that he had promised only to try to help her, and that he might not succeed. And he reasoned that the possession of such innocuous information as he had offered to procure could not do her much harm. Such musings so soothed his scruples that he set forth inquiries the following day and, having fulfilled his obligation, determined to spread his interest to other young ladies, for his friendship with Miss Breckinridge, though enjoyable, would not bring him closer to his goal of finding a wife.

Thus, he conscientiously participated in a flurry of outings to the maze at Richmond, Sadler's Wells theater, and Windsor Castle, and promised himself to attend a string of balls, routs, and even a masquerade put on by a dashing but respectable matron. These afforded him much pleasure, and many interesting exchanges with any number of eligible maidens, but in the midst of his consideration of which of these he should most like to pursue, he was obliged to turn his attention back to his lordship, who one day informed him roundly that he did not much like being neglected for petticoats.

After pronouncing his language uncouth, Geoffrey said, "However, you are right, George, and I shall make it up to you. Why do not we go for a ride in the park?"

"I'm tired of riding in Hyde Park!" cried George. "Such tame doings, and always the same people coming to smile and fawn over me, and the dowagers pinch one's cheek so! Ugh! I had rather do my lessons than abide such treatment!"

"Well then, my lord, what do you propose? How may I redeem myself?"

The earl bounced in his chair. "Take me to the races at Galleywood Common! It is not as if it were Newmarket, and a den of iniquity, like Mrs. Smith says. There's a fair, so lots of children are there, and it's thoroughly respectable! And the races go for only three days, you know, so it may be done in less than a week!"

Impressed at the thought his lordship had put into the scheme, Geoffrey agreed, saying, "But you must take care not to hobnob with the jockeys, George, for you know why Mrs. Smith thinks the way she does, after what trouble you got into at Newmarket."

"That was a hum, Captain!" insisted his lordship disdainfully. "I never hobnobbed, whatever that old cat Mrs. Skillins says, just asked a question or two. And if it makes you more easy, I'll engage never to leave your side during the whole of the races."

Captain Mantell owned that it did make him more easy, and they planned the remainder of the trip with the eagerness of sportsmen, the captain trusting that his friends would not fail to deliver the information he had sought on Miss Breckinridge's behalf before he and the earl set out.

As he awaited a reply from his informants, other information came in his way in the form of a note from Mr. Adkins, the Runner.

Dear Sir,

I write to confirm that the last property under investigation has indeed been resold, and is in the hands of new owners. Two of the investments Sir Anthony made are worthless, one a trade ship that disappeared and the other a factory that apparently failed, though I was unable to visit the actual site. A detailed list is enclosed. I can discover no evidence of the outcome of the remaining investments. However, I have been put in the way of information which leads me to suspect that Sir Anthony made further investments with the proceeds of the property sales.

I hope I am not impertinent, but believing you an honorable man, sir, I feel to inform you that everywhere I speak the name Crowther, I am met with annoyance and suspicion. It seems that your client was involved in all sorts of dubious doings, and if the several reports I have received are to be believed, ought not to be trusted. The name Snipson is also held in aversion wherever I have inquired. I cannot find out that he has done anything against the law, but he is known to be a slippery fellow, and his fingers seem to be in all Crowther's pies. If this is no surprise to your honor, then I am glad, for then you would not have been previously imposed upon.

I will write more when there is something regarding the investments to report.

Respectfully,

J. Adkins

This news did surprise him somewhat, for though Crowther had shown himself capable of double-dealing with Sir Anthony, Geoffrey had not considered that this could be his normal habit. Clara's representations of Crowther's changeable manner gave truth to the assertion that he was not to be trusted, and Geoffrey himself had never felt the desire to do so. The persons from whom Adkins had got his information may, however, have exaggerated the matter, as people who are unlucky in business often do, and so he chose to defer judgment for a time.

He also elected to postpone relaying the information of the failed investments to Crowther, for he had no wish to precipitate another scene such as Clara had overheard. He thought perhaps to write to Clara, who could then relate the information to Mrs. Crowther so that she could determine in what way to break the news to Crowther. But in the end, he decided that any action could wait until he had returned from Galleywood Common, and he endeavored to put the matter from his mind.

Though the Runner had not given the information for which he had hoped, the captain was not disappointed on Miss Breckinridge's behalf. On the day previous to that appointed for his journey, his lordship's secretary handed him a letter which contained the information that Lord Helden had made his application, and was awaiting only some few pieces of corroborating evidence in his favor. He duly presented this information to Miss Breckinridge, whose fluttered state upon hearing it rather corroborated his suspicions of her having a deeper interest than she claimed, and it was with varied emotions that he took his leave of her.

He was pleased to be of service to her but he continued to fear she courted disappointment. In plighting herself to a man in whom she had not the slightest dependence, she would likely experience the same shocking outcome as Geoffrey had done, and though he had known the woman with whom he had fallen in love, his reliance upon her returning his affections and being available to fulfill them had been his undoing. Miss Breckinridge was a sweet girl, and he did not wish her the unhappiness that had been his upon discovering all his hopes and plans were vain.

Chapter 17

THESE SOMBER MUSINGS accompanied Geoffrey as he walked along Picadilly toward his club, until he was jerked from them by the sight of Mr. Crowther walking through the throng on the flagway. The tenor of his thoughts were such that when Mr. Crowther greeted him with all the obsequious friendliness he had shown in Warwickshire, Geoffrey did not trust himself to do more than extend his hand.

"My dear Mantell!" Crowther cried, shaking his hand vigorously. "Fancy meeting you here, when I am only come to this part of the city for a trifling thing, and should have missed you entirely in another minute."

Geoffrey, commanding himself, agreed that it was extraordinary. "What has brought you back to London, Mr. Crowther? I hope all is well at home."

"Yes, yes! All is well there. I've settled what I can of the estate at last, and Mrs. Crowther and I have come back to Town to see what I can do about that unfortunate mortgage," he said, his eyes roving eagerly over the captain's face. "You've no more news from that Runner of yours?"

Geoffrey corroborated this, thinking quickly that it would be wise to relay the disappointing news through Mrs. Crowther, if she was in Town to bear the consequences.

Mr. Crowther's stare faltered, but he said with unabated cordiality, "A confounded muddle it's been, poorly managed from the outset, but I hope for my poor Emily's sake we shall soon set it to rights."

"I hope Mrs. Crowther bore the journey well," said Geoffrey in a civil tone.

"You're kind to ask. Poor old girl's quite done for, as always, but she wished so much to come. Insisted on closing up the old house and arranging for the removal of our things to the Manor. I tried to dissuade her, for I know how badly travel affects her, but she begged me to believe she would not regard the trouble if only she could come with me." He turned his head, but kept his eyes on Captain Mantell. "Never thought she had much heart for the city before this, but I'm not one to deny my poor Em anything, though she's as bad off as ever she was. I've done what I can for her, even going out of my way to get these special powders for her, that my own good doctor prescribes, just here at the apothecary. But she will be obliged to rest a few days before going about on her own legs."

Geoffrey was instantly alert. "If you have deemed it necessary to consult a physician, sir, I fear it was an ill-judged thing to let her come. But I hope there is no harm done, and that she will be able to perform her duties well enough that her present ill health will be thought worth the trouble."

"As do I, sir, as do I." Crowther licked his lips and smiled in his disconcerting way. "A visit from an old friend such as yourself would do her a world of good, I know. She has few enough friends here in Town—but if you cannot spare the time..."

"Nonsense! I am only too happy to oblige an old friend," Geoffrey replied. Then, conscious that such a visit should inevitably produce a recrudescence of the emotions he had striven these many weeks to suppress, he added, "That is, if you do not feel it an unnecessary risk to her health."

The denial of this was voluble and decided, and though Geoffrey was obliged to postpone the promised visit until after his return from Galleywood Common, Crowther left in excellent spirits.

Not so Geoffrey. Crowther's continued dismissal of Emily's welfare grated upon him, and he wished that he had not arranged just now to go out of town. If she was ill, he could not enjoy himself by any means, and would chafe until he could be assured that she had recovered. In addition, Crowther's excessive friendliness made him concerned lest the man's social aspirations would lead him to encroach on his wife's acquaintance. Geoffrey did not care for his own consequence, but such a mushroom-like habit would alienate those who otherwise might have become Mrs. Crowther's friends, through proper introduction. But Geoffrey would be gone for nearly a sennight, and whatever Crowther sought to do during that time would be past mending by the time of Geoffrey's return.

Thus, Geoffrey made certain of Lord Chesterfield's prognostication, and they were back in London within a week, having lost no more than they had won, and seen a great many fine animals that George was intent upon convincing his trustees should grace his stables. In this cause, Geoffrey was in no mind to interfere, and after depositing his lordship safely at Chesterfield House, he gave the coachman the Crowther's address.

Lost in his thoughts, Geoffrey scarcely noticed where he was until he alighted outside number 64, Jurston Street. The row of houses was a long, flat wall of brick in an indiscriminate shade of brown, intermittently divided by scuffed doors with one wide window beside each, all in need of paint. Another dirty window looked bleakly out from under a low, jutting roof on the first floor of each dwelling. Geoffrey noted the slinking dogs and lounging men and heard the muted cries of children and answering shouts of their mothers, and comprehended perfectly why Crowther would wish to close up this residence. Jurston Street had all the look of a losing battle during the War—as hopeless as it was pointless, yet it must be fought to the end.

Directing the coachman to wait, Geoffrey knocked on number 64, and his consternation was great upon discovering Mrs. Crowther to be not at home. Mr. Crowther was likewise out; however, his inquiries as to Mrs. Crowther's health were answered satisfactorily enough by the slatternly serving girl who answered the door, and he went away with the reassurance that she was much better, for she was even now out on errands about town.

With time on his hands, he desired his lordship's coachman to take him into the City to pay a visit to his bank. The chaise deposited him in Fleet Street, but no sooner had he alighted from the vehicle than he perceived a familiar but most unexpected face amongst the crowd who walked up and down the street. He watched the young man for some minutes, disbelieving his eyes, for the last time he had seen Private James Ingles had been on a battlefield in Belgium, just after Waterloo. The private's dress had then been bloodied and tattered, but even before experiencing the rigors of battle, it had never been of such high quality as now clothed his person, and the air of fashion which clung to him was as foreign to Geoffrey's memory of the private as was his gentlemanly mien.

"Ingles?" he said, when the young man had come up beside him. "James Ingles—is it really you?"

The young gentleman blinked at him, then a grin split his face and he thrust out his hand. "Captain Mantell! How good it is to see you!"

"And you—though you could have knocked me down with a feather! What are you doing here? I thought your regiment was called to Ireland."

"It was," said Ingles, his smile faltering a trifle. "But I was discharged, due to my rank, sir."

Geoffrey nodded, looking down. "Right. There's been a lot of that since the peace began. Suppose it can't be helped." He glanced up again, his eyes taking in the excellent cut of Mr. Ingles's coat. "You seem to have found your way well enough, however."

With a wry smile, Mr. Ingles agreed that it appeared so, and suggested they take themselves somewhere less public to renew their acquaintance. Geoffrey instantly agreed and, descending into the rabbit warren that was the Cheshire Cheese tavern, the two men found a corner table and ordered mutton pies and porter. They were made to wait some time for their dinners, owing to the popularity of the house—and their not being well-known to the host—but passed the time exchanging reminiscences of the Peninsular War and Waterloo.

"You may have been discharged, James, but that doesn't explain how you got manners!" said Geoffrey, continuing to be amazed at his friend's transformation from rough soldier to fine gentleman. "Come, open the budget! Who've you bumped off to get that fine suit of clothes? Did you steal his breeding as well?"

Mr. Ingles laughed. "You're not far from the truth, Captain. However, he died without help from me and there was not much breeding there to be desired, for it was only my disreputable grand-father, so there's no harm done."

"James! Don't tell me your grandfather was a highwayman, and these clothes were his spoils!"

"No! Oh, no. Though he may as well have been! He left me a worthless estate and a title, but neglected to leave anything else, except a bag of gold he had hid from my father, God rest him. It was that purchased these clothes, but if I do not soon find some luck, this may be all I end up with."

Geoffrey, who had been caught at "estate and title," was aghast. "Never tell me you're a lord? But how—wait a moment, I recall your cousin Woodley mentioning you had a noble grandfather, but the chances of your inheriting were almost nil. He said you ought never even to think of it, if I recall correctly. But it did fall to you! If that don't beat the Dutch!"

"Indeed, I was as astonished as yourself, Captain, for though I knew my father was a gentleman, he told me nothing of his family, and when he died, I thought I was left alone in the world. But for my father's cousin, that is, who got me my place in the regiment."

"Lieutenant Woodley was a good man," said the captain. "His death was a great loss." They were both silent in remembrance of the fallen lieutenant, then Geoffrey inquired, "If your father was a gentleman, why did you act as a common soldier?"

Mr. Ingles sighed and recruited himself at his pint. "With no home, no prospects, and no relations, it seemed foolish to cling to my education, but now..."

The captain nodded, clapping his friend on the shoulder. "What are you lord of, then? Ought I to exchange my preference from Lord Chesterfield to you?"

"Heavens, no! You'd be in a hobble then," cried Mr. Ingles. "I'm merely lord of Helden Hall, a wasted estate in the middle of Gloucestershire, and as Lord Helden am a penniless cipher among nobility."

Geoffrey nearly dropped his mug, favoring his friend with an incredulous stare. "You are not serious! You are Lord Helden?"

At his friend's positive insistence, the captain demanded to be told the entire tale of Mr. Ingles' antecedents, at the end of which he took a great gulp of his porter, which seemed to work a charm on him. A smile overspread his features.

"Well, bless my soul and call me betwattled. Now, if you will satisfy me on two points, I shall know how to act. Do you wish to redeem your estate?"

Mr. Ingles's brows drew downward in puzzlement. "Of course I do, but—"

"Excellent!" cried the captain, not allowing him to finish. "And did you get a wife along with all that finery?"

"No." Mr. Ingles looked warily at him. "I did not."

Geoffrey clapped his hands exultantly. "Never did I dream of such felicity! Do you know, James, I have a notion I am about to make not one, but two friends exceedingly happy?"

Mr. Ingles blinked at him. "I don't follow you, Captain."

"Little do you know, my lord, that your reputation proceeds you!" said Geoffrey, bending toward his friend with a conspiratorial look. "Your history is so interesting that a certain young lady has been wild to meet you, but did not know how."

"Truly?"

"Yes," said the captain, barely containing his glee. "And I am the lucky man whom she has tasked with finding you." He sat back in his chair, pulling at his porter with immense satisfaction. "A job well done, I should say."

"But who is this young lady, Captain? Or am I never to know?"

"Oh, you shall know, for I doubt anyone could stop her from finding you, even if I refused to introduce you—which I will not! How could I refuse such a thing when I know it will bring you both satisfaction? For I tell you, James, she is a fine creature, and well worth knowing, though she does show a disagreeable tendency toward being busy, at least in your case."

Mr. Ingles slapped his hand on the table top in agitation. "Her name, Captain! What is her name?"

"Miss Lenora Breckinridge, my friend," said Geoffrey, laughing. "Though it will do you little good only to know that."

Mr. Ingles stared intently at him but did not speak, settling slowly back into his chair and refreshing himself at his pint. His gaze became abstracted, and a very silly smile transformed his face.

"James! Don't go off into raptures just yet," recommended the captain. "Your trust is moving, but really, you ought to meet the girl before you begin to fantasize over your future together."

Mr. Ingles' gaze flicked to his friend's face. "Oh, I have met Miss Breckinridge, Captain. But it was before I had made up my mind to pursue the title. She believes me merely to be the caretaker of Helden Hall."

"You dog!" cried Geoffrey, drawing several interested eyes their way. Commanding his exuberance, he hunched over the table and pressed his friend to divulge all.

"When I got word that I was Lord Helden," said Mr. Ingles, "I had been working at the docks for over two years, and had descended into the most pathetic self-pity imaginable, and even though the solicitor informed me of the exact state of my inheritance, I felt that anything was better than where I was then situated. I went to live on the estate—and I tell you, Captain, it is an utter ruin—and try though I might to be hopeful, my already battered spirits were easily depressed. I had no money but what I could earn selling game from the estate, and as time wore on, I wondered if I could ever make anything of my inheritance. My reception in the village, too, was unamiable. The people mistrusted me, though they took me for one of their class, and I did not have the courage to reveal that I was their lord, for they should have disdained me all the more." He looked up at his friend. "I was not a man to be respected at that time, to be sure. But Miss Breckinridge was kind to me. She gave me hope, and would not leave me alone until I saw potential in the Hall, and in my inheritance. It is to her I owe my present state, though she never had an idea of it."

Geoffrey grinned. "This is quite a romance! Who could have guessed that I should be privileged to play a part?"

"Will you help me, Captain?" asked Mr. Ingles urgently. "I want nothing more than to meet Miss Breckinridge as Lord Helden, and yet I am terrified that she will spurn me. I allowed her to believe I was nothing more than a caretaker, and even if she forgives me for that, I have nothing yet to legitimize me in the eyes of the world."

"A title can go a long way in Society, James," said Geoffrey, but added, "You've truly nothing else?"

Mr. Ingles drank the last of his porter. "My father had some property in India, but I've not had the means to discover what has become of it. When I found the gold left by my grandfather, I sent to India to inquire, but it may be months before I receive a reply."

"I am persuaded Miss Breckinridge is not the sort of girl to require a fortune, James," said Geoffrey ruminatively. "She appeared entirely taken by the thought of Lord Helden."

"Perhaps, but she may have quite a different idea of Lord Helden than what I am."

Geoffrey gazed at his friend, who sat tracing the knots on the table top. "I cannot see what she will find wanting in you, James. I hardly recognized you as Private Ingles just now, and if you had fallen as low as you claim when Miss Breckinridge knew you, then I'll wager she'll not recognize you when you meet. You may test her feelings without revealing yourself as Mr. Ingles, and have nothing to lose."

Mr. Ingles looked up. "There may be something in that."

The hope in his eyes set Geoffrey's brain to thinking. "You already have the look of a lord, but we must give you more of an air. Do you ride as well as you did in the army? Lord Chesterfield has more cattle than he can care for, and it falls to my lot to exercise them all. It is more than I engage for, I assure you! It would be a great favor to his lordship if you would take one or another of his animals out every day or two."

"It would be my honor," said Mr. Ingles.

"And you must be seen at all the *ton* parties. There is one tonight—Lady Wishforth's ball. I had not thought to attend, for I'll own I'm fagged to death by the journey from Galleywood Common, but I believe I shall make an appearance—albeit a late one—and you must be my guest."

Mr. Ingles smiled. "You are as good as a *djinn*, Captain. You have granted me two wishes already."

"Then your third wish is about to be fulfilled," said Geoffrey, arching an eyebrow. "I do believe Miss Breckinridge will be at the ball, and I will seek an introduction for you."

Chapter 18

GEOFFREY'S OFFER WAS met with some reticence, for James Ingles, Lord Helden, would not be so sanguine as to his reception at Miss Breckinridge's hands. However, with some little persuasion on his friend's side, his lordship was brought to recognize the benefits of taking the plunge, now or never, and agreed to meet the captain at Wishforth House at midnight.

Both gentlemen were punctual to their agreement, and Geoffrey hastened up the steps, hardly waiting for the footman to take his hat and cane before taking the stairs up to the first floor two at a time. No hostess awaited them, the hour being late enough that she had abandoned her post, and he motioned forward Lord Helden, who adjusted his cravat nervously as his eyes searched the small groups clustered about the landing for any sign of Miss Breckinridge.

His lordship had just suggested to Geoffrey that perhaps theirs was an ill-judged errand after all when Lady Wishforth came forward from the milling ballroom at the back of the house to demand pleasantly of Geoffrey why she had been relegated to his latest priority that evening.

"I had quite given you up, Captain," she said, tapping him playfully on the wrist with her fan, "and had begun to believe that you had been kept away by that dear Lord Chesterfield. How is young George, by the by?"

Bowing with his best grace, Geoffrey said, "His lordship does very well, Lady Wishforth, and would beg to be remembered to you, if he were not exhausted by his adventures at Galleywood Common and already fast asleep in his bed."

"Galleywood Common! Well, I declare his lordship has been to many a horrider place. You take very good care of him, Captain, and I believe I speak for his dear departed parents when I say that you shall be well remembered for your kindness to a poor orphaned boy."

Smiling with appropriate humility at this encomium, Geoffrey pulled Lord Helden forward to make the introduction, which was very graciously received by her ladyship. She looked him up and down with intense interest before linking her arm through his and towing him resistless into the ballroom. Here, she brought him to the notice of some few of her acquaintance, who with friendly curiosity surrounded him and rendered a withdrawal from his purpose impossible.

Geoffrey, perceiving his friend's courage returning at his kind reception, left him to his new acquaintance and looked about the crowded room for Miss Breckinridge. He glimpsed her across the room and made his way to her, preparing in his mind the speech that would inform her of the delight in store, for he anticipated her raptures at finding her way clear to finally meet and speak with the heir to her beloved Helden Hall.

Miss Breckinridge greeted him brightly, turning pointedly away from her former partner, who hung about her like an eager puppy, and Geoffrey smugly suspected that his would be a welcome distraction. The rumors of her fortune had become rampant, and Miss Breckinridge had been obliged to put up with the attentions of several gentlemen who, only a month ago, would not have looked twice at her, and he could tell it had become very wearing. It was well that she already knew the master of Helden Hall may be suffering under financial hardship, even preparing herself to offer her fortune for the redemption of his estate, so Geoffrey need not allay her fears on that head; he was confident that James Ingles was no fortune hunter.

Taking her hand and answering her inquiries as to his trip to Galleywood Common, he said, "I should not have come here at all, but that I have met someone—that is, I have information that I know will interest you excessively, and I could not wait."

Her response was entirely unexpected; instead of breathless curiosity, he was met with a dilating stare, and she blanched so dreadfully that he feared she may be unwell. Leading her quickly to a chair, he took up her fan, plying it vigorously until she began to recover some of her color, but her aspect was still one of shock, and he wondered if he had misjudged his errand. If she suspected what he had to say, her response hinted either at a total change of heart toward Lord Helden, or a sudden comprehension of the enormity of her hopes, and he greatly wished the latter to be true, rather than the former, for James Ingles's sake, if not her own.

Within a very few minutes, she claimed that she was much better, and had merely been overcome by the heat, and looked so very much improved that he began to feel confidence that his second conjecture was correct.

"Pray, Captain," she said when still he hesitated, "what could be so pressing that you would go to the trouble of putting on ball dress and coming to find me?"

He smiled, returning her fan. "It may be a trifle, but I do believe it is better that you hear it now from me, rather than in the gossip columns tomorrow."

She swayed a little, her fixed smile wavering, and he hurried on, eager to put her at ease. "I have met Lord Helden. He is here in London, and his Writ has been delivered. He will take his seat in the House of Lords at the end of the month."

He watched her closely, and though her chest rose and fell with rapid breath, her color did not fluctuate and, taking courage, he plunged on, "If it is not too much to ask, he has expressed a desire to meet you."

She blinked rapidly and nodded, murmuring something disjointedly about it being agreeable to her, but he believed this rather abstracted response was merely the result of a heightened state of nerves. He could easily imagine that she was feeling much the same distress that he had done when he had at last presented himself at Chandry Manor to declare himself to Emily. But she had no such barriers to her happiness as he suffered, and grasping at this conviction, he dismissed his fears that he had been precipitate, and had ruined Mr. Ingles' chances with her.

Looking round, he found Lord Helden almost at his shoulder, and the introduction was made. Geoffrey retreated from the couple, watching with breathless interest Lord Helden's gaze fixed on Miss Breckinridge's face, and her confusion as he took her hand and led her into the dance. His compassion for her anxiety was great, but he had reason to hope for a happy issue, once the initial shock and embarrassment were got over.

It seemed his hope was misplaced, however, for soon after one o'clock, Lord Helden sought him out to declare his intention of retiring for the evening, and to thank him for his kind offices with a look so dejected as to raise concerns in the most sanguine breast.

"You are blue-deviled," observed Geoffrey, eying his friend's countenance. "Surely she did not scorn your acquaintance. Or did she recognize you after all?"

"No," said his lordship, glancing back to where Miss Breckinridge stood with her group. "But I do not know if it would have been better if she had. She was offhand to me, almost cold! I had convinced myself that she would be eager to make the acquaintance of Lord Helden, yet I could not get more than a few words together out of her. I must be nothing more to her than a curiosity. I have wasted my time and yours."

On this bitter exclamation, he strode from the ballroom, and Geoffrey, gathering his wits, caught him up on the stairs. A hand on his lordship's arm could not stop him, so the captain descended with him to the ground floor, saying, "Think, man! She has awaited this introduction since she arrived in London. It was too sudden, I am persuaded. She had no proper time to prepare and was flustered and embarrassed. The fault is mine in that, but it is not the end of the world. She merely wants time to command herself and to adjust to your presence."

"Perhaps," was all his lordship would say, as he collected his hat and coat from the footman at the door.

Geoffrey retrieved his own headgear and followed his friend down the steps to the street, doggedly remaining at his side. "You must carry on as we planned. She will come around, you will see. The *djinn* has spoken! You must mingle in Society and be seen everywhere, just as Lord Helden would be."

"Puffing myself off will not earn her regard," said Lord Helden, scornfully.

"That it will not," replied the captain promptly, "so you'd best take care not to puff yourself off."

Lord Helden only glanced sideways at him, but his expression had softened and Geoffrey continued to work at him in this vein until they parted ways.

His efforts were not fruitless. Lord Helden availed himself of the captain's advice, and was to be seen at the fashionable hour in Hyde Park astride one of Lord Chesterfield's high-bred hacks, and met with at many of the *ton* parties. Within a few days, Geoffrey was pleased to perceive Miss Breckinridge's reserve melting away, and determined that his two friends were in a fair way to happiness.

Opening his mail one morning at breakfast, Geoffrey set aside two bills for later and opened a letter from Clara that had been delayed over a week. In it, she helpfully informed him that the Crowthers had gone up to Town, and begged him to write her instantly of any interesting news regarding the investments.

But, Geoff, the oddest thing happened yesterday. We were in Southam, and as I came out of the milliner's shop, I saw that my mother, who had awaited me outside, was standing stock still, as if she were stuffed, and when I inquired whether she were unwell, she shushed me and whispered out the side of her mouth, "He's coming."

I looked round for some disagreeable person, but could see only Mr. Noyce leaning on the butcher's boy and coming up to us. My mother did not alter her astonishing attitude, however, and I could not conceive of what it could mean, so I shielded her from their notice as much as I was able, and bid Mr. Noyce good day in as natural a manner as I could contrive. He tipped his hat most graciously, but is such a gentleman that he would not go on without greeting my mother.

Geoff! I have never seen her so discomfited! She screwed up her mouth and would not speak, and blushed like anything, and hardly had the sense to return his bow. I fancied, then, that perhaps my mother had taken some sudden illness, but thankfully Mr. Noyce mounted his horse and rode away, and after a few moments she had regained her composure.

"Well!" she said, walking the opposite way, "That is over! Would that I could never to meet him again!"

She said this of Mr. Noyce! A man who would not hurt a fly, and who has a civil word for everybody, Geoff! Everybody! And if her disapprobation is for his being a cripple, I cannot see what that has to do with anything! Well, I was stunned enough not to say a word on all the drive home, and know not what to think.

Geoffrey did not know what to think of this strange behavior as well, unless his mother's charity for Mr. Noyce had given her a disgust of him. She had ever been incomprehensible, however, so he put her odd crochets out of his mind.

Lord Chesterfield being in lessons, Geoffrey went out, intending to visit his club when he met suddenly with Mrs. Crowther, coming out of the apothecary's shop on Picadilly. Her face was pale and drawn, and she wore mourning dress under a black pelisse, walking with an air of resignation that instantly awoke his deepest concern. The rush of emotion he experienced upon seeing her discomposed him greatly; she did not perceive him for a few moments more, however, giving him time to pull himself together.

"How do you do, Mrs. Crowther?" he said tolerably evenly. "I heard you were in Town. Are you on an errand? May I escort you?"

She had lost color—no small feat in one so pale—and appeared as though she knew not where to look, but after a moment said quietly, "You are so very kind, but I am only going to Hookham's to return a book."

"Then it will be my pleasure to accompany you, if you will have me," he said, gallantly offering his arm.

Two spots of pink came into her wan cheeks, but she accepted his arm and said, "I own I would be glad of company."

"I see Mr. Crowther does not accompany you," he said, taking the book and a small parcel she had been holding and turning with her to walk toward Old Bond Street.

She shook her head. "He has business of his own. But it does not signify, for I am used to going about London on my own."

He kept his inevitable conclusions to himself, instead asking what it was that she had been reading. She indicated the book he held, saying it was titled Emma, by an anonymous author, and was dedicated to the Prince Regent.

"It sounds intriguing," he said, "and I hope it has given you many hours' enjoyment."

She nodded, "Reading is my only luxury, and I do so love this author's style. It is unutterably comfortable."

He continued talking commonplaces until the library was reached, where she returned the book, turning instantly to go. He inquired if she had not meant to borrow another, and at her admission that she did not wish to put him to any trouble, he insisted that she take what time she wished, for he was at her service.

The two spots of color burned in her cheeks again, but at last he persuaded her, and she took some few minutes to find another book, discovering with the aid of the clerk a new novel by the same author, who was revealed to have died only the previous summer.

"Her name is Jane Austen," she said, glancing over the biographical notice included in the first volume, as he escorted her from the library and out onto the street. "Thank you, Captain. I should not have found this treasure but for your kindness."

"It was my pleasure," he said, gently guiding her through the crowd. She turned once more to smile at him, and with a mighty effort not to lose himself in her luminous eyes, he said briskly, "And now where do we go? Have you more errands, or am I to have the honor of escorting you home?"

She sighed. "I suppose it must be home. I am unequal to much of anything these days, though Mr. Crowther wishes me to close up the house and I have ever so much still to do."

"And you have been unwell, or so Mr. Crowther told me. Did he mention our having met ten days or so ago?"

She told him he had, saying, "I do not do well in fast coaches, and had rather have stayed behind to see to repairs and things at the Manor, but Mr. Crowther could not do without me. In general, I am unwell no more than a day or two, but have not been much better this sennight."

Without another word, Geoffrey stepped off the flagway to summon a hackney coach, giving the address to the driver and adjuring him to take care and drive slowly before joining her within.

"Though it is a lovely day for a walk, I cannot believe it would be as beneficial to your health as a calm drive by way of the Green Park," he said.

"And then we will be obliged to take St. James's Park in the way, as well," she said with a smile. "For the Westminster Bridge cannot be got to any better way."

Wholeheartedly agreeing to this, Geoffrey let down the glass so that she could gaze out on the cool, green precincts of the parks with pleasure.

After a few minutes, she said, "I have been unable to thank you for your kind offices to us regarding the oddities of my father's estate. Your willingness to undertake the investigation is most appreciated."

Geoffrey started a little guiltily. "I am glad you have put me in mind of it, Mrs. Crowther, for I have a confession to make. I withheld some new information on that matter from Mr. Crowther, but with the best of intentions. My sister—you will forgive her, I hope—informed me more particularly of your circumstances, and I wished to find a way of delivering the news without your being in harm's way—for I fear it is not good news."

"Clara is a dear, though I could wish she had not made you uneasy. I am in no danger, sir, of that I may promise you. What is the news, pray?"

He tried to see into her face to determine if she spoke truly, but it was averted, so he told her what Mr. Adkins had found out about the failed investments. She was silent for some time, considering.

"Then there may be still more investments?" she said at last. "How odd of my father. This is all very strange." She paused again, then inquired if he had spoken again to Mr. Adkins.

"No, for I desired to know your mind first. If you wish it, I will engage him to try if he can discover these new investments, and if they are worth anything to you."

She sighed, but said, "If it is not too much trouble, Captain, I do wish it. I wish very much to understand what my father has been about. It is all so unaccountable."

"It is no trouble at all, for I own I am most curious myself. But what will you tell Crowther?"

She thought a moment before saying, "I will tell him all. It will relieve him to know the trail has not gone completely cold. He will believe that my father cannot have hidden his money so completely that it shall not soon be uncovered, and so will have every cause to believe himself richer than he is at present."

"Which must relieve your burdens excessively, I am persuaded," he said dryly. "This is what has brought him to town, if I am not mistaken."

"Yes. He is most anxious for money. He believes he has discovered a way to release certain securities so that he may pay the mortgages."

"And you must close up the house." Geoffrey's jaw tightened for a moment, but he merely glanced at the parcel on the seat beside her. "I hope the parcel from the apothecary may be of use to you."

She looked out the window as they neared the river. "It is stomach powders, and I take them for Mr. Crowther's sake. He swears by those sold only in that shop, for his doctor has told him never to trust any other. I cannot be certain they are any more than a placebo, but he believes them to cure any number of ills. He has urged me to take them for my nervous fits, but I have never done so. My present disorder had convinced me to try; however I have yet to feel a benefit."

"Mr. Crowther must have received no little benefit from them at some time or other to warrant such loyalty," said Geoffrey.

She gave a fleeting smile. "Perhaps. His drinking habits often render him bilious, and he claims the powders are a charm. It has become something of a habit with him to take them, I imagine, and to prescribe them to others. He even went so far as to press them upon my father in the days before his death. He thought they might help his indisposition, but they seemed to be as efficacious for my poor father as they are for me."

Geoffrey considered this as the hackney stopped to pay the toll to cross Westminster Bridge. "Perhaps his new wealth will give him more to do than to be busy about other's health. He at least can make the Manor more comfortable for you. It is your money, after all."

She huffed lightly. "My husband has no such notions, and the law sustains him. As soon as we spoke our vows, I lost all rights of my own. But he has what he wanted, and I have little to complain of. In any event, if I had not married, I do not know that I could have found the means to unravel my father's affairs, and so I would be no better off."

He did not trust himself to speak for a long moment, at last saying somewhat tersely, "Surely Mr. Crowther will use some of his money to furbish up Chandry Manor, where you will enjoy the benefits."

"Yes, but I do not believe I could ever be happy there. We stay only for a short while. Crowther has determined to sell the estate, or to let it. His business requires that he spend too much time in London."

"Then why does not he keep the house in town?"

"He must find a new residence, sir, for a man of his ambition deserves better," she said, with a wry look.

Chapter 19

ON THE FAR side of Westminster Bridge, the verdant greenery of St. George's Fields had been covered over with fine new stone buildings, which lined Westminster Bridge Road to the Obelisk and beyond. The side-streets, however, were filled with cheaper structures thrown up in the frenzy of expansion some fifteen years earlier, and already bore depressing marks of neglect and decay. Jurston Street, which branched off the main road within sight of the unfinished St. George's Circus, was one of the worst of these, its dingy, two-storey row houses sagging as if under the weight of depressed pretensions.

"I'm told this area was not always disreputable," remarked Mrs. Crowther, glancing at a nearby house that had been transformed into a tavern. "Indeed, it was known to be quite lovely when it first was built."

With some effort, Geoffrey could imagine so, but wondered aloud at Mr. Crowther's deigning to live there in its present state.

Mrs. Crowther gave him a wry look. "Recollect that Mr. Crowther and my father were business partners, sir, and very much alike. They neither of them could countenance the waste of good money, unless it was directly for their own gain."

"But now that Crowther expects to be a rich man?"

"He plans to take a house in Mayfair, in order to attract a nobler clientele. He believes the cost will be well worth the recompense."

"At least, then, you will be more comfortable."

She gave a desultory smile and extended her hand, thanking him for his company before turning to go.

He retained her hand in his clasp. "I promised Mr. Crowther that I would visit you and have already tried once in vain. May I not come in now?"

She hesitated, glancing up and down the street. "I should enjoy that, Captain; however it would look very particular, as I am alone," she said, coloring slightly. "Snipson is out with Crowther, and I have given my maid the afternoon off."

He accepted this, for though she was a married woman, she could not entertain a gentleman so utterly alone without occasioning remark. They had already attracted notice as they stood talking in the street, and much as he desired to stay with her, he did not wish to cause her discomfort. He had indulged himself too long in her company as it was.

Stepping back, he bowed over her hand. "Then it is with regret that I leave you, Mrs. Crowther. I hope you will rest while you may, and that you find yourself in better health very soon. If in future you are in need of escort, do not hesitate to inform me. I have had a very pleasant afternoon, and am ever at your service."

She smiled, her gray eyes regretful as she pressed his hand, and he watched her safely into the house before turning to the waiting hackney. His dismay upon leaving her at this forlorn abode was eased only by the knowledge that she would not long stay there. Indeed, he flattered himself that she would never be in so dismal a situation again, for Crowther intended to refurbish Chandry Manor, and when she was obliged to leave there, it would be for a fine home that Crowther could not but make comfortable for her, if he truly wished to move upward in Society.

His thoughts as he rode back to South Audley Street, though tempered by these convictions, were somber, and it was with an effort that he wrenched them away from Emily's disagreeable situation—over which he had no power, he sternly reminded himself—and reflected upon his own. He was no closer to finding a proper wife than he had been upon coming to town. The temptation to blame his continued concern in Emily's affairs for keeping him from forming any real intentions he refused, for though he had spent some time helping her, he had not otherwise been remiss in putting himself about in Society. If he could find another love in London, he thought he would have done so by now; and he was inclined to believe she did not exist, in Town at least.

Geoffrey sent off a note to Mr. Adkins at Bow Street, relaying Mrs. Crowther's request for more information, then, to distract himself from thinking unduly of her, he threw himself into another round of gaiety. The warmer weather prompted many hostesses to ambitious outdoor entertainments, and Geoffrey attended picnics, rides to Wimbledon, and evenings at Vauxhall Gardens. But after a sennight of frenetic activity, he called a halt for a day, seeking out the quiet and sanity of his club, where it was impossible that he be expected to make himself agreeable to the female sex.

After greeting some old friends, he took up a newspaper and went to the reading room, ensconcing himself in one of the comfortable chairs near the window. The articles of news were uninteresting enough, and his mind continually drifted across Westminster Bridge, to a dingy little house in Jurston Street, when a murmur of voices speaking Miss Breckinridge's name caught his attention.

"It's sure, then, that she has thirty thousand pounds?"

"Dead sure, man, as I'm standing here! Got it out of Mintlowe, who knows the chit's father—which is why his son and heir is hot on the girl's heels, or I'm a chub."

Having heard enough, Geoffrey turned over the leaves of the paper, hoping the noise would alert the speakers to his proximity, but they continued on, speaking of whether the odds offered on the matter were fair, or if chance would ruin everything. He turned another leaf with a snap, eying the gentlemen in palpable disdain, but the abrupt cessation of their discussion was prompted only upon the entrance of Miss Breckinridge's brother into the room.

Mr. Thomas Breckinridge favored the two gossips with a curdling stare, and Geoffrey, who had met Tom only briefly after his arrival in town a week previous, could only hope the young man would not lump him into their lot. It seemed not, for after the precipitate retreat of the offenders from the room, Tom turned toward the captain and made for the chair beside him.

"How do, Captain?" he said, pleasantly enough for a man whose temper was seething. "I can see you've been getting an earful. What a pleasant way to while away the afternoon."

The captain chuckled grimly. "I had just determined upon calling one of them out when you walked in and settled the whole business with that stare. You must cultivate it, sir—as effective as a ball to the chest, and far less complicated."

"I've had about enough of these fellows, I'll tell you," said Tom, eying the door out of which the gentlemen had slunk, lest any more of their ilk should appear. "None of their business to be bandying my sister's name about, and making bets on her chances with Lord Who's His Face, and Mr. What's His Name."

"Certainly, sir, but they don't care a button for that. What they do care for is whether or not their last night's gaming debts may be repaired, compliments of the latest *on dit*."

"Yes, well, my sister ain't it, even if she does go parading about town with every gazetted fortune hunter on her arm." Tom leveled a challenging gaze at him.

Captain Mantell cocked an eyebrow. "Surely you do not believe me to be a fortune hunter, Mr. Breckinridge, though your sister does spend an awful lot of time on my arm."

"Yes, and I begin to wonder why, Captain."

The humor in the situation overcame Geoffrey, and he let out a laugh. "If you think that my intentions are dishonorable, you are greatly mistaken, sir! In fact, I facilitated her introduction to the man with whom she will find lasting happiness, or I am much mistaken."

Tom glowered. "Lord Helden."

This unpropitious response sobered Geoffrey. "You have little reason to trust me, sir, but I hope you will consider that I have nothing to gain by your sister's marrying Lord Helden but the satisfaction of seeing two dear friends well settled. Please believe that your inclusion of Lord Helden in the ranks of fortune hunters is ill-judged. I know him from the army, and would vouch for his being an honorable man, and quite in love with Miss Breckinridge."

Tom gazed keenly at him for several moments, during which the captain wondered if his words had been taken amiss, but then Tom dropped his gaze and sighed.

"I'm glad my goose of a sister has had someone to look after her while I've been away. My step-father does his best, but she's so often out of his reach that anything can happen!" He hit a fist on the padded arm of the chair. "That dashed fortune! It's been no end of trouble. I'd give a monkey to know how it leaked out."

"Depend upon it, your sister had nothing to do with it," said Geoffrey. "I only knew of her fortune by the merest chance, and that from a lady scarcely known to your sister."

"It cannot have been told by my mother or step-father," Tom said, chewing his lip, "for they intended that even she should not know of it. Some romantic nonsense about her being unburdened by the knowledge of her wealth as she made her choice of a husband."

Geoffrey shrugged. "It doesn't seem so far-fetched, however, when one considers how much of a burden the rumor of her fortune has turned out to be. She would not have such unsavory fellows to deal with if there had been none of it."

"You're a man of sense, Captain," said Tom, turning speculatively to him. "You are certain you do not mean to develop a tendre for Lenora?"

Geoffrey chuckled. "You cannot conceive of how I wish it were possible. But it is not. I have tried to change my heart, but it is not to be."

Tom opened his eyes at him. "Heart's lost already? I sympathize, sir. Devil of a business."

"Yours, however, is not a hopeless case, I trust," said Geoffrey.

Tom shrugged. "Not yet, but it seems I have stiff competition.

You are acquainted with Miss Marshall? Yes, well, the lady's father is inclined to believe I'm a good for nothing like my late father, though I've worked six years and more to repair my fortune—the fortune my dear father so zealously strove to destroy."

"Fathers are often difficult to please," murmured the captain.

"Yes, and all too often throwing a rub in one's way, for they know one cannot take a miff without jeopardizing one's position," said Tom bitterly.

Geoffrey nodded knowingly. "Her father's refused his consent?"

"Not in so many words, but he's taken his family away to Brighton, supposedly for his health. He's healthy as a horse, until his favorite takes it into his head to remove to Brighton."

"Competition makes the chase all the more fulfilling when it is won."

"I suppose your competition is a mere trifle, Captain," said Tom, eying him with dislike.

Geoffrey blew out a sigh. "Not so, my friend. Unless you call 'til death do they part' a trifle."

Tom's eyes widened, and he whistled. "My condolences, sir. That is a hard thing to bear. I do not think I shall look upon my trial in the same light again."

"Glad to be of service," said the captain wryly. "Truly, though, I wish you well. How long do you suppose until your estate is solvent?"

They talked some time over the ins and outs of redeeming an estate, and the measures which Tom had taken over the years to right his pecuniary difficulties, and Geoffrey felt no compunction in encouraging his new friend to hope.

"If Miss Marshall's heart is even partly yours, with your estate so near to being profitable, I am persuaded you can have very little to fear. Even a doting father cannot hold out against his daughter's wishes forever."

Tom thanked him, but remained skeptical. "This old friend of Miss Marshall's that's come out of the woodwork is a puzzle. She seems to like him prodigiously, but he's nothing but a frippery game-ster. Never could understand the draw of the rascally sort to women."

Geoffrey expressed his own confusion in the matter—thinking of Francis—and reassured him as far as he was able, accepting with real pleasure Tom's invitation to take Branwell Manor in his way at any time he might be passing. He took his leave, and as he received his hat and cane from the footman at the door, he thought how ironic it was that he had been denied domestic felicity and yet found himself in the role of facilitator and confidant to others. It was pitiable, to be sure, but it did, at least, offer him the satisfaction of being useful, and assuaged some part of his grief at not being in their positions.

He met with Miss Breckinridge the following week, having agreed to accompany her to a balloon ascension. Lord Chesterfield had again lent Geoffrey his phaeton, though declining to attend such a "tame affair" himself, and Geoffrey had pulled up in a fine viewing spot. As they awaited the filling of the balloon, Miss Breckinridge spoke of Lord Helden's vacillating fortunes, and Geoffrey was impelled to ask if she still viewed his lordship's situation favorably.

Miss Breckinridge blushed, but only said, "I have always felt a—a connection to Helden Hall that will not be denied."

She went on to describe her hopes for the Hall, and though her words did not precisely relieve his concerns for Lord Helden, he was again struck by the similarity of their situations: they both knew what it was to be tied to something—someone in his case—that would always be a part of them, whether the connection was completed or not. Miss Breckinridge could no more help pursuing a relationship with Lord Helden, for the sake of completing her connection to Helden Hall, than he could help pursuing every avenue that would secure Emily's health and happiness.

"There is much in what you say," he said, when she had finished. "I do not believe in fate, but I have felt a connection like what you describe, and which has persisted through all my attempts to suppress it. I begin to feel that this connection is one I must endure, for I fear it will never be requited."

Here, he was obliged to pause, for he perceived that a distant relation of his mother—a rail-thin old spinster with a sharp eye—had stalked up to them.

"Here you are, Geoffrey! I told your dear mother I'd look in on you, but I vow you are never to be found at Chesterfield House, and I had all but given you up!"

Geoffrey suppressed a sigh and took the lady's proffered hand. "A thousand pardons, Cousin Blanche! I have been fulfilling my mother's dearest wish, and attempting to find me a wife—a task which, as you may imagine, involves much venturing from home."

"You are ever the dutiful son, I am persuaded." Cousin Blanche's gaze flicked to his companion. "This must be she! I may tell your mother that you have done well."

She held out her hand to Miss Breckinridge, who had gone stock still. "I'll not stand on ceremony, Miss Breckinridge, for though we have not met, your circumstances are known to me. As Geoffrey's relation, I presume upon the relationship to claim your acquaintance."

"Cousin Blanche—she is not—you are grossly—" stammered Geoffrey, but to no avail.

His relative plunged on, oblivious to his or Miss Breckinridge's discomposure. "It's a fine family with which you're privileged to ally yourself. The Mantells, though untitled, have an illustrious heritage, and Captain Mantell's fine accomplishments, coupled with your fortune, make a fine contribution to so respected a tradition."

Geoffrey could only stare, white with horror, as Cousin Blanche swept away, and Miss Breckinridge made not a sound. He hardly dared look at her, for though ten minutes ago he had been persuaded her heart was falling for another, his cousin's words filled him with dread that he had greatly misjudged the affair. Had he, in the name of friendship, encouraged Miss Breckinridge to form an attachment to himself? Could her interest, all this time, have rested merely in Helden Hall, and not at all in Lord Helden, because her heart had been reserved for himself?

A wave of despair washed over him at the thought of such terrible mismanagement, and he jerked his head to look at his companion. Her expression, however, relieved him on the instant, for it was every bit as horrified as his own.

"Captain, pray do not think—I have never—there has not been the slightest hope—Oh, dear!" She closed her eyes and took a steadying breath. "I lay no claim to your affections, nor should I ever wish to!"

Heaving a great sigh, Geoffrey said, "Oh, Miss Breckinridge, you relieve my mind excessively! For one terrible moment, I thought that I had given you reason to expect—I should never wish you to believe my intentions to have been—in short, I have never cherished romantic feelings toward you!"

She gave a shaky laugh, and the sudden release of tension was so welcome that he joined her, and soon they were laughing so hard together that they drew some censorious looks. With a concerted effort, they regained command of themselves, and settled once more to watching the preparations for the balloon launch.

"What was the connection you were speaking of, before we were interrupted, Captain? Or shall I not ask you?" she inquired, turning to him. "You need not share if you would rather not. I will not press you, but I own I am curious."

"If I had no wish to share it with you, I should not have mentioned it. That would be badly done, don't you think?" he said lightly, but his levity gave way to somber reflection. It would relieve him to be able to share something of his situation with her, for she stood in the unique position of having something of the same circumstance. He was persuaded that she, of all his acquaintance, could be trusted to sympathize with him.

"Her name is Emily," he said. "We were childhood friends, but were separated when I went to school, and I did not see her again until I returned home from the Peninsula."

She took this just as he had hoped, saying only, "But you thought of her."

"Indeed, I did, every day. But thinking was not enough. She is lost to me, and I do not know that it is not my fault. I never told her of my feelings."

Miss Breckinridge grasped his meaning. "She is married? I am truly sorry. I like to believe that a connection based on love is fastened at both ends. If you cannot forget her, it should follow that she, likewise, cannot forget you."

She paused, and for a brief moment, Geoffrey wished that Emily did pine after him, that he could know she loved him as much as he loved her, to requite some little part of his longing. But he dismissed this idea as quickly as it had come. He could not wish Emily such pain only to soothe his own, and he valiantly hoped—though without much fervor—that she truly was content with only his friendship.

"I suppose that notion would not comfort you," said his companion, her eyes searching his face.

Smiling to reassure her, he said, "Not under normal circumstances, Miss Breckinridge, but at this moment I will take comfort in the kindness of your intent."

Chapter 20

THE FOLLOWING DAY, as Geoffrey was changing his dress after a hard morning ride, Mr. Crowther's card was brought up. Geoffrey subdued a craven instinct to claim he was not at home to visitors, dreading that by inviting Crowther into Lord Chesterfield's house he should encourage the man to believe himself part of his lordship's circle. However, Lord Chesterfield's being so well guarded by his servants greatly diminished the likelihood of Crowther's getting any foothold in the household, and Geoffrey told the butler to show his visitor into the library.

There he met Mr. Crowther, who smelled of spirits and smiled his toothy smile as he rubbed his hands together.

"Captain! What a bang up place this is! Fancy your being invited to stay here whenever you are in Town! What fine luck to know an earl." His eyes roamed the room. "Fine luck indeed. What excellent friends my Em has."

Swallowing his revulsion at this ill-breeding, Geoffrey asked after Mrs. Crowther's health.

"It's kind of you to ask after Emily, for she's in poor shape, so poor she has gone home."

Geoffrey was startled. "If she is in such poor shape, how did you imagine her well enough to make the journey?"

"Oh, it was because of her illness that I sent her home, sir," said Crowther, tutting and shaking his head. "She never seemed to improve, though it had been a fortnight, and knowing that London never agreed with her, I sent her back to Chandry Manor in the hopes that she'd have some comfort there. She's got her maid and Snipson to care for her. They'll soon set her to rights."

"You do not intend to follow her?" inquired the captain, with more force than civility.

"Oh, you think me remiss, but it went against the grain with me to send her, I declare. I've got some loose ends to tie up here before I can go into the country again. That mortgage, you see, is nearly settled. Em told me what your Runner found out—I'm obliged to you, sir, very much obliged. But that's what I've come about. Has that Runner discovered anything more?"

"No, sir. I am sorry to say he has not."

Crowther's smile stiffened, his piggy little eyes going hard. "A pity. But I thank you again. You've been a great help, but needn't trouble yourself more. I'll be taking this matter off your hands, and should like you to inform your Runner of it."

Geoffrey assured him this was wholly agreeable to him, and offered to furnish him with a note of introduction to Mr. Adkins. However, Mr. Crowther declined.

"No, no, I thank you, sir. I have a man of my own I'll employ."

"Very well, sir," said Geoffrey. "Best of luck to you."

Mr. Crowther, after making some few more encroaching references to fine friends, took his leave, and Geoffrey lapsed into a brown study. That Emily had been so ill as to require a removal to the country had shocked him, for she had seemed merely tired during their visit together the previous week. It was possible that Crowther's over-nice solicitude for her had sent her away, but if she was truly ill, Geoffrey wished to know how she went on. After considering for a few moments, he went to the desk by the large front window and wrote a letter to Clara, asking her to resume her visits to Mrs. Crowther as soon as was possible, and to apprise him of her situation. He gave the letter to the footman to post, but still, his thoughts were unsettled.

As he ruminated, he recalled the powders Crowther prescribed for her, and he wondered all at once if they had caused her more harm than good. She had told him she had never taken them before, and perhaps they did not agree with her constitution. If the powders contained ingredients that could be irritating, it could account for her never recovering. Geoffrey further imagined that Crowther, in his zeal, had pressed her to take more than was good for her, for he had every faith that they would cure all ills.

These thoughts resolved him to inquire after the powders, and he was receiving his hat and coat from the footman when Lord Chesterfield thundered down the stairs to remind him of his promise to take him to Tattersall's.

With a heavy sigh, Geoffrey forced an indulgent smile. "Certainly, my lord. I am, after all, a man of my word. We must only make one stop before we go, if your lordship is agreeable."

Lord Chesterfield declared himself game for anything, if only the captain would show him again how to tell if a horse was touched in the wind, or would be forever throwing out a splint, and Geoffrey, smiling more naturally, led him from the house.

They made their way along Picadilly to the apothecary's shop where Mrs. Crowther had purchased her powders, and the captain entered, a nonplussed Lord Chesterfield in his wake.

"Are you unwell, Captain?" he asked, glancing uneasily about the shop.

"No, no, George, just looking into something curious," replied Geoffrey, in a nonchalant tone.

Leaving George to inspect a jar of leeches, he approached the counter and said, "I believe you have an almost magical treatment for disorders of the stomach."

"Certainly, sir," said the highly gratified apothecary, dusting his hands on his apron and taking a box down from the shelf behind the counter. "A mixture of my own concocting, and guaranteed to soothe the most deranged stomach."

"Excellent. A friend of mine, however, has been taking your powders and has experienced the opposite effect. I wonder if there can be a problem with them."

A flush crept into the man's cheeks. "My patients have never experienced a problem before, I assure you, sir. I take every care to measure and mix with exactness, for my patients come from the cream of Society, and demand the very best. My business would not have survived this long if it was not so."

"I see," said Geoffrey, striving for a conciliatory tone. "I suppose your powders have all the usual ingredients to promote their efficacy?"

The apothecary's high color receded. "As you say, sir. However, I've added a few special ingredients beyond the chamomile, poppy leaves, bole armoniac, nutmeg, and arsenic you'll find in other preparations."

"Arsenic?" interrupted the captain, surprised. "But is not that used for poisoning rats?"

The apothecary smiled condescendingly. "Rats are an inferior species, sir. Rest assured that arsenic, when properly used, is quite efficacious for various disorders of the human system, principally of the stomach. Accelerates the purging effect, you see, and rids the body of bile."

Geoffrey, assimilating this information, asked if the powders sold there were likely to exacerbate symptoms if taken in larger quantities, and was told unequivocally that, while other concoctions may have such an undesirable effect, his own mixture was faultless.

"I take great care to provide my customers with explicit instructions. When used accordingly, there can be no ill effects. I've customers from far and wide that swear to my mixture as a no-fail cure. Lady Gidgeborough herself uses my powders," he said, nodding again for emphasis. "A long-time customer, her ladyship, and never a bad word for the effects."

Geoffrey's brow lowered, but he simply nodded, requesting some of this magical medicine. The apothecary measured out a speckled greenish powder into a small packet, tying it up with string and tucking in a gold-leafed label which proclaimed the contents to be "Mr. Stephens Powders, compounded with Plant Extracts and Minerals for the Relief of all Disorders of the Stomach, or of the Kidneys, or Bowels." Clear instructions for dosage and use were printed underneath.

He handed over the packet, his teeth flashing in a smile. "Sixpence, if you please."

The captain paid him and quitted the shop, young Lord Chesterfield trailing behind.

"If you have a stomach complaint, Captain, I'll eat your dinner," his lordship offered manfully.

"Thank you, George," said the captain, placing the small packet into his pocket. "I am well enough at present, and will undertake to finish my own dinner, but if my courage should fail me when the time comes, I will reconsider the offer. Now let's be off to Tatt's."

After the outing and dinner were accomplished—with George eying the captain for any unpleasant aftereffects—Geoffrey excused himself to join a party at the opera. This event was touted next day as "a triumph," and the principal artists "sensations;" however, Geoffrey knew nothing of it, for his mind was unable to hear any note but what he could do for Emily.

The following morning, he took himself to Gidgeborough House, where he was shown into the opulent drawing room in which her ladyship received visitors.

"I thought not to see you this morning, Captain Mantell," observed her ladyship, giving him a languid hand.

He bowed over it before taking a seat at her invitation. "Forgive me for coming unexpectedly, my lady. I hope that you may assist me, for I have a question which I fear you will find rather strange."

She looked sharply at him. "If it concerns my daughter Athena, you may rid your mind of it instantly. She is presently being courted by the Marquis of Foxham, so you need not trouble yourself."

"I do not think of Lady Athena, my lady," he said, blinking. "I have never thought of her, to be sure." Then, recalling with whom he had to deal, and not wishing to affront her, he explained, "I should never aspire to so august a hand, for I know myself to be unworthy."

"Very well, then," said her ladyship, softening visibly. "What is it you wish to inquire?"

"I had occasion to speak to the apothecary, Mr. Stephens, about his powders, and he mentioned that you are his customer. I have a dear friend who has been taking Mr. Stephens' powders, but they do not seem to be helping her condition."

"Nonsense! Mr. Stephens' powders are excellent. I have taken them time out of mind, and have always found them to be effective. Her condition must be something quite extraordinary if she does not find relief."

"Have you never experienced ill effects from the powders, my lady?"

"Never," she said unequivocally.

He opened his mouth to ask further, but the dagger-look she gave him changed his mind. Instead, he rose and took his leave of her, thanking her for her most gracious reception and wishing her the best of health.

He went about his business, trying to put the matter from his mind, reasoning that Emily's illness was beyond his knowledge and his help, and that Crowther had done all he could for her. But in recalling that Crowther had sent her away in the care of Snipson, whom Mr. Adkins had stigmatized as untrustworthy, Geoffrey was unable to feel easy. He made a very poor showing at Manton's shooting gallery, and was so inattentive at a musical soiree that he complimented a young lady who had played the harp on her fine voice. His abstracted mood was only aggravated by a letter from Clara with the intelligence that Mr. Crowther had returned to Chandry Manor, and that she had made three or four visits, finding each time that Emily's condition had worsened.

I've no doubt her indisposition is owing to that horrid
Mr. Crowther's black mood, which has never abated since
he came home. He has been disagreeable even to me,

*whom he has always treated with the utmost obsequi-
ousness, which circumstance obliged Emily to confide
to me what had angered him so dreadfully (or perhaps it
had something to do with our new degree of intimacy).*

*Those investments, which he set you to discover, and
which had promised so much wealth, were all failed. And
Sir Anthony had also sold those properties your Runner
found, and not a soul but those involved knew anything
of it. So Crowther is nearly mad with anxiety. The investments which he encouraged Sir Anthony to make before
his marriage to Emily are untouchable for some months
yet, and so the man has nothing with which to pay the
mortgage.*

*I still cannot believe that Sir Anthony orchestrated all
this to spite Crowther. It is right out of a novel, I declare,
and so righteous a judgment on so odious a man! For I do
not scruple to tell you, Geoff, that Crowther is growing
more and more odious to me. He drinks excessively, even
when in company, as if he does not care anymore what
people think. But I suppose that since I am the only guest
they entertain, besides the solicitor who comes from time
to time, he feels himself safe.*

*If I were not so anxious for Emily's health, I should
be delighting in his discomfiture, but she is in a terrible
state. So pale, and weak, and scarcely able to shuffle from
one room to another. She insists it is only a passing illness,
brought on by the rigors of the journey, and I must say
that a journey of a hundred miles, even broken into three
days, can be trying, but I do not believe it could be so*

rigorous as to cut up one's health in this manner. But perhaps I am merely a robust person myself, and can have no notion, but it does strike me as odd; however, not so much if the recovery be aggravated by an odious husband.

For he is ransacking the house, and distressing Emily by his rants over her father's treachery and deceit. He apparently believes Sir Anthony purchased yet other investments, and hid the evidence somewhere in the Manor. I have offered to take Emily out in the barouche, but she declines, saying she dare not be far from the chamberpot (crossed out) must lie down upon her bed. Poor soul! Instead, I went with my mother into the village to see if there were not something the apothecary could recommend. He gave me some stomach powders, which I will give Emily directly.

This letter greatly increased Captain Mantell's anxiety for Mrs. Crowther, and after some time of pacing up and down the room, he made a resolution, and asking the butler for the address of Lord Chesterfield's physician, he set out. The address was in Hanover Square, and Dr. Knighton, who was a physician-ordinary to the Prince Regent, seemed entirely capable. Geoffrey put his questions about stomach powders to him and received much the same answers.

"But what if there were a mistake in the proportions used?" he inquired urgently.

Dr. Knighton shrugged. "Any number of problems may arise then, sir. However, I know Mr. Stephens to be an excellent apothecary, and prescribe his powders myself. They have given relief to many of my patients."

"And they have no ill effects?" Geoffrey pressed.

"Perhaps an isolated occurrence, but nothing to throw a shadow on the medicinal value of Mr. Stephens Powders. If patients were dying from it, I think I should have known it by now," the doctor added with a wry smile.

Such reasonable answers from an eminent physician did something to ease Geoffrey's anxieties, and he returned to Chesterfield House, determined to lay his fears at last. To this end, he settled down with a book in his lordship's magnificent library, but he could not concentrate, and was relieved at the entrance of the footman, who proffered a salver with a letter. Seeing that it was from Mr. Adkins, Geoffrey opened it at once.

> *Dear Sir,*
>
> *I have discovered two investments entered into by Sir Anthony after those I've previously investigated. They were extremely large investments, and would have been worth much, had they prospered; however, they did not. One was in a mining concern that has since closed down, and the other in an invention to improve corn harvest, which failed.*
>
> *If this information is distressing, I am only sorry to have been the bearer of it.*
>
> *J. Adkins*

This information merely corroborated what Clara had written, and Geoffrey assumed Crowther's agent had been before Mr. Adkins in its discovery. So Geoffrey took up his book and attempted again to lose himself in it but could not, for his mind chased about with Crowther and investments and Snipson and rats and arsenic and apothecaries. And Emily—always poor Emily standing against all this without proper support.

At last he gave it up. He would have no rest without knowing that Emily was being suitably cared for. He would run mad if he did not go back to Southam and do what he could toward restoring her to health and ensuring her peace. How could he pursue romance with eligible young ladies when Emily was in such dire straights? He could not, and he would not. When she was well again, and Crowther had settled the mortgages, Geoffrey would return to Town and do what he could to forget her.

Replacing his book on the shelf, he went in search of his batman, who was to be found in his bedchamber, arranging freshly starched cravats in a drawer.

"Ah, Chalmers, you are excellent. I hope that what I am about to say will not vex you, for it involves undoing much of what you have just done. I am returning to Warwickshire. Please make preparations for my departure, tomorrow."

Chalmers, having witnessed much of his master's abstraction, and guessing what was in the wind, merely bowed and left the room. Captain Mantell wrote a short note to Clara, informing her of his intention to return home within the week, and another note to Tom Breckinridge, accepting his kind offer of lodging at Branwell Manor, which lay on his road to Southam.

Chapter 21

Though Geoffrey wished to begin his journey with all possible haste, there were some civilities that could not be left unobserved. It was with real regret that he took his leave of Lord Chesterfield, as the young earl was a true friend and an excellent host, even at only twelve years of age. Geoffrey thanked him profusely, promised to return as soon as he was able, and bade him not to purchase anyone's breakdowns, no matter how showy the animals were made to look.

He bid Miss Breckinridge a regretful goodbye as well, for her romance had not yet come to a happy conclusion, and he saw the strain that she was under. Again, he was struck by the similarity in their circumstances, and after giving what encouragement he could, took some comfort in imparting to her the true cause for his sudden departure. She instantly shared his concerns, but trusted that Mrs. Crowther would be the better for his visit. Grateful for her faith, he seconded this hope and left her with a lighter heart.

His journey to Branwell was accomplished with little trouble, though he was obliged to ask directions more than once, for the roads off the King's Highway were horridly rutted and in dire need of repair, and he was forced to take several detours. His sighting of the lodge gates of Branwell Manor was a source of both relief and impatience, for it grated upon him that he must stop at all. But a journey of a hundred miles must needs be cut up somehow, for the postilions and their horses must be allowed sleep at some point, and he very much appreciated Tom's generous invitation.

Mr. Breckinridge welcomed him into his home with obvious pride, and Geoffrey saw that he would be obliged to curb his impatience and play the gracious guest.

"If you'd come even five months ago," said Tom, pouring out Madeira in a comfortably appointed study, "I'd have been obliged to welcome you at the Cottage, for that is where I've been living these six years, with tenants paying the bills here. It was a grand day, I tell you, when I saw the last of them—though they were, in and of themselves, good sort of people."

"It's a fine house," remarked Geoffrey, accepting the wine and taking care to drink it unhurriedly. "Though I wonder if it doesn't feel a bit lonely, with only you rattling around inside it."

Tom chuckled. "I'm certain it may, once I've slowed up enough to pay any heed. For now, I'm too busy seeing to all the repairs and running the farm to think about my solitary state. I never eat in the dining room, but take my meals in here, where, you can see, I have plenty of work to bear me company."

Geoffrey eyed the paper-strewn desk near the fireplace without envy. The lack of such business was one consolation of having no property of his own. But in the spirit of congeniality, he encouraged Tom to talk about the improvements he meant to have made, and heard with real pleasure the young man's details of the profitable farm he had established before inquiring, "You've incredible motivation for one so young. Has it been always so, or is this a more recent development, with a more romantic motive?"

"I'll not deny the emergence of a greater motive," said Tom, coloring. "But I've always been fascinated by farming. I learned estate management by necessity, when my father died suddenly. He had never been prudent—indeed, he'd never cared for anything but his own pleasure—so there was much to be learned, and quickly, if we were to retain ownership of our estate."

"It's a fine thing, to bring about your fortune," said the captain, manfully commanding his thoughts to remain on Tom's prospects and not on Emily's. "And now you have every right to be proud, for you have a very pretty property here, and a growing independence with which to impress the father of a certain young lady."

Tom smiled at this, but without conviction. "Miss Marshall has ten thousand pounds, and includes the daughter of an earl in her circle. I do not think that I, who have scarcely begun to realize a profit in my estate, am quite what Mr. Marshall had in mind for a suitable *parti*. My mother remarried a man with plenty of wealth, it's true, but it does not come to me, and I would not wish it to. I've worked hard enough to build up my own success, and don't wish to lean on anybody, but I cannot imagine Mr. Marshall should consider such a scruple as a positive, particularly when a far more eligible suitor has lately presented himself."

"One who presently resides near Brighton?" asked the captain, recalling their discussion from White's club.

Tom nodded, taking a judicious gulp of wine. "I cannot forget that Mr. Marshall has never discovered an ailment that can only be cured by Berkhampstead air, just so his daughter may be within easy reach of Branwell."

Geoffrey was forced to concede this point, and Tom changed the subject.

"You're on your way home, aren't you? I wonder what could have dragged you away from the Metropolis?" he mused. "Family matters, boredom, or romance the culprit?"

It was Geoffrey's turn to color, and he set his glass down on the table beside him. "A mixture of all, I suppose. There are some things I feel I should attend to at home, though I ought, I suppose, to stay away at all costs. But I feel I must convince myself of the safety of my very dear friend, which makes it hard to behave rationally."

Tom waited, but when more information was not forthcoming, he let the subject drop, moving on to the health of various of their mutual friends. Geoffrey appreciated his circumspection, and was confirmed in it when after dinner Tom did not keep him chatting long over their port but sped the captain off to bed, insisting he must be exhausted.

In the morning, Tom's indulgence continued, and Geoffrey was on his way betimes. He pressed on through the day and into the night, having good luck in his horses at every stage and a full moon to guide him, and he arrived at Gracely Hall before ten o'clock. His family, who kept country hours, had gone to bed, so he could not hope for a report on Emily's welfare before morning, and retired to his bedchamber to collapse into restless slumber.

His weeks of exertion and worry had taken their toll, and Geoffrey slept late into the morning. Directly after taking breakfast, however, he sought out Clara, discovering her in the garden, cutting flowers.

Her greeting to him was matter-of-fact. "Ah, Geoff! I must say I am glad to see you here. It is the devil of a coil."

Raising his brows at her language, Geoffrey said, "How is Emily—that is, Mrs. Crowther?"

"Emily," she said, looking pointedly at him, "is quite well. She began suddenly to improve three days ago, upon her deciding, not without my considered influence, to leave off those horrid powders she had been taking." She placed the last of the blooms in her basket and stood, casting him a dignified look under her bonnet brim. "Perhaps you did not know that her odious husband has been practically forcing her to take a certain preparation which has been acting in the form of poison to her."

He surprised her by announcing that he did know it, or at least that he had suspected the powders to be the culprit in her sudden indisposition, and begged to be informed how they came to suspect it.

Clara gave him a look of approbation. "I suppose that is why you came hotfoot from London? It is just as well, for Emily, I am persuaded, is in need of protection. But I am getting ahead of myself. I wrote that I had decided to procure some powders for her from our own apothecary, having no notion that she had been taking powders all along. Well, when I went to so much trouble for her, she felt obligated to take them, as the other powders did not seem to be helping her the least bit, and she was ready to try anything to feel better."

They had reached the house now, and before they entered, Clara guided Geoffrey to a bench on the veranda and sat him down beside her, turning to him with grim animation. "And from almost the moment she changed those horrid powders for mine, she began to improve! Geoff, though she does not wish to believe it, I am convinced—convinced!—that Crowther had been trying to poison her, and when you see her you will believe it as well, for she is so altered—poor creature! She could hardly stand the day I brought her the powders, and now she has recovered some of her color, and her energy, and has begun again to eat. Oh! When I think how close he got to killing her—"

Geoffrey took her hand in a firm grip, looking gravely at her. "Clara, you are not serious. You will not have me believe your dear friend is in dire peril—indeed, at the mercy of a murderer—while you are calmly cutting roses."

She huffed. "Well, I suppose I am merely suspicious of it, but so must you be, for why else should you come so urgently?"

"You know why I came, Clara," said Geoffrey simply. "I could not stay away while Emily's health was so uncertain. But I think that if you truly suspected Crowther of being a murderer, you should not be able to recite it to me as if it were a scene from a novel."

Clara glared at him, crossing her arms and pursing her lips. "What a killjoy you are, to be sure, Geoffrey! I did suspect it—I do suspect! At least—he is a scoundrel, Geoff! I tell you, he is horrid and selfish and continually foxed—"

"That does not make him a murderer, Clara."

She rolled her eyes, taking a flower from her basket and viciously plucking off the petals. "Perhaps not. She was ill while he was still in Town."

"Precisely." Geoffrey patted her hand. "I am excessively relieved by your report of Mrs. Crowther's improvement, and grateful for your watchcare, Clara. I own that for some time I could not get the idea out of my head that the powders were to blame for her illness, but I discovered, through the aid of the physician-ordinary to the Prince Regent, that it could only be the case in isolated occurrences. Perhaps this is one such case—I do not know, for it could just as easily have been a mistake by the apothecary, or a reaction limited to the Chandry family. Did you know, Sir Anthony looked as horridly pathetic before he died as you described Mrs. Crowther? Perhaps the two circumstances are linked."

"If you will be a dead bore, then yes, I imagine his ailment was something he passed on to poor Emily, and that is all there is to it."

"Do not look so glum, Clara, as if you wished for Emily to be in real danger. No, I know you do not—indeed, I know it to be the reverse, for you will wish to continue your support." He paused. "You say she is much altered."

Clara looked at him, all fancy gone from her thoughts. "Yes, Geoff, very altered. It was a close run thing—you cannot fault me for considering her a victim of foul play when you see how she looks."

"You may depend upon my whole desire being to do what we can to see that she is properly cared for in her recovery," he said. "You are already in the way to being a fixture in her house, and I believe my presence will be acceptable as well. We may keep a good watch over her in that way, by frequent visits."

Clara approved this idea, and differed from Geoffrey only regarding the speed with which it ought to be executed.

"We must not look too particular, Clara," he cautioned, "for if we were to descend upon Mrs. Crowther on the very day that I have arrived home from a protracted absence, then Crowther may justly suspect a deeper motive than disinterested friendship."

"You are right, Geoff. I was not thinking. We must keep him comfortable, or the game will be up before it is begun."

"There is no game, Clara," reminded her brother firmly. "You must not allow your imagination to run wild."

"At least there is still the question of the investments," cried Clara. "I will not forget Crowther's great distress over money just now. That I can enjoy, for it is the greatest suspense to see if he will die of frustration or triumph over Sir Anthony in the end."

"Very well," said Geoffrey, washing his hands of her. "I ask only that you do not forget in your excitement to ensure Mrs. Crowther's well-being, and that you do not become an annoyance to her husband."

Clara agreed to this, giving it as her considered opinion that, for a military man, Geoffrey was decidedly craven when it came to tactical maneuvers, and it was a wonder to her that he had even distinguished himself enough in the field to rise to Captain. Geoffrey, wisely unheeding, agreed with her that they should pay a call to Chandry Manor the day after the next, and left her to arrange her flowers, which she did with rather more violence than was necessary.

Chapter 22

AFTER A REFRESHING ride to fully release his pent up anxiety, Geoffrey went up to change his dress, but was arrested mid-stride in the corridor by the sound of weeping coming from his mother's apartments.

Knocking tentatively on the door, he called, "Mother? It's Geoffrey. Are you unwell, Mother?"

A rather incoherent response led him to turn the handle, and he stepped into his mother's sitting room, where she sat wiping ineffectually at swollen, red eyes with a shred of a handkerchief. He went to her, too shocked to think of hesitating, for he had never witnessed his mother crying.

"Mother, pray do not weep," he said gently, taking her hand as he sat beside her on the settle where she had, from the evidence of wet patches on the cushion, cast herself some time before. "What can be the matter to have upset you so? Will you not tell me? Perhaps I may help you."

Her answering sobs were eloquent of her misery, and he was forced to wait some time for anything coherent to come out of her mouth.

"My—life—is—ruined!" she managed at last, in a hiccuping sob, as she grasped the lapels of Geoffrey's coat and wept profusely into his neckcloth.

Utterly discomfited, Geoffrey offered, "Perhaps if I bring Clara to you—"

"Nooo!" wailed his mother, emerging from his neckcloth for a brief moment. "She mustn't see me like this!"

Startled and utterly bewildered by this unaccountable behavior, Geoffrey held his mother as she wept, patting her back awkwardly until her sobs began to die down, and she pulled away from him to dab at her face with the bedraggled handkerchief. Geoffrey quickly produced his own and she took it gratefully, blowing her nose and sighing deeply.

"I suppose I must go on living," she said, gazing bleakly out into the room, "for without me, neither you nor Francis shall ever get properly married, and if Clara does not mend her odd ways, she will be left an old maid, and will have no home to call her own when her brothers die."

Geoffrey blinked at this. "Mother, what ridiculous start is this! Of course Clara shall marry! And Francis too, and—" But he could not promise it for himself, so he said instead, "And you shall live to a good old age, and be peaceful and comfortable with all your grandchildren about you."

She eyed him askance. "Children do not make one peaceful and comfortable, especially when they are forever setting their will against one's own. I ought never to have borne children, for I was not made for it," she added in a voice of deepest gloom.

"Come, come, Mother," cried Geoffrey, entirely out of his depth. "Do you miss Father? I daresay you do, for he was used to make everything easy—"

"No! I do not miss your father!" she interrupted, with such an angry look that Geoffrey cringed back. "For he was not used to make everything easy, excepting for himself! He was used to take no consideration for my feelings, and to ride rough-shod over anyone who did not give him his way, and to—and to—" Her voice became suspended by tears again, and Geoffrey was obliged to fight the craven impulse to flee before she seized his coat again.

But she merely stared ahead as the tears rolled gently down her cheeks, saying tragically, "He courted me with such grace, bringing me the most beautiful flowers, and writing me the most exquisite letters! How could I not choose—but I was entirely taken in! I suppose I only got my desserts, for I desired consequence and position, and—and—" She gulped, her chin trembling, "that is what I got."

Geoffrey was poised to ring the bell for assistance, but his mother did not succumb to her sorrow again, only closing her eyes on her grief and clutching the damp handkerchief to her bosom.

"It was not your father's fault," she whispered. "You mustn't think that, Geoffrey. He only did what came naturally to him. And so did I." Her eyes opened, tears sparkling on her lashes, and she turned to gaze mournfully at him. "I am glad he is gone. We are both of us free of our loveless marriage. And yet I press my own children to enter into the same arrangement—to value position and consequence more than love." She shuddered, her shoulders slumping. "I ought never to have married, for I am a most unnatural parent."

At this astonishing confession, Geoffrey was moved to relinquish his discomfort and once more take his mother's hand, pressing it between his own. "My dear Mother, it is not so. Your feelings are very natural. Every parent must make their children's comfort and provision in life the first priority. Sometimes that requires a more prudent approach to marriage. You merely have recognized too late for yourself what that means, in truth."

She glanced sadly up at him, and he smiled hearteningly. "Indeed, you have caused us no harm, for Francis, you know, has disregarded your admonitions entirely, and Clara has told me in no uncertain terms that she means to marry a man who worships her, and I—" Here, he stopped uncertainly.

"And you will never marry," supplied his mother.

Startled, Geoffrey looked an inquiry, but she merely patted his hand and stood, blowing her nose defiantly and tossing the handkerchief onto a side table. "I had thought to change your mind, but doubted the likelihood of my success. It is for the best, I suppose. For now we both know unequivocally that where one cannot have love, there is no point in marriage."

On these words, she swept out of the room, leaving Geoffrey to blink after her, for he really did not know what to think. He had been used to consider his mother as devoid of all tender emotion, but apparently he had wronged her. All along she had only been guarding her broken heart from further injury, and storing up her emotion for this moment, when she at last felt it safe to release.

"My poor mother," sighed Geoffrey, standing and going to his own room, and considering how his future might mirror her own, should he force an attachment with any one of the number of girls toward whom he had directed his attentions. Even a marriage with a young lady of Miss Breckinridge's quality could have been penury after a few years, when they had both realized his inability to forget his first love. For as long as Emily Chandry was married to Crowther, he would be anxious for her—of that he was certain.

The visit to Emily, when it occurred, was almost too much of a success. They were ushered into the house not by Marsden, the ancient butler, but by Crowther's manservant, Snipson.

"He's been acting as butler, footman, and general factotum since their return from London," Clara hissed in Geoffrey's ear, as they trailed Snipson into the saloon. This apartment had been cleaned, dusted, and generally brightened up, insofar as it could be and still retain all its faded and outdated furnishings and hangings. Mrs. Crowther, looking worn but not nearly as close to death's door as Clara's letter had taught him to fear, made to rise upon their entrance, but was quickly and firmly commanded by Clara to retain her seat, while her visitors made themselves comfortable near her.

The subject of her health, uppermost on their minds, was broached first, and she was able to give a satisfactory answer:

"I continue to improve, little by little, each day. The powders Clara brought for me," she said, looking a little conscious, "are nothing short of miraculous."

"Emily, you goose, it was not my powders that cured you," said Clara, not mincing matters, "but that you stopped taking those horrid ones from London."

"Indeed, Mrs. Crowther," said Geoffrey, "I wondered if there might not have been something in the powders you were taking in London, that did not agree with you. But whatever the cause, I am glad you are on the mend. I hope," he added, with feeling, "that you will take prodigious care what medicines you take in future."

She gazed gratefully at him, her large gray eyes rendered larger from the effects of her illness. "Yes, Captain Mantell. I have not been wont to take medicines, for though I am often nervous, I have never experienced much trouble in recovering from my various illnesses. I believe this may have been the cause of my violent reaction to the stomach powders Mr. Crowther insisted I take—merely my digestion is unfamiliar with such coddling, and will not abide it."

At that moment, the door was opened, and Crowther came in, smiling and bowing in his usual way to the Mantells.

"Such a delight to see you again so soon, Captain!" he said, shaking his hand. "I had no idea of your returning into the country before the end of the season, and yet here you are!" He let his smile linger on Geoffrey for a moment before bestowing it upon Clara. "And Miss Mantell is so regular a visitor here that I count her as one of the family! Practically a sister to my dear Emily, if I may be so bold."

He did not seat himself beside Emily, instead taking a chair on the other side of the fireplace. "Don't know what we should have done without Miss Mantell these many days, Captain. She has been as a guardian angel to our Emily, who was as sick as could be, and I not knowing what to be done. Even prescribed her my favorite powders, that never fail to bring me around, but to no avail. Nothing would cure her but Miss Mantell's goodness in scarcely leaving her side. You've thanked Miss Mantell, I am sure, my love."

He fixed Emily with a look much like a teacher to a recalcitrant student, and she looked down at her hands, which clung together in her lap, and murmured her gratitude to her kind friend. He seemed satisfied, for he went on.

"Thought she was done for, I did, for she looked just as her poor father did, before he turned up his toes. It chilled my heart, to see just how alike they were, and no one could fault me for fancying they'd got some sort of disease that ran in the family. My heart was almost breaking, but then we got a miracle, and here she is, as you see her, pinking up and as hearty as she can be, poor soul. Our new cook-housekeeper's good food has done it's part, but it's your condescension and goodness that did the rest."

He ran an eye over his company, as if to gauge their attention, and rubbed his hands together. "Now you are here, I cannot think it anything but providence, for I had just taken a notion into my head to celebrate Em's recovery by redecorating some of her favorite rooms, but I knew too well she could not stand the noise. Anything of that nature just rattles her, poor old girl, and she'd like as not be obliged to take to her bed again, just after she had risen from it as from the dead. I couldn't have that happen, not for the universe, and I had all but given up my grand idea when I had the happy notion to beg Miss Mantell to take her as a visitor to Gracely Hall, and here you are to give your answer directly!"

Clara gaped at him, while Geoffrey merely blinked at this extremely ill-bred, though not unwelcome request. That Crowther had suggested it was what only was wrong, for it was Geoffrey's dearest wish that his sister take Mrs. Crowther into her care, and to have her ensconced in their home would ensure her successful recovery.

But that Crowther would wish to foist his wife onto them was very strange indeed—though it blasted Clara's suspicions, for he could not murder his wife if she was to be removed from his power. His very urgency for the scheme argued his innocence, and Geoffrey smiled inwardly at the irony. He still could not understand what Crowther could be about, however, until he considered that Crowther may wish to search for anything that may be of value in the Manor, unhampered by her presence—though he considered she was too weakened and weary to be meddlesome. Perhaps he imagined she should object to his looking in certain places, and having her out of the way would give him impunity.

Whatever the cause for this sudden start, Geoffrey was not about to refuse it, for he was of much the same mind as Crowther in that it was as the hand of providence. It would be difficult for him to be in the same household as Emily, to have her so close but always out of reach, but he thought that knowing exactly how she fared would be worth the cost. And being so often in her company just might inure him to his fascination with her, and teach him to be content with their separate circumstances. With a quick look to Clara, he communicated his approbation of the plan, and she, recovering her countenance, quite adequately expressed her joy in the scheme.

"It is what I most could wish, sir," she cried, reaching to take Mrs. Crowther's hand in her own. "And the delight shall be twofold, for we will nurse her to health, and enjoy her company, for as long as we may have her!"

Crowther smiled on them like the lion at the Exchange. "Excellent! Excellent. There now, my love," he said, sparing a glance for Emily, "you will be well cared for while we make a noise and bustle here. It ought not to be above a month or two. And then, when all is put to rights again, you may come home to enjoy the improvements."

What Emily thought of the scheme was uncertain, for her face had gone white as a sheet, then pink, and no speech could be got out of her as long as her husband stayed in the room. He was gone in another moment, however, to order his servant to take Mrs. Crowther's trunk to her rooms, and as soon as the door had closed behind him, Clara pounced.

"Emily! Do not look so! There can be nothing to distress you in this scheme, indeed, it is of all things excessively lucky, for you shall be wholly out of his reach—"

"Clara, you know that I am in no way in danger from Crowther," Emily said in a desperate undervoice, pressing hands to her heated cheeks. "Indeed, this proves to the contrary, for if he wished to harm me, why should he let me go? It is most perplexing, for it is not his way to consider my comfort, nor to think up schemes for my entertainment!"

Clara waved away her reasoning with an airy hand. "It does not signify, for you are to be safe at Gracely Hall, with only friends around you. Come, my dear, let us go and pack your things."

"No, Clara!" cried Emily, in the same urgent whisper. "You can have no notion how a stay of this kind would pain me—" She stopped abruptly, her eyes flying for an instant to Geoffrey's face.

Geoffrey, more of her opinion than he could show, stepped away to the window, and looked out at the riotous lawn that had not been mown for two decades, while Clara continued her whispered conference with Emily.

"If my brothers' being at Gracely Hall will cause you discomfort, then they will remove themselves, for I am still of the opinion that it will be best for you to be there."

He did not hear what Emily said in reply, but Clara continued in a pleading tone, "Please come. Even if you are not convinced that your husband intended harm, you know that he does not generally have your welfare at heart. His requesting this visit is most surprising, but why he does so does not interest me so much as your wellbeing."

Glancing over, he saw that tears had welled up in Emily's eyes, and she blinked them away, searching in her pocket for a handkerchief. "Very well," she said quietly, after dabbing at her eyes.

"Excellent," said Clara, casting her brother a look of triumph. "We'll not keep you waiting long, Geoffrey."

Chapter 23

THEY DID NOT keep him waiting above a half hour, for Clara was possessed of the notion that Crowther would change his mind at any moment and snatch away his approbation. This would once more ruin Emily's peace, for she was every minute becoming more resigned to the scheme, even beginning to speak with pleasure of the delights in store. By encouraging such thoughts, Clara sped their packing and talked her friend down the stairs and out into the carriage before any thoughts of reversing the plan could occur to Mr. Crowther.

Clara kept up a lively chatter during the short drive home, and upon their reaching the Hall, sent Geoffrey away directly to inform their mother of her surprise visitor while she set about making Emily as comfortable as possible in the drawing room. Mrs. Mantell, though somewhat astonished at this sudden visit, did not give more resistance than to look annoyed and comment on the singular notions of civility obtaining in certain circles. Had she desired to scotch the whole business, she could not have done so, however, for Clara, well-versed in her mother's odd humors, had eliminated doubt by ordering a room to be made ready and the cook informed of the necessity for an extra cover at dinner.

By the time the family gathered in the drawing room, Emily had so composed herself that none of her earlier agitation was apparent. She greeted her hostess with such humility that Mrs. Mantell was moved to thank her for coming to them, and to speak civilly to her until dinner was announced. Then she sat Emily at her right hand at the formal dining table, with Francis at the far end and Geoffrey and Clara on the left, and chatted away about the comings and goings of the neighborhood, and how unusual it was to have a decent neighbor at Chandry Manor.

Geoffrey was anxious to rejoin the ladies after they had left him and Francis at their port, but he needn't have worried, for Clara had taken Emily to the pianoforte and had encouraged her to play through some of the pieces piled on the top. He took his seat in appreciative silence, surprised that he had had no notion of Emily's having learned to play. And she played very well, even singing a little, though without any pomp or show. Her skill lay in revealing the beauty of the music, without drawing undue attention to herself. Even Francis, who had taken up a newspaper on the other side of the room, could not keep his attention wholly absorbed in reading, and let the paper fold once or twice in his distraction.

At the first sign of fatigue in their guest, Clara announced her intention to seek her bed, and Emily did not want much coaxing to join her. She smiled fleetingly up at Geoffrey as he bowed her out of the room, and he returned to his chair to listen to his mother recount her utter astonishment at Sir Anthony's daughter's pleasant manners.

The success of this first evening set the tone for the remainder of Emily's visit. She settled quickly into Clara's routine, chafing only at the very little work that she could find to be done.

"I wish you would give me something plain to do, for you will find my embroidery abominable, I daresay," she confided to Clara, as they bent over such work. "You must know that I am used only to darn stockings and to mend linens. In my experience, there is no need for such fancy work as this."

"Nonsense, my dear," replied Clara with an impish look. "If one is not allowed the opportunity in girlhood to sew deplorable samplers, then one must make up for it sometime."

Geoffrey observed this exchange with delight, but also with pain, for the vision of Emily as Clara's sister had instantly obtruded itself into his brain. Other exchanges were difficult as well, from Emily's kind notice of the servants to her gentle skill at handling his mother.

Since his return from London, Geoffrey had remarked a change in Mrs. Mantell, which he connected to her strange outburst just after his arrival. Upon inquiry, he had been told that his mother, the one-time belle of every occasion, had seemed over the last few months to shrink in upon herself, wandering the Hall with a languor wholly incompatible with her former energetic efficiency. Geoffrey himself had noted that, for hours at a time, she would sit in her drawing room, her embroidery forgotten in her lap, and her eyes turned unseeing either on a point outside the window, or at her immobile hands. When discovered at these moments by her children, or one of the upper servants, she would rouse herself sufficiently to allay their fears by her quick, sharp tongue, and they withdrew from her under the impression that they had allowed their imaginations to run away with them. But after many weeks, their certainty that something was not right began to assert itself, and if her firm denials had not made them equally certain of the futility of seeking the cause for her decline, something might have been attempted to reclaim her. As it was, the upper servants knew their place too well to do more than mutter direfully, and her children would risk only the exchange of bewildered looks.

But Emily, when confronted with this odd behavior in her hostess, perhaps from not knowing differently or perhaps from that kind intuition so inherent in her character, simply sat quietly with Mrs. Mantell, responding gently to any abruptness and acting as though nothing were untoward. Geoffrey, amazed but not surprised, wished to thank her but knew not how.

He came upon her in the stables one day, stroking the nose of a white mare and murmuring to her.

"You are full of surprises, Mrs. Crowther," he said to announce his presence. "You play the pianoforte, you sew beautifully, and you speak to horses. I did not imagine you to be so talented."

She looked conscious but smiled. "There are some benefits to attending a private seminary, I suppose. One of the young ladies there had an uncle in town, and he allowed us to come see the horses. He would have allowed me to ride, but I had not been taught, and did not have the time to be or, for that matter, a riding habit."

"Should you like to learn to ride?" asked Geoffrey, thinking only that this was how he could show her his gratitude.

She glanced quickly at him. "Would you teach me?"

"Certainly, if you wish it." But the look of disquiet in her gray eyes brought him to a sense of the intimacy of such an endeavor, and he amended, "Or perhaps Clara could do so."

She looked down, her hand absently brushing the mare's cheek. "I thank you for the kind offer, Captain, but I fear I am not yet well enough for exercise. I will simply enjoy the horses' company at present."

Geoffrey replied that he was agreeable, and after offering to take her and Clara out in the barouche at any time they desired, he fled the stables.

Clara made it known to her friends that she had a visitor, and several subsequent invitations included Mrs. Crowther, but she could not be prevailed upon to accept them. She shrank from the attention, begging to be forgiven for the refusal of such civility, but insisting that she was still recovering from her indisposition, and was more than content to stay quietly at the Hall, reading or playing the pianoforte or tending the garden, or most often, walking in the woods.

Geoffrey, sensible that he was every moment in danger of betraying his feelings—which had not unsurprisingly come perilously close to the surface since Emily's arrival at the Hall—did not dare to offer himself as her companion on these sylvan rambles. He had been at great pains to keep her at arms' length, and had hoped that by his deliberately friendly demeanor and Clara's lively company, Emily would feel at home. But he could not rejoice in his success. Whenever he came into a room where she was, it seemed necessary for her to hold her breath, and her eyes, though seldom meeting his own, were often turned toward him. It was a kind of exquisite torture to both of them.

He did not know what to do, for he could not leave the country again, not while she had been entrusted to his family's care. And he would not leave her again without the certainty of her good health and at least relative peace, which would only be ensured when Crowther had been enabled to pay the mortgages. Better to try and make her stay at Gracely Hall as pleasant as possible, for soon enough Crowther would call her back to Chandry Manor, and her fate would once more be out of his hands.

So he took long rides in the countryside, and accepted all invitations to dine away from home. In the evenings, he played at billiards with Francis—whenever Francis was not otherwise occupied—and endured veiled hints on the advisability of seducing married women.

Just when he thought he could abide his worldly-wise brother no longer, Mr. Simpford came down from London after a disastrous run at play, "to rusticate, dear boy, until the quarter, for besides my vowels—don't ask the total, Geoff! Just don't—my tailor has been making my life devilish uncomfortable since I ordered three new coats and never paid him!"

"Well, Lawrie, it's dashed good luck you're here, for I've a sudden inclination for male company, and I can stomach only so much of Francis," said Geoffrey.

Mr. Simpford gave him a knowing look. "Been sent to the rightabout, have you? I saw how you went after that heiress in town. Left mighty quick, you did, and I thought, I'd lay odds her father don't look too kindly upon second sons."

Geoffrey gazed blankly at his friend for some moments, until his meaning became clear. "Oh! Miss Breckinridge! Devil a bit—" He paused, as a new thought came to him. "That is, you've the right of it, Lawrie! Clever, as always. Yes, I've been rusticated as well, though for blighted hopes, and I'd be forever grateful if you'd assist me in forgetting all about her."

This Mr. Simpford was all eagerness to do, and whiled away the following fortnight in filling every spare moment of Geoffrey's days with sporting events, long nights of piquet, companionable trips to the village pub, and spirited attempts to excite his poor friend's interest in likely young ladies in the neighborhood. That he was bound to failure in this Geoffrey never let on, for he was grateful to him for the relief his absence gave to Emily—and, after a fashion, himself.

The quarter came, however, and with it the means for Mr. Simpford to return to town, leaving Geoffrey again to his own devices. Unwilling to upset the balance he hoped Emily had found in his absence, he continued to avoid her company, though it chafed him to be so poor a friend. He felt that there must be something he could do for her, without cutting up her—or his own—peace. He conjectured that her walks often led her to the faerie clearing, and that the state of things must pain her, and at last he determined to steal away—when he knew she would not be there—to do what he could toward repairing the neglected village.

Sure enough, when he entered the little clearing, he detected amidst the ruins evidence that she had been there, working to repair the injuries that time and the elements had done. He inspected her work, conjuring up a vision of her kneeling there, a lock of her pale hair falling across one cheek as her deft hands created something fascinatingly lovely. It was almost too much—he wanted her there with him, sharing the magic of this place, and to combat this rush of emotion, he fell to his knees and threw himself into a repair of his own.

He was hard at work when he heard footsteps and looked around. Emily stood at the entrance to the clearing, and at sight of her he started up, coloring, and begged her pardon for his intrusion.

"You have as much right to come here as I," she said, betraying no hint of the reticence that had become usual in his presence. She gazed about her. "It is a wretched prospect, is not it? I had not returned since my father died."

"I have made some pathetic attempts, as you see." He paused, then raised a hand, saying with a rueful look, "My fingers have never been half so clever as yours."

"No," she said, smiling. "But you have helped to mold this place all the same." She bent to touch the remains of the post office then looked up at him. "I should like it if you would stay."

Her manner was strange, but not eerily so. She was peaceful and confident, and it warmed his heart to see it, after the weeks of discomfort between them. But the clearing seemed to have that sort of effect on her—it was its own kingdom, and detached from the outside world. They were simply two dear friends again within its boundaries.

He settled back onto the ground, picking up a horse that lay damaged beside him, and began to bind its broken limbs with some twine from the treasure box. Emily sat also, taking up a tiny hut that had been crushed by the elements.

As she sought for a twig with which to repair it, she said, "Your mother has been most kind to take me in at such short notice."

"I hope your stay has been enjoyable thus far."

"To be sure. Clara is a dear friend, and so thoughtful. I would be a selfish creature indeed to find fault with any of your family. Even Mr. Mantell is not so strange to me now."

He laughed, as much with delight at her honesty as with agreement. "He is a rare one, is not he? I am glad you are growing inured to his devil-may-care ways."

"I am certain he is a good man at heart, but—" She hesitated, taking up a piece of bark and fitting it to the roof of the hut. "Does he always ogle the maids so?"

Geoffrey blinked. "No—that is, not all the maids." He coughed and dug into his waistcoat for his penknife.

"I expect it is boredom, from having no vocation," she remarked pensively. "It is likely that he will outgrow such flighty behavior, now that he is master of Gracely."

Geoffrey choked on a laugh. "Outgrow it? He is close on thirty!"

"It is not uncommon for a man to take quite a long time to outgrow childish things," she said, looking pointedly at the village that surrounded them.

"Yes, and women also," retorted Geoffrey, grinning. "I suppose that is a symptom of difficult circumstances."

She paused. "I suppose it is."

They both fell silent for a time. She reached into the brush for another twig and Geoffrey saw the stone he had given her, still reposing on its chain, slip out from her neckline. He caught his breath, for he had not thought she would still wear it after her marriage. He wondered if Crowther knew of it.

"Is your marriage what you expected, Emily?" he asked abruptly.

She hesitated, coloring, and he cursed his impudence. But she said, "Not entirely; however it has its advantages. I knew it was no love match, and did not expect to enjoy—certain aspects of marriage." She gazed resolutely at the villager in her hand. "But as it turns out, Crowther has no interest in such things. I told you once he treats me as a sister, and it is so, for which I find reason to be glad."

He gazed steadfastly at her profile. "Then it was not so much of a sacrifice."

"I did not think of it as a sacrifice," she said. "It was marriage to Crowther or subservience to my father. Though it would seem I should have been free of my father far sooner than I had anticipated."

"But you don't know that he would not have served you the same trick as he has served Crowther."

"Perhaps you are right." She sighed somewhat wearily. "It is neither here nor there, for I am married and my father's hatred of my husband reaches beyond the grave to vex me." She gave a rueful smile. "He forgave me as he lay dying."

"Much good it did him, as he would have done better to ask your forgiveness."

She shrugged, replacing the now repaired villager and taking up another. "He was a different man at the end. We talked as we had never done before, as father and daughter."

"I hope it gave him comfort," said Geoffrey amicably. "It is unfortunate that he did not show such feeling when you were in his care."

"The nearness of death can soften the heart, or so I understand," she murmured, still not looking at him.

He sighed, relinquishing his irritation at the men who had so ill-used her when they ought to have cherished her. He could not insist upon hating them if she did not.

"You are a better person than I, Emily," he said. "I wish I had your goodness, for it seems to make things almost easy."

She looked quickly at him then. "It is not easy. It was not without difficulty that I bade my father goodbye just as he had learned to think well of me. It is not easy to accept that I will never know love as I dreamed one day I might. My goodness, as you call it, does not save me from dark and mortifying reflections."

Geoffrey, horrified that he had spoken so insensibly, cast about for some way to apologize, but she forestalled him by saying in a softened tone, "It has never made things easy, Captain, but it has given me the strength to continue to try."

Chapter 24

THIS SOBER CONCLUSION to their dialog was long in Geoffrey's mind, causing his thoughts to hark back to Clara's admonitions last winter in the wood as they were shooting. She had told him then that he was selfish to think himself the only sufferer, and he saw again how she had been right. In his self-pity, he had turned Emily's burdens into a grievance to himself, and in doing so had enlarged her burden. He was chastened, not only by his own weakness, but by her willingness to forgive him, and he resolved to do better.

Though the magic of the faerie clearing and their uninhibited discourse could not follow them into the Hall, Geoffrey found that from this time Emily was easier in his company, and he gradually came to be more and more at home, determined that his love for her must learn to be chivalric and nothing more.

Indeed, after a month, Emily—as she begged to be known to them all—had become so comfortable in the family circle that she no longer apologized for any inconvenience she felt she had placed upon them, and even twitted Francis on his new green coat, which she said quite took her breath away. Mrs. Mantell, having jerked out of an abstraction, primly agreed to this, wondering aloud what the Colonel would have thought of his son's frippery taste, and Francis replied that he cared not a button. Then he stunned them all by saying he meant to wear it at the Banfield's ball Tuesday sennight, and would Emily give him the honor of the first dance?

Emily sat motionless as all eyes in the room went to her. Geoffrey half expected her to subside into mortified blushes, but after a ruminative pause, she said in her quiet way, "If you will promise not to wince if I tread on your toes, then yes, I will, Francis."

Francis's answering grin broke the tension in the room, and the family began chatting about the upcoming ball, to which they all planned to go. Geoffrey alone held any reservations regarding the treat, for he had only just learned to trust himself in the same room with her, where he could admire her from several feet away. Not only did she look well, both from improved health and from superior society, but her gentle presence had become almost indispensable to his own happiness, and he knew not how he would react to hold her hands in a country dance, or—terrors!—to feel her in his arms in a waltz.

Thus it was with a painful mixture of excitement and dread that Geoffrey accompanied his mother, brother, sister, and guest to the Banfield's villa on the night of the ball. Emily too, it seemed, suffered some anxiety, for though she had stated her perfect willingness to attend, and had practiced the steps in the drawing room, and even acquiesced to Clara's insistence that she borrow one of her gowns, she grasped Clara's arm with trembling fingers, and her eyes were as wide as a child's as she entered the ballroom. Geoffrey wished to be the one to soothe her, but knew it ought not to be, and so excused himself upon entering the ballroom to mingle with his friends.

Clara took Emily's enjoyment into her own hands, introducing her to a few of her acquaintance who could be trusted neither to overwhelm her nor to look upon her as an oddity. This approach answered so well that by the time the first set was being formed, Emily had a partner for the next set but one, having reserved the second set as a reprieve to herself, in case she should be fatigued. As she entered the first set with Francis, however, her chin was held well up, and her partner had no cause to hide a wince from his feet being trodden on.

Indeed, thought Geoffrey, watching her progress down the line from his vantage point in the next set, she seemed to take greater enjoyment as the night wore on, and to greet each new partner with a glow of spirits he had seen only in the faerie clearing. He had long known that her reserve hid a bright, joyful woman, and he was at first inclined to be jealous of the secret's getting out. But a recollection that she was not his to be jealous of soon put flight to that emotion, and he was instead so fascinated by her inherent loveliness that he forgot his resolution to keep her at arms' length and requested her hand in a dance.

He was at leisure to consider his rashness during the interval of rest before their dance, and to feel all the anxiety at the probable outcome—that he would betray his feelings and she would be wounded beyond recovery. So terrified was he of this engagement that he sought refuge at the refreshment table, and was embarking upon his second glass of champagne when a hearty voice sounded over his shoulder.

"Steady, my boy, or you'll not have the wits to stand up with anyone, let alone that sweet Mrs. Crowther."

Geoffrey turned to find Mr. Noyce leaning on his crutches at his elbow. "Pardon me, sir, but it is composure I want and not soberness if I'm to manage at all. Do not be anxious; I don't mean to over-indulge. I'm sensible that I'm nothing to my father, who could drink three bottles of port at a sitting and still be as grave as a judge."

Mr. Noyce readily agreed he was nothing like his father, saying, "I'd approach the lady myself, if I'd two legs willing, for she's always been a favorite with me. I had not thought to see her at a ball such as this. How comes it to be?"

"Providence and Clara's forceful personality, sir," replied Geoffrey, his eyes finding his sister chatting to Emily nearby. "She carries all before her, heedless of the inclination of her victims."

"Don't you wish to dance with Mrs. Crowther?" inquired Mr. Noyce, watching him steadily.

Geoffrey swallowed more champagne, his eyes fixed on Emily, whose hair Clara's maid had styled in ringlets cascading from a knot on the top of her head, with one trailing down the side of her neck. She smiled at something Clara had said, and the beauty of her luminous eyes made his heart beat a frantic tattoo in his chest.

"The unattainable prize, and you must dance with her," said Mr. Noyce quietly, following his gaze. "It's like facing death, I'll be bound, but a soldier like you ought to manage it, and remember why you do it. She's worth every moment of heartache, sir."

Geoffrey tore his eyes from Emily to gaze at his companion, whose percipience had begun to unnerve him, but before he could resolve whether to thank him or refute his words, his mother's voice turned him about.

"There you are, Geoffrey," she said in a huff. "Good heavens, what a horrid squeeze this is! I can hardly catch my breath. I should not have thought Althea Banfield capable of such a triumph, but such it is, and I must commend her. Bless me!" she cried, snatching the glass from Geoffrey's lips. "How can you swallow this stuff? It is one thing to gather all the great and low together at once, but quite another to serve them terrible wine. If your father had tasted such stuff from our cellars, he should have ordered it destroyed instantly! But Lord Banfield was ever indiscriminate. The Colonel always said it was because he preferred rum, but I would not know."

Her gaze slipped past Geoffrey and she executed a start. "Oh! Mr. Noyce! I had not perceived you there! Dear me! How rude you must think me." Smiling dazzlingly, she held out a hand to him, which he took and bowed over with the grace of a courtier. Her eyes glistened and, blinking quickly, she said, "How long it has been, sir, since we have been in company!"

"Yes, ma'am, for though I have received innumerable baskets from your emissaries, I do not think we have met since before your honored husband died. No, no, I mistake—I had forgotten our meeting in the street some weeks past."

Mrs. Mantell colored deeply, her eyes flitting everywhere but his face. "Oh, that! You will forgive me, for I was unwell, and scarcely recollect it! I beg you will forget all about it—so stupid of me! Well! It has been lovely to see you again, sir. Good evening! Geoffrey, your dance is about to begin."

She went away, not looking back, and Geoffrey, blinking at her, came to himself with a start only when Mr. Noyce nudged his arm, indicating that the set had begun to form and his partner awaited him.

Gathering his resolve, Geoffrey closed the distance between Emily and himself and, bowing, took her hand to lead her into the set. He felt her fingers trembling within his own, and glancing quickly at her, noted the paleness of her cheek and the tightness of her lips.

Commanding his own anxiety, he smiled down at her, pressing her hand. "You are all kindness in allowing me this dance."

She returned his smile and the pressure of his hand, and her shoulders straightened. They took their places and Geoffrey, having done what he could for Emily, now did what he could for himself, and was able, during the bustle of the other couples joining them, to bring himself to that state of detachment he had learned to achieve before each of the battles on the Peninsula.

The music commenced and their eyes met, and Geoffrey's determined smile was returned by Emily. They went through the steps of the dance almost automatically at first, but gradually seemed to gain a measure of tranquility, and within a few minutes were able to show real pleasure.

"Are you enjoying yourself tonight, Emily?" he then asked.

"Very much."

"I am glad you consented to come. I hope that Clara did not press you too much to do it."

"It was not her doing. When Francis was so obliging as to ask me for the first two dances, I felt a sudden resolve to do something bold. So I accepted him, and was obliged to abide by the consequences."

"They are not too disagreeable, I hope."

She glanced warmly up at him. "Oh, no. It is a breath of fresh air, almost as if our faerie clearing has made its way into this ballroom. I can almost believe myself to be just like any other woman."

"You will never be like them," he said, with feeling. Then, seeing her quick, searching look, added hastily, "I know you far too well to compare you with the generality of females."

A blush overspread her cheeks and she averted her eyes, and Geoffrey cursed his unguarded tongue. Further conversation was interrupted by the movement of the dance, and Geoffrey fought to gather the remnants of his crumbling self-control.

"You dance very well," he said, in as conversational a tone as he could manage. "Were you used to attend assemblies in London?"

"Oh, no." Again, she colored and looked away. "I learned to dance at school, but had never put my tuition into practice. Clara insisted that we go over the steps together, and I am glad that she did, for I should never have had the courage to go through with it if she had not."

"Then I am indebted not only to you, but to both Francis and Clara, for enabling me to enjoy this dance with you."

The look that she gave him was at once full of pleasure and pain, and he was obliged to swallow down his own emotion. That a girl as lovely as she must be held back from happiness by the odious circumstances of her life was almost more than he could bear. If only he stood in a position to relieve her burdens, and to make her happy—but he did not, and would not, as long as Crowther lived.

Their dance ended, and the rest of the evening passed in somewhat of a blur, for Geoffrey, once the thought of Crowther's demise had entered his head, could not get it out. His recent inquiries into poison filled his brain with all manner of evil ideas, and it was only after great exertion and many more glasses of champagne that he was able to dismiss the insidious conviction from his mind that a man such as Crowther, who cared more for riches and consequence than for his own wife, deserved to die.

❧

After two months, Crowther called Emily home, but before another week was out, Clara received a note from Chandry Manor.

"It is from Emily!" she cried, pulling open the seal. She perused it quickly, her expression changing from eagerness to confusion. "We are all of us invited to dinner. Mother and Francis and you and I. How odd."

She gazed away from the letter, pondering, and Geoffrey twitched it from her fingers. "It is not so odd when Emily has now been introduced into society." He set the letter on the table and stared at it, troubled. "Crowther has long desired to capitalize on Emily's social standing. I only hope he does not force her to it."

"Perhaps he has discovered a hoard of treasure and is putting on airs," sniffed Clara.

Geoffrey cast her a disapproving look but was thoughtful some moments longer. "We must accept."

"Certainly we must accept! Emily would be mortified if we did not." She glanced quickly at him over her teacup. "If you expect me to believe you do not feel equal to it, Geoff, after having Emily in the house for two months, I wash my hands of you."

Geoffrey denied anything like discomfort, and even expressed some excitement at the prospect of enjoying Mrs. Crowther's hospitality, to which Clara haughtily approved and the discussion closed. In the event, Clara and Geoffrey were the only ones who set out on the day appointed, for Francis had other engagements, and their mother declared herself unwell and disinclined for society, a circumstance which had occurred more and more often.

On this occasion, Geoffrey's mind was too full of Emily to dwell much upon his mother's malady, and he could only hope that his good breeding would carry him through the evening. Both Mr. and

Mrs. Crowther welcomed their guests, Emily with gentle reserve and Crowther with his usual heartiness. But nothing untoward passed during the dinner, and after the ladies had retired, Crowther was most civil over port, even suggesting to Geoffrey the early closure of their *tete-a-tete* in order that they may rejoin the ladies in good time.

"Almost, he seems a different creature," murmured Geoffrey to Clara over their tea.

"As much as a snake can resemble a toad, I suppose," responded his cynical sister.

When they rose to take their leave, Emily accompanied them both to the door, stepping out onto the porch to smile her gratitude without the leering presence of her husband over her shoulder.

Geoffrey and Clara had much to discuss on the drive home.

"I cannot conceive of what he can be up to," began Clara, as soon as they were past the lodge gates.

Geoffrey looked wryly at her. "Cannot you? Has your prodigious imagination failed you at last?"

With a withering glance, she said, "Depend upon it, he is up to something, and we ought to try if we may find it out. If not for our own sakes, for Emily's."

"He merely is making his way into society, Clara, as I have told you before."

"But he did not make the attempt before their return from London. What can he be about, do you think?"

"I do not believe it matters, for Emily was as happy tonight, almost, as during her stay with us—there can be no two opinions on that point. And there can be no two opinions that it is good that she be happy, no matter the motive."

"Perhaps," allowed his sister, eying him askance. "However, I believe you are excessively poor-spirited, not to wish to do all in your power to get to the bottom of this mystery."

Geoffrey pulled up his pair in the middle of the road and turned to gaze sternly at his sister. "There is no mystery, Clara. I wish you will cease insisting there is, for if I were to believe Emily were in danger, I should go mad."

Clara blinked at him and he continued in a gentler tone. "I must believe that she will be safe enough, for it is all the comfort I have."

Averting her eyes, Clara said a little glumly, "Very well. But I will keep a weather eye open."

"To be sure," said Geoffrey, urging up his team and continuing home.

Interactions with Chandry Manor became regular after this night, and even Mrs. Mantell had occasion to welcome the Crowthers into her drawing room and saloon. Emily was additionally encouraged—or allowed, depending on the way one wished to look at it—to be of the Mantell party at various gatherings in the neighborhood, to which Clara was assiduous in gaining her invitations after it was borne in upon her that Crowther truly wished her to mix more generally in society. When Emily protested that she ought not to be putting them continually to the trouble of sending their carriage for her, Clara silenced all argument by pointing out that, as a single young woman, she must have a chaperon when her mother was disinclined for society, thus Emily would make her the obliged.

Geoffrey was in a quandary, for their intercourse with Chandry Manor had become so friendly, and Emily's manner subsequently so cheerful, that he really believed Crowther had come to a realization of his duty as a husband, and meant to make his wife happy. His emotions on this conviction were so disparate as to cause him some pain, for he wished nothing more than for Emily's happiness, but he had insensibly counted it his own privilege to make her so. His brain told him this had never been the case, and that he was a clodpole of the first degree to ever fancy it, but his heart had always cherished the hope that she would somehow be his, even if only in the way of the knight errant to his lady—in chivalrous performances only. That Crowther would be credited with Emily's happiness grated sorely against him, and he fought strenuously to suppress his desire to believe Clara's ongoing conviction that the man was up to something, for once he gave in to that, it was only a step to losing both his head and his honor, he feared.

After two gloriously painful months, however, a distracted note from Emily put flight to all his restraint.

> *Geoffrey (crossed out) Captain Mantell,*
>
> *Please forgive the familiarity with which I write this, but I can hardly think. I have but a moment, for this note must go by the carter or all is lost. I must speak to you. Will you, can you meet me in the faerie clearing at once? I pray you can, for else I do not know what I will do.*
>
> *In haste,*
>
> *Emily Crowther*

Chapter 25

GEOFFREY LOST NO time in donning his coat and hat and slipping out the side door and into the wood. His heart beat fast in his chest and he scarcely perceived his surroundings as he ran at full speed to the clearing, fearing what he may find there. Horrid images of Crowther giving Emily violence, or threatening her with some terrible retribution for imagined offenses belied Clara's influence on his own thoughts, and he swore aloud.

Telling himself it could not be as he feared, he entered the clearing to find Emily, in a drab cloak with the hood thrown back, her hair in disarray and her cheeks tear-stained, pacing restlessly and wringing her hands. At his arrival, she stopped still, staring at him with such a look of despair that he lost all sense of decorum and took her into his arms, pressing her to him and murmuring comforts into her hair. She clung to him for several minutes, shaking with sobs, until at last, whether from exhaustion or from a renewed sense of their impropriety, she drew back from him and accepted his handkerchief in lieu of her bedraggled one.

"Thank you, Geoff—Captain Mantell."

"Emily, we are fast friends. Cannot you call me Geoffrey, as you have done these many weeks?"

She shook her head vehemently. "I cannot. I must not. There must never be any sort of familiarity between us again, for then Crowther's ends will be answered, and you will be undone."

"What do you mean?" Geoffrey urged, reaching a hand to her, but she stepped back, turning away. "What has Crowther done?"

"He has played us both for fools," she said, closing her eyes and swallowing painfully. "He sees our friendship—your kindness to me— and seeks to twist it and use it for his own evil purposes. Oh!" she cried, clutching at her cape and drawing it around her as if to shield herself. "I have been blind, and let him ensnare not only me, but you as well! You, who have ever been my friend! I could not live with myself if he were to hurt you!"

"Emily—Mrs. Crowther, I do not understand!" pleaded Geoffrey. "How could I be in danger? You must tell me what Crowther means to do."

She was some moments collecting herself, breathing deeply to do so, before she said in a flat, controlled tone, "I happened to overhear him talking to Snipson. He believes that you are not my friend, but my lover, and throws me together with you for the purpose of contriving our downfall." She pressed a hand against her forehead. "But it is absurd, preposterous even, and I shall tell him so a thousand times if he so much as hints at it again."

"Preposterous," repeated Geoffrey, stunned.

"Singularly, for nothing could be more proper than your attentions to me. Yet Snipson has been spying on us, to alert my husband if any of our actions merit suspicion. Crowther imagines it is only a matter of time before he will have proof of an indiscretion, and then he will serve you with the choice to be publicly charged with Criminal Conversation or to pay handsomely to keep him quiet."

Geoffrey turned away, numb, as much by her revelation regarding Crowther's plot as by her opinion of the absurdity of their being lovers.

"Pray forgive me, Captain!" said Emily, emotion again overcoming her. "I know him well—I ought to have seen that he was up to something. Indeed, I never felt quite comfortable with his complaisance at our friendship, but I wished so much—"

She stopped abruptly, and he raised a hand to wave away her protestation. "I am as much to blame as you, Mrs. Crowther."

They were both silent, then she said quietly behind him, "It is all in his imagination, Captain. You have never given me cause to believe you are anything more than my friend, and I have never expected it of you."

"Never?"

There was a pause. "Never."

He closed his eyes, breathing deeply against the sudden hollowness in his chest. Emily had never wished for his love, had never dreamed of it, and now was only too mortified that the hint of a deeper relationship than friendship could be thought to exist between them.

"What do you suggest be done?" he said, subdued.

She hesitated. "You must draw back from the acquaintance."

"You wish me to draw back?" he said, turning once more to face her.

She did not raise her eyes from her tightly clenched hands. "It is for the best. I will dearly miss your company, but Crowther must not harm you, on that I am determined."

"Surely I may still be your friend—"

"No!" she cried, her gaze urgently meeting his. "Please, Captain. You must draw back. It is the only way."

He gazed at her, his emotions suspended from pain. He noted the rigid set of her jaw, and thought absently how he had long known her to be possessed of a fierce determination, and that he loved her the more for it. He looked at her tousled hair, glinting in the slanted sunlight, and down to her interlaced fingers, so small and delicate. He saw the smudges on her gown where she had knelt in the clearing, working at their village. At last, he returned his gaze to her large gray eyes, whose luminosity was now almost feverish with intensity.

"Very well," he said. "I shall draw back from the acquaintance."

She blinked quickly as something like a shudder ran over her, and dropping her gaze she said, "It would be advisable as well for you to be seen to give your attentions to some—some other young lady."

He murmured in agreement and she hurried on, "You ought to, you know. You ought to be spending your time in finding a wife, and settling down, and producing fine grandchildren for your mother."

"Yes, perhaps that is what she has been pining for these many weeks," he managed to say at last.

She raised her eyes to his again, and he perceived that they were filled with tears. His heart leapt a little at the idea that perhaps she did love him, and wept for their parting, but he sternly repressed this notion, for of what use was it to hope? Her emotion could easily be put down to her mortification at what her husband had stooped to do.

Reaching suddenly behind her neck, she undid the clasp of the moonstone necklace and held it out to him. "Take this, I beg. I can no longer keep it, but no more can I bear to throw it away."

It winked in the sunlight, and he gazed at it dumbly until she said, "I fear it is what gave Crowther the notion that you—that you feel more for me than a friend. I must be rid of it."

He blinked, raising his hand to take the necklace, and placing it carefully in his pocket. "Well then."

"Well then," she repeated, her gaze once again refusing to meet his.

He put out his hand and she gave hers into it, and he noted how it trembled. Swallowing convulsively, he bent swiftly to kiss her fingers, then let them go.

"Good bye."

"Good bye," she said, clenching her hand into a fist at her chest and closing her eyes tightly.

He turned and compelled his feet to walk away from the clearing and into the wood, but rather than go home, he wandered unknowing for some hours, his thoughts a cacophony of pain and irony and regret. At last, when it grew too dim for him to see, he made his way back to the stream and returned to the Hall.

He went up to his room and sat numbly at his dressing table, pulling out the moon stone necklace and gazing at it. All its associated memories came jumbling into his mind, and he wished for a moment that he had never found the clearing, had never offered the stone, had never met Emily. Coiling the chain in his hand, he opened the lid of his dressing case and dropped the moon stone next to the heart stone and closed the box.

Rising quickly, he paced down the corridor and found his mother and sister in the small saloon, seated at separate employments. Mrs. Mantell was gazing out the window with a half-knotted fringe forgot in her lap, while Clara worked at a scrolled paper box on the table. With a glance at his mother, Geoffrey went to Clara, sitting heavily beside her.

"How good of you to return to us, Geoff," said Clara in a miffed undervoice. "I had it from the footman, oh, hours since, that you went out of the house like a shot after he gave you a letter. I considered coming after you, but foolishly believed that if you had anything exciting to tell, you would come instantly back to me. I hope you intend to reward my faith in you, or I shall never speak to you again."

Geoffrey ran a hand across his eyes. "Emily asked that I withdraw from her acquaintance, and begged me to put all my energies into finding a wife."

Clara's hands stilled and she turned to him with an incredulous gaze. "You're bamming me!"

"Clara, you really ought not to repeat all the phrases your imprudent swains utter in your presence," said Geoffrey impatiently. "No, I am not bamming you. She discovered that Crowther meant to catch us in Crim. Con., with the intent to blackmail or prosecute me, and she would not risk further interaction."

This revelation bereft Clara of speech, and it was some minutes before she was able to say, in a harsh whisper, "Well! And what did I tell you? Did not I suspect him of some villainy? Did not I say he was up to something?"

Geoffrey acknowledged her superior intelligence by settling back against the chair and crossing his arms over his chest, allowing her to run on.

"For anyone who knows Crowther must recognize that he never did anything but to benefit in some way. You imagined it was merely to insinuate himself through his wife into better society, but this—Oh! It goes beyond all bounds! And Emily! Oh, poor, dear Emily, to be forced to such an action. She was, I am persuaded, mortified in the extreme—to discover it, and then to be obliged to relay it to you! How awful for her."

She subsided into uneasy silence.

"Emily was mortified, but not precisely, it seems, for the cause you imagine," said Geoffrey quietly. "She was excessively affronted by Crowther's conviction that we were something more than friends."

Clara glanced quickly at him and he went on, "So you see I was mistaken in her feelings for me. She never loved me. She told me she had never hoped—" He swallowed down a sudden lump in his throat. "She has never wished for my affection."

"Geoffrey!" Clara put a hand on his arm. "I cannot credit it. Are you certain you did not mistake her meaning?'

He shook his head. "If you had seen her manner toward me—so horrified at the very idea of our being closer than friends that she could scarcely look at me—you would not ask."

"I am sorry," Clara sighed, her shoulders slumping. "So very sorry. But it is all for the best, I suppose. As it is, you may never wound her, and it is not so tragic that she married before you understood your own heart, for she would not have accepted you in any case."

Geoffrey shut his eyes against this poor comfort, but was forced to agree. It was for the best. He had loved in vain, and if Emily had never desired his love, then there was nothing to feed the hope that he had hidden so carefully in his heart, that someday, somehow she would be his. He ought now to be able to move on in earnest, to find his true love. But the notion did not console him. He had no heart for lovemaking if it could not be to the one woman he truly loved.

"I suppose you are right," he said with a sigh. "Perhaps I ought to return to Town."

She huffed. "Only if you take me with you, Geoffrey."

"But Emily needs you."

"Very well, sir," she said after a pause. "I do love Emily, despite her poor taste in men, and will stand her friend through thick and thin. But you will be the greatest beast in nature if you abandon me to go to Town."

"It will be very thin of company, Clara, hardly more exciting than here."

She pursed her lips. "You forget I have been to London, and even were none of my acquaintance there, I am persuaded I should get on very well. Dearest Geoffrey," she said, altering her tone, "please do not go away. With our mother acting so strangely, and Francis gone away to his horrid friends in Leicestershire, my situation really will be most pathetic. Please stay."

"You do understand that if I stay, I must make every effort to attach myself to a young lady."

"What young lady?"

He shrugged. "Miss Thornton is as good as any—I did like her once."

Clara rolled her eyes. "That will not do! If you think to forget Emily, your fancy must alight on a more worthy specimen than Arabella Thornton."

"She is most eligible," he offered.

"Well, I detest her."

"You did not seem to detest her last winter, when you and Mother all but threw her at my head."

"Perhaps 'detest' is too strong a word," she sniffed, "but now I am persuaded that I could never stomach such a flimsy intellect in my sister."

"Her intellect is hardly flimsy, Clara. She can be very thoughtful, and is very sweet."

Clara turned narrowed eyes upon him. "Stop there, I beg, or I shall be sick."

Geoffrey could not resist a laugh. "If you must know, I am well aware that it will not answer. I doubt very much if I am more than a fascination for her. She did not seek me out in London, though she was there for the Season, if I am not mistaken."

"Then of what use is it to pursue her, pray? For I can think only of one kind of use, and I distinctly remember having offended your honor by suggesting such an arrangement."

"Heaven preserve me from your worldly wisdom!" cried Geoffrey, rolling his eyes. "It would be nothing like that. I may not be able to marry her, but I can fulfill my promise to Emily."

"Fulfill your promise?" she exclaimed in an incredulous whisper. "In what possible way can your making love to a—a gilflirt fulfill your promise to Emily?"

Raising his brows at this cant phrase, Geoffrey glanced pointedly toward their mother, who sat at the other end of the saloon, absently knotting her fringe. Clara hunched an impatient shoulder and requested to be satisfied.

"It will be just the sort of mad flirtation you delight in, Clara. Indeed, you may be my tutor."

"And what if you make poor Miss Thornton fall in love with you?"

"Then you will assist in extricating me from her toils."

"If a man of your courage and experience is unequal to the task," she replied tartly, "then I suppose I shall be obliged to help you."

As it transpired, Clara's help was unnecessary. Miss Thornton, dazzled by a brilliant Season, had all but overcome her interest in the charming captain—which had merely grown out of his having soundly beaten her childhood tormentor, Shelby Frean, when they were boys. But faced with the prospect of being immured for the summer months in the country, she readily responded to Geoffrey's advances, and quickly gave him to understand that a flirtation—no more, no less—was what she desired.

Free of any guilt, Geoffrey did his part, and Clara, who saw no cause to cease her visits to Chandry Manor, was able to report on the success of his endeavors.

"Crowther is as sulky as a bear. He is back to his horrid habit of drinking far too much, though he does not join Emily and me in our visits—I am only privileged to smell him when he happens to be there to greet me. And he is back to ransacking the place. He is desperate to find anything that will ease his pecuniary discomfort. Well, I hope he works himself to death."

Geoffrey heard this in silence. "And how is Emily?"

"Emily seems a trifle grim, but she assures me she is well enough. She is often abstracted, which I teased her over, but she said only that she wonders why Sir Anthony went to such lengths. He has certainly revenged himself, for if his ploy does not drive Crowther into an early grave, I do not know what will. I have always said it is like a novel up at the Manor, but I vow I would never have credited Sir Anthony with the imagination to do anything so interesting."

"No, nor would I," mused Geoffrey.

"Emily never neglects to ask after you, Geoffrey," remarked Clara, eying him askance. "She seems peculiarly interested in your health, for a woman who cares nothing for you but as a friend."

"Clara! Please do not—" Geoffrey shook his head impatiently. "Much as I appreciate your motives in saying such things, it does not help me. Emily is lost to me, and I must accept it."

She huffed, pushing to her feet and tossing her head. "Well, I hope Crowther dies of apoplexy, and then what will you say to it?"

He was spared the effort of an answer by her flouncing from the room.

Chapter 26

The arrival of a letter from Emily after ten days apart from her immediately overturned Geoffrey's resolution. Clara found it in the pile of morning post and, after only a brief hesitation on seeing the handwriting of the sender, gave it over to Geoffrey. He took it somewhat warily, having noticed her hesitate, and gazed for some moments at the handwriting.

"I wonder what it can be about?" he said at last, slowly breaking the seal. "This does not look like her hand."

Clara raised her brows at this, and waited expectantly as he perused the note.

> *My dear Captain Mantell,*
>
> *I do not know what I can have done to drive you away, for I believed us to be the best of friends, and your protracted absence from my society has pained me exceedingly. Forgive me, I beg, any incivility which I may*

have shown you, for it was done unknowingly, and if I have given offense, it has been likewise. Will you not resume our friendship? For I have missed you terribly, and cannot be comfortable until either the cause of your retirement is known to me, or it is vanquished.

Yours in anguish,

Emily Crowther

Geoffrey gazed so long at this astonishing letter that Clara at last was obliged to take it from him in order that he may recover his wits while she read it.

"Good heavens!" she muttered at the end. "Can he think to deceive us by such a performance?"

"It cannot be Emily's hand," repeated Geoffrey.

"Certainly not. I remarked it instantly. But Crowther's rascally servant is just such a man as would agree to write something like this, only to lure you back into his master's clutches. Think, Geoff, he must despair of ever getting hands on those investments, and believes your inevitable indiscretion to be his next source of income."

Geoffrey blinked slowly, turning his thoughtful gaze to her. "But what must I do? Mrs. Crowther cannot be very comfortable in all this. If I do not respond, what will keep him from blaming her?"

Clara frowned, returning his steady gaze. "You must not write, for that could be used as evidence against you, but you may visit if I go with you. It would certainly lessen his cause to blame her. Would it pain you very much?"

"I do not know until I see her again."

"Then we will visit this morning, and get it over," she said briskly, rising and moving toward the door.

They arrived to find a post chaise and four standing ready on the drive in front of the Manor, with a trunk loaded on the back. As they approached the house, Crowther appeared in the doorway, blinking in the light until he recognized his visitors.

"Ah, Captain and Miss Mantell!" he cried, pulling on his gloves as he trundled down the steps, his oily grin splitting his face. "Well met! For I am off to London on urgent business—can't be helped! But now I may leave my poor Emily with a lighter heart, for I know her friends have not, as I had once believed, forsaken her."

This was said with a direct look at the captain, who did not reply as he shook Crowther's hand. Crowther turned to briefly bow to Miss Mantell, then expressing his apologies for his haste, recommended they go into the house and comfort his Emily as best they could. He was up and into the coach on the words, and the driver set the horses to almost before the coach door was shut.

The visitors did not gaze after their host long, but did as he recommended and went into the house, where Snipson directed them into the saloon. Emily was there, pacing in front of the fire. She stopped to greet her guests in a voice that was calm enough, but Geoffrey detected a trembling in the hand that was held out to him. He motioned her gently toward a chair.

"Please, sit, Mrs. Crowther. Surely you will increase your anxiety by pacing. Snipson, won't you bring your mistress some wine? Your husband will return shortly, Mrs. Crowther. No need to distress yourself on so slight an occurrence as a trip to London."

Emily, who had glanced quickly at him at the suggestion of wine, waited until Snipson had gone before making a reply. "I do not want wine, Captain. Indeed, I do not want anything that Snipson may give to me."

The firmness in her tone made Geoffrey look hard at her. "Has something occurred, Emily?"

"Snipson dropped something into my tea this morning at breakfast," she said, crossing her arms protectively over her chest. "You will think me mad, but so it is."

Her two visitors exchanged a speaking look before assuring her, as one, that they should never think her so.

"It is only what I have suspected all along," said Clara.

Emily's eyes closed, but she recounted the scene at breakfast, where Crowther had insisted she wanted sugar, and Snipson had instantly placed a lump into her cup, but Clara had seen a fine white powder sift from his hand at the same time.

"It was not an hallucination, I assure you," she said.

Geoffrey reached out to her, but thought better of it, pulling back his hand and saying, "We believe you, Mrs. Crowther. You need not be anxious on that head. Only tell us what you wish us to do for you. Do you wish for me to send Snipson away?"

"I do not know if it will answer, for Crowther will only recall him when he returns," she said, turning glittering eyes to him.

She was undoubtedly furious, a mood Geoffrey had never beheld in her. "What do you wish us to do?" he repeated.

Snipson entered at that moment, bearing a tray with wine in a glass. Geoffrey rose and took it from him, thanking him smilingly, and dismissing him. With a furtive glance at his mistress, and another at the captain, he withdrew.

Watching him depart, Emily said in a low tone, after the door was firmly shut, "I have had time to think, and I believe Snipson has been trying to poison me. Indeed, I believe he tried to poison me in London. My illness began there, and only worsened after we had returned home. I do not know why he should wish me dead, other than his extreme dedication to Crowther."

Clara sucked in a breath, whispering, "Of course they both are in it! Crowther has made no secret of his disappointment in your marriage. And you foiled his scheme to blackmail Geoffrey. He may have become convinced that his only hope to repair his fortune is to rid himself of you and take another wife—a rich one."

"Clara!" Geoffrey chided. "You are run away with—"

"This is not my imagination, Geoff! I read in the Monthly Museum how a woman made herself a widow seven times over, by poisoning each of her husbands only to get another. She was a very rich woman before they caught her!"

Emily's voice silenced them. "I do not know if Crowther is involved, but I know what I saw this morning. I will no longer trust Snipson."

With an oath, Geoffrey strode to the fire and tossed the wine in, where it hissed and steamed on the logs. "Why does Crowther go so urgently to London?"

"He found some documents last night, in a lock box in my father's bedchamber, well hidden under the floorboards. They seem to be deeds of investment and he is certain, from their location, that they are valid."

She suddenly swayed in her chair, her eyes rolling back in her head. Geoffrey leapt to catch her, lifting her in his arms and carrying her to the sofa, where he laid her with her head upon a pillow. Clara knelt beside her and took her hands, chafing them.

"Good God! Geoffrey, you do not think they have succeeded!" she cried.

Geoffrey could not answer, his whole attention on Emily, watching her shallow breaths and the frightening pallor of her face. She could not die—she could not! Her eyes fluttered and she blinked, and her companions gasped, watching her intently.

She sighed. "Forgive me. I am so distressed, and I have not dared eat."

Clara gripped her hands in patent relief, and Geoffrey, letting out a ragged breath, passed a hand over his face.

"Geoffrey!" cried Clara. "Why are you so stupid? Fetch something for Emily to eat!"

"On the instant," he said, adding quickly, "Your new cook-house-keeper—do you trust her?"

Emily nodded and with two strides, Geoffrey was at the door, wrenching it open. Snipson nearly toppled into the room, recovering himself at the last instant before colliding into Geoffrey's chest.

"Sir! I thought the missus would like some food. She ain't had nothing all morning, and—"

"I'll see to it, Snipson," said Geoffrey curtly, closing the door tightly behind himself. "Your mistress feels herself unequal to remaining alone while her husband is gone to Town. Please arrange for a portmanteau to be packed. She will be staying with us for several days."

With that, he swept past the startled servant and made his way to the servant's stair, descending into the nether regions in search of the cook-housekeeper. He found her at her ease in her apartment.

"Mrs. Patton, pardon my interrupting you in your sitting room, but your mistress is in need of sustenance, and quickly."

The cook-housekeeper, startled over her sherry, declared she was at the mistress's service, and inquired if he would condescend to be seated.

"Only if I may not be of assistance to you. Mrs. Crowther is very ill, and cannot be left waiting a moment too long."

Mrs. Patton jumped to her feet. "The poor dear, so put upon as she always has been. You go back upstairs and tell her I'll send up bread and tea just as soon as the water boils."

"No, ma'am. If you don't mind, I will stay and take it up with you."

She blinked at him, but said she was agreeable. "If you will fetch me that loaf there, and poke about in the larder for some cheese, sir, the tray'll be ready in two shakes of a lamb's tail."

True to her word, Mrs. Patton put together as hearty a meal as could be done in five minutes, and she and Geoffrey brought it to the saloon, where Clara took it upon herself to minister to Emily. Geoffrey, whose mind had been working, followed Mrs. Patton back down to the kitchen.

"Mrs. Patton, I trust you will not think me very odd, for all I have a very odd question to put to you: what do you use to kill rats?"

She blinked at him, demanding to be told whether he had seen a rat in the upstairs rooms, but when she had been reassured on this head, she answered readily enough. "We does it with arsenic, of course, sir. Some will bludgeon the vermin to death, but I don't hold with violence, and in this house there's only Marsden and Snipson, and I don't need to tell you they neither of them's up to such a deed. So I sends to the apothecary for arsenic, and bait some cheese in the larder with it."

"May I see it?"

Having the arsenic close at hand, she gladly showed it to him. It was a fine white powder, with a tendency to clump.

He rubbed it between his fingers, letting it sift back into the packet. "How much do you use?"

"No more'n a pinch or two."

"And the rats do not notice it?" he asked.

"Oh, no, they can't taste it. It hasn't a flavor, or smell, you know, for I've tested it."

"You've taken arsenic, to no harm?" the captain asked, watching her keenly.

"Certainly! It don't harm us, only rats. My husband, God rest him, had all sorts of preparations made with arsenic, for it's good for the human constitution, in small doses. Though it didn't help him, poor soul. Bad liver," she said confidentially. "Never did feel comfortable after he ate, no matter how many powders he took."

Geoffrey digested this. "Fascinating—but for your poor husband's condition, that is. Thank you for your information, Mrs. Patton." He turned to go, but bethought himself of one more thing. "Mrs. Patton, I wonder if you would do something for me. Would you mind very much keeping that arsenic in a safe place, and not to allow anyone else to use it?"

She agreed, and leaving the cook-housekeeper to shrug her shoulders at the oddities of the Quality, Geoffrey returned to the saloon. He found the door locked and tapped lightly, calling to Clara to open to him. She came directly, closing and locking the door again, and stuffing a handkerchief into the keyhole for good measure.

"That rat-faced servant will not spy on us again," she declared, returning to her place beside Emily.

Clara had set the tray on a table near the sofa, and had been engaged in feeding Emily strips of bread in between sips of tea. Emily's color had significantly improved, and she looked up when Geoffrey pulled a chair close to her side.

"I have told Snipson that you will be coming to stay at Gracely Hall for several days," he said. "I hope you do not mind, Clara."

"Mind?" she cried. "I had already determined upon it, even if we had to spirit her away from this place."

"Thank you," murmured Emily. "It will give me great comfort not to be in Snipson's power. However, I fear that Crowther may think too much of it." She did not say more, but Geoffrey saw the color rising into her cheeks at the very thought of what her husband had plotted to do.

"Do not fear. I shall remove to Simpford's, if necessary. But I do not believe such an exigency will present itself. Clara and my mother are constantly in the house, and Clara shall never leave your side."

"Certainly, Emily," put in Clara. "Depend upon it, your odious husband shall have no opportunity for vexing you in that manner."

"Yes," said Emily, sitting up. "He shall not vex me again, for I mean to beat him at his game."

Chapter 27

A TAPPING ON THE door drew their attention, and Geoffrey went to open it. Snipson stood there, Emily's maid behind.

"Madam's portmanteau, sir," he said, with a sour look.

"Thank you, Snipson. We will go when she is recovered enough."

"I am ready now, Captain," said Emily, rising to corroborate this. Clara stood beside her, taking her arm.

Geoffrey was about to argue, but saw the stubborn jut of Emily's chin and, agreeing inwardly that the sooner she got out of Chandry Manor the better, turned to Snipson and said, "Please order the carriage."

As soon as they were out of the rutted lane and on the road, Emily relaxed, leaning her head on Clara's shoulder. "Thank you," she said simply.

They arrived at the Hall, and once again Geoffrey relayed the news of their unexpected guest's arrival to his mother, who merely eyed him narrowly and gave her permission. Clara saw Emily's things settled in her old room, and then took her to the drawing room, where they met Geoffrey.

"There must be a way to prove Snipson put poison into your tea," declared Clara almost as soon as they had sat down. "If that could be done, he would be taken by the magistrate and tried for attempted murder."

"The tea is no doubt thrown out now, my dear," said Emily, her hands fidgeting in her lap. "But it is no matter. I believe he is frightened by your speedy action in getting me away."

"He may think the game is up and fly," said Clara, "and then we do not know what he would do!"

"Clara, he cannot harm Emily while she is with us," put in Geoffrey.

Emily stood and began pacing. "Yes, but I cannot stay here forever. I will not go back to Chandry Manor, for as long as Crowther trusts him, Snipson will have a place with him. I must find a way to convince Crowther to let Snipson go, or allow me to live apart."

"It may be simpler to request a separation than to deprive him of his loyal henchman," pointed out Geoffrey. "Crowther does not seem to require your presence for much more than social advancement, but he does rely almost entirely on Snipson."

"Yes," said Emily. "That is why we must find out what my father did with the money from those investments. I know it is somewhere, for he was always a shrewd businessman, and would never lose or squander it."

"You do not think those documents valid that Crowther carries to London?" asked Geoffrey.

"I am almost certain of it, and that my father reinvested the money in something even more secure, though it seems incredible," said

Emily, resuming her seat on the sofa. "In the weeks before my father died, as I tended him, he became very thoughtful and restless. He spoke to me almost kindly—he had never been kind, and so did not know how to be, but he meant well. And as I told you, he forgave me for my elopement. That was the most shocking thing, for my marriage had turned out to be nothing less than a betrayal. But he said he knew I was innocent, and had been deceived, and he no longer blamed me."

She gazed into the distance as she spoke. "He grew worse and worse, and near the end he lost his reason—or so I thought. He would grasp my hand and pull me close to him, his eyes burning into mine, and say things that meant nothing to me at the time, for they were only nonsense, but now they begin to be clearer."

Clara's eyes were fixed on Emily, her mouth open in disbelief. "A deathbed confession! Oh, how disagreeable of him not to make himself plain. What did he say, Emily?"

"It was all so long ago, and I did not pay him much heed." Emily closed her eyes, clasping her hands in her lap as she tried to recall her father's words. "He ranted like a madman about my childhood, and that he 'had done it,' and that I was worth more than Crowther knew. Now I see he was trying to tell me something, without letting Crowther or Snipson know what he meant, for they continually spied upon us. Only his communications were too cryptic even for me to make sense of."

"You believe he was speaking about the investments?" breathed Clara.

Emily sighed, "Yes, but try as I might, I cannot decipher his meaning. He spoke of my cleverness as a child, in making my own games and toys—"

"The nursery!" cried Clara, jumping up. "We must look there!"

"Crowther has already done so," said Emily, "During my visit here. He also has searched my room, in the guise of refurbishing it."

While Clara made disgusted noises at this violation of feminine dignity, Geoffrey moved from his station at the fireplace to sit beside Emily on the sofa. "Then there must be some other clue. Think, Emily. What else did your father say?"

"He said that where I was, his treasure was also. But I lived in London—do you think the documents could be there?"

"If he wished to hide them from Crowther, he could not choose a better place, for London is a large city; however, it does not seem likely, for you would have just as much trouble as your husband in finding them. Unless he gave you some sort of clue as to where."

Emily shook her head. "He gave no names or places or even hints as to something like that. And he never stirred from the Manor after my marriage. All his business dealings he carried out from here." She rubbed the spot between her eyes. "I've gone over and over my memories and can recall nothing more specific. My cleverness, my games, his treasure."

"What if he did not reinvest the money?" inquired Clara, her eyes gleaming. "What fun if there is a treasure trove of gold or jewels hidden somewhere about the property?"

Geoffrey opened his mouth to chide her, for he was of the opinion that she was enjoying herself far too much in the business, but Emily looked gratefully at her.

"My dearest Clara, I am so glad you are here. Your lightheartedness is just what I need to keep from becoming maudlin. It is ridiculously like a romance, is not it? And the wonder is that my father was the author of it!"

"Then you do not think he kept the money about him?" said Geoffrey.

Emily shook her head again. "No, for if Crowther's estimation of the value of those investments is correct, it would be so large a pile of gold or jewels as to be impossible to hide. It could only have been put back into properties, or into new investments."

"Then we are looking still for documents, which could be hidden in almost any small space in the house."

Sighing, Emily acknowledged this, and Clara wrinkled her nose. "It would have been so much more romantic if the treasure had been buried, like a pirate's trove. However, we should never find it, I am persuaded, for your property is every bit as extensive as ours."

"At least in that event, Crowther should have as little luck as we seem to be having," said Emily, with the ghost of a smile.

Geoffrey lifted a finger, his expression thoughtful. "Emily, did your father know of the faerie clearing?"

She looked at him in surprise. "No, not at all. I never told him of it, and he never asked me where I went. He knew only that I walked about the wood."

"And yet, if I am not mistaken, that is where you passed the majority of your childhood hours, and where the cleverest of your games were played."

She gazed keenly at him, her eyes focusing beyond him, in the realm of possibility. "I am persuaded he never knew of the clearing before my marriage, but I was away for more than two years afterward. It is possible that he discovered it during that time." Then she shook her head. "It does not make sense! My father's desire for revenge included me all the while he was buying and selling and investing after my marriage. He did not experience a revulsion of feeling until just weeks before his death. How could he have arranged anything when he was sick in bed?"

"Did he never leave his bed?" inquired Geoffrey. "The day I called on you, when he fell ill in my arms, you said he had got away from Snipson—"

"Good heaven, yes! That was the second time. He had done so previously, and had got outside, for we found him wandering in the back garden. He seemed particularly gleeful, too, and it was soon after that he began speaking riddles to me."

Clara squeaked, pressing her hands over her mouth. She bent toward Emily and said, her eyes bright, "I fancy we must take a walk in the wood."

They went directly to the gardener's shed and retrieved a shovel before setting off over the lawn to the wood. As they trod the well-worn path, Geoffrey's pulses quickened with both anxiety and exhilaration. If they found what they were seeking, Emily could possibly barter for a sort of freedom from Crowther; however, then she would go away to live in seclusion, and though he knew he ought to rejoice in the prospect, he could not.

"If we find the treasure in this clearing of yours, Geoffrey," said Clara as she jumped nimbly over the stream, "then perhaps I shall finally forgive you for deceiving me three years and a half ago."

Emily, receiving gratefully Geoffrey's assistance over the stream, inquired as to the possibility of his ever deceiving anyone in his life, and Clara turned to regard them both, her gaze becoming speculative. Geoffrey was instantly wary.

With an impish sparkle in her eye, Clara continued on her way, saying carelessly, "Before he left for Belgium, he came often to the wood, and we were all of us convinced he was meeting a lady clandestinely."

Emily's color rose, and Geoffrey begged Clara to hush, but she went brazenly on. "As you know, I prefer action to conjecture, so I went into the wood, determined upon finding his lady love and talking some sense into her. However, I found the faerie clearing instead."

Emily looked up at that and Clara, with a secret smile, continued.

"Geoffrey shamelessly allowed me to believe the faerie village to be his creation alone, which I suppose was honorable and all that, for I was obliged to discard the notion of clandestine meetings," she said airily. "However, circumstances eventually forced him to reveal to me the existence of a co-creator."

"What circumstances?" inquired Emily, with a quick glance at Geoffrey.

Clara, with a flash of triumph in her blue eyes, answered blithely, "He requested me to deposit a letter for you in the post office—while he was abroad, you know." She skipped ahead of them, saying casually over her shoulder, "An important letter."

Geoffrey, who did not know where to look, gestured civilly for Emily to go before him, wondering if murder of one's sister could be thought justified, in the face of such provocation. It was barefaced treachery to reveal to Emily the existence of his letter, the contents of which she had herself instructed him must be carefully guarded from Emily's knowledge.

As Clara disappeared into the wood, Emily observed with downcast eyes, "I suppose this was after I was married, for I received no letter."

He cleared his throat. "No, it did not reach you."

There was a pause, during which Geoffrey's heart thudded in his ears.

"I do not suppose you would wish to relate to me the substance of the letter?"

He opened his mouth, shut it again, pulled at his collar, and then said, "It was moot, by the time I had written it. You need not regard it."

"I see," she murmured. "After I was married."

"Yes, about that time, I do not precisely recall—" Looking everywhere but at Emily, he said, a trifle to loudly, "This affair with your father has been so surprising, I do not know if I am on my head or my heels. To think that all this while, we may have been sitting on the key to your future happiness."

She paced beside him, a thoughtful look on her face. "The clearing has always held the key to my happiness, so the notion is not so fantastic to me."

Geoffrey's agitation was too great to consider her words, and he merely suggested they hurry along. They reached the clearing just behind Clara, who was bent almost double as she searched the ground for any indication of buried treasure.

"I fear we shall be obliged to dig up all this area. I cannot perceive anything like disturbed earth."

"Geoffrey and I have been frequently here, trampling the ground, I fear," said Emily.

"I came here in the days after Sir Anthony fell ill," said Geoffrey. "The village was in disorder, but I imagined it to be no more so than when I had come formerly. But there was something odd— if I can only recall—the post office! There was a deal of dirt turned up about the post office. I thought it was an animal that had dug under it."

Clara fell to her knees to remove the post office, clearing the space around it. "Here, Geoff! Dig just here!"

Scrambling out of the way, she watched as her brother thrust the shovel into the ground and turned up the earth, over and over. Clutching Emily's arm in excitement, she murmured, "Forgive me if I seem overeager, but this is such an adventure! I have anticipated that something extraordinary should happen ever since we first became friends and I sensed some mystery about the Manor, but never did I imagine hidden treasure, and such intrigue!"

Emily's reassurances were interrupted by a loud thunk made by the shovel in the now deep hole. Geoffrey scraped and dug a bit more, then went to his knees to brush away the dirt, revealing a wooden box, black with damp. Clara squealed with excitement and Emily knelt beside the hole, assisting Geoffrey as he dug away the dirt around the box, which proved to be quite small. Wedging the shovel between the box and the side of the hole, Geoffrey gave a mighty heave, and the box lifted free.

Emily helped him to lift the box from the hole and place it on the ground. Laying the shovel down, Geoffrey knelt beside her and Clara, who were gazing in amazement at their discovery.

Geoffrey gestured to the box. "It is your treasure, Emily."

She bit her lip. "It is Crowther's, by law, if he discovers its existence."

Nevertheless, she reached out and pried the lid off the box, setting it to the side. Inside was an oilskin packet which, when opened, contained the deeds to three properties—the names of which, Clara maintained, sounded expensive—and several shares of stock.

Geoffrey read the documents with interest. "These names— Holbrook Heath—the Holbrook Mine was on the list of investments Mr. Adkins, my Runner, discovered. He said it was abandoned, but apparently the land still has great value. And these shares in Frampton's Patent Gear—it must have been Frampton's Corn Cycler, which was a failure. I'm much mistaken if the Corn Cycler was not turned to better purpose as a Gear, and these shares are worth quite a lot."

He turned to Emily. "Sir Anthony was not only leading Crowther a dance, he was hiding his fortune where no one would think to look for it, except with these documents. His investments seemed to be failures, but were in fact deviously hidden successes!"

Emily, after gazing over each document in bemusement, carefully returned them to the oilskin, staring at the packet for several long moments.

At last she raised her eyes to Geoffrey's. "Will you take them? Will you keep them safe for me? I do not know yet what to do, but if I know these are safe from Crowther, I can at least hope—" She took a deep breath. "I can at least plan for my future."

"Certainly," said Geoffrey, taking the packet and placing it in his coat. "We ought to rebury the box, I suppose, for that is what conspirators do, is not it?"

Clara, smiling on this notion, agreed, and they all helped to tamp down the dirt again and to spread leaves and twigs over the space so it looked untouched once more. Then, taking an arm of each lady, Geoffrey led them from the clearing and back to the Hall.

Chapter 28

WITH THE DISCOVERY of the documents, Emily's agitation all but fled, and she settled into the flow of regular activity at Gracely Hall. After a sennight, however, her enjoyment was ended by the precipitate return of Mr. Crowther to Chandry Manor. The Mantells were apprised of it by the report of the upper maid, whose cousin was a potman at the village pub, that two casks of the finest Nantes brandy had been sent up to the Manor at Mr. Crowther's request. This news, though depriving them at an instant of much of their peace, only strengthened their resolve that Emily should stay out the fortnight, as planned.

A note from Crowther civilly requesting the return of his wife was answered by an equally civil note explaining that she was wanted for several entertainments that week, and so they simply could not do without her until the following Saturday. Another note arrived, less civil, and more insistent that Emily return posthaste to Chandry Manor.

"You will not go, Emily," said Clara, throwing down the note.

"Perhaps not now; however, as my husband, Crowther may require my obedience. Indeed, that is what I expect he will do, for he seems angry. He is very desperate for money, I am certain. The documents he found were, as we know, invalid."

"It is unfortunate for him, but you shall not be made to bear the brunt of his disappointment. We ought, perhaps, to pay him a visit," suggested Clara.

"But if I go, he will insist that I stay," said Emily.

Clara considered the matter, then said, "If Geoffrey and I accompany you, we may try what our influence may do. Crowther is still eager for our good opinion, I am persuaded."

After some hesitation, Emily agreed to the plan, and the following day they set out together in the sultry August weather toward Chandry Manor. They were bowed in as usual by a narrow-eyed Snipson and let themselves into the saloon.

Emily gazed about the room. "I hate this place. I have no fond memories but that are tarnished by the misery I have almost constantly experienced here. If I could leave it forever, I would."

Before either Clara or Geoffrey could respond, the door crashed open and Crowther stood on the threshold, swaying slightly, his bloodshot eyes taking in the scene before him. "What is this? I am told I have visitors, and come to find the wife of my bosom thus supported by her friends! It moves me beyond tears."

Geoffrey gazed in disgust at Crowther, fists clenching, while Clara put her arms about her friend's shoulders.

Crowther stumbled a few steps forward, his bleary eyes roving from one face to another. "Yes, you are forever in company, so I hear, and stuffing handkerchiefs into keyholes, and whispering secrets.

What friendship is this!" He lurched toward Geoffrey and punched a finger at his chest. "You claim you are not in love with my wife, and yet you will be so familiar as to take her hand and use her Christian name. I believe I know your ilk, sir!"

A muscle by Geoffrey's eye twitched, but beyond that, he made no response.

Emily, however, said, "Crowther, pray do not expose yourself in this manner. I have come to show you that I am in good hands at Gracely Hall, and to satisfy myself that you are in good health. I cannot do the latter, however, and encourage you to take better care when and how deeply you imbibe."

Crowther turned on Emily. "You are to blame for my shocking state, my dear! You and that devil of a father of yours—he set you on to trap me into marriage, just so he could torment me forever! Well, I won't have you living in good style at Gracely Hall while I waste away in poverty in this hulk of a house."

"She is not coming back, sir," said Clara, moving in front of Emily. "We cannot possibly give her up for another week at the least."

"But my dear Miss Mantell," said Crowther, as silkily as a drunken man could do, "I cannot possibly spare her until then. I must have her here, under my eye, for she is a cunning one. You do not know."

With a gentle but firm hand, he put Clara aside, gazing narrowly at Emily. "You like your secrets, don't you, my sweet? Whispering and smiling and going off to Gracely Hall. You knew just who you could trust when you came here, with Sir Anthony ailing. Such great friends as they are," he said with heavy sarcasm.

He reeled away, staggering about the room. "Poor Emily, losing a father to illness, and enjoying such ill health herself. He was raving before he went, did she tell you? Did she say how he raved about his treasure? At first I thought he was mad, then I discovered how he had cheated me, and then, oh then I saw just what he had done! Father and daughter, so alike, so enamored of their secrets! He choked and died on his, but she shall not die—" He had returned to Emily, and thrust his face close to hers, his eyes roving over her impassive countenance. "No, for she must tell me her secret."

She remained impassive, and he laughed, turning to Geoffrey. "Did she tell you he called her a treasure? He really was raving." He reached suddenly to grasp Emily by the shoulders and shook her. "He called this worthless piece of goods his treasure."

Clara cried out and Geoffrey came forward to pull him away, but Crowther shoved him back, shaking Emily again. "Nothing but an ugly, sneaking, trullish wh—"

He got no further, as Geoffrey whirled him around and felled him with a hard left to the jaw. He crashed to the floor, upending a small table, and lay there, senseless. Geoffrey stared down at him, breathing heavily as rage still colored his vision, until Emily drew a shuddering breath beside him, breaking the spell. With an effort, he blinked away his anger and, swearing under his breath, knelt to inspect the fallen man.

Crowther lay still where he had fallen, but other than a cut to his forehead from his fall and an abrasion to his right jaw from Geoffrey's fist, there seemed to be no other injury. Geoffrey turned him onto his back and watched his chest for movement.

"He lives," he observed grimly and stood up.

A cry sounded from the doorway, where Snipson had appeared, his eyes round. "You've killed him! You've done and killed the master!" he shrieked, advancing into the room with a shaking finger pointed at Geoffrey. "I knew you for a lying, sniveling cur, out to get what's rightfully my master's, but this is murder, and you'll hang for it, sure as fire!"

Geoffrey moved to confront him, but Emily stopped him with a hand against his chest. "No, Geoffrey. He is not killed, and so there is no crime."

"I'll go for the doctor," Geoffrey said.

But Snipson uttered another cry. "You'll not! He's murdered, and so I shall tell everyone! I'll summon the constable!"

"You'll do no such thing, Snipson." Emily's voice filled the room with surprising authority. "You see his chest rises and falls. He is still alive. He was drunken, as you well know, and lost his reason. He is likely only stunned, and will wake in the morning. Get Marsden to help you carry him to his bed. Captain Mantell will go for the doctor."

"I'll not! I'll go for the magistrate!"

"Snipson," said Emily, in a voice of steel, "Do what you must, but when you leave this house, you leave my service. I have tired of your sniveling, sneaking ways and have no more use for you."

Snipson glared at her, breathing heavily. "You've no authority! Crowther's my master!"

"Your master may be Crowther, but he is insensible, and I must be his deputy. Captain Mantell, will you be so good as to see Snipson off the premises?"

Snipson looked belligerent, but only muttered vitriolic curses on Captain Mantell as he swung round and out of the room. Geoffrey followed, and the sound of the front door closing echoed with finality through the house.

Geoffrey returned and went to Emily. "He is gone, but I do not know that he will stay away. Perhaps I ought to remain—"

"If you lend me some of your menservants to keep watch, all will be well," said Emily. "Now we must carry Crowther to his bed."

In answer, Geoffrey took the unconscious man under the arms and dragged him ungently out of the saloon, calling to Marsden for his assistance.

Clara came to Emily, taking her hand. "I will stay with you, Emily."

"No, my dear. There is nothing you may do here. I would not have you stay under this roof for any length of time. It is odious and horrible."

Clara attempted to convince her that she should delight to stay in a horrid, haunted mansion, but Emily was firm. "Please, go now. I must tend to my husband. There is no more you can do to help me, and your leaving now will be for the best, depend upon it."

Geoffrey came into the room and she turned to include him in her plea. "You have done more to help me these few months than you will ever know. I thank you, again and again, but go now. I shall be well."

"Well enough?" he said roughly.

Her luminous eyes raised once more to his, filled with determination. "No. I have hope for my future! Well enough shall never do again for me."

Clara moved to Geoffrey's side, taking his arm. "Yes, Geoff, it's best that we go now. We'll not be far, Emily, should you need us."

"We shall send some servants to guard you, Emily," he said, as Clara at last prevailed upon him to move.

He and Clara let themselves out the front door, and Geoffrey was obliged to hitch up his own cattle to the curricle, as Snipson had been the Crowther's groom. They got away quickly enough, however, and Geoffrey stopped only to let Clara down at Gracely Hall before driving himself into the village after the doctor. Mr. Sloan, being in, insisted on taking his own gig to the Manor, so as not to incommode the captain, and Geoffrey, having done everything in his power for Emily's sake, went home.

Mrs. Mantell, when apprised of the events at Chandry Manor, remarked briskly, "I hope he does not wake, for a more odious, encroaching, vulgar man I never met with. If he thinks he can go about with his red nose so high in the air, then he deserves such an end. He will not be missed by anybody, I daresay."

"Mother!" cried Clara. "You mustn't say such things! Geoffrey knocked him down, and if he dies, just think what that will mean for Geoffrey!"

"Pooh! A man does not die from some trifling fall."

"It was no trifling fall, madam, I assure you!" rejoined Clara, in misled defense of her brother's prowess.

Geoffrey, fully alive to all the implications of what had happened, and what may yet happen, inserted himself at this point to remind them both that Crowther had been very much alive when they had left him, and that they must hope, no matter how vile a man he was, that Geoffrey's violence had not unduly harmed him, and that he would survive the night.

A tense three days passed, with no word from Chandry Manor. The cook, however, whose sister lived next to Mr. Sloan in the village, reported that things looked very bad, for Mr. Crowther hadn't awoken, and was pale as death. A rumor started—circulated they had no doubt by Snipson—that "murder foul had been committed, and no one need look far for the villain what perpetrated it, though he called hisself a gentleman."

Then word reached Gracely Hall that Crowther had revived, but only to be gravely ill with brain fever, and the doctor had been to the

Manor to bleed his patient, in the hopes of reducing the pressure on the brain. When this was ineffective, purging was the next course of treatment, but dire whispers began to circulate that the blow to the head had occasioned this dreadful state, and if death followed, so he who had administered the blow would be a murderer.

Geoffrey's mental state was acutely painful, and he rode often in the fields to find relief. He did not dare go to the faerie clearing, or anywhere on Chandry Manor for that matter, as it caused him intense anxiety to be reminded of how much he had lost, and how much he could yet lose. At last, after five more days, a brief note was had from Emily:

> *Dearest friends,*
>
> *He is dead, and the doctor believes the brain fever to have been caused by the blow to the head occasioned by his fall. But have no fear. I go to London to bring down Crowther's doctor, and Mr. Adkins. Pray for my success!*
>
> *Emily Crowther*

As neither Clara nor Geoffrey could imagine what Crowther's doctor or Mr. Adkins could do to ameliorate Geoffrey's case, their prayers were with little faith. The next day, they sustained a visit from the village constable who, impressed with his own importance in this extraordinary case, could not be said to possess a conciliating manner toward Geoffrey.

"I've come merely to inform you, Captain Mantell, of the inquest opened on the question of Mr. Crowther's death. As you and Miss Mantell were witness to the, er—" Here he coughed, and continued with barely concealed smugness, "incident, you both will be required to give a deposition. I thereby issue you this summons, to appear before the coroner and his inquest."

"Certainly, sir," said Geoffrey, his jaw tight as he took the summons. "We've nothing to hide."

Brows raised, the constable informed Geoffrey that, as he was under suspicion of murder, he must not leave the country until the inquest was over. The constable turned and strode to his gig, whistling as he went, and Geoffrey, returning into the house, asked for his dinner to be sent up on a tray to his room.

Chapter 29

NOT ONLY DID Geoffrey remain in the country, he scarcely left his room during the two days preceding the inquest. His mind was fully occupied in speculation, regarding both his fate and that of Emily. Had she given a written deposition before she went to London? If she had, he did not doubt she had given it in his favor, but what good it would do, he could not tell. When seen in the light of Snipson's testimony, her veracity would be highly suspect. Snipson had every cause to blacken both their reputations, and would spare no effort, he was certain. Emily would be painted as an unfaithful wife, practically Geoffrey's mistress, while Geoffrey would be shown as nothing but a rogue and a rake. That he had been defending Emily may stand to his advantage; however, Geoffrey would not rely on this to sway the jury.

His only visitor, apart from Clara and his mother, was Mr. Noyce, who had been summoned to the jury, and came with sober countenance and shuffling gait to discuss the business.

"I could have hoped you were not involved, my boy, for a more decent young man one doesn't often find. I'd give my verdict today in your favor, for I'd bet my life there were extenuating circumstances; however, it can't be done, and so it's neither here nor there. No, no, don't tell me how it happened, for though there's no law against it, it'd just as well not be done, and I'd as soon hear your story at the inquest."

"Thank you, sir," said Geoffrey, moved by his support. "Do you happen to know who else has been appointed to the jury?"

"Those you'd expect—the squire and Mr. Thornton, and Mr. Crane at the Blue Pig. I can't imagine they'd rule unfairly, for they've known you for a good lad all your life. Lord Wraglain and young Mr. Simpford have been summoned as well, so you know they'll be for you. It's those from the surrounding boroughs that may be a problem. Murder don't often come in the way of these country gentlemen, and it might go to their heads, if they're not acquainted with you. They think nothing of a sentence of transportation for as little as poaching, whether the accused was feeding his starving family or not, and it might seem even more fitting in this case, to hear Snipson put it."

Geoffrey's jaw tightened. "Is his story so credible, sir?"

Mr. Noyce huffed. "Not a bit, but you never can tell what people will believe. He's a long-time servant, and what with his being turned out just after he witnessed the thing—well, I could have wished Mrs. Crowther had not been so precipitate."

"If you knew all, sir, you'd not think she'd been remotely precipitate. Snipson is a villain and a scoundrel, and means all sorts of harm."

Mr. Noyce's brows went up, but he merely shifted his weight in his chair. "I've some idea of that. He's whispering of an *affaire* between you and Mrs. Crowther. He must be incensed enough to want you hanged, for all the fuss he's kicked up."

Geoffrey blew out a breath. "It's a bleak prospect. The noose or Australia."

"Now, now, my boy, don't be blue-deviled!" said Mr. Noyce in a heartening tone. "Mrs. Crowther's got something up her sleeve. She's off to London, if you didn't hear, to bring down witnesses who knew Snipson, I'd wager. If she can prove his unsavory character, then his testimony won't be worth that."

Geoffrey greatly appreciated his kindness, but was not sanguine. "It may help my case to prove him untrustworthy, to be sure, but will it sway those who know nothing of my own character?"

Mr. Noyce shrugged. "With so much high emotion in the case, one never can tell. But if one fury can be vanquished, perhaps the rest will fall in line. We shall do all we can for you, Geoffrey—that's what Mrs. Crowther aims to do, and I with her. We'll not abandon you, depend upon it. You've more friends here than enemies."

Slumping in his chair, Geoffrey put a hand over his eyes. "I did not mean to kill him, though I was incredibly angry, Mr. Noyce. That day, if you had heard what he said to Mrs. Crowther—and I am not sorry I defended her, but what will be the cost?"

"Oh, my boy," said Mr. Noyce, laying his hand on Geoffrey's shoulder. "Love is never easy. But it is strong, where it is real, and that sort of connection has a power that is not easily broken. She will find a way to save you, I'm sure of it."

Geoffrey blinked at him, recalling Miss Breckinridge's words to that point, back in London—that a connection based on love was fastened at both ends. If he did not know that Emily's feelings for him were purely friendly, perhaps he could find comfort in this fine notion of love conquering all. But as things were, he felt nothing but uncertainty and dread. He had knocked a man down, and the man had died soon thereafter—there was not much to be said in his defense. Whether he had wished to kill Crowther or had done it accidentally, Crowther was still dead, and at Geoffrey's hand. Only the jury could decide what his motive was worth.

"All there is to do is to tell the truth, my boy, and trust to Providence," said Mr. Noyce, straightening. "Not much more you could do, anyhow."

There did not seem to be anything to say after that, and Mr. Noyce took his leave. Geoffrey accompanied him through the hall to the door, but they were met halfway by Mrs. Mantell, who bustled out from the breakfast room with a large basket in her arms.

She gave a well-feigned start at sight of them. "Oh, Geoffrey, Mr. Noyce! I had not thought to see you here. That is, Geoffrey, of course, lives here, but Mr. Noyce, you do not!"

She colored up to the roots of her hair as Mr. Noyce acknowledged the truth of this, but embarrassment did not deter her for long. Averting her eyes, she said, "You are here about that horrid inquest, no doubt, and I must thank you for being a support to Geoffrey. Did you know, these excellent pines are taken from our succession houses. Such a harvest as has been! And all our tenants declare they are sick of them—at least, they should if they were so rude as to say so, I am persuaded, though they are not—rude, that is. We have the best tenants imaginable, to be sure."

Mr. Noyce smilingly expressed his satisfaction with her good fortune and wished her a delightful morning, but she stayed him by the simple expedient of hastening before him and blocking his way to the door.

"Would you take them, Mr. Noyce?" she cried, thrusting the basket toward him with a beseeching look in her eyes. "I would be so grateful."

"I really could not presume—It may be seen as a bribe, you know."

"Nonsense! I insist! Truly, we have enough and to spare, and I would be so grateful to you—you must take them as a favor to me—as an old friend."

Mr. Noyce had seemed ready again to refuse, but that last moved him to take the basket into his hands. "You are too kind, Mrs. Mantell. And you know just the way to work upon one. I could not refuse such a friend as you have been."

She blinked quickly at this, her features covered in chagrin, then recollected that she blocked the door, and moved aside with a bow of the head. She went quietly away and Mr. Noyce, watching her retreat as he adjusted his hold on the basket, murmured, "A rose by any other name would smell just as sweet—but a friend? I do not know."

Geoffrey took the basket from him and accompanied him out the door, the canes clicking on the stone steps. Once Mr. Noyce had mounted, Geoffrey handed up the basket and returned to the house, going up to his room with a heavy heart.

Bless Emily, he thought, for going to such lengths to secure his release, but he did not see that anything could be done. From all he had heard, public opinion already was ranged against him, and even if it were not, the rumor that he and Emily had been entangled could not improve matters. Emily had been so long a cipher in their society that even her late acceptance into it might not be accounted in her favor. Scandal was exciting and enticing in so small a neighborhood, and he did not trust that the jurors, upstanding gentlemen though they were, could hold themselves entirely aloof from the general view.

A soft knock on the door interrupted these depressing thoughts, and at his invitation, Clara entered the room.

"I heard Mr. Noyce was come to see you," she said, crossing to sit beside him on the bed. "Did he have anything encouraging to say?"

After Geoffrey related the pertinent points of the recent conversation, she sighed. "I am persuaded Emily will do all she can, but we cannot be certain it will be enough. I must think long on my deposition!"

"I beg you to do nothing but tell the truth, Clara. You are a co-conspirator, after all, and any embroidery of the facts will not mend matters."

"Co-conspirator? I like the sound of that," she said, with a smirk. "I am more important than I knew. In that case, we ought to consider our depositions together, for they must match."

"If we tell the truth, they will match, Clara," said Geoffrey, casting her a long-suffering look.

She dropped her gaze. "Forgive me. I know this is a very serious business; however, I cannot make myself believe it to be, for I cannot but feel that you will be let off, somehow. Emily must succeed in her endeavor, whatever it is, and all the jurors will be made to see that it all had nothing whatever to do with you."

He tried to disabuse her mind on this point, but she merely shrugged and looked belligerent. "If you are convicted, it will be entirely unfair, Geoff. Crowther was an odious man, and it is my belief that God struck him down, and your hit—which was an excellent one, by the by, and I am so glad to have witnessed it—was merely a coincidence. Do not they say such things in an inquisition, that "by the visitation of God" he died? Indeed, he was offering violence to Emily, and if that is undeserving of death, I do not know what is!"

Abandoning the point, Geoffrey said, "It is nothing to the purpose, for what you and I think does not matter. It is the jury who will need to be convinced."

"Oh, I could knock some heads together on that jury—and I would, if I were a man! Lawrence Simpford came down from London as he was summoned, and only stays away from you because Shelby Frean claimed he would be fraternizing with the enemy! I told Lawrie he was chicken-hearted, but perhaps he cannot be blamed, for you could not conceive of the lies Shelby is telling about you! That you have always had a temper, and were a violent child, and were sent into the army to put your thirst for blood to good use! But it is all of a piece, for he was always the horridest boy. The poor squire can't know what to do with him—perhaps he should be sent into the army!"

She hopped down from the bed. "It is not as if you did not grow up here, and everybody knows you for the mildest, most correct boy in the world! And our military men are not bloodthirsty! Perhaps some are, but you cannot say the generality of them are, for none with whom we are acquainted are, and Father was not—only odiously pompous—and yet everyone is ready to believe that you are!"

"Everybody?" inquired Geoffrey, a trifle discomposed at this revelation.

Clara shrugged. "Well, perhaps not everybody, but the whole village can think of nothing else but this inquest, and wherever one turns, someone is tearing your character to shreds. It shall come to nothing, however, you may depend upon it. Mr. Noyce will take the jury in hand, I am persuaded, and has assured me he will move heaven and earth to get you off. You have nothing to worry you."

On that valediction, she kissed her brother's cheek and went to dress for dinner, leaving him uncertain whether she had heartened him or cast him even farther into despondency. Simpford's defection he was not sorry for, as he had rather be alone with his thoughts than be made to entertain others' thoughts as well. And he would not allow himself to believe that the majority of his neighbors could believe him bloodthirsty in the least. Shelby Frean's persistence in representing him so outrageously might even have the opposite effect on the jurors, many of whom had known both young men from the cradle, and could guess which one to believe.

But it was all useless speculation until the verdict was read, and Geoffrey put his energies into making his sister and mother easy, coming down to dinner as if all was well and speaking comfortably on casual topics throughout the evening.

The day of the inquest came and Geoffrey and Clara duly presented themselves at Chandry Manor, where the jury had viewed the body and made their observations. They were made to wait with the other witnesses in the small drawing room, which had been cleaned and furbished up a bit by Mrs. Patton. Snipson eyed Geoffrey and Clara with malice as they awaited their turn to give testimony, and Geoffrey did his best to ignore him, but the others in the room seemed to take great interest in the animosity between them, as if expecting them to suddenly pounce at each other's throats.

Geoffrey, being the defendant and principle witness, was called first. He was ushered into the library and stood before the jury and gave his story, then answered their questions, which were few. Then he signed the written record of his deposition, and was told he may retire to the drawing room or wait at his home for the verdict, as there were several witnesses yet to hear. The whole experience was less than a half hour, and though he was heartened by the respect and forbearance of the jury, he left them feeling deflated and ill.

He returned to the drawing room only to bid Clara good luck, for she was to be next. She marched out, head high, and Geoffrey prayed her impetuosity would not get the better of her. Snipson resumed his glare from across the crowded room and Geoffrey, determined to remain unrattled, went to a window and looked out.

He was in time to see a carriage pull up in front of the house, with four sweating horses and dust caking its frame. The door was thrown open and a portly gentleman in a black coat stepped down, turning to offer assistance to someone inside. As Geoffrey watched, Emily descended from the coach and hurried into the house, closely followed by the man. Then, Mr. Adkins hopped out of the coach and ran in behind them.

They came into the drawing room with much bustle, and as soon as Emily spied Geoffrey, she went to him, gesturing for her companions to follow.

"Captain Mantell," she greeted him, her large eyes anxiously searching his face. "You are unwell, I believe. It has been a hard two days."

He denied it, but not very convincingly. The sight of her had almost taken his breath away, for he had not had much time to think of her for all his troubles. She brought Mr. Adkins forward and Geoffrey shook hands, thanking him for coming.

Then she introduced the other gentleman. "This is Mr. Carson, Crowther's doctor from London. He knows my husband's disposition well, and can testify to his state of health better than a doctor who saw him only for his last ailment."

Geoffrey said all that was proper, but his situation had become overwhelming, and he could scarcely think. Emily, somehow sensing this, stood quietly beside him, murmuring occasionally to Mr. Conrad or Mr. Adkins. She was called when Clara came out from the library, and reaching quickly to press Clara's hand, she flashed her and Geoffrey a brave smile and left the room.

With her gone, Geoffrey suddenly felt unequal to his surroundings. Snipson's glare and Clara's concern and Mr. Adkins' sober look and the interested stares of the other occupants of the room unnerved him. With a resolve to take advantage of the coroner's suggestion that he await the verdict at home, he took leave of Mr. Adkins and Mr. Carson and shepherded Clara out the door.

Chapter 30

THE REMAINDER OF the day was passed in much agitation, for even in the quiet of his own home, Geoffrey could not find peace. Clara, sensing his mood, forbore to speak to him of what was transpiring at Chandry Manor, but sat at her sewing in the corner, watching him pace out of the corner of her eye. At last, feeling he could not stand her gaze on him longer, he excused himself and went up to his apartments.

Late in the afternoon, the footman fetched Geoffrey from his room.

"You've a visitor, sir—a right important-looking man, what's a solicitor, sir."

Geoffrey took the card proffered to him. Mr. Page, it read in flowing script, and underneath it, Campbell and Tooms, London. His heart skipped a beat. Had it come to this? Was the verdict in, and so dire that his family felt he was in need of legal assistance?

Geoffrey entered the library to find a tall, thin man dressed entirely in black inspecting the shelves from a respectful distance.

"Mr. Page," Geoffrey said, announcing his presence. "Will you take some refreshment? If you are down from London, you have been traveling some time."

"Thank you, no. I arrived yesterday."

His accents were clipped and formal, and Geoffrey's heart sank further still. His family had apparently summoned Mr. Page previously, in the event the verdict of the inquest was unfavorable.

Mr. Page went on, "You no doubt know why I am here."

Geoffrey poured himself some Madeira and downed it with one gulp. "I believe I do. What happens now?"

"It is an odd business, but as long as everything is legal, there shouldn't be much to it. A few days to verify the documents, but as Crowther is dead, we need not wait upon his will."

"Documents?" said Geoffrey, a trifle confused. "Do you mean the depositions? The evidence?"

"Certainly, the documents are evidence in themselves, are not they?" Mr. Page's brow furrowed, as if it had just occurred to him that he was dealing with a stupid man. "Do you have the documents, sir?"

Geoffrey, bewildered at this point, said, "Forgive me, but I must have made a mistake. Are you not here regarding the inquest?"

"No, sir," responded Mr. Page, slowly and patiently. "I am sent from Mrs. Crowther. My firm represents her interests. She would like for you to give into my possession certain deeds." He took from his coat a letter and handed it to Geoffrey. "She assured me you would know of what I am speaking."

The letter was from Emily, explaining that this solicitor would take the deeds off his hands and convey them to her agent in London.

Enlightenment dawned, and Geoffrey begged his guest's pardon, excusing himself to retrieve the deeds, which he had placed in the locked desk in his bedroom.

As he removed the oilskin packet from the desk, he felt a heaviness in the pit of his stomach. Emily must have recognized that he was beyond her help now, and determined that she must make what she could of her life. The properties and stocks were now hers outright, and he had always hoped that she would find happiness through the use of them. He descended the stairs at a sedate pace, sobered by the realization that he would never see her again. He must be pleased for her, however. She had escaped her terrible fate, and now was her own woman, just as she deserved.

He re-entered the library and handed the packet to Mr. Page, who took it and opened it, spreading the contents on the desk. For several minutes, he examined the deeds, making small noises in his throat as if taking notes in his head. More than once, Geoffrey saw his eyes go wide, and heard him murmur in surprise. At last he gathered the deeds together again, placing them in a black bag that he had brought with him.

"Is everything in order?" asked Geoffrey.

Mr. Page tipped his head, unwilling to commit fully. "The deeds shall have to be verified; however, if they are valid still, Mrs. Crowther is a rich woman."

The library door opened and the footman stepped in to announce the constable. Geoffrey's heart gave a convulsive thud, but he took possession of himself and thanked Mr. Page, desiring the footman to see him out as the constable was shown in. Just as Mr. Page had exited the room, however, Geoffrey ran after him.

"Mr. Page, will Mrs. Crowther remain for a time at Chandry Manor?"

Mr. Page looked up from his gloves, which he was adjusting. "For a short time, sir. Now the inquest is over, Mrs. Crowther must see to funeral arrangements for Mr. Crowther, and then there is the estate to be settled."

Again, Geoffrey thanked him and bid him good day. Perhaps she would come to see him before his trial at the assizes. At the very least, he hoped she would visit him in prison, but he knew it was folly to look so far ahead. The assizes may find him innocent after all. Squaring his shoulders, he turned back to the library, to face his fate at the hands of the law.

The constable stood at the desk, slapping his gloves against the hat in his hand. He cast Geoffrey a darkling look as he entered. "No need to call in a solicitor, sir. It's not as if he'd have anything to do."

"You mistake, sir. The solicitor was sent from Mrs. Crowther, regarding another matter entirely. He has nothing to do with me."

"Humph. Well, you know what I've come to say, with tongues wagging all around. But I must come to tell you for the legality of the thing. Doesn't look good if it don't come from the proper authority!"

"Certainly not, sir. But again, you mistake. I do not know what precisely you've come to say, and if you'd only come out and say it, I'd be excessively grateful."

The constable eyed him deprecatingly. "You're off, sir. Scot free! Verdict of death by poisoning."

Geoffrey blinked at him. "But how can this be? Poison?"

"Alcohol poisoning. Mrs. Crowther got Crowther's doctor to give a deposition that he was already half dead from drinking, and what Mr. Sloan diagnosed as brain fever was actually *Delirium tremens.* Man killed himself, to whit."

"Good God," uttered Geoffrey, sinking into a chair.

"Won't scruple to tell you some tried to get you charged for assault, but the jurors came to the resolution that even that would be self defense, for you hit him in defense of Mrs. Crowther, after all. And the post-mortem proved the blow to the head to be hardly a bruise, and so it was found to be irrelevant. Nothing for it but to let you off."

Geoffrey, his head in his hands, merely nodded and murmured, "Thank you, sir."

The constable, watching him, softened a bit. Placing his hat on his head and drawing on his gloves, he said, "Never would have come to the noose, by the by. But transportation—well, congratulations, sir. Must have been hell for you these three days." And with that thought to cheer him, he took his leave.

For many minutes, Geoffrey sat cradling his head, too overwhelmed by relief to move an inch. He knew the constable had said he had been let off, but he had allowed the evidence, and the rumors, and Snipson's and the townspeople's ill will to keep hope at bay for so long that he could scarcely believe it. Alcohol poisoning! And Emily had known it all along, but had lost no time in explanation that could be more efficacious in action. She was the most excellent of women, and he was honored to call her friend.

"Love conquers all," he said aloud, bringing himself out of his reverie. But he still dared not hope that her love was anything more than that of a good friend.

"Geoff?" Clara peeped into the room. "Geoff, what did he say? He was smiling when he went, and oh, I wished to box his ears! Geoff, what did he say?"

Geoffrey turned to greet her with a bemused smile. "I'm off, Clara. Innocent as a babe."

"I knew it!" she cried, running to throw her arms about him. "I knew it would be so! Did I not say it would be so?"

"Yes, you did, but you had little enough to go by."

"No, and it did look black for you, but there it is! Emily's mission must have prospered."

His smile faltered. "There was a solicitor who came from her, to retrieve the deeds. She will be rich, Clara, if Sir Anthony did not cheat her as he did Crowther."

"It would be very bad of him indeed, if he did. But she is still mistress of Chandry Manor, and the whole of the estate, is not she? With Crowther dead, it all reverts to her."

"Yes, it would. I do not know if he made a will, but it is usual that the wife inherits any unentailed property. It is heavily mortgaged, but we will suppose the investments to be valid, and she will be her own mistress now."

Clara tipped her head, gazing at him. "How can you say so, Geoff? She is free! Go and tell her that you love her—that you have loved her for years!"

"I cannot do that, Clara," he said, putting her from him. "She never loved me in that way. She is finally free, as you say, and will not desire attentions from me, or any man. And who can blame her, with a father such as Sir Anthony, and a husband such as Crowther? Her circumstances have taught her that men are only thoughtless and overbearing, if not cold and cruel, and she will be glad to have done."

"Not you, Geoff! She knows you are not thoughtless or overbearing! If she does not, then she is a simpleton!"

"Do not say so of her, Clara. You know she is no simpleton. Her quickness is what got me off the charge of murder. As soon as Snipson began threatening after Crowther's death, she went instantly to

London to get Crowther's doctor. We all knew Crowther was a drunk-ard, but it was worse than we knew. He died of alcohol poisoning, Clara. It was *Delirium tremens* in the end."

"Then I was not so far off. It may not have been the hand of God, but it was a just reward."

Geoffrey, learning again to smile, shook his head. "I am glad you were not on the jury, Clara, for you are entirely too hard-hearted for me."

"Nonsense! I am only hard-hearted toward those who deserve it. But you are trying to fob me off. What do you mean to do?"

He was spared a response, for Mr. Noyce was announced. He came in with his uneven gait, a beaming smile on his face, and stretched out a hand to shake Geoffrey's.

"We've done it, my boy! It was touch-and-go there for a while, but your friends still outnumber your enemies. And Mrs. Crowther saved the day! What a fine woman! First she had that Runner testify to Snipson's bad character. Then that doctor she brought down from London was up to all the tricks! He had never doubted but Crowther would drink himself into his grave, and when Mrs. Crowther told him what short work her husband had made of two casks of brandy, well, he said that was proof enough, even without the *Delirium tremens*!"

They laughed and talked out the whole business, until Geoffrey began to feel that it had been nothing but a nightmarish story that he would tell his friends over half a daffy once or twice a year. "Tell us how you were nearly hanged, Mantell!" they'd say, and he would willingly oblige, for they would not believe it had really happened, after all.

"All's well that ends well," said Mr. Noyce, rising to take his leave. "And what are you going to do now, young man? That Mrs. Crowther will be in mourning, but not for long, I'd wager."

Geoffrey kept his smile with an effort. "We will see, sir. Plenty of time. She may not wish to remarry, having had such a poor go of it."

"But she could have an excellent inducement, could not she?" Mr. Noyce said, elbowing Geoffrey's ribs.

"She could, if he would take the trouble, sir," broke in Clara, with a deprecating glance at her brother. "My brother's gentlemanly modesty, it seems, has deprived him of all the courage he gained in the Peninsula. How he ever faced an enemy regiment, I cannot tell, for now his tail is firmly between his legs."

Mr. Noyce regarded Geoffrey with something like compassion before transferring his gaze to Clara. "We mustn't be too hard on him, Miss Mantell. It is up to the lady, after all. And not every lady is ready to take on the gentleman that loves her best. Some of us are simply meant to be alone. But you, lad," he said, slapping Geoffrey's shoulder, "you have the world at your feet—two feet that do your bidding, I'll warrant! Not like me—too pitiable to promote attachment."

"Never say so!" came a cry from the open library door, where their astonished eyes perceived Mrs. Mantell, who had apparently been listening to their conversation for some time. She strode in now, fearful to behold, with fury in her blue eyes and ribbons flying from the cap in her glorious blond hair.

"You are not pitiable—unless you count the way you do not wrap yourself up against a chill. Geoffrey, how can you keep Mr. Noyce standing in the draft in this thoughtless way? Go build up the fire—"

"Mother, it is August, and sultry—"

She silenced him with a look. "Older persons are more susceptible to drafts, as you would know if you had an ounce of perception! But you are always worried for yourself—as if there was ever a doubt you would be let off, with Mr. Noyce on the jury. He is twice the gentleman to the squire, or to that insipid Jasper Thornton, and would never have stood to have an innocent man blamed for what was undoubtedly an accident. There, Mr. Noyce," she said, pressing him into a chair by the now roaring fire, heedless of his protestations that he had been perfectly comfortable where he was, and he was just leaving at any rate. "Where may I put your canes, sir?"

"You are very kind, Mrs. Mantell, but I will keep them by me. I can't have you waiting upon me hand and foot, for these crippled legs of mine—"

"How dare you call them crippled?" she cried, eyes flashing. "For shame! Every man of fashion uses a cane, and I must say it is refreshing to see one who tries to make his useful. These frippery fellows who sport about town with their Malacca canes swinging at their sides, they are but a poor imitation of a true gentleman like you, Mr. Noyce."

Geoffrey and Clara glanced at one another with dawning comprehension. Their mother continued to fuss about Mr. Noyce's chair while he made polite but ineffectual attempts to stop her.

"I will not leave you be, sir, so you may as well be quiet and let me take care of you. I have had enough of watching you go about making everyone else happy, with your fine manners and your delightful smile—it is time someone made you happy for a change."

Geoffrey and Clara, as one, began to inch toward the door as Mr. Noyce looked gravely up at his benefactress. "Mrs. Mantell, it is a long time since I gave up all desire for someone to make me happy."

"Then you are a foolish old man, sir," she replied, her voice slightly thickened.

"I think I am a wise one, for only a foolish man would hold to a dream that has been utterly denied him."

Mrs. Mantell stilled, and something like a sob issued from her throat. "Oh, William, will you never forgive me?"

Geoffrey and Clara, who had not yet reached the door, became as statues, unable to move or breathe. All eyes were fixed upon Mrs. Mantell as she collapsed to her knees, sobbing into her hands before Mr. Noyce.

"I have always loved you," she wailed, "but did not know it until too late! Oh, how I have been made to regret the past thirty years!"

Mr. Noyce, who had gone quite as still as Geoffrey and Clara, gingerly reached to touch Mrs. Mantell's hair. "Anamaria, do not say so. Your children, surely—"

"They have been my only consolation, truly, William," she said, raising her tear-streaked face. "But even that has been tainted, for if I had not been blinded by ambition, you would have been their father, and a far better, I daresay."

He stared at her. "I am all amazement. I never knew. You were only ever civil to me after your marriage."

"Oh, do not remind me!" she cried, reaching to grip his hands. "At first it was pride, to show the world that I had done right, but then it was mortification at knowing I had made an everlastingly tragic mistake. Robert was not cruel, but no more was he kind. He did not love me, nor I him, and so—" Her voice became again suspended by tears, and she burst out, "And so to cover my gross fault, I chose a life of pretense."

As she sobbed into his knee, Mr. Noyce regarded her with some bemusement, and Geoffrey and Clara made their escape. The library door closed, but not before they heard him say quietly, "You know just the way to work upon one, Anamaria."

Chapter 31

MR. NOYCE STAYED to dinner, which was served in the small dining room, with Mrs. Mantell smiling mistily from her place at one end of the table as he carved from his place at the other. Clara and Geoffrey had much to do, introducing appropriate subjects for conversation, and eating, and training their eyes away from each other to keep from laughing. It was the pleasantest evening they had spent in some time.

Emily was not far from Geoffrey's thoughts, for all he tried to keep her from them. She was doubtless kept very busy with Crowther's affairs, and would be for some time longer, but it was difficult for him not to wonder where she was and what she was doing at any given point in the day. He wanted to thank her for her exertions on his behalf, but he did not wish to encroach on her new freedom. She would be looking forward to an unencumbered existence now as her own mistress, and able to enjoy all that her father's fortune promised.

He had only just succeeded in reducing the wanderings of his thoughts to her to a handful of times each day when a letter came for him in the morning post.

Captain Mantell,

My happiness in hearing the news of the verdict in your favor knows no bounds. I am only sorry that the urgency of my travel kept me from lending you and Clara my support before the inquest. I have come to the end of my estate business and, having much to think of, would be glad of your counsel. Is it too much to ask that you meet me one more time, for old times' sake, in the faerie clearing? I shall await you there after breakfast.

Yours, etc.

Emily Crowther

P.S. If you do not mind it, I should like to take the moon stone back.

The effect of this letter was not extraordinary to any who were familiar with Geoffrey's feelings. He instantly went to his rooms and retrieved the necklace from his dressing case, then set out to the clearing, his heart pounding to think that he would be so soon in her presence again. What she could have to consult him about, he had little idea, for she had already retained the services of a land agent and a solicitor, who would no doubt put her in the way of whatever assistance she was in need of. But very far from questioning her need of his advice, he determined to help her in any way she asked, for he could refuse her nothing. Though she could not love him, he had her to thank for his present liberty, after all.

He reached the clearing before she did, and paced its confines for some minutes while conjectures came in and out of his mind as to the conversation to come, but this proved too much for his nerves, so he knelt down in the moss and began to craft a new citizen for the village in an attempt to divert his energy. He was hard at this task when a gentle laugh sounded behind him.

"The new owners will be delighted with this addition," said Emily, smiling down upon him as she removed her gloves. "I hope they have children."

He started to get up, but she forestalled him by kneeling beside him, though her walking dress was new, as was her pelisse. Taking up some twigs and twine herself, she began twisting and tying them into a small animal. He watched her nimble fingers, a slight ache in his chest, until her words registered fully in his brain.

"New owners? You plan to sell the Manor, then?"

She nodded, her eyes fixed on her creation. "The thought of living there fills me with loathing. Every room holds another horrid memory, even those places that used to be dear to me." She glanced up. "This clearing is the only place I will miss—and I will miss it dearly; however I must get away from my life here—put it squarely behind me."

He was silent, busy at his work for a while. "Where will you go?"

"I do not know. Perhaps not far, but I have always wished to travel. I long to see Paris and Rome, Greece and India. Even to travel about England would be delightful. Now that I am independent, I shall be able to indulge all my fancies."

He forced a smile, saying, "You shall realize all your dreams."

She paused. "It is my hope to do so."

The possibility of her going away had occurred to him, amongst the many possibilities that had crowded his mind while she had been settling her husband's estate, but now that it was a reality, he was overcome with pain. He would never meet her at an assembly, or come upon her in the village. He might never see her again. He did not know if he could survive such a loss.

Swallowing, he pulled the moon stone necklace from his waistcoat pocket. "It gives me great pleasure to restore this to you."

"Oh, thank you," she said, delightedly accepting the stone from him and cradling it in her hand. "I have missed it terribly. I am grateful to you for taking such good care of it." She clasped the necklace around her neck, touching the stone fondly. "Do you—do you still have the heart stone?"

"I do," he said.

She looked down. "You never wear it. Did not you intend to have it set in a pin?"

"I did, and I wore it often—until I discovered you were married." He faltered, grasping for an adequate explanation. "Then I felt it inappropriate that I wear it."

"I see." She went back to her work at the small animal.

Agitated, he shifted to a sitting position and said, "I have wished to speak to you for some time—"

She looked up enquiringly and he was shaken by the expectant brightness of her gray eyes. She looked almost as if she wished—but no, she had made herself clear weeks ago. And yet—

He shook himself inwardly and continued, "I would thank you for your part in my exoneration. If you had not brought Crowther's doctor down, I should very likely have been transported."

Instantly, her gaze fell. "It was a gamble," she said, resuming work on the small creature in her hands. "When Crowther did not wake up after his fall, I feared it was to be the end—for though I wished so dearly to be free of him, I could not bear that you be his murderer, as

Snipson had sworn you were. So when he awoke the second day, I was greatly relieved, but it was dreadful. He started shaking and sweating, and seeing things—horrible things. I called the doctor back to the house and he said it was brain fever, brought on by the blow to the head. He bled him and gave him purgatives—which he assured me are the usual course of treatment—but it was to no avail."

She finished her creation and set it down near a small house, dusting her hands on her dress. "But I was thinking, during those nightmarish days. Crowther's doctor had often warned him against his drinking habits, and he had drunk such a quantity of brandy on his recent return from London that it struck me. Where we lived in Jurston Street there were several drunkards, and I had seen two or three in the grip of *Delirium tremens*—though I did not know its name. It seemed so like the brain fever that I wondered if it was not the strong drink that had caused it, rather than the fall. As soon as Crowther was dead, I posted up to London to see his doctor."

"You were very brave," Geoffrey said, his voice husky with varied emotions.

"I suppose I was, but I could not bear to lose you in that way."

He looked at her, but she was gazing at their little village. He cleared his throat. "You do not wear mourning."

"No," she said simply. "I will soon be where I am unknown, and will not be under the necessity of mourning for one who does not deserve it. It would be a shame to waste my newfound wealth on such a hypocritical undertaking."

He chuckled in spite of himself. "Am I to suppose those deeds were valid?"

"Yes, you are. It was no small delight to hear the solicitor describe to me my holdings, each one more splendid than the last, his deference growing in pace with my consequence." Her eyes danced as she recounted how the office clerks had scarcely noted her coming, but had bowed to a man on her going. "They were listening at the keyhole, I expect. But I do not refine too much upon my sudden elevation. It is only wonderful that I have my father to thank for it. Of a surety, his first thought in making such elusive investments was for cheating Crowther, but his decision to hide them here and give me clues was all for my benefit. Doubtless, he knew I could keep them concealed until such time as they became useful to me, either to barter my independence from Crowther, or to free myself from debt at his death. In any event, he discovered at the last where his treasure truly lay, and I forgive him with a whole heart—"

She was interrupted at that moment by a violent rustling in the hedge, and a snarling figure flew into the clearing, knocking her aside as he barreled into Geoffrey. Geoffrey was thrown onto his back where, in utter shock, he locked gazes with a furious Snipson, who closed claw-like fingers around his throat. They rolled to and fro, crushing the faerie village as they struggled against one another, Geoffrey's greater reach all that kept him from succumbing to his assailant's grip. But Snipson was a man possessed, and managed to knock his victim's head against a rock, dazing him. As the hold around his throat tightened, Geoffrey's vision began to blur and fade, and he feared he had not avoided death after all.

Then a shadow moved behind his attacker and a thud sounded, and Snipson's eyes rolled back as he slumped to the side. Geoffrey gasped for breath and blinked up at Emily, who held a short, thick branch in her hands. She let this fall to the ground as she fell to her knees beside him, helping him to sit up and pushing his dampened hair away from his eyes.

"Geoffrey! Oh, my love, are you alright? Did he harm you?" Her anxious eyes found the red marks on his throat, but returned quickly to his face as he coughed.

"I am not much hurt," he rasped, clutching at her hand as he closed his eyes and took great gulps of air. "Where did he come from?"

Moaning behind Emily made her jump up and, wrenching the hat from her head, she pulled off the ribbons and bent to secure Snipson's hands behind his back. "Geoffrey, are you able to help me? My knots may not be strong enough to hold him."

Shaking his head to clear it, Geoffrey shifted forward and tied the ribbon tightly, and they added one around the unconscious man's ankles for good measure. As they finished, Snipson's eyes opened and his gaze, at first bleary, turned malevolent as it focused on Geoffrey.

"Murderer!" he spat. "You stole my master from me! He was in a fair way to riches and consequence, and I his right hand man! But you took it all away by murdering him! I hated you from the moment I laid eyes on you."

"Silence, Snipson!" said Emily firmly. "You heard the verdict of the inquest. Your master killed himself with drink."

His fury turned on Emily. "You tricked him! You trapped him with your wily ways, so your sneaksby of a father could ruin him! He ran his heart out trying to find those investments, and you had them all the time! You're nothing but a tramp and a trollop! I oughtn't to have tried so to make your death look natural—"

Geoffrey silenced him with a scientific jab to the face, and with a deep breath, sank back onto his heels, feeling his throat again. "He almost had me, there."

"Dearest, dearest Geoffrey," said Emily, putting her arms around him and hugging him tightly.

Holding her to him, Geoffrey whispered into her hair, "You saved me again, Emily."

She did not answer, only burying her face in his cravat, and Geoffrey slowly came to the realization that she had thrown herself into his arms and called him dearest. Before he could consider what to do, however, Snipson began to moan and stir again.

"We shall have no end of trouble from him," muttered Geoffrey, pulling himself to his feet and offering Emily a hand. "You had better go to the Hall and bring back Daniel and Sam, the two footmen we lent you, to carry him off to the constable."

"But if he should get free after I am gone–"

"Better I than you be here," said Geoffrey. "I will not be taken unawares. Now go!"

She did go, and Geoffrey stood sentinel over his prisoner, who became vociferous again once he had regained full consciousness.

"Hush, you," commanded Geoffrey, "or I'll have to send you to sleep again."

"You like to knock people on the head, don't you, Captain! You're as bloodthirsty as they say you are—a murderer at heart!"

Geoffrey deigned not to answer this as Snipson thrashed about on the ground, his words becoming more and more vitriolic.

"You always hated my master! You wanted his consequence, his property, his wife! You had her, too, I know it! Always together as you were! I never caught you at it, but you—"

Geoffrey loomed over him, his fist pulled back. "One more word against Mrs. Crowther's virtue and I shall not be responsible for what I do to you, you foul-mouthed, vile-minded fiend!"

Snipson burst into tears. "I only wanted what was best for the master! He was so clever, he'd've gone to the top, and I with him! If I'd known what that varlet Sir Anthony meant to do, I'd not've bumped him off, and we'd still be happy in London, without a care in the world!"

"Good God!" cried Geoffrey, gazing at his prisoner with loathing. "I should have guessed it."

He walked to the other side of the clearing, wishing to put distance between himself and the loathsome criminal, but was forced to endure the man's wailings until Emily returned with the footmen.

"Take this wretch to the constable," directed Geoffrey, as the two sturdy young men hefted the now resigned Snipson between them. "He has confessed to the murder of Sir Anthony Chandry, and to the attempted murder of Mrs. Crowther."

Emily stared at Geoffrey as the young men left the clearing with their sobbing burden. "No, Geoffrey! It cannot be!"

"I'm afraid it is true, Emily. It must have been an easy thing, with your father already ill, to slip some arsenic into his food. I imagine it would have done the job, and quickly."

"Oh, no," she murmured, covering her mouth with her hand, and Geoffrey put his arms around her, pulling her to him.

"I am sorry, Emily."

"I ought to have suspected it. My father had never been so ill." She was silent for several minutes while he held her. Then she said, "But my father had his redemption in the end, for he learned to care for me, so I must be reconciled."

"The wonder is that he never cared for you before," said Geoffrey, holding her more tightly.

She was so good and kind, so forgiving and generous that he could not comprehend anyone not loving her as he did. And she was here, willingly within the circle of his arms, recalling to his mind that he had reason to hope.

Speaking haltingly, he said, "Did you—Emily, before—did you call me your love?"

She pulled away slightly, not looking at him, and hesitated. "I did, Geoffrey. I love you. It is a secret I have guarded for many years. Only you may tell me if it is well to be revealed."

His heart thudded as it refused to believe—but she had said it. He touched her cheek, and when she raised her eyes to his once more, his heart tumbled over itself at what he saw there.

Almost too overjoyed to speak, he managed, "Oh, Emily, it is well."

"Well enough?" she said, her voice hitching.

He bent his head to press his forehead against hers. "Oh, no. Well enough will never again do for you."

He kissed her then, and she met his kiss with all the passion he knew she possessed, that had been stifled and suffocated and refused for too long. It was a torrent that flooded the parched places of his soul, and he drank her in. So starved was he that he felt he could never get enough, and he kissed her eyes and cheeks and nose and hair for good measure.

At last, Geoffrey paused for breath, and Emily laughed up at him. "I fear the villagers are shocked."

"Let them be shocked!" said Geoffrey, kissing her again. Then he stepped away, eagerly taking both her hands in his. "Emily, will you—"

But then he stopped, closing his eyes. "But I dare not ask you."

"Why do not you dare?" she said gently. "Have not I told you I love you?"

He shook his head. "But you have wished for your freedom for so long! Now you are your own woman at last, and rich, and able to do all you ever wished to do. How can I ask you to give that all into my hands?"

She reached up to kiss him soundly. "Geoffrey, have no fears on that head, for I have known to trust you from the day we first met.

Nay, before we met, you made that lopsided little horse and the boy as an offering from your good heart. You, of all the men I have known, have never sought to use me ill, or seen me as less than I am."

"But I have! I have been so blind—when I think that you might have been spared the ignominy of these three years, had I recognized my feelings for you sooner—"

She kissed him again. "I never faulted you for that, Geoffrey. While I cannot say that I would not have changed my circumstances if given the chance, all that I have experienced has made me stronger. All the heartache has had the mercy of your friendship to temper it. Your care has kept me from despair."

"It was love, Emily, not care," he said, pulling her to him again. "I tried to act as though I merely cared for you as a friend, but all along—ever since we met again after all those years, even without knowing it—I have loved you. Even when I tried to forget you, and to find someone else to love, I couldn't do it. It was you or no one."

She looked up into his eyes. "I have loved you at least as long, Geoffrey. I felt a connection with you from the day we met. Now that we understand one another, how could I wish to live without you? Paris and Rome and India will be desolate indeed without my true love."

Geoffrey gathered her hands into his and kissed them. "Emily, will you marry such a block-headed gudgeon as myself, and allow me to do penance for my mistakes by making you happy for the rest of your life?"

"Need I even answer that?" she inquired, drawing his head down to her again, and the citizens of the faerie village, scattered and crushed as they were, were subjected to yet another shockingly extended display of romantic sentiment.

If you enjoyed this book, I hope you will share it with others! Please consider leaving a review on Amazon, Goodreads, Bookbub, or any other review site you like. Reviews are the best way to help people find their next favorite book, and are incredibly appreciated. Thank you! To get started, scan the QR code and scroll down to the review links:

For more on the other books in the Branwell Chronicles series, including sneak peeks, announcements, and more historical tidbits, scan the QR code above or visit my website at judithhaleeverett.com.

Author's Note

IT'S ALWAYS AMAZING to me just how much I don't know about the Regency. Even stuff I thought I knew has details that are new to me when I come across them in my research.

Before 1837, cerebral palsy was lumped with various other conditions in a general diagnosis of "deformity." But if the doctor was more specialized, he may diagnose "spastic paresis or paralysis," with or without "idiocy" or "imbecility." These definitions sound harsh to us today, but at the time doctors had very little knowledge of how the brain worked and could only identify issues from how a person appeared or acted. Children with intellectual disability or quadriplegia were often sent to asylums, which varied widely in quality of care, depending on funding and the involvement of trustees. Children with only motor dysfunction, like Mr. Noyce, could more easily be cared for at home and had a good prognosis for health and happiness. Dr. John Little, himself affected by neural disease, was the first to connect neural defects with birth injuries or lack of oxygen. Due to his pioneering work, what we know as cerebral palsy was termed "Little's Disease" until 1887, when Dr. William Osler coined the term we use today.

Regency mourning was not nearly as strict as Victorian mourning—which was popularized by Queen Victoria at the death of her beloved Prince Albert—and often depended on the family's personal preferences. Women tended to bear the outward burden of mourning, wearing black or gray dresses and pelisses for the entirety of the mourning period, while men would only wear black cravats, armbands or gloves. Widows and widowers were generally expected to be in full-mourning for six months, and then half-mourning for another six months, while children were only required to be in mourning for six months. Mourning for other relatives was even shorter, from two weeks to three months. Half-mourning dress was muted colors like lavender or gray, but occasionally red was worn. As far as exclusion from social events was concerned, a period of four to six weeks after the death of the family member was sufficient. Widows were expected not to remarry during their year of mourning (so that paternity issues could not arise), but some did anyway. And people who wished to send a message about their feelings toward the departed would sometimes choose to curtail mourning or forgo it altogether.

Not much is known about the Bow Street Runners because all their records were destroyed—not accidentally, but because they were thought to be unimportant. The Runners were begun by Henry Fielding in 1749, as a private police force operating from a house in Bow Street. Police in general were looked on as a threat to English freedom, therefore the Runners did not wear uniforms, and restricted their activities to detective work-for-hire. They did not exact a fee from those who hired them to find and bring in criminals; rather they were rewarded by the bounties they could collect from the government upon turning in criminals, though they did receive a small annual salary for their efforts. Any detective work or other work that did not involve a bounty would require a fee.

Arsenic has been used as a medicine almost as long as it has been used as a poison. This seems to defy logic, but arsenic was used by Hippocrates on ulcers, and countless medical men over the intervening centuries have used it to treat asthma, anemia, syphilis, eczema, cancer, dyspepsia and more. Arsenic is even now used to treat some types of leukemia. It was easily obtainable at the apothecary's shop all through the 18th and well into the 19th century, even though accidental poisonings were common. It was even added to things to give a distinctive green color; fabrics and wallpaper contained arsenic that could be absorbed through the skin or breathed in. It's odd how so many in the legal and medical fields turned a blind eye to the dangers of arsenic, even with known murders by the poison coming to trial. Death by arsenic poisoning was horrific: when given in high enough doses, the stuff burned the lining of the intestines and stomach, caused severe pain, vomiting, and diarrhea, wreaked havoc on the organs, and made all the teeth fall out. But it would not be until 1851 that public alarm became acute enough to convince lawgivers and doctors to place restrictions on its sale.

As church and state were almost inseparably intertwined through the Regency period, laws predominated to discourage divorce for any reason. Besides the Biblical sanctity of marriage, however, concerns of rightful succession kept lawgivers from relaxing the rules, even in cases of abuse, when the court was more likely to grant a legal separation than they were to recommend a divorce. The only body with the power to grant a divorce was Parliament, and one of the few legal bases for divorce during the Regency was Criminal Conversation, which was the legal term for adultery. If a man could provide proof that his wife was engaging in sexual relations with another man, he could sue that man for Crim. Con. and win monetary damages along with a divorce. This process could be so lucrative, however, that it was not uncommon for a man to forgo the divorce and simply hope that his wife would slip up again. Unfortunately, this solution benefited only husbands; a wife could not sue her husband for Crim. Con., no matter how blatant his indiscretions, because she was not legally recognized as an individual.

In the 18th and 19th centuries, people drank alcohol in surprising quantities. Some men persisted in drinking ale or beer with breakfast well into the Regency, and wine in its various forms was a common refreshment at social gatherings and during and after dinner. Men, especially, drank excessively; it was considered manly to acquire a "hard head" and to be able to hold your liquor well. In consequence, many people suffered from gout, which is a severely painful form of arthritis (usually in the big toe), caused by the purines present in alcohol being broken down into uric acid. High rates of alcohol poisoning, known during the Regency as *Delirium tremens*, was another, worse, outcome. Alcohol poisoning is caused by extremely high amounts of alcohol in the body, and will lead to vomiting, erratic breathing, delirium, coma, and death. Contrary to medical belief at the time, alcohol poisoning can be reversed by slowly weaning the patient off alcohol over several days. However, because the common Regency treatments for *Delirium tremens* were total abstinence from liquor, purging (inducing vomiting or sweats), and bleeding, most people died from it.

Whenever there was a suspicious death during the Regency, the coroner was called in for an inquest, which was a preliminary investigation to determine if murder had been committed. The inquest generally took place within forty-eight hours of the death, and jurors were chosen from among the gentry and principle inhabitants of the area where it occurred. The first order of business was to view the body, which was supposed to have been untouched since the death; hence, all the jurors would troop up to the bedroom or into the backroom or over the fields to see the dead person and make what they could of it. Then the group adjourned to somewhere close by—a room in the house or the local inn—to hear the depositions. Anyone with any knowledge of the situation was called in to give evidence, and could be heavily fined if they refused to cooperate. Suspects were only detained in jail if they seemed to be dangerous or likely to flee, and jurors were not forbidden from speaking to any of the witnesses (including the suspect) before the inquest. The only time the jury could not speak to anyone outside the court was after all the evidence was heard and they were deliberating over their decision. If the inquest found the suspect guilty, he would be ordered to appear for trial at the assizes, which came around every couple of months and only in principle towns.

Sources:

Panteliadis C.P., Vassilyadi P. "Cerebral Palsy: A Historical Review." *Cerebral Palsy.* Springer, Cham. 2018.

https://www.cdc.gov/ncbddd/cp/facts.html

Trumbach, Randolph. *The Rise of the Egalitarian Family.* Academe Press. 1978.

https://janeausten.co.uk/blogs/womens-regency-fashion-articles/regency-mourning-an-in-depth-look

Goddard, Henry. *Memoirs of a Bow Street Runner*. Quaystone Books. 2021.

https://www.historic-uk.com/HistoryUK/HistoryofBritain/Bow-Street-Runners/

Whorton, James C. *The Arsenic Century: How Victorian Britain was poisoned at home, work, and play*. Oxford University Press. 2010.

Hughes, M. A. "Historical Perspective on the Dichotomy of Arsenic as a Poison and Medicinal Agent." Society of Toxicology, San Antonio, Texas, March 11–15, 2018.

Stone, Lawrence. *Road to Divorce*. Oxford University Press. 1990.

https://pubmed.ncbi.nlm.nih.gov/782235/ and https://pubmed.ncbi.nlm.nih.gov/26444921/

Bynum, William F. "Chronic Alcoholism in the first half of the 19th century." *Bulletin of the History of Medicine*. March-April 1968, Vol. 42, No. 2, pp. 160-185.

Impey, John. *The practice of the office of sheriff; also the practice of the office of coroner*. W. Clarke and Sons. 1817.

https://www.londonlives.org/static/IC.jsp

Acknowledgements

THIS BOOK HAS been a long time coming. The plot idea was my first when I began writing Regency romance, and I wrote a rough draft of it several years ago, but got sidetracked by two other books before coming back to this one. It's a joy to have it finally published, and I hope you are as satisfied with it as I am.

Thanks are always in order. First, to my excellent reading buddy, cheerleader, and friend, Nichole Van Valkenburgh, I wouldn't be here without you! Your extensive knowledge of the Regency and of writing have been almost as invaluable as your encouragement.

To my wonderful beta readers, Diane Paredes, Liz Prettyman, Emily Menendez, and Cynthia Hart, you guys deserve a medal! Thanks for taking time out of your busy schedules to help me be a better writer.

To my friends, neighbors, and family members who are always so interested in my success, thank you for believing in me!

To Rae Allen, who designs my book covers, your talents are awe-inspiring. Thank you for coming back to my books from the exciting world of comics and commissions!

To my kids, who are so patient with my busy writing days and who can't wait to see another book published. You guys are the best!

And of course, to my husband Joe, without whose support I could never survive this crazy, hectic, joyous, wild ride. Thank you for reading everything I give you, making great suggestions, bragging me up to everyone you meet, letting me cry on your shoulder, and being everlastingly patient when I've got a deadline. I cannot love you enough!

Judith Hale Everett is one of seven sisters, and grew up surrounded by romance novels. Georgette Heyer and Jane Austen were staples, and formed the groundwork for her lifelong love affair with the Regency. Add to that her obsession with the English language and you've got one hopelessly literate romantic.

You can find JudithHaleEverett on Facebook, Twitter, and Instagram, or at judithhaleeverett.com.